Praise for *The Blue Hour*

"Douglas does it again! This is the kind of novel you absolutely cannot put down, the kind that gets your pulse racing, to such an extent you have to switch off your phone, ignore your entourage, and devour to the very end. Brilliantly compelling, startling, and exotic, definitely one of Kennedy's best works."

—Tatiana de Rosnay, Author of *A Paris Affair*

"A gripping thriller, this book poses a universal question: How far are we prepared to go in pursuit of the truth, and do we really want the answers when we find them?"

—Louise Doughty, Author of *Apple Tree Yard*

"Kennedy has a knack for portraying characters readers love to hate."

—*Kirkus Reviews*

"Douglas writes with verve, and plot twists, several sharply drawn characters and an exotic locale give the novel a cinematic quality. Hand this to readers looking for a page-turner with a strong female protagonist."

—*Booklist*

"The best book about Morocco since *The Sheltering Sky*. Completely absorbing and atmospheric."

—Philip Kerr, Author of *The Other Side of Silence*

"*The Blue Hour* sits firmly in the mode of existential crisis pioneered by Paul Bowles' *The Sheltering Sky*. With the added value of Kennedy's far more equitable eye: his scrutinizing but empathetic sensibility looks at Morocco in the round, with an admirable respect for its nooks and crannies."

—*The Arts Fuse*

"Skillfully written page-turner . . . Recommended for readers looking for an entertaining roller-coaster of a read featuring a strong, modern female protagonist."

—*Library Journal*

The Blue Hour

A Novel

DOUGLAS
KENNEDY

ATRIA PAPERBACK

New York   London   Toronto   Sydney   New Delhi

ATRIA
PAPERBACK

An Imprint of Simon & Schuster, Inc.
1230 Avenue of the Americas
New York, NY 10020

First Atria paperback edition May 2017

ATRIA PAPERBACK and colophon are trademarks of Simon & Schuster, Inc.

For information about special discounts for bulk purchases, please contact Simon & Schuster Special Sales at 1-866-506-1949 or business@simonandschuster.com.

The Simon & Schuster Speakers Bureau can bring authors to your live event. For more information, or to book an event, contact the Simon & Schuster Speakers Bureau at 1-866-248-3049 or visit our website at www.simonspeakers.com.

Interior design by Dana Sloan

Manufactured in the United States of America

10 9 8 7 6 5 4 3 2 1

The Library of Congress has cataloged the hardcover edition as follows:

Kennedy, Douglas, date.
  The blue hour : a novel / Douglas Kennedy. -- First Atria Books hardcover edition.
     pages ; cm
  I. Title.
  PR6061.E5956B58 2016
  823'.914--dc23
                                        2015028299

ISBN 978-1-4516-6637-3
ISBN 978-1-4516-6639-7 (pbk)
ISBN 978-1-4516-6640-3 (ebook)

Again for Christine

Run up the sail, my heartsick comrades;
Let each horizon tilt and lurch—
You know the worst: your wills are fickle,
Your values blurred, your hearts impure
And your past life a ruined church—
But let your poison be your cure.

—*Louis MacNeice, "Thalassa"*

The Blue Hour

ONE

FIRST LIGHT. AND I didn't know where I was anymore.

The sky outside: was it a curved rotunda of emerging blue? The world was still blurred at its edges. I tried to piece together my whereabouts, the exact geographic location within which I found myself. A sliver of emerging clarity. Or maybe just a few basic facts.

I was on a plane. A plane that had just flown all night across the Atlantic. A plane bound for a corner of North Africa. A country which, when viewed cartographically, looks like a skullcap abreast a continent. According to the flight progress monitor illuminating the back-of-the-seat screen facing me, we were still seventy-three minutes and 842 kilometers (I was flying into a metric world) from our destination. This journey hadn't been my idea. Rather I'd allowed myself to be romanced into it by the man whose oversize frame (as in six foot four) was scrunched into the tiny seat next to mine. The middle seat in this horror movie of an aircraft. No legroom, no wiggle room, every seat taken, at least six screaming babies, a husband and wife fighting in hissed Arabic, bad ventilation, bad air-conditioning, one-hour line for the bathroom after the plastic meal they served us, the rising aroma of collective night sweats hanging over this hellhole of a cabin. Thank God I had made Paul pack his zopiclone. Those pills induce sleep in even the most sleep-impossible conditions. I had put aside all my concerns about pharmaceuticals and asked him for one. It gave me three hours' respite from this high-altitude sweatbox confinement.

Paul. My husband. It was a new marriage—just three years old. Truth be told, we loved each other. We were passionate about each other. We often said we were beyond fortunate to have found each other. And I truly believed that. Never mind that the day before we legalized our relationship and committed to each other for the rest of our lives, I was silently convincing myself that I could change some of Paul's worrying inclinations; that, in time, things would tick upward, stabilize. Especially since we had decided that the moment was right to become parents.

Out of nowhere, Paul suddenly began to mumble something in his sleep, its incoherency growing in volume, indicating serious subconscious agitation. When it reached a decibel level that woke our neighbor—an elderly man sleeping in his gray-tinted glasses—I touched my husband's arm, trying to rouse him out of his nightmare. It took several further unnerving moments of shouting before he snapped awake, looking at me as if he had no idea who I was.

"What . . . where . . . I don't . . . ?"

His wide-eyed bemusement was suddenly replaced by the look of a bewildered little boy. "Am I lost?" he asked.

"Hardly," I said, taking his hand. "You just had a bad dream."

"Where are we?"

"Up in the air."

"And where are we going?"

"Casablanca."

He appeared surprised at this news.

"And why are we doing that, Robin?"

I kissed him on the lips. And posed a question:

"Adventure?"

TWO

FATE IS BOUND up in the music of chance. A random encounter, a choice impulsively made . . . and fate suddenly has its own interesting momentum.

And fate had certainly brought us to Casablanca.

The fasten-seat-belts sign was now illuminated. All tray tables stored away. All seats upright. The change in cabin pressure was wreaking havoc with the eardrums of all the babies around us. Two of the mothers—their faces veiled—tried to calm their children without success, one of the babies staring wide-eyed at the cloaked face in front of him, his anguish growing. Imagine not being able to see your mother's face in public. Or does it just become a part of a child's everyday décor: mother is visible at home, but in the world beyond, all that can be seen is a slittish hint of eyes and lips. For an infant jolted awake by a change in cabin pressure, it's even more reason to cry without limits.

"Little charmers," Paul whispered, rolling his eyes.

I entwined my hand with his. "We'll be down on the ground in just a few minutes."

Paul suddenly put his arms around me. "Am I still your love?"

I clutched his hand more tightly, knowing how much reassurance he craves and needs.

"Of course you are," I said.

3

From the moment he walked into my office three years ago I knew it was love. What do the French call it? A *coup de foudre*. The overwhelming, instantaneous sense that you have met the love of your life; the individual who will change your entire trajectory because you know . . .

What exactly?

Now there's a major speculative question: How and why do you fall in love? What triggers the realization: he's the one? Even if, some weeks or months down the line, the reality of the other person (and of all the needs and desires you have projected onto him), makes you begin to wonder . . .

Was it really love that made me swoon? I certainly thought so at the time.

Let me restate that. Honestly.

I fell in love with Paul Leuen immediately. And he told me later, much to his surprise, he too fell in love on the spot . . . with the woman he'd been sent to in order to make sense of his messy financial affairs.

That's right, I'm an accountant. A numbers cruncher. The person you call to form a barrier between yourself and our friends at the Internal Revenue Service. Accountants are usually grouped with dentists as purveyors of a profession that they privately loathe. Now, I happen to know quite a few fellow Certified Public Accountants. The majority of them—from the gray bookkeepers to the corporate high-flyers—tend to like their work.

I like the work too—and I speak as someone who came to the numbers-and-tax game in her thirties. No one grows up proclaiming, "I want to be an accountant." It's a bit like driving down an open road, then veering into a cul-de-sac that, from a distance, looks staid and humdrum. But then, much to your surprise, you find it has its own intriguing allure; its own singular sense of human narrative. Money is that fault line along which we pirouette. Show me an individual's numerical sum total and I can develop a portrait of their immense complexities: their dreams and aspirations, their demons and terrors.

"When you look at my financial records," Paul asked me, "what do they tell you about me?"

Such directness. A flirtatious directness, even though—when the question was posed—we were several weeks off from becoming intimate. He was still just a prospective client—with wildly disorganized books. Paul's tax problems were considerable, but not insurmountable. His salary at the state university had been taxed at source. His problem was when it came to sales of his artwork, he'd frequently been paid cash and had never thought much about paying taxes on this income, which was reasonably modest—maybe fifteen thousand dollars per year. But, stretched over a ten-year period, it became not so insignificant to a sharp-eyed IRS inspector who now wanted it declared and paid for. Paul was being audited—and the local mom-and-pop bookkeeper who'd been handling things for him for the past ten years ran scared once the IRS started knocking on Paul's door. He told his client that he needed someone who was skilled at negotiating with the tax man. And he recommended me.

Paul's financial problems, however, weren't limited to undisclosed income. His spending habits had landed him in severe cash flow difficulties. Wine and books were his principal vices. A part of me privately admired someone who had such an apparently unfazed approach to life that he thought nothing of spending $185 on a bottle of Pomerol 1989, yet was being chased by the electricity company for forgetting to pay his quarterly bill, and also that he chose only the finest French-made charcoals, pencil leads, and other materials for his etchings. These art supplies alone accounted for another six thousand dollars in annual outlay. And when he went off to the South of France for an annual vacation, though he would stay in a friend's guest cottage outside the medieval village of Èze—which cost him nothing—he would easily rack up another ten grand's worth of gastronomical indulgences.

So, the first impression I had of Paul Leuen was someone who—

unlike the rest of us members of the workaday world—had somehow managed to avoid all the pitfalls of routine life. And I had always wanted to fall in love with an artist.

We are often attracted to that which runs contrary to our nature.

Did I see in Paul—this rail-thin, six-foot-four-inch artist, with long gray hair, his black leather jacket and black jeans, his black hoodie, his Converse high-top sneakers—the possibility of change; a way out of the humdrum that so much of my life had become?

During our first professional meeting Paul made a joke about his financial affairs being somewhat akin to a Jackson Pollock painting, and then said that he was the living embodiment of the French word *bordélique*—which I looked up after our meeting and discovered meant "like a brothel" and "all over the place." Then there was the way he was almost apologetic about his "financial absurdities," and how he needed someone to take him in hand and "turn me into a proper functioning grown-up."

"The books will tell all," I said.

What the books did tell me was that Paul Leuen was accruing serious debt. I was direct with him: "You like to show yourself a good time. The fact is, your income from the state university leaves you—after state and federal taxes—with around fifty thousand a year to live on. Your house has been mortgaged twice. You could be facing a tax bill of sixty thousand plus penalties if the IRS has its way. And since you have virtually no savings . . ."

"So what you're saying is I am a disaster area."

He was all smiles as he said this; a certain bad-boy cheerfulness as he acknowledged his imprudence, his need to mess up. I well knew this smile, as my father had been charming and witty, with no ability to get the bills paid. He was a so-called entrepreneur; a corporate guy who could never hold down a job, who always had a get-rich-quick scheme on the go, who made me and my mother move five times during my adolescence in his search for the next executive position, the next break scheme that was going to finally get us "on easy street" (an expression he used so often). But that reversal of fortune, that manna from heaven moment, never materialized. My mother found ongoing work as a geriatric nurse everywhere we went, as infirmity and ageing are two of life's great constants. She kept threatening to leave my father whenever he bumped into another setback, another financial loss that propelled us to yet another city, another rented house, a new school for me, a sense of ongoing uncertainty that was counterbalanced by the fact that my Dad loved me and I adored him. He was the sort of guy who, when he had money in his pocket, would indulge me and Mom relentlessly. God knows I preferred my father's absurd sunny outlook on life to my mother's bleaker perspective, even though I knew that hers had a certain credibility. When my father died of a sudden heart attack the first week I started college at the University of Minnesota, I was beyond crushed. Phoning me with the news my mother masked her distress with steely coolness.

"There was a will. You'll get his Rolex. The one thing he never hocked, along with his wedding ring. But don't cry for him. No one—not you, not me—could have saved your father from himself."

But cry I did, long into that night and many thereafter. After my father's death, my mother and I began to detach from each other. Though she was the parent who got the bills paid and somehow kept the roof (or series of roofs) over our heads, I never felt much in the way of love from her. I still spent part of most major holidays with her and dutifully called her once a week. I remained the responsible daughter. And embraced, in my own way, her rigorous standards when it came to financial caution and saving for a rainy day. But when, just a few years ago, I got together with Paul—and finally brought him to meet her—my mother afterward was bluntness itself.

"So you're finally marrying your father."

"That's not fair," I said, my head reeling from the slap-across-the-face nature of her comment.

"The truth is never fair. If that makes you think that I am being, as usual, merciless, so be it. Don't get me wrong, it's not that I don't find Paul charming. He's charm itself. For a man eighteen years your senior he's not in bad shape, even if he dresses like Woodstock was last week. Still he does have a certain charm. And I know how lonely things have been for you since Donald walked out."

Donald was my first husband—and it was I who ended our three-year marriage, as she well knew.

"I left Donald," I heard myself telling my mother.

"Because he gave you no choice but to leave him. And it destroyed you. And now you are with a man much older and as irresponsible as your father and . . ."

"Paul isn't as irresponsible as you think."

"Time will tell."

Mom. She died a year ago; an out-of-nowhere stroke that killed her at the age of seventy-one.

Turbulence in the cabin. I peered out the window. The plane was trying to break cloud cover, rocking with its downward shift toward land. The man in the aisle seat shut his eyes tightly as the plane lurched in a treacherous manner.

"Do you think the pilot knows what he's doing?" Paul whispered to me.

"I'm sure he has a wife and children he'd like to see."

"Or not."

For the next five minutes the aircraft was like a prizefighter having a bad night, as it took ongoing body blows from the storm enveloping us. The children's cries hit new levels of discord. Several of the masked women began to keen. Our neighbor's eyes remained tightly shut, his lips now moving in what seemed to be silent prayer.

"Imagine if it was all to end right now," Paul said. "What would you think?"

"If you're dead you're not thinking."

"But say this was the moment before death hit. What would your last thought be?"

"Is this line of questioning supposed to distract me from the fact that the plane might crash?" I asked.

Paul laughed and was quickly silenced as the plane seemed to go into momentary free fall. I gripped the armrests so tightly my knuckles felt like they just might perforate the skin. I kept my eyes slammed shut until, out of nowhere, order and calm descended on the world. We had hit calm air. Moments later, we had the runway beneath us.

I opened my eyes. Paul's fingers remained gripped around the armrests, his face now the color of chalk. We reached for each other's hands. Then my husband spoke.

"I wonder: Is this all a mistake?"

THREE

CUSTOMS AND IMMIGRATION at Casablanca. Controlled chaos. Hundreds of new arrivals being corralled into two different lines—one for Moroccans, another for the rest of humanity. Every historical epoch—from the Middle Ages to our current hyperconnected, cyberworld reality—seemed to be represented. There were sharply suited businessmen and -women everywhere—and at least half of those I saw, with their Italian tailoring and their black iPhones, were from North Africa. There were backpacker types, all grungy and twenty-something, eyeing the suits with zonked amusement. Just in front of me was a rail-thin man in a dusty brown suit—his teeth blackened by cigarettes—who must have come from Mauritania, as he was holding a travel document from that country in his right hand.

"What's the capital of Mauritania?" I asked Paul.

Without a pause for reflection he replied: "Nouakchott."

"The things you know," I said.

"This line is insane. When I came last time it was thirty-three years ago, when there were no computer checks, when the world wasn't as paranoid as it is now."

"Zen, Zen, Zen," I said, stroking my husband's face.

"This is Casablanca Airport, not some fucking Buddhist retreat."

I laughed. But he stood there, bouncing from foot to foot, an ongoing fugue of impatience and anxiety.

"Let's go home," he suddenly said.

11

"You don't mean that."

"I do."

I felt myself tense.

"How will we go home?" I asked.

"Get the next plane."

"You're not serious."

"I think I am. This is all wrong."

"Because of the long line?"

"Because my instinct tells me: go home."

"Even though your 'instinct' told you to make us come here?"

"So you are angry at me."

"If you want to go home, we'll go home."

"You'd think me a loser if I did that," he said.

"I never think you're a loser, my love."

"But I know I am a liability."

Liabilities. That was the word that ricocheted around my head when I discovered, nine weeks ago, the extent of his debts. Having promised me, eight months earlier, that he would curb his spending habits, a knock on our door came one Friday evening around six p.m. A gentleman from a collection agency was standing on our front porch, asking to speak with Paul Leuen. I explained that my husband was at the gym. "Ah, so you are Mrs. Leuen? Then you might be aware of the sixty-four hundred dollars that your husband owes to the Vintners Wine Society." I was speechless. My mind was racing. When had he bought all that wine, and why hadn't I seen it anywhere in our house? The collection agent went on, explaining that the Wine Society had sent close to ten letters demanding "a conversation" about the unpaid sum that had accrued over two years. Now they had run out of patience. If the bill wasn't settled forthwith, legal action would follow, and could involve a lien on our home.

But instead of going inside and getting my checkbook and solving the problem on the spot (as I had done on several past occasions), I simply told the collection guy:

"You'll need to speak directly with my husband. He's at the Gold's Gym on Manor Street—which is about five minutes from here by car. Ask for him at the reception desk: they know him."

Repeating the address of the gym again I excused myself and closed the door. As soon as I had ascertained that the collector had pulled off down the road in his car, I went into our bedroom, packed a small weekend bag, called my old college roommate, Ruth, at her home in the Cobble Hill section of Brooklyn, and asked if I could use her foldout sofa for a few days. Then, after leaving Paul a note—*If the wine debt isn't somehow paid off by the time I am back late Tuesday night the marriage is over*—I got into my car and drove the eight hours south to the city I had always promised myself I would one day call my own. I deliberately kept my cell phone off all weekend. I never went online and spent the next four days trying not to bore Ruth with the cocktail of anger, guilt, and sadness that was coursing through me. Ruth—a professor of English at Brooklyn College, divorced, no kids, single, disappointed in love, wickedly funny, and hyper-cultural ("High art is God's apology for men," she noted at one point between the three plays, two concerts, and two art exhibits we saw when I was there)—was, as always, a great friend. She steadied my resolve when I broached the idea that perhaps I should check in on Paul, see how he was bearing up.

"When he landed himself in debt nine months ago," she asked, "what did you do?"

"I dug into my retirement fund and found the ten grand to get him out of trouble."

"What did he promise you in return?"

"You know very well what he did. He admitted that he's got a sad pathological compulsion when it comes to spending, spending, spending . . . and he promised to curtail that destructive impulse."

"An impulse that is corroding your marriage. It's all so sad."

Ruth was aware of the fact that, when I met Paul three years earlier, I was thirty-seven and entering that last lap of possible fertility.

Within six months of declaring love for each other, and talking about the wondrous possibilities of a shared future together, I delicately raised the fact that I did not want to pass through life without becoming a mother; that I was entering the now-or-never phase. I knew that I was bringing a certain degree of pressure to our relationship, and said that I would perfectly understand if Paul felt this was all too much too fast. His response astounded me.

"When you have met the love of your life, of course you want to have a child with her."

Yes, Paul was a great romantic. Such a romantic that he proposed marriage shortly thereafter, even though I told him that, having been in that institution once before, I wasn't anxious about a return visit. But I was so swept up in the wonder of finding love at my age, and with such a talented and original man, and in Buffalo (!), that I said yes. He did say that, though he realized time was of the essence, we needed at least two years together before becoming parents. I agreed to his request, staying on the pill until eight months ago. At which point we seriously began to "try" (what a curious verb) for a baby. We went about the task very robustly—though sex was, from the outset, one of the aspects of our marriage that always worked. It wasn't as if we were having to motivate ourselves into making love every night of the week.

"You know, if I don't get pregnant naturally, there are other options," I said six months later when nothing had yet happened.

"You'll get pregnant," Paul said.

"You sound very certain about that."

"It's going to happen."

That conversation took place ten days before the debt collector arrived on our doorstep. As I headed south in my car toward Brooklyn, my cell phone off, my piercing sadness about Paul was underscored by the realization that he was my last chance at having a baby. And that thought . . .

Ruth splashed a little more wine into my glass. I took a long sip.

"He's not your last chance," she said.

"I want a baby with Paul."

"That's a definitive statement."

Friendship is always a complex equation—especially a friendship where it had been agreed early on that we would never sugarcoat things; that we would speak what we felt to be the truth.

"I don't want to be a single mother," I said. "If I can get him to just accept that he has certain obligations . . ."

"Paul had problems with money before you. Even though you've tried to organize his personal finances, he refuses to play smart. At the age of fifty-eight, he is not going to have some sort of epiphany and transform himself. He is what he is. Which therefore begs the question: Can you live with his ongoing recklessness?"

All the way home that question nagged at me. We project onto others that which we need and seek at a given moment. Life, they say, is a great teacher. But only if we are truly willing to shake off the illusions and misnomers within which we dwell.

Love, however, always muddles clarity of vision. And a life without love is a bit like the balance sheets over which I gaze every working day: far too concrete, too reasoned. And my love for Paul was as bound up in his recklessness as in his talent, his intelligence, his ardor for me.

When I got home, it was just after six p.m. I saw his car parked out front of the nineteenth-century Gothic place we'd bought together two years ago. When I entered the house I was startled to find that order had descended upon chaos. In recent weeks Paul had started treating our home as a happy dumping ground. But in the days I had been out of contact, not only had he divested the house of his mess, but all windows glistened, all wood surfaces were free of encroaching dust and smelled of lemon polish. There were fresh flowers in several vases. And I could smell something pasta-esque in the oven.

As the door slammed behind me, Paul emerged from the kitchen, looking just a little sheepish. He couldn't make direct eye contact with me. But when he did once look up in my direction I could see his encroaching sadness and fear.

"Smells good," I said.

"I made it for you, for us," he said, dodging my gaze.

"How did you know I'd be home tonight?"

"Called your office. They told me you'd be back at work tomorrow."

"Yes, I came back. But . . ."

He held up his hand.

"I sold all the wine."

"I see."

"I found a guy here in town. Big-deal collector. Offered me six thousand dollars for my cellar."

"You have a cellar?"

He nodded, looking so much like a little boy who had just been caught out in a very big lie.

"Where?" I asked.

"You know that shed behind the garage? The one we never use?"

The "shed" was something akin to a bomb shelter, with two folding steel doors that lay flat to the ground. When we were in negotiation to buy the house we naturally had the shelter opened for us, and found a damp semilined cave. As the house already had a renovated basement, we simply put a lock on the shed doors after we bought the place and left it unattended.

Or, at least, that's what I'd thought.

"How long have you been building up this wine collection?" I asked, sounding most reasonable.

"A while."

He came over and took me in his arms.

"I'm sorry," he said.

"I don't want apologies. I just don't want a repetition of all this financial mess again."

"And I don't want to lose you."

"Then don't. Because I do want you, *us*."

To Paul's credit he became industrious again after the wine debt incident, spending all free nonteaching hours on a new series of lithographs. It was the first time that Paul had settled down to serious creative work in over two years. Though his gallery owner in New York was enthusiastic, the general downturn in the market and Paul's lack of visibility over the past few years had meant that the sort of prices he could demand had shrunk decisively. Still, he did manage to find a buyer, and though Paul was disappointed with the negotiated price, part of him was clearly thrilled with the fact that he still "had the chops" when it came to his art. After paying off most of his credit card debts, he then took me out to dinner at a very upscale (for Buffalo) French restaurant. He ordered a far too expensive bottle of Pauillac, telling me that his gallerist had another client interested in a new series.

"The buyer is willing to plonk down fifty percent up front—so that should be another ten grand to me in a couple of weeks. What's a bottle of Pauillac compared to ten grand?"

I'm not that into wine. Still . . . why not celebrate? Especially since Paul was making good on paying off all his debts. When we got home that night, he lit candles in our bedroom, put on a CD of Miles Davis playing "Someday My Prince Will Come," and made love to me with the ferocity and sensuality that only he could bring to the act.

My first husband, Donald, had always had issues in the intimacy department. He was a superbright, endlessly anxious man; a journalist on the *Buffalo Sun Times* who covered local politics and was widely considered to be one of the great specialists on municipal corruption in the state. I was just out of college, having done a stint on a paper in Madison, Wisconsin, after getting my BA from Minnesota. I was very pleased to have landed the job on the city desk of the *Sun* and was immediately in awe of this five-foot-six-inch whirlwind and old-school journalistic muckraker. Donald was committed to Buffalo.

I was so smitten with him that I too became committed to Buffalo. But the sex—when it happened—was, at best, perfunctory; at worst, it flatlined.

"Not good at this, never been good at this," he whispered the first night we slept together and he had what could be politely described as "performance-related issues." I reassured him that this was something that happened to all men from time to time, that it was no big deal, that things would come right. The truth is . . . even when he was able to complete the act, it was never satisfying. He was endlessly anxious, caught up in his fears about appearing inadequate and inferior, and no amount of reassurance on my part could assuage such ingrained self-doubts. But I chose to overlook the fact that our bed became a sort of metaphoric cross upon which Donald crucified himself. By the end of the first year of our marriage, our lovemaking (if you could call it that) had dwindled down to twice a month. I suggested that Donald seek counseling. He agreed and then refused to go. Our problems deepened further. Though he remained brilliantly engaging company, that crucial part of our married life went into permanent decline.

But I continued to reason that, given even more love and support, all those intimacy issues would vanish and our marriage would steady and . . .

It is extraordinary, isn't it, the way we convince ourselves all will be well in a relationship that we privately know to be doomed? In the case of my marriage to Donald, the end came the evening he showed up late from the newsroom with eight whiskies too many in him, and informed me, "The fact is, even if I did get counseling or go to my doctor and let him prescribe me something, all the little blue pills in the world wouldn't stop the repulsion I feel every time you come near me."

As soon as this line was uttered, I snapped my eyes shut, trying to tell myself that he had not said what he had just said. But when my eyes opened, there was a strange little half-smile on Donald's face. The sight of him, quietly enjoying the hurt and confusion now ricocheting within me, led me to the following uncomfortable truth: he said all that because he knew, once uttered, we would pass the point of no return.

"Now you can really hate me," he finally whispered.

"I just pity you, Donald."

I asked for a meeting with our newspaper's editor in chief the next morning. I told him that, if the paper was still offering the voluntary redundancy packages that had been mentioned some months earlier during a wave of cutbacks, I would be willing to accept one.

Ten days later—with one year's salary in my bank account—I got into my car and drove north to Montreal. I'd decided to learn French and live in a city that hovered somewhere between a European and new-world sensibility. It was also cheap. I found a small apartment in the decidedly francophone confines of the Plateau. I went to daily French lessons at the Université de Montréal and worked hard at mastering that challenging and intricate language. My proficiency improved considerably when I started having an affair with a man named Thierry, who ran a used record shop on the rue Saint Denis and was intermittently trying to write the great Quebecois novel. His charms and reasonable sexual prowess—especially after Donald—were subsumed by unapologetic laziness. After a year I was able to renew my student visa. As my prowess in French grew, I began to hatch plans about perhaps moving to Paris and working out some way of landing a *carte de séjour* and reinventing myself professionally as . . .

This was the dilemma. What was I going to do next in my life? I set up an appointment at the French consulate in Montreal and found myself facing a very *petit fonctionnaire* who discouraged me from even thinking about finding work in Paris without a European passport or a French husband. My Canadian student visa allowed me to take on work for the length of my sojourn there at the university. I found a temporary post as an administrative assistant in a firm of bilingual accountants—and started finding myself fascinated by the world of numbers. I knew that, by retraining as a CPA, I was landing myself in the world of other people's narratives that I said I would dodge once I left journalism. Nonetheless, after eighteen months in Quebec, I decided to recross the American frontier and enter a CPA course in Buffalo. Privately I knew why I had run back there. Buffalo was safe. Buffalo was the only place, to date, where I had put down roots. No longer being at the newspaper meant that my chances of running into Donald were slim. I still felt a deep lingering sadness about the end of the marriage, coupled with the thought that I should have been able to change him. In Buffalo I had some good friends and many contacts—so there was also the prospect of being able to set up my own small accountancy firm and have enough people to reach out to as prospective clients.

Just to prove that I was a responsible young woman, I found a job with a local CPA while doing the two-year accountancy course. This allowed me to take what was left from the redundancy money and buy a nice apartment in an old Victorian-style house outright (Buffalo is so cheap), and even renovate the kitchen and bathroom while furnishing it with funky secondhand items. When the time came— and I was indeed an official Certified Public Accountant—I had seven initial clients who joined me on the day I first opened my office.

Then, two years later, Paul walked in.

"I wonder: Is this all a mistake?"

His words as we landed in Morocco. A journey that was his idea, his surprise—and one that he sprang on me just two weeks after he had cleared a significant portion of his debts and had sworn off compulsive spending. I'd just come home from my biweekly yoga class to find Paul at work in the kitchen, the aromas of North Africa wafting everywhere. Approaching him at the stove I gave him a kiss. "Let me guess: a tagine?"

"Your powers of observation are formidable."

"Not as formidable as your culinary skills."

"Your self-doubt is touching, but not founded in fact."

As always Paul's lamb tagine was splendid—he made it with preserved lemons and prunes; a recipe he'd learned during the very formative two years he'd spent in Morocco in his midtwenties.

That was back in the early 1980s—when, after graduating from Parsons in New York and trying to make an early go of it as an artist in the then-still-demimonde world of lower Manhattan, he decided that a radical change of scene was required. Through the careers office at Parsons he learned that an art school in Casablanca was looking for an instructor in drawing. A two-year contract. Three thousand dollars a year, plus a little apartment near the school.

"They told me it was probably the best art school in Morocco," he said during one of our early dinner dates. "But that wasn't saying much. Still, they said it would give me the chance to live somewhere exotic, escape the workaday world, travel, and get a considerable amount of my own work done under that white-hot North African sun."

So Paul quit his job and took the cramped overnight flight to Casablanca, and hated everything about the place on sight. In no way resembling the fabled, mythic city of the movie, he described it as sprawling, concrete, ugly. The art school turned out to be second-rate, the staff demoralized, the students largely untalented.

"I had very few friends at the beginning—outside of a Franco-Moroccan artist named Romain Ben Hassan, who was a talented abstract expressionist as well as a budding alcoholic. But it was Romain who got me a French teacher and forced me to speak with him all the time in the language of everyone around me. And it was Romain who got me to stop feeling sorry for myself, and let me into his social circle of local and expatriate artists. He also forced me to get on with my own work."

By the end of his first year, Paul had found a life for himself in Casablanca. He had a circle of fellow artists—Moroccan and expatriate—with whom he hung out. He had one or two students whom he thought promising. Most of all he worked rigorously on an amazing portfolio of lithographs and line drawings that chronicled his quarter of Casablanca. Though the art school wanted him to stay on he used this portfolio—which he called "The White City"—to get himself a gallery in New York and to start looking for teaching work. While on a three-week break between school terms, he headed south to a walled seaside city called Essaouira. "Like going back to the Middle Ages and landing yourself in the ultimate artist's colony."

Essaouira was always one of Paul's conversation pieces: how he found a room in a fantastically cheap and "atmospherically seedy" hotel. It too had a great balcony off his room, from which he could see the sweep of the Atlantic and the medieval walls of this strange, alluring city where "Orson Welles shot his film version of *Othello* and Jimi Hendrix smoked far too much dope while chilling out on the Moroccan Atlantic vibe." Paul spent his weeks there working on a second collection of line drawings—"In the Labyrinth"—depicting the spindly alleyways of Essaouira, and landing him a decent art dealer–gallery owner in Manhattan, Jasper Pirnie. He managed to sell thirty of his lithographs.

"The money I made from the lithographs could have paid for me to stay another two years in Essaouira, it was so cheap back then. But what did I do? The State University of New York in Buffalo had a position open in their Visual Arts Department. The fact that I knew the chairman of the department, who actually rated me . . . well, there it was: an assistant professorship with the possibility of tenure in six years if I kept getting my lithographs and drawings exhibited. But even as I packed my bags in Essaouira, after sending a telegram back to the department head that I was accepting the job, I knew this was a decision I would come to regret."

I remember distinctly that this was the moment when I covered his hand with my own; the first time either of us had made an intimate gesture toward each other. Strange, isn't it, how I reached out to comfort this man after he admitted to me that he had fenced himself in? Perhaps because I too felt self-fenced (is there such a word?), and because he was someone with a creative, bohemian streak who would pull me away from my innate cautiousness, my need to make lists in my sleep and keep the books balanced. He leaned over and kissed me as I covered his hand, then threaded his fingers into mine and said, "You are wonderful." That was the first night we slept together. After all the years with Donald, it was both revelatory and heady to be with a man who was so sexually confident, so adept at giving me pleasure.

He made me a lamb tagine the second night we slept together. And he made me a lamb tagine just six weeks ago, to celebrate his paying off his debts. That night he also dropped a little surprise into my life.

"What would you say to spending a month this summer in Essaouira?" he asked.

My initial thought was that we'd put five hundred dollars down on a cottage near Popham Beach in Maine. Reading my mind, Paul said, "We can still do the two weeks in Popham. I've booked us to leave Morocco on August thirteenth, which is a few days before we're due in Maine."

"You've actually bought us two tickets for Morocco?"

"I wanted to surprise you."

"Oh, you certainly did that. But you could have at least asked me if I was free."

"If I had asked, you would have found an excuse to say no."

He was, alas, right about that.

"Did you even consider the fact that I have a business, and clients? And how are we going to afford this trip to Morocco?"

"Jasper sold four more lithographs last week."

"You never told me this."

"The nature of a surprise is to keep things secret."

I was already intrigued. Except for my time in Montreal and a trip once to Vancouver, I had no experience of the world beyond American frontiers. Here was my husband offering to whisk me off to North Africa. But my alleged financial caution was, I knew, underscored by fear. The fear of foreignness. Of being dropped into a Muslim country that—for all of Paul's talk about its modernity—was (from everything I had ever read about it) still locked in the North African past.

"We can easily live for a month in Essaouira for two thousand dollars," he said.

"It's too long to take off."

"Promise your staff a nice bonus if they hold the fort for six weeks."

"And what are my clients going to say about this?"

"Who consults an accountant between mid-July and Labor Day?"

He did have a point. It was my slowest season. But six weeks away? It seemed like such a huge block of time . . . even though I also knew that, in the great scheme of things, it was nothing—and that, yes, Morton (my bookkeeper) and Kathy (my secretary) could manage to run everything very well while I was away. One of the hardest lessons for anyone with control freak tendencies to absorb is that the world actually goes on very well without them.

"I'm going to have to think this over."

"No," Paul said, taking my hand. "You're going to say yes now. Because you know this will be an amazing experience which will take you out of your comfort zone and show you a world you've only imagined. And it will give me the opportunity to work on a new portfolio, which Jasper assured me he can sell for at least fifteen thousand dollars. So there's a big financial incentive. Most of all it will be very good for us. We could truly use some time out of here, time to ourselves, and away from all that day-to-day stuff."

Morocco. My husband was bringing us to Morocco. To Essaouira. How could I not overlook my qualms and give in to the idea of a North African idyll in a walled medieval city facing the Atlantic? The stuff of fantasy. But aren't most fantasies all rooted in one great hope: that we will land, even temporarily, in a better place?

So I said yes.

The immigration line inched forward, slowly, inexorably. Almost an hour had passed since we'd landed. Only now were we the next in line to have our passports inspected by the police. In front of us the man from Mauritania was being rigorously questioned by the cop in the booth, the discussion getting heated, voices raised, the policeman picking up the phone to call someone, two other plainclothes officers (guns bulging under their suit jackets) showing up and leading the now angry and frightened man into a side interrogation room. Glancing away from this little drama toward my husband, I could see that he was regarding these proceedings with dread.

"You think they'll let me in?" he whispered.

"Why wouldn't they?"

"No reason, no reason," he said, sounding uneasy. At that precise moment the cop in the booth called us forward, his hand out for our passports and landing cards. As he scanned each of our passports and peered at the computer screen, Paul was working hard at masking his distress. I reached over and took his hand, squeezing it, willing him to calm down.

"You stay how long?" the cop asked in choppy, cadenced English.

"*Quatre semaines,*" Paul said.

"You work here?" the cop asked.

"No way," Paul said. "We're on vacation."

Another glance at the computer screen. Then a thorough inspection of all the pages of our respective passports, during which I could feel Paul tense even more. Then: stamp, stamp . . . and the cop pushed the passports back to us.

"*Bienvenue,*" he said.

And we stepped forward into Morocco.

"See, they let you in," I said, all smiles. "Why so nervous?"

"Stupidity, stupidity," he said.

But as we moved forward toward the baggage carousels I caught him whispering to himself one word:

"Idiot."

FOUR

JULY IN NORTH Africa. Heat and dust and gasoline fumes enveloping the parched air. That was the first aroma to hit my nostrils as we left the airport terminal: petroleum intermixed with arid, motionless oxygen. Up in the sky the morning sun was at full wattage. It didn't matter that Casablanca was on the Atlantic coast. The first sensation on leaving the somewhat cooler confines of the arrivals hall was "welcome to the blast furnace." The sort of torridity that immediately stung the eyes and parched the mouth.

"We would have to arrive in hell," Paul said as we waited at the packed bus stop for the coach into the city center.

"Well, you did once live here in July, right?" I said.

"It will be cooler in Essaouira."

"And we'll be there in just a few days. No doubt our hotel here in Casablanca has air-conditioning."

"Don't be so sure of that. This is North Africa. Discomfort at the cheap end of the spectrum is part of the deal."

"Then we can find a hotel with AC."

"Or we can change our plans now."

"What?"

"Back in a moment."

With that he disappeared off into the crowd. I wanted to follow him. But our suitcases were there in front of me. They were four sizable pieces of luggage, as they had clothes for many weeks and

Paul's art supplies and the collection of twelve books I had envisaged myself reading while facing the waters of the Atlantic. Were I to leave the suitcases and pursue my husband, I would be inviting theft and a proper disaster at the start of what was already shaping up to be a rather dubious adventure. So all I could do was shout Paul's name several times over. My voice was drowned out by everyone crowded around the bus stop: veiled women, men of varied ages in ill-fitting suits, one or two backpackers, two grandfatherly types in long flowing robes, three very dark-skinned Africans carrying their worldly goods in cheap canvas bags, causing me to wonder if they were guest workers here looking for work and, from the bewilderment sketched on their faces, very much as adrift here as myself.

Buses came and went, most of them elderly, all belching further clouds of exhaust as they heaved away toward assorted destinations. I peered into the distance but could see no sign of my vanished husband. Ten, fifteen minutes passed. God, he really has decided to do a geographic about-face and head for home. He is probably back inside the terminal building, using a credit card to dispatch us back to the States.

But then, amidst the crowded theater of this street scene, a tall man emerged. Paul. Walking toward me, accompanied by a diminutive fellow. He was half shaven, with a small knitted skullcap on his head, a cigarette clenched between blackened teeth. In one hand he carried a battered tin tray on which sat two stubby glasses, while his other hand clutched a pot of tea.

"*Laissez-moi vous présenter ma charmante épouse,*" Paul told the gentleman as he approached us.

The man smiled shyly. Placing the tray down on the empty space next to me on a pockmarked bench, he then raised the teapot a good foot above the glasses and began to ceremoniously pour a green liquid into the two glasses. I immediately discerned the heady, aromatic properties of the tea.

"*Thé à la menthe,*" Paul said. "*Le whisky marocain.*"

Mint tea. Moroccan whisky. The man smiled and offered me the tray with the two glasses. I lifted one of them. Paul took his glass and clinked it against mine.

"Sorry to have disappeared like that," he said.

He leaned forward and placed a kiss on my lips. I accepted it, as I did his hand, which he entwined with my free one. Then I took my first sip of *le whisky marocain*. The mint was palatably strong, but undercut by a certain sugary sweetness. I usually dislike anything overly sweet—but this tea worked because of its aromatic strength and its honeyed undercurrent. After that horrendous flight and the wait in the sun, it was balm.

"You approve?" Paul asked.

"I approve."

"Our friend here loaned me his cell phone. There is a change of plans."

"What sort of change of plans?"

"We're going straight to Essaouira. There's a bus that leaves here in twenty minutes."

"What about Casablanca?"

"Trust me, you're not missing much."

"It's still Casablanca, a place you've talked about endlessly from the moment we first got together."

"It can wait."

"But Essaouira is . . . what . . . four, five hours from here?"

"Something like that, yeah. I checked just now—the Casablanca hotel doesn't have air-conditioning. Nor will they let us check in until three p.m. . . . . which would mean sitting in a café for almost five hours. Why not take that time getting to Essaouira? And the guy who was selling the bus tickets told me the coach we're taking is air-conditioned."

"So it's a *fait accompli* that we're going to Essaouira? You decided for us?"

"He told me the bus was getting full. Please don't take this badly—"

"I'm taking nothing badly. I'm just . . ."

I turned away, feeling beyond tired after the sit-up-all-night stint across the Atlantic, the heat and the toxic air even more oppressive, a further sip of mint tea doing wonders for a throat gone parched again.

"Fine, fine," I said. "Essaouira it is."

Twenty minutes later we were aboard a bus heading south. It was absolutely packed, but Paul slipped the guy taking tickets a ten-dirham note to find us two seats right at the back of the coach. It was not air-conditioned.

"*Ça se déclenchera dès que le bus aura démarré*," said the guy who managed to squeeze us on when Paul asked, in his rather good French, if the stifling heat inside the coach would be alleviated by cooling air. *It will come on once the bus starts*. But when the coach pulled out, there was no arctic blast from the vents. The bus wasn't very old, but it wasn't very new either. And it was crammed with people and their many possessions. Two women in niqabs sat opposite us with a young girl whose hands were elaborately painted with signs and symbols denoting things beyond my knowledge. Nearby was a wire-thin man well into his seventies, his eyes baffled by dark glasses, praying semisilently, rocking back and forth in his cramped seat, so clearly bound up in the intensity of his beseechings to a power higher than this sweatbox of a bus. Next to the praying man was a young guy—sallow, peach-fuzz beard, don't-mess-with-me eyes—listening to some pop Arab number on an overlarge set of headphones that leaked sound. He sang along with the song's lyrics, unaware of how loud he was, his off-key drone accompanying us all the way south.

The seats were tightly packed, allowing for little legroom, and so unsuitable for Paul's six-foot-four-inch frame. But we did have the long-benched backseat—which let him angle himself in such a way as to stretch out. He pushed himself up against the window. I slid in next to him. Putting his arms around me, he said, "So I got it wrong about the AC."

"We'll survive," I said, though after ten minutes on the road my clothes were drenched.

"We always survive," he said, tightening his arms around me and kissing my head. Nearby the young guy caught a glimpse of this moment of marital affection and rolled his eyes while simultaneously singing that same toneless lyric over and over again. I peered out the window. North African–style urban sprawl. Chipped white apartment blocks. Chipped white stretches of congested houses. Car dealerships. Warehouses. Congealed traffic. Chipped white strip malls. Chipped white villages. And then . . .

Sleep.

Or an approximation thereof.

I passed out.

Then there was a jolt. The bus had hit a pothole or something akin to that. We were in open country, stony, empty, bleak. Low-lying hills on the horizon. The world vanished again, then woke up when . . .

A baby was screaming. The mother—young, in a multicolored head scarf, sitting in front of us, looking sleep deprived and fearful—kept trying to calm the child. He couldn't have been more than three weeks old. And he was miserable. Understandably so. What little oxygen there was in the bus had been sucked away by the reek of communal sweat and malodorous exhaust fumes, the heat curdled so that it actually felt tactile, weighty and doughy like four-day-old bread.

Shifting around in the space between Paul's legs where I had parked myself, I could feel his limp penis. I suddenly had a huge stab of desire—not just for the sensation of abandonment making love with my husband, but also with an overwhelming need to have a baby.

There had, of course, been women in Paul's past. One was a colleague at the university, with whom he'd lived for around two years. He talked little about her, except to say that it didn't end well. Otherwise he made it known that he didn't want to talk much about his romantic past. He did tell me one crucial detail: I was the first woman with whom he could imagine having a child.

As the bus hit another bump my husband jumped awake, finding my hand on his crotch.

"You trying to tell me something?" he asked.

"Maybe I am," I said, leaning up to kiss him on the lips.

"Where are we?"

"No idea."

"How long have we been on the bus?"

"Too long."

"And the AC?"

"Never showed up. It's not your fault."

He reached over and touched my face.

"How did I get so lucky?" he asked.

"We're both lucky."

"Do you really mean that?"

"Yes. I do."

"Even though I've driven you mad sometimes?"

"Paul . . . I love you. I want this marriage to work."

"If we can get through this fucking bus trip together we can get through anything."

I laughed—and gave him such a full and deep kiss that, when the bus hit another bump and disengaged me from my husband's lips, I saw that everyone around us was either embarrassed or disapproving.

"Sorry, sorry," I whispered to the elderly man sitting just in front of us. He turned away, showing me his back. Paul whispered to me, "They'll be a little more open in Essaouira, as they're far more used to hippie-dippie foreigners."

"We are hardly hippie-dippie."

"Correction: *you* are hardly hippie-dippie."

I found myself laughing again and causing more disapproving glances by kissing my husband once more. A moment like this—

when all seemed right between us—was so pleasing, wondrous, reassuring. Paul was right: if we could get through this bus ride we could get through anything.

Around ten minutes after Paul snapped back into consciousness, the bus pulled into a tiny concrete depot off the side of the road. The landscape here was rocky, scrubby, flat, uninspiring.

"You think there's a toilet here?" I asked Paul.

"No idea—but that line over there looks huge."

He nodded toward a group of about a dozen women, all but three hidden by niqabs, lined up in front of a single hut.

"Maybe I should just try and hold it," I said.

"But there's at least another hour and a half to go. We should try to slip around the back of the depot."

Which is exactly what we did—finding a patch of ground festooned with trash, broken bottles, two burned-out fires, even a dead mouse charred by the sun.

"You expect me to pee here?" I asked Paul.

"There is the toilet option."

The stench enveloping us was nothing short of toxic; an aroma of fecal matter and festering rubbish. But I was desperate to empty my bladder. So, finding a patch of ground that was free of glass shards and trash, I undid my loose-fitting cargo pants, squatted down, and let go. Paul meanwhile was standing some feet away, peeing against a wall, laughing.

"Gracious living, eh?" he said.

The driver began to beep his horn. We had to get back on the bus. But as we came aboard we discovered that two young men— they must have been around twenty years old, both scowling and menacing, both wearing nylon bomber jackets and black plastic sunglasses—had taken our seats. They saw us heading toward them as we negotiated the tiny aisle, sidestepping all the bags and two very parched dogs (German shepherds, rendered inert by the heat). When we reached our places, Paul informed them in French that they were sitting where we had been sitting. Their response was to ignore us. I glanced around. Every other seat on the bus was taken. Paul quietly asked them to move. Their response again was to act as if we didn't exist.

"*Vous êtes assis à nos places,*" Paul said, his tone getting edgier. "*Vous devriez en chercher d'autres.*"

Again, nothing. Paul tried again, adding, "*S'il vous plaît.*"

The two guys exchanged a cool, amused glance. They continued to say nothing.

At this point the other young guy, who'd been singing along tonelessly to his iPod all the way south, turned around and said something in Arabic to the two toughs. One of them shot back a short response—which, from its menacing vehemence, was a warning to stay out of this. The young guy remained cool in the wake of this exchange. He just quietly shook his head, then popped his earphones back on his head.

Meanwhile, the elderly man seated nearby heard this exchange and suddenly erupted in an angry flow of Arabic; so angry that all eyes in the bus were on us, the two foreigners standing in the aisle. The same one who had hissed at our friend with the headphones now said something so unpleasant to the elderly man that several people nearby—including a large woman whose face was completely covered by a niqab—began to shout back at the pair. Again they sat there silently, refusing to budge, refusing to listen to reason, determined to play out this scenario to some sort of unpleasant conclusion.

"I'm getting the driver," Paul said to me.

But the driver—a harassed, constricted man with sunken eyes and a pencil-thin moustache—was already en route toward us, looking less than pleased. He walked into a sea of raised voices, as the elderly man, the woman with the niqab, and three others began to tell him what had just transpired. The driver asked Paul something in fast French. Paul responded equally fast, indicating that he had politely asked these two boys (they couldn't have been more than seventeen) to vacate the seats that we'd had since Casablanca. Now the driver got vehement, yelling at them, staring into their menacing black sunglasses, which made them appear even more sinister. But, as before, they refused to respond. The driver's voice now ticked up another angry octave. As he put his face close to them, the more verbal of the pair—the one who had spoken back to the young guy and the elderly man—did something startling: he spat at the driver, catching him directly in one eye.

The driver looked beyond stunned. To his credit he didn't lash out, didn't explode into understandable fury. Rather, with immense quiet dignity, he pulled a handkerchief from his pocket, wiped the spittle from his eye, then hurried down the aisle, leaving the bus and heading into the depot building opposite where we were parked.

Immediately the young dude with the headphones stood up. Gently touching my shoulder, he motioned that I should take his seat.

"*Ce n'est pas nécessaire,*" I said.

"*J'insiste,*" he said. The man seated next to him—a quiet businessman-type in his forties, bespectacled, wearing a light-blue striped suit—also slid out of his seat.

"*J'insiste.*"

"*Mille mercis,*" Paul said, as he gently directed me toward the window seat, then positioned himself next to me, ensuring that I was out of range of the aisle should anything violent happen.

"You okay?" Paul whispered as I reached for his hand.

"What's this about?"

"Macho bullshit. Showing they can stand up to a Western woman."

"But I said nothing to them."

"Doesn't matter. They're idiots. Fortunately everyone else around us thinks that too."

At that moment two policemen entered the bus, both looking as hot as the rest of us. The driver was right behind them. Seeing us now seated he explained something to the officers in rapid-fire

Arabic. One of the officers turned and actually saluted us. The elderly man now began to get angry, pointing an accusatory finger at the two toughs, expressing his outrage at what had transpired with the driver. The second officer picked up the nastiest of the pair by his shirt, whipped off the kid's sunglasses, threw them to the floor, and stamped on them with his foot. With his eyes exposed, the boy's gangster image suddenly vanished. He was just a sallow adolescent. The other officer did likewise with his cohort, only this time, when the dark glasses were pulled from his face, all I could see was fear.

Within moments they were both being frog-marched down the aisle and out of the bus. As soon as they were clear of the front door, the driver was back in his seat, revving the engine, wanting to put immediate distance between himself and all the events that had just transpired. Paul and I stood up, offering to move back to our previous seats. But the businessman and the young headphone dude insisted we stay put. I glanced out the window and regretted doing so. Because I saw the tougher of the tough guys trying to break free of the grasp of one of the officers. Immediately the cop had his baton out and slammed it directly in the boy's face. As soon as he fell to his knees the cop responded with a direct blow to the head. The other tough began to cry out, but was slapped across the mouth with an open hand by the officer holding him. The bus picked up speed, shrouding this brutal tableau in a cloud of dust. Behind me the young headphones dude began to sing his toneless song again. I buried my head in Paul's shoulder, feeling profound guilt. As if my presence here had caused it all. Sensing my distress, Paul tightened his arm around me.

"It's all in the past now," he said.

And the bus sped off into the future.

FİVE

IF THE CAT could talk, she would have said: How did this happen? She looked dusty, grubby, world-weary; a cat who lived on the streets and had no human home to which to retreat. And tonight she was hanging off a wall. The way her claws were digging into the chalky texture of the brickwork made it appear as though she had been glued into place, her back in perfect parallel with the wall. There was something spectral and unsettling about the way she seemed to be frozen. I was reminded of images I'd once seen of wildlife that had been caught in volcanic lava flow and had fossilized into place; their final steps as sentient creatures frozen in time. I must have spent a good minute looking at the cat and the place in which she now found herself. How was she able to sustain this absurd, improbable physical position? And what fear or apprehension had forced her to take refuge on a crumbling bit of whitewashed stone down a dark alleyway within the labyrinthine confines of a walled city?

How did this happen?

And what was I doing down this black passageway in the middle of the night?

To jump back around twelve hours . . .

The bus deposited us at its terminus—the depot at Essaouira—just before two p.m. As we staggered off that motorized steambath, the headphones dude—still singing that wonderful ludicrous tune (was that the only song on his iPod?)—gave us an amused wave goodbye. The bus driver, smoking what was evidently a much-needed cigarette, also nodded farewell as we grabbed our luggage and fended off several touts who were trying to convince us to take up their offer of cheap accommodation.

"You want room . . . very clean . . . good price."

"*Nous avons déjà une chambre,*" Paul replied, steering me toward a line of beat-up taxis nearby.

"But I have better room . . . you come with me I show you everything in Essaouira."

Paul waved him away while I sidestepped several women holding up woven shirts and multicolored shawls and cheap beaded necklaces. The afternoon sun was still punishing. This concrete plaza was thick with gas fumes and dust. I grabbed my scrunched-up field hat out of my shoulder bag, then pulled it down so squarely over my head that it shielded my eyes. The crowd of hawkers followed us as we moved toward the taxis. They were relentless in their need to hound us. They wouldn't take no for an answer.

"Just keep walking," Paul told me. "They are a nuisance, but harmless."

The first cab we approached—a blue-colored Peugeot that appeared to have been in a demolition derby—was driven by a man who looked like he'd last slept in 2010. He had a cell phone to his ear, and was shouting into it. Paul approached him and gave him the name of our hotel.

"Two hundred dirhams," he said in English, even though Paul addressed him in French.

"But the hotel is maybe ten minutes' walk from here," Paul said.

The cabbie put down the phone for a moment.

"That's the price. You don't like it, walk."

"*Charmant,*" Paul said.

The cabbie just shrugged. Paul, shaking his head, led us to the car behind this unpleasant fellow. When the first cabbie saw us approaching the next driver, he was immediately out of his taxi, shouting. The new cabbie—a rather stubby man with a look of fatigued resignation on his face—ignored the protestations of Mr. Charm.

"*Où allez-vous?*" he asked Paul.

"*Vous connaissez l'hôtel Les Trois Chameaux?*"

"*Bien sûr. Ça vous coûtera environ trente dirhams.*"

Thirty dirhams. An honest man.

"*D'accord,*" Paul said and we loaded our bags into his truck. As we drove off we ran into a small flotilla of geese and chickens, herded alongside the city walls by a man in a white djellaba and skullcap. The driver honked his horn in a short, nonchalant manner, indicating that the shepherd should get his livestock out of the way. Nearby was a man wheeling a barrel filled with unrefined cotton. And—this was hallucinatory—a fellow sitting in front of a basket, intoning a tune on a reedy instrument as a python ascended upward from the straw hoop.

Paul could see me taking this all in. The taxi followed a route along the walls of Essaouira; walls that looked like fortifications from some medieval bulwark.

"It gets even stranger," Paul said, clearly at home amidst the vivid chaos.

We hugged the road adjacent to the wall for another minute, then turned under a narrow archway and down a back alley, notable for its blue walls and the tiny lanes that branched off it. At the end was a doorway, also painted a deep blue. This was the entrance to our hotel. Les Trois Chameaux. The Three Camels. The lobby was dark, shadowy, austere. An elderly man was asleep behind the reception desk. He was dressed for a day out at the races: a flowery shirt, a gold chain with the Moroccan star heaving up and down with his snores, gold rings on his fingers, heavy dark sunglasses hiding his eyes.

I looked around. Old Moroccan furnishings—all heavy wood and once-luxuriant brushed velvet upholstery—now dust-ridden and showing serious signs of neglect. There was a loud 1920s railway station clock hanging next to the reception area that counted off each passing second with an ominous click. And there was a half-starved cat on top of the counter, eyeing us warily.

As we approached, Paul took the initiative, at first whispering "Monsieur," then raising his voice several decibels with each additional attempt. When this proved pointless, I tapped the hotel bell near the open guest register. Its loud clang jolted the man back to life, the shock on his face coupled with bemusement, as if he didn't know where he was. As he tried to adjust his gaze on us, Paul said, "Sorry to have woken you so abruptly. But we did try—"

"You have a reservation?"

"Yes."

"Name?"

Paul gave him this information. The man stood up and, using the index finger on each hand, spun the register around toward him. He peered at today's page, rifled back through several pages, shaking his head, muttering to himself.

"You have no reservation," he finally said.

"But I made one," Paul said.

"You received confirmation from us?"

"Of course. I made it on the internet."

"You have a copy of the confirmation?"

Paul looked sheepish. "Forgot to print it," he whispered to me.

"Surely if you went online," I said, "you'd find it."

"I think I deleted it."

I stopped myself from saying, "Not again." Paul was always clearing out his files and frequently removing essential correspondence that he needed to hold on to.

"*Mais il vous reste bien des chambres, non?*" I asked the guy behind the desk.

"*Oui et non.*"

He now picked up an ancient house phone—the sort that seemed to belong in some movie set during the German occupation—and started speaking Arabic in a loud, fractious voice. This was something I was beginning to notice: how Arabic was often a language declaimed in a stentorian manner, making it seem aggressive, swaggering, bordering on the hostile. It reminded me that I should try to resuscitate my still-reasonable, if rusty, French while here. The desk clerk finished his conversation. Turning back to us, he said, "My colleague, he gets the owner now."

We had to wait ten minutes for the arrival of the man in charge. His name was Monsieur Picard. He was French, in his midfifties, short, fit, dressed in a crisp white shirt and tan trousers, formal, chilly; his face reflecting, I sensed, a lifetime of enforced diffidence and the dodging of emotion.

"There seems to be a problem?" he asked, his tone borderline supercilious.

"We booked a room, but you don't seem to have a record of it," Paul said.

"Do you have the confirmation?" Monsieur Picard asked.

Paul shook his head.

"Nor do we. So a reservation mustn't have been made."

"But I made the reservation."

"Clearly not."

"Well, you do have rooms, yes?" I asked.

"Has not Ahmed here told you that we have just one room free?"

"And how much does that cost?"

"It is a room with a balcony and a sea view. And you will need it for how long?"

"A month," Paul said. "That's what we booked it for."

He pursed his lips, then turned to Ahmed. He directed him in French to scan the ledger. Ahmed thumbed through its many pages, glancing down, clucking his tongue against the roof of his mouth, seeing whether they could house us for all that time. I began to wonder: Did Paul actually make the reservation, or was this one of his many "little oversights" that seemed to decorate our lives? Now I was starting to feel angry with myself for not checking up on the reservation before departure. Another part of me was castigating myself for questioning his veracity; given the sliminess of the hotel owner and the sleepwalking style of his desk clerk, who's to say they didn't lose the reservation or weren't playing games to get a better price from us?

This latter scenario began to seem more plausible after the next exchange. Ahmed turned to the owner, nodding his head, saying something that sounded positive. The owner now spoke to us.

"I have good news. We do have that room available for the entire period you desire. The other good news is that it is the best room in the house—a minisuite with a balcony that faces the Atlantic. The price is seven dirhams per night."

Paul's face fell. Immediately the adding machine in my brain was whirring away. That was almost one hundred dollars: double the price Paul told me he had negotiated.

"But the room I booked cost three-fifty," Paul said.

"You have no record of this offer, do you?" Monsieur Picard said. "As we too have no record of this reservation and are trying to accommodate you—"

"I booked a room for a month at three hundred and fifty dirhams," Paul said, angry, stressed.

"Monsieur, if there is no proof, all we have is words. And words—"

"What are you, a fucking philosopher?" Paul hissed.

I put a stabilizing hand on my husband's left forearm.

"He didn't mean that," I told Monsieur Picard. "We are both exhausted and—"

"I did fucking mean that. This guy is playing with us."

Monsieur Picard smiled thinly.

"You act as if you are doing me a service by staying here. By all means find another hotel—and one of this quality and cleanliness that can offer you a suite of this size for a month. The door is there. *Bonne chance.*"

He turned and started heading up the stairs.

"Could we see the suite, please?" I shouted after him.

"As you wish," he said.

I started following him upstairs. Paul lingered by the reception desk, fuming.

"You coming up?" I asked.

"Looks like you're the one in charge now."

"Fine."

I continued up the stairs. As we reached the first landing Monsieur Picard turned to me and said, "Your husband does not seem to be a happy man."

"And what business is that of yours?" I asked.

The sharpness of my tone startled him.

"I meant no offense," he said.

"Yes you did."

The upstairs corridors were narrow, but reasonably well painted, with ceramic blue tiles surrounding the door frames. We reached a corridor and walked up a set of stairs barely wide enough to accommodate a modest-size person.

"Splendid isolation," Picard said as we reached a wooden door carved with lattices. He opened it.

"*Après vous, madame.*"

I walked inside. Picard turned on a light on a side table. At first I thought: Oh, God, this is small. We were in a narrow sitting area with carved wooden tables, a sofa in heavy red brocade, and a small armchair. The entire room couldn't have been more than around ten square feet. Tiny slits of light from the blue wooden shutters caught the dust in the air. Sensing my disappointment, Picard said, "It gets better."

Opening a connecting door, we were now in a high-vaulted room augmented by wooden beams. The centerpiece was a king-size bed with huge round cushions propping up the carved wood headboard, upholstered in faded red velvet. Everything here was heavy dark wood and maroonish: the bedspread, the large desk with a matching carved chair, the large chest of drawers, the sultan-throne armchair with a matching footrest. Stone walls. The bathroom was acceptable and clean, with a shower stall enhanced by an intricate painted design. I turned on the knobs and discovered there was reasonable water pressure. When I returned to the bedroom area I was taken aback. Picard had opened all the shutters, allowing light to flood in everywhere. This darkened enclave was suddenly awash with crystalline sun. I followed Picard's request to follow him onto the balcony, out into a day that was still white-hot, incandescent.

The balcony itself wasn't substantial. Perhaps ten feet long by three feet wide. But its prospect was ravishing. Turn right and you peered directly over the walled fortress that was Essaouira. The absolute wild originality of the place—its medieval bunkers, its spindly alleys, its visual and human density—was laid out in front of me with a near-cartographic clarity.

Then, when you turned left, the entire spread of the Atlantic enveloped the eye.

Is there anything more balming than the sight of water? Especially this body of water, linking us to home?

There were two folded deck chairs on the balcony and a small table. I quickly envisaged Paul here, his sketchbooks and pencils and charcoals spread out in front of him, engaged with the sky, the sea, the jagged rooftops, the strange scenic concoction laid out directly beneath us. I would be in the next chair, hunched over a French grammar book, fresh from a language lesson I'd had that morning, working my way through the subjunctive case.

"Not bad, is it?" Picard said, his voice more diplomatic since I'd snapped at him a few minutes earlier.

"It will do."

I stepped back inside. Never negotiate a price when facing a peerless view. Picard joined me.

"I saw the email that my husband received from you," I said.

"He never received anything directly from me."

"From your reservations person, then."

"*Madame*, we have no record—"

"But I saw it. I know that you agreed to a price of three hundred and fifty dirhams for a room with a balcony and a sea view."

"It was not this suite. And as this suite is the only room we have left . . ."

"Be smart here."

"You think I am stupid?" he asked, the tone shifting back into superciliousness.

"I'm beginning to think that I should send an email to the person running my accounting firm back in the States and get her to find the email and send it over here. Then I can find the local tourism authority and report you for price gouging."

"Now I must ask you to leave."

"A pity. Not a bad room—and you could have had us here for a month. But your call, sir."

With that I turned and headed for the door. Halfway out he said:

"I can accept six hundred per day."

Without turning back to look at him I said, "Four hundred."

"Five-fifty."

"Five hundred—breakfast and laundry included."

"You expect us to wash your clothes every day?"

"Twice a week. We have little in the way of clothes."

Silence. His thumb was rubbing up against his forefinger, a sure-fire sign of anxiety.

"And you will be here for the entire month?" he asked.

"I can show you our return tickets."

"For this price I will need payment in full in advance."

Now it was my turn to feel as if the tables had turned a bit. But looking around the suite, the hard radiant blue of that North African sky clarifying everything, I decided that a decision was in order. Throw in breakfast and laundry and the savings of two hundred dirhams per night, and I had just saved us well over a thousand dollars.

I also sensed that Picard would be relatively civilized from this moment on. So I reached into my bag and pulled out a credit card and said, "All right, sir. You have a deal."

A small tight pursing of his lips.

"*Très bien, madame.*"

"By the way, you wouldn't know somebody who might want to give me a daily French lesson? I've decided I'd like to improve my fluency in your language."

"I'm certain I can find somebody."

We went downstairs. I found Paul, sitting at a corner table, drinking a mint tea.

"Can you please have our bags sent upstairs?" I asked Picard.

"*Très bien, madame.*"

He signaled the front desk man to bring up our luggage.

Paul was now on his feet, incredulous.

"Don't tell me we're staying," he said.

"Come see the suite."

Then I turned back and headed upstairs. After a moment Paul was right behind me. We reached the next floor, then walked down the narrow corridor and up the final set of tiny stairs. When we reached the suite I walked straight through the two rooms and out onto the balcony. Standing outside, the sun full frontal on my face, the blue contours of the rooftops mirroring the bleached azure of the sky, the choppy waters of the Atlantic luminous with reflected light, I wanted to marvel at this exceptional vista. Marvel that I was here on the eastern lip of North Africa, high above a medieval enclave, about to spend a full month immersed in such an alien but strangely compelling corner of this planet. What a privilege to escape the humdrum and be here. I owed all this to the man in the other room, a man with whom I so wanted things to go right.

I felt Paul's hands on my shoulders. "This view is wondrous," he whispered.

"And the suite?"

"Couldn't be better."

"So you're staying?"

He spun me around and kissed me deeply. Feeling his body so close to mine, his hands sliding up my T-shirt and caressing my back, his penis thickening against my thigh, I had a strong charge of desire, of wanting to obliterate the fatigue, the anger, the doubt, through the wonder of losing myself in him.

So I pulled him closer. And reached down and felt him grow even harder as my hand covered his crotch. Looking briefly over his shoulder to ensure that the door was closed and our bags now in the room, I walked him backward to the bed. The two of us fell on top of it. And then we were pulling off each other's clothes. I was already wet, so in need and want of him. I immediately pulled him inside me. And threw my legs around him to take him even deeper. The desire, the hunger, was immediate, all-encompassing. I came twice within moments. That only seemed to embolden Paul even more, his thrusts deeper, slower, bringing me again to the edge of a certain crazed abyss, over which I tumbled again, every nerve ending beyond electrified, every endorphin amok. I could feel, as always, the slow, relentless buildup within Paul of his own release—and how he held back, like the extraordinary lover that he was, the moment of climax for so long, wanting us to remain fused, deranged, manic for each other. When the buildup became unbearable, and his moans grew louder, I could feel his loins tensing wildly and his penis within me becoming even more rigid, more penetrating. Suddenly he burst forth, letting out a cry amidst subsequent shudders, and I whispered, "Love of my life, love of my life," feeling that to be the truth right now. And hoping against hope that, this time, a baby would come of it all.

As Paul fell off me, I glanced at the watch on my wrist. Almost four in the afternoon. After over thirty hours of travel—and all the inherent tension accompanying that long, difficult journey—a siesta was desperately needed. So I reached down and pulled the white sheet over us; the ceiling fan was circling overhead at a speed reasonable enough to generate a bit of chilled air against the heat. Putting my arms around my already passed-out husband, I shut my eyes.

Then it was pitch dark. Drifting back into consciousness, I had absolutely no idea where I was for several strange moments, the clip-clip rotor movement of the ceiling fan overhead intermingling with a voice of incantation discerned from a loudspeaker. I opened my eyes, noticing the windows still open, no curtains pulled against the stars shining with astonishing clarity in the night sky. And then that voice started again—a loudspeaker crackle, then *"Allahhhhhhhhhh-hhh,"* the last syllable held as a long intoned note, wafting through the darkness. Reality began to reassemble itself. Morocco. Essaouira. The hotel. The suite where we would be spending the next month. My husband, now curled up in a corner of the bed, still closed down and unconscious. And me holding up the dial of my watch close to my face and discovering from the glowing hour and minute hands that it was three forty-three. But if we had started our siesta around four . . .

Could we have been asleep for almost twelve hours? I sat up and squinted again at my watch. I had an urgent need to pee. I got to my feet, my balance just a little askew after such deep sleep. The fan overhead kept up its percussive rattle as my bare feet touched the cool stone of the floor. The middle of the Moroccan night was temperate; an antidote to the immense heat through which we had traveled yesterday. I reached the bathroom, taking in the fact that it was decorated in blue tile; an ultramarine that called to mind the sky above, the Essaouira rooftops below. Like everything else about the suite, the bathroom was clean. The floor was also an intriguing ceramic of blue and white. Monsieur Picard may have been an oily customer, but there was something raffishly stylish about his hotel.

I was feeling very awake. Twelve hours of sleep does that. Having last washed almost two days ago in Buffalo, I was also rank. I dug out my toiletries and made a beeline for the shower. There was proper hot water. It remained hot throughout the twenty minutes I stayed under its spray. When I got out, wrapping my hair in a towel and using the other spare towel around my body, I caught sight of myself in the mirror and shuddered. Not because I looked wretched and aged and beaten up by life. All that sleep had actually restored some vitality to eyes previously adorned with dark rings. But, no doubt about it, what the mirror told me that morning was that I too was up against the inevitable forward momentum of time.

When grappling with uncertainties, there is only one solution: organize. I opened my bag and got dressed: loose linen pants, a blue linen shirt. Then I opened the wardrobe and spent the next fifteen minutes hanging up and arranging all my clothes, before turning to Paul's bag. I hesitated for a moment, but also knew how grateful he was whenever I took charge of the domestic details of our lives. So I unzipped his bag and found chaos. Shirts, underwear, jeans, socks, pairs of shorts, all in an unwashed, beyond-disordered state. Dumping them into the room's wicker laundry basket, I put on a pair of sandals, then, hoisting the basket, let myself out and down the two flights of darkened stairs to the reception desk. A different man was asleep behind the counter: rail-thin, brown teeth, dressed in a djellaba, middle-aged, a lit cigarette still fuming away between two fingers, his mouth open wide. I put the wicker basket down beside him and reached for a notepad and pen on the reception counter to leave him a note, asking him to get our clothes washed. But suddenly he mumbled something in his sleep, then snapped awake, squinting at me.

"Sorry, sorry," I whispered. Then, pointing to the basket, I said, "*Linge.*"

The man's watery eyes began to snap into focus. He glanced at the clock on the wall. It was now four twenty-eight.

"*Maintenant?*" he asked. "*On est au beau milieu de la nuit.*"

Before I could tell him the laundry could wait until later, he disappeared off through a back doorway, returning a few minutes later with a shy young girl—I guessed she was around sixteen—in a simple gingham dress, her hair covered by a head scarf. She looked half awake.

"There was no need to get her now," I told the man.

He just shrugged, then turned to the young girl and pointed to the wicker basket and spoke in rapid-fire Arabic. She answered back, her voice hesitant, demure. The man asked me, "*Laver et repasser?*"

"Yes, yes," I said. "And I need them this morning."

More Arabic to the little girl. She gave a shy, quiet answer. The man turned to me and said, "You will have to wait for the sun to dry your clothes."

"I can't argue with that," I said, smiling at the young girl. She smiled back.

"*Shokran,*" I said, Arabic for *thank you* and just one of a small handful of words I knew in that language.

"*Af wan,*" she replied. *You're welcome.*

And she disappeared with the laundry basket.

"I have one last favor to ask," I told the man. "Since all my husband's clothes are being washed, do you have a robe or something he could wear?"

"*Une djellaba pour votre mari?*"

"*Oui, oui.*"

"*Attendez là,*" he said, and disappeared through the door behind him.

At that precise moment, the voice began to incant again over the loudspeaker. *Allahhhhh.* The *ah* was held so long and in such a haunting, mellifluous way that I felt compelled to step outside and see if I could discern from where it was coming.

Leaving the blue carved archway of the hotel I discovered we were in a back alley, unpaved, narrow enough for one vehicle but little else. The amplified voice started chanting again. I moved away from the doorway. Just ten or so paces away from the hotel and I was enshrouded in darkness: hostile doorways, shuttered shops, tiny alleys filtering off this constricted street. I knew I shouldn't be here. It was like falling into a blackened maze. But the voice kept beckoning me forward, inviting me deeper into the shadows, making me fearless.

Then I saw the cat. Hanging off a wall directly in front of me, as if he had been glued onto its crumbling stone surface. So emaciated, so grubby, so spooked. Had something terrifying thrown her against that wall? She was now clinging to it, paralyzed perpendicularly. Catching sight of her threw me. The impossibility of her position was so unnerving that I felt as if an ice-cold hand had been placed on one of my bare shoulders.

Then an ice-cold hand was placed on one of my shoulders.

I found myself surrounded by three men. They had come out of nowhere. A guy in his fifties with a grizzled half-shaven face, three teeth, wild eyes. A plump kid—he couldn't have been more than eighteen—wearing a T-shirt that failed to cover his hairy stomach, his face oleaginous, his eyes darting up and down my body, a goofy smile on his lips. The hand belonged to a hunched young man, sallow-skinned, his countenance glassy, disturbed. The touch of his fingers made me jump. I shrugged him off, spun around, saw him gazing at me with loonlike eyes, the plump kid then whispering, "*Bonjour, madame,*" the grizzled old guy puffing on a stub of a cigarette, a half-smile on his face. Immediately the hand reattached itself to my shoulder. Immediately I shrugged it off.

"Leave me alone," I hissed.

"No problem, no problem," the plump kid said, his face even more greasy as he came right up to me. "We're friends."

I tried to move forward, but the hunched guy had his bony fingers around my arm. Not in a restraining way. More as if he just wanted to touch me. My mind was racing. I figured the plump kid would make a grab for me, though at the moment he was simply hovering behind me, laughing a low laugh. And the old guy, though now in close, was just watching, clearly enjoying my fear.

"We like you," the plump kid said with another unnerving laugh. The hunched guy's hand was tightening around my right forearm. I took a deep steadying breath. I quickly sized up that I was close enough to catch him squarely, cripplingly, in the groin. I began to count to myself: one, two . . .

Then all hell broke loose. A man came running toward us, a stick in his hand, shouting one word over and over again:

"*Imshee, imshee, imshee!*"

It was the night man from the hotel, now brandishing the cane over his head, ready to lash out. All three men scattered down dark alleyways, leaving me there, alone, frozen to the spot, terrified.

As soon as he reached me, the night man took me by the arm the way a father would reach for a child who had gotten herself into deep trouble, pulling me along the narrow alley and out of danger.

When we reached the hotel, he all but pushed me inside. He had to sit down for a moment and compose himself. I too slumped in a chair, shocked, and feeling beyond stupid.

The night man reached for his cigarettes, his hands shaking as he lit one. After taking a steadying drag, he spoke two words: "*Jamais plus.*"

Never again.

SIX

JAMAIS PLUS. JAMAIS plus. Jamais plus.

I sat on the balcony of our room, watching light break through the night sky, still reeling from that incident in the alleyway.

Jamais plus. Jamais plus. Jamais plus.

But my "never again" exhortations had less to do with the behavior of those men and were focused more on my arrogance and inanity. What was I thinking? Why did I even dream of following the loudspeaker voice out into the shadows? The accountant in me was trying to separate the menace and dread of the scene from the hard cold facts of what I'd walked into. Would they have actually attacked me, tried to rape me? Or was I just an object of curiosity for them?

My hero from the front desk served me mint tea, deftly entering the room and placing it on the balcony table without managing to wake up Paul. He was still collapsed flat out in the bed, oblivious to all that had just transpired. Sitting there, looking out at constellations diminishing with the emerging dawn, I came to the conclusion that, though deeply creepy and offensive, there was no serious sexual threat behind this encounter. But there was, without question, some sort of recklessness on my part that had sent me out into the shadows. And I wouldn't forgive myself for such impetuousness until I understood what had pulled me toward trouble.

"Well, hello there."

Paul was standing in the doorway of the balcony, dressed in the white djellaba that the night man had brought up along with the mint tea.

"You really slept," I said.

"And you?"

"Twelve hours versus your fourteen."

"Fourteen hours?"

"You needed it."

"So did you. And I see that I have no clothes."

"They're being washed as we speak. That djellaba suits you."

"The French have a word for an aging hippie still dressing as if he's just walked off an ashram: a *baba-cool*. Even during my year here I never wore a djellaba."

"But it now suits your 'aging hippie' look."

He leaned down and kissed me on the lips.

"I walked into that, didn't I?" he said.

"Indeed you did."

Now it was my turn to lean over and kiss my husband.

"Tea?"

"Please."

I poured out two glasses of the mint tea. We clinked them.

"*À nous*," he said.

"To us."

He threaded his hand in mine. We both stared up at the emerging daylight.

"Do you know what this time of day is called?"

"You mean, besides 'dawn'?"

"Yes, besides 'dawn' or 'the break of day.'"

"The last one's poetic."

"So is 'the blue hour.'"

I let that phrase resonate for a moment or so. Then I tried it out myself.

"The blue hour."

"It's rather lovely, isn't it?"

"Indeed. Neither darkness nor light."

"The hour at daybreak or dusk when nothing is as it seems; when we are caught between the perceived and the imagined."

"Clarity and blur?"

"The pellucid and the obscure? Simplicity masking enigma?"

"Nice image," I said.

He leaned over and kissed me. "*J'ai envie de toi.*"

And I so wanted him. Especially right now. After all that restorative sleep. After that business in the alley. With the blue hour enveloping us.

He lifted me right out of my chair, his hands under my T-shirt. I pulled him toward me, feeling his hardness against me. Then he was steering us to the bed. And some time later, every neutron in my body was electrified as I bit into his shoulder and I came and came again and again. And then he let out a cry and shot into me.

We lay there, arms around each other, bewildered and, yes, happy.

"Our adventure begins now," I said.

"In the blue hour."

But, in the world beyond our bedroom window, emerging sunlight had already eradicated the dawn.

"The blue hour has passed," I said.

"Until sunset this evening."

"The beginning of a day is always more mysterious than the onset of night."

"Because you don't know what lies ahead?"

"At sunset you are more than halfway through the day's narrative," I said. "At dawn you have no idea what will transpire."

"Which is perhaps why the blue is always bluer at dawn. And why a sunset is always more wistful. The entry into night, the sense of another day of life spinning toward its end."

Paul leaned over and kissed me on the lips.

"As the Irish would say, 'There's a pair of us in it.'"

"How do you know that expression?"

"An Irish friend told it to me."

"What Irish friend?"

"Someone long ago."

"A woman?"

"Perhaps."

"Perhaps?"

"Okay, since you asked, her name was Siobhan Parsons. She was a professor of art at University College Dublin and not a bad painter. At the SUNY Buffalo for a year. Unmarried. As mad as a lamp, to use another of her favorite expressions. It lasted between us maybe three months. It was all around twelve years ago, when neither you nor I was aware of each other's existence."

Paul kept so much about his life before me in a room marked off-limits. And there was a part of me that was jealous about his past. Jealous of the women who had known him intimately before me. No man had ever pleasured me the way he had, so I didn't like to think there were others who'd felt what I'd felt when he was inside me. Yet thinking all this here, now, I couldn't help but feel ridiculous. *Stupid. Stupid. Stupid.* As stupid as wandering off down that murky alleyway.

"I'm sorry," I whispered.

"Don't be sorry. Just try to be happy."

"I am happy."

"That's good to hear," he said, kissing me.

"Hungry?" I asked.

"Famished."

"Me too."

"There's no way I'm going downstairs dressed like this."

"But the outside world beckons. And do you really think anyone will care that you've gone native?"

"I'll care."

"I won't," I said. "And that must count for something."

"It does—but I am still waiting for my clothes."

"Isn't there a movie where someone says, 'Come with me to the Casbah'?"

"Charles Boyer to Hedy Lamarr in *Algiers*."

"So come with me to the Casbah."

"They don't call it the Casbah here. They call it the souk."

"What's the difference between a casbah and a souk?"

"Mystery," he said.

SEVEN

A PITILESS SUN overhead. The sky cloudless, a hard cobalt blue. But down here, in Essaouira, everyone except us seemed to be oblivious to the punishing heat. A heat so intense that the unpaved ground beneath our feet felt nearly molten.

The souk at midday. A backstreet labyrinth of stalls and shops and hidden alleyways containing more back streets, more spindly precincts where every sort of merchant was plying his trade. The sense of human density was extraordinary. So too was the prismatic concentration of color. The piles of auburn, maroon, crimson, scarlet, chestnut, sorrel, even chartreuse spices along an entire alleyway, displayed side by side, fashioned into almost minaret-style anthills; the contrasting aquamarine, ultramarine, turquoise, and lapis lazuli in the intricately designed tiles on display by a vendor who had created a mosaic on the ground, which the passing crowd seemed to effortlessly dodge; the searing reds of the butcher meats on display, hanging limbs and fatty flanks, dripping blood, around which flies congregated in mercenary clusters.

The burned-yellow, sea-green, ocher, jet-white, electric-pink, salmon-pink bales of fabrics. The stalls selling intricately patterned leather goods in every shade of brown, tan, khaki. Then there was the melding of aromas, some enticing, some extreme. Fetid sewage interplaying with the redolence of the spice market; the pungent tang of the salted sea overhanging the flower stalls; the brewing mint tea at every curbside stand we passed.

Add to this the souk's crazed acoustics. Loudspeakers blaring French and Moroccan pop music. Hawkers shouting everywhere. Merchants beckoning us forward, blurting out, "*Venez, venez!*" At least two competing muezzins—the men who cried Koranic prayers in distended voices—intoning high-noon prayers from a pair of strategically located minarets. The lawn-mower chop of motorbikes and scooters, their drivers beeping manically as they negotiated the dirt-surfaced potholed terrain, dodging stands piled high with van Gogh-ish oranges and mangoes, and vegetable stalls where the tomatoes were primary in their redness. And here was a man trying to reach for my hand and pull me over to a corner of the souk where soaps in many hues—ivory, copper, scorched cream, ebony—formed a geometric sculpture several feet high.

Even with the Atlantic nearby the air was still so parched, so arid, that after twenty minutes of exploring the souk's early byways, my loose-fitting T-shirt and linen pants were sodden. So too were the T-shirt and shorts that Paul had pulled on when our laundry was delivered to our room just after eleven (he held firm to the "no djellaba outside" rule). By that time we'd had a large breakfast on our terrace. Then we set up his outdoor studio—Paul getting me to help him move the desk from the outer room to a corner of the balcony where it was shaded by an overhanging roof, but where he had a direct view of the Essaouira rooftops. He excused himself for a moment, returning ten minutes later with a brightly striped parasol he said he'd bought at a local shop. Positioning its plastic stand to ensure that his desk was fully shielded, he began to ready himself for work. A sketch pad was opened. Eight pencils were laid out with great formality on the varnished wood surface of the desk. Pulling his khaki safari hat on, he sat down, peered out at the rooftops in the immediate distance, and then began his intricate architectural rendering. I stood inside, watching him for a good ten minutes, marveling at the precision and intensity of his vision, the amazing sense of line that he maintained, the way he seemed oblivious to everything but the work at hand, the ferocious discipline that rose up within him as he drew. All I could feel was a strange rush of love for this very talented, off-kilter man.

Then I set up my own little workspace: my laptop, a very nice Moleskine journal I bought before my departure, and an old Sheaffer fountain pen that had belonged to my dad. It was red, with the sort of chrome appointments that recalled the fins on a vintage Chevy. Dad always kept it filled with red ink. His choice of color was a source of dry amusement to my mother. "Your whole damn life is about the accumulation of red ink," she told him on more than one occasion. But Dad once explained to me the reason he loved that color was the richness of its imprint: "It really does look like you've been writing in blood."

But before I was able to make my first crimson entry in my note-book, the phone by the bed jumped into life. I answered it to hear the guy at the front desk telling me, "Your French professor is down-stairs."

M. Picard clearly worked fast, as I'd only asked him to find me a teacher the previous afternoon.

Before going downstairs to meet him or her, Paul told me, "Who-ever is going to be giving you the lessons will need the work. Don't agree to more than one hundred dirhams an hour."

"But that's only fifteen dollars."

"It's great money here, trust me."

When I entered the lobby, I saw a demure young woman waiting by the reception desk. Though wearing a hijab—a head scarf that allows the face to be shown—she was nonetheless dressed in blue jeans and a floral blouse that wouldn't have been out of place in a 1960s commune. A touch of retro-hippie chic. You could tell im-mediately that this was a young woman who was very much caught between disparate worlds.

When she accepted my outstretched hand, the softness of her grip and the dampness of her palm hinted that she was anxious about this meeting. I tried to put her at her ease, motioning to two dusty armchairs in a corner of the lobby where we could talk undisturbed and asking the man behind the desk to bring us two mint teas.

She was intensely shy and seemed keen to please. Her name was Soraya. A Berber from the extreme south of the country, deep within the Sahara, Soraya was just twenty-nine and a teacher at a local school. Through gentle probing I discovered that she'd studied at the university in Marrakesh and had even done a year in France. When she couldn't get her visa extended she had to return home. Languages were her passion. In addition to her native Arabic and French she had mastered English and was working on Spanish now.

"But the Moroccan passport makes it difficult to actually live or work anywhere else."

"So you've never lived in England or the States?" I said, completely amazed by her English.

"That's my dream—to find my way to New York or London," she said with a shy smile. "But with the exception of France, I've never been out of Morocco."

"Then how on earth did you get so good at my language?"

"I studied it at university. I watched all the American and British films and television shows that I could. I read many novels."

"What's your favorite American novel?"

"I really liked *The Catcher in the Rye* . . . not that I completely understood it."

"What didn't you understand?"

"All the local New York references. I tried looking many of them up. What's that place he goes to see the Christmas show?"

"Radio City Music Hall."

"The dancers are acting out . . . what do they call the birth of your savior?"

I found myself laughing.

"It's called the Nativity, and the dancers dressed up like people from the Holy Land are called the Rockettes."

"Is there a French word for 'Rockettes'?" she asked.

"No, the Rockettes are truly beyond translation."

I told her about having first learned French in Canada, and how I was here with my artist husband this summer and was very determined to rejuvenate my French in four weeks.

"But you speak it well already," she said.

"You're being far too kind."

"I'm being accurate—though a foreign language is one you must continue to work at, otherwise it does fade from memory."

She asked me how I'd found my way to Essaouira. She was interested to know about Paul's time in Morocco over thirty years ago, and where we lived in the States, and might Buffalo be a place that she would like?

"Buffalo is not what one would call a particularly cosmopolitan or elegant city."

"But you live there."

Now it was my turn to blush.

"Where you end up may not be where you wished to live," I said.

Shutting her eyes for a moment, she bowed her head and nodded agreement.

"So, if I wanted to regain fluency in French in a month, how many hours a week would I need?" I asked.

"That depends on your schedule."

"I have no schedule here. No obligations, no commitments, no pressing engagements. And you?"

"I teach at what you would call 'lower school.' Children between the ages of six and nine. But I am free from five o'clock onward every afternoon."

"If I were to suggest two hours a day . . ."

"Could you afford three hours?" she asked.

"What would you charge per hour?"

Now she turned an even deeper shade of crimson.

"You don't have to be shy about this," I said. "It's just money—and it's best to get these things settled at the beginning."

God, how American I sounded. Cards on the table. Name your price and let's talk.

After a moment or two she said, "Would seventy-five dirhams per hour be too much?"

Seventy-five dirhams was around ten dollars. Immediately I said, "I think that's too little."

"But I don't want to ask for more."

"But I want to offer more. Would you accept one hundred and twenty-five dirhams per hour?'

She looked shocked. "That's almost two thousand dirhams a week."

"Trust me, if it was not affordable for me I would tell you."

"Okay, then." She looked away but now with a small smile on her face. "Where shall we do the lessons?"

"I have a suite upstairs. I'll have to check with my husband—but I think that should be fine."

"And if I may ask . . . what do you do professionally?"

"Nothing very interesting," I said. When I told her about my work as an accountant I could see her maintaining a neutral pose about it. I could also sense that she was wondering if I had children, and where were they right now? Or was this just me projecting my own concerns and insecurities onto this quiet but observant young woman?

"I'm sure your work is very interesting," she said.

"When it comes to money, you do get to know a great deal about how other people function. Anyway . . . can you start tomorrow?"

"I see no problem with that."

"Brilliant—and can you get me all the books I'll need?"

I handed her three hundred dirhams, telling her that if they cost more, I'd reimburse her after our first lesson.

"Three hundred dirhams will buy them all," she said. "I'll bring them tomorrow."

"Do you want payment every day or once a week?"

Again she looked away.

"Whatever is easier for you. If you pay me on Friday the bank here is open until nine o'clock, so I can deposit most of it then."

Ah, a saver.

"Payment every Friday it is, then. One last thing—how do you know Monsieur Picard?"

"My mother is a cleaner here."

I considered my response for a moment before saying, "I'm certain she's very proud of you."

Soraya averted her gaze as she nodded acknowledgment. I told her how much I looked forward to being her student and that I would see her tomorrow at five o'clock. Then I went upstairs. Paul was still on the rooftop under the umbrella, a good half dozen drawings strewn across the table. His face was swathed with sweat; his shellshocked eyes indicating the onset of heat exhaustion. I grabbed the water bottle that was by the bed and insisted that he drink it. He drained half a liter in moments, staggered inside, and collapsed onto the bed.

"Are you insane, courting disaster like that?" I asked.

"Inspiration trumped perspiration."

"But you, of all people, know what the sun is like here."

"Can you rescue the drawings before they get bleached by the light?"

I went outside to gather up the six drawings exposed to the sun and brought them inside. As I shuffled through them one by one, I felt myself sucking in my breath, floored by what I saw. They were a half dozen variations on the same theme: the rooftops in the immediate vicinity of our balcony. What made these depictions so remarkable was the way that, in each drawing, Paul had reimagined the minarets and water towers and crumbling roofs and dangling laundry and satellite dishes that defined the Essaouira skyline. I glanced up at one point and stared out at the actual panorama on which Paul had based this sequence of work. Then I returned to his highly detailed drawings, marveling not just at their sheer refined technique, but also at the way these six scenes reminded me that there is no such thing as a correct vision of the state of things; that the act of looking is utterly subjective; that none of us ever sees the same objects, the same landscape. And when it comes to a vision of life . . . everything is, by its very nature, an interpretation.

"These are . . . extraordinary," I told him.

"Now it's you who's suffering sunstroke. They are a couple of sketches I knocked off in a few hours."

"Didn't Mozart often write a piano sonata in a morning?"

"He was Mozart."

"You are incredibly gifted."

"I wish I could share your fulsome opinion of me."

"I wish that too. But in my humble opinion I think that these mark an entirely new direction for you."

"You're biased."

"Take the compliment. They're brilliant."

But Paul just turned away, unable to accept such praise. I quickly changed the subject.

"I start French lessons tomorrow," I said, then told him all about Soraya.

"How much is she charging per hour?" he asked.

"She asked for seventy-five, I'm paying her one-twenty."

"You're a soft touch."

"Only when it's the right thing to do."

"Even seventy-five dirhams an hour is a huge amount of money for her already."

"And not that much money for me. So what's the big deal?"

"None whatsoever. Your generosity is admirable."

"So too is your concern about our finances."

"Do I hear a tone?" he asked.

"Can we drop this?"

"Of course we can," he said, getting up and heading into the bathroom. A moment or so later I heard the shower being turned on.

When he came out ten minutes later, a towel wrapped around his midsection, he said, "I really wish we could get beyond these exchanges."

"So do I."

"Let's try to steer clear of all stupidity."

"It gets corrosive, doesn't it?" I said. "Kindness is the better option."

He considered this for a moment.

"That just might be a solution."

He came over and put his arms around me.

"A fresh start, okay?"

"Fine by me." I kissed him lightly on the lips, simultaneously wondering if I would be replaying this dialogue a day or two from now. Maybe I simply needed to accept that this was how our marriage operated; that this was our weather system as a couple, and one in which the moments of inclemency were supplanted by periods of genuine tranquility and, indeed, amazing love. The word *adventure* came to mind yet again.

The next day, during my first lesson with Soraya, I asked her whether *adventure* had multiple meanings in French. She blushed slightly, noting:

"Yes, '*une aventure*' is the word. But also it's a very French expression for a love affair. *Par exemple, 'J'ai eu une aventure avec Jacques . . . seulement une aventure, rien de bien sérieux.*'"

She didn't need to translate. *Une aventure* was just that: a fling that wasn't love. When I asked about the semantic difference between adventure and love, Soraya said, "In French if someone says— as they often do—C'est *l'amour*, it indicates its profound seriousness, for the moment, anyway. When I lived in Lyon I had several French friends who always seemed to be exclaiming the fact that they had fallen in love after seeing a man for two or three weeks. Then when it ended a few months later the next fellow they got involved with . . . *oh, c'est l'amour*, after the fourth night. The way I heard it used so frequently made me think that to exclaim 'I'm in love' is to express immediate emotions that haven't been allowed to deepen. It's also to admit: I am in love with the idea of being in love."

"And in Morocco?"

Now her shoulders tightened. "We need to return to other things," she said, tapping the textbooks. I didn't protest, because I realized that I had mistakenly traversed an invisible boundary, one that Soraya was going to maintain.

So back we went to the pluperfect subjunctive.

We sat together on the sofa in the small living area of the suite, the French books she'd brought along spread out across the little coffee table. Paul was at work on the balcony, shaded by the big umbrella and his wide-brimmed hat, the sun still at high wattage at five thirty in the afternoon. He had come out to say hello when Soraya earlier knocked on the door of our suite. I could see that she was taking in his lankiness, his long gray hair, the age difference between us. Just as she was also impressed by his French and by the drawings that I had now placed around the room.

"Your husband did all these?" Soraya asked.

"You approve?"

"They're superb. And they so capture Essaouira."

"Or at least the rooftops of Essaouira."

"Will he start doing street scenes as well?"

"You'll have to ask him."

"Imagine being married to such a talented man. Your children . . . ?"

"We have none."

Now Soraya looked as if she wished the floor could open and swallow her whole. I quickly added, "None yet."

Her relief was immense.

"I'm so, so sorry," she said. "I should never have pried like that."

"That was hardly prying."

"But it was an inappropriate question. Even though I well know that, in the West, having children is not obligatory for married couples."

"That's true. My first husband didn't want children."

Soraya seemed thrown by my directness.

"Is that the reason you left him?"

"One of the many reasons."

"I see . . ."

"But Paul definitely wants children."

Soraya seemed to approve of this.

"He's had none before now?" she asked, but then added, "If that isn't another totally inappropriate question on my part."

"Not inappropriate at all," I said.

"In Morocco, marriage is so much about having children," she said.

"Is that how you see it?"

She considered this for a moment. "How I 'see it' and how things are . . . those are two very different things entirely."

Over the first ten days of my lessons with Soraya the non-French-grammar conversations were an intriguing game of verbal Ping-Pong, in which her innate caution and cultural reticence were frequently undercut by her immense curiosity not just about my life but about the way a woman like me functions in modern America. A fast sense of trust developed between us, though it was not until the second week of our lessons that some of the more private aspects of her life began to be revealed. I sensed very quickly on that her time in France had completely altered her way of thinking, and that her return to Morocco was a reluctant one.

"So when you went to university you actually lived on the campus itself?" she asked in wonder when I started telling her about leaving home for the University of Minnesota.

"Isn't that the usual way in France or here?" I asked.

"In Morocco, if you go to another city for university, it is arranged that you will live with family there."

"And when you were in Lyon?"

Her lips tightened.

"The only reason I was allowed to go to Lyon was because my

paternal uncle Mustapha was there. He and his wife have lived there for thirty years. He has a rather successful taxicab business and she is a teacher in a *lycée*—so they are both, on a certain level, quite assimilated. Except when it comes to their responsibilities as guardians of their niece from Essaouira. The entire year was a power struggle. Especially when they discovered I was not wearing the hijab when I went off to class, and was even using a friend's place to change my clothes. When it came to staying out late, which I started to do when Fabien came into my life—"

"Who's Fabien?" I asked. But at that very moment Paul came in off the balcony, en route to the bathroom. The subject was abruptly dropped.

Later that night, in a little backstreet restaurant that had quickly become a favorite, I told Paul how Soraya had mentioned the name of a Frenchman whom I sensed she was involved with during her year in Lyon.

"That's what most educated Moroccan women dream of," he said. "Meeting a Westerner who can get them out of here."

"So speaks the voice of experience."

"Was I indicating that I had any experience of that whatsoever?"

"Surely there must have been a Moroccan woman or two in your life back then."

"What makes you say that?"

"Because you are a most attractive man now, which means you must have been even more so in your twenties. And you were probably hanging out with fellow artists, the Casablanca bohemian circle, right? Wasn't there some gorgeous abstract painter who—"

"What's the point of this?"

"The point is that I want you right now."

An hour later, back in bed in our hotel room, his body entwined with mine, the two of us sharing the most extraordinary metronomic symmetry, him whispering to me just how much he loved me, promising wondrous times ahead, free of the shadowy recesses of the past, what else could I do but also proclaim my love for him; as actual and veracious a love as I had ever known.

Afterward, lying next to each other, our arms interlocked, keeping us close, I said, "Maybe we did it this time."

Because it was right in the middle of my cycle. And because, tonight, our normal level of passion hit an even more dizzying summit.

Paul kissed me lightly on the lips.

"I'm sure it happened this time. We're blessed, after all."

Outside the muezzin sang praises to his Almighty. *Allah akhbar! Allah akhbar!*

To which I could only think:

Your timing, sir, is impeccable.

EİGHT

THE NEXT TWO weeks were supremely happy ones. Happiness has always struck me as a fleeting event—a moment here or there when all the dreck of life washes away for a few precious hours. You're free of all the fears and neuroses that seem to act as a subtext to everything you are trying to do and accomplish in life. The problem when you are a couple is that you are also in thrall to your partner's fears and neuroses. So if there is a period when you are both outside the reach of all the emotional baggage you each cart around with you . . . well, that is one of those rare, sublime junctures when you can truly think: we are blessed.

Those fourteen days in Essaouira were magic. Paul got into a serious, high-end creative groove when it came to his work, spending close to six hours a day on his line drawings, moving from the panoramic eyrie that was our balcony to a café table right in the heart of the souk. There he became something of a local celebrity. Its manager—a young guy in his midtwenties named Fouad—saw the work that Paul was producing and made it his business to keep him free of unnecessary distractions, especially from hawkers and tourist touts. Fouad was a shrewd, cool customer. His "patron" was his father, who owned the café but spent much of the time in Marrakesh—where, as his son once intimated to Paul, he had a mistress. Fouad had studied in France—at the École Supérieure d'Art et de Design in Marseille. He'd fallen in love with a fellow painter there from Toulon. She wasn't a Muslim. And Fouad's father—though willing to pay for his son's three-year adventure on the other side of the Mediterranean—pressed the paternal guilt button and insisted, at the end of his course, that he drop all hopes of a life of art and love with the Frenchwoman. He had to return home to Morocco and learn the family business.

So now Fouad managed this café and a small hotel in the souk for his largely absent father. He was most welcoming to Paul when he discovered that he was not just an artist but an exceptional one at that. The café was located right at a corner of the medina, where spice and fruit merchants plied their trade next to butchers with animal carcasses bleaching in the midday sun. It gave Paul a ringside seat on all the manic, chromatic action—which he captured in edgy black pencil and charcoal on off-white cardstock. Fouad—clearly in need of an older brother (especially one who was a fellow artist)—insisted on setting up Paul at a shaded corner table, which became his office, and on keeping him supplied with mint tea throughout the hours he worked there. He also provided us both with a daily lunch. He refused to take any payment for it, which is when my husband began to pay with a daily original postcard. Paul told me that he was borrowing a trick from Picasso—who paid for his hotel and bar bills in the French seaside town Collioure by leaving a sketch with the patron every few days . . . in the process making him the possessor of a very lucrative art collection.

"I doubt Fouad will eventually be able to retire to the Côte d'Azur on the proceeds of my scribbles," Paul noted after lunch one afternoon when we had retreated back to the hotel to make love and nap.

"Don't underestimate your market value," I said. "This new sequence of drawings you're doing is such a breakthrough."

I was making progress myself. My classes with Soraya were always rigorous. Most of the mornings I would spend hunched over my textbooks, forcing myself to learn ten new verbs and twenty new words per day. I also read local newspapers in French and bought a

small radio so I could hear RFI—France's version of the BBC World
Service.

"You really are committed," Soraya said when, around ten days
into our lessons, I surprised her by asking all sorts of questions about
langage soutenu—the most elevated and formal version of French.

"Bravo for your diligence," she told me. "To be able to speak *un
français soutenu* is the key to so much. If you can master it, the French
will be most impressed."

"If I ever get to France."

Soraya looked at me quizzically. "Why do you think you'll never
get to France?"

"I've never traveled much before."

"But you're traveling now."

"It depends on certain things happening in my life."

"Of course it does."

"Still," I said, "children are portable . . . *les enfants sont portables*."

"You used the word *portable* incorrectly here. *Un portable* is a cell
phone or a laptop computer. The verb to use here is *transporter*. So
try rephrasing it."

I was obsessed about getting my French back in working order. I
needed the sense of accomplishment; of using the time here in a positive, beneficial way. Watching Paul so focused and involved in his work
made me push myself even harder to immerse myself in the language.

Meanwhile, Essaouira became a home for us. I figured out, by
and large, the maze-like geography of the old city and was able to
find my way unencumbered through the souk. I also learned how
to deflect attention from the occasional tout or young tough guy
playing macho. But though I began to feel as if I had a true handle
on Essaouira's exuberantly twisted realities, the city after dark was
a place I never ventured alone. This precaution did not dim my ap-
preciation of the place. Or the fact that, as I discovered, its residents
were supremely welcoming and pleased to see that we had decided
to spend time among them.

I became a beach walker, setting off most afternoons after our siesta along the endless strip of sand that fronted the Atlantic. Once past the bathers, there would be the women in hijabs lifting up their djellabas to wade in the water. Nearby the camel guides were offering a half hour on top of one of their haunted beasts for a negotiable fee. Another mile farther south, all traces of habitation fell away. I was alone. The beach stretched into geographic infinity, the Atlantic mirroring the declining summer sun, its horizon boundless. How I always wanted to live on a strip of beach, with hardly a hint of the twenty-first century in sight, walking it daily, reveling in the way that the metronomic pounding of the surf always seemed to smooth out, for a time, all the stress and doubt and anxiety that we haul around with us. We're a bit like Bedouins when it comes to the trappings of our lives. No matter where we roam, or how far we venture away from our place of birth, we still haul with us so much of the past.

On an empty beach—especially *this* empty beach—you could almost convince yourself that it might just be possible to detach yourself from your history and all its weight.

Given what a productive place Paul found himself in right now—and how free of shadows he also seemed to be—when I got back from my daily two-hour beach hikes, he'd greet me with a smile and a kiss and the suggestion that we watch the sunset from the rooftop of a very elegant hotel situated just inside the city walls. It was called L'Heure Bleue (of all things); very much an old-style travelers' hotel of the 1920s, redone in subdued, chic, five-star style. Totally out of our league, budget-wise, but *un kir* at the open-air bar on its roof didn't break the bank. And it did provide the most ravishing panorama of the red globular sun slowly liquidizing into a tranquil ocean.

"Interesting, isn't it, how the Atlantic is so becalmed here," Paul noted one evening as we sipped our kirs and sat in awe of the wide-screen sunset.

"Especially when compared to Maine."

"We'll be there in a couple of weeks."

"I know," I said.

"You sound less than enthusiastic about that prospect."

"You know how much I love Maine. It's just . . . well, it's home, right?"

"My thoughts entirely. So why don't we stay here for another two weeks?"

"But that means losing Maine—and we put down twenty-five hundred dollars for the fourteen days there. Our airplane tickets are nonexchangeable and nonrefundable . . . and, yes, I know I'm sounding like an accountant."

"You're right to do so, especially given my behavior in that department."

I reached out and took his hand.

"That's all behind us now," I said.

"Because you forced me to grow up."

"It wasn't about you 'growing up.' It was about just exercising a bit of restraint."

"I know I have this compulsion to spend," he said. "And I know that the compulsion is rooted in the fact that I allowed life to turn out in a way I never truly wanted. Until, that is, I met you. You saved me . . . from myself."

I kissed him lightly on the lips. "Happy to be of service."

Just beyond us the sun had been rendered fluid, thawed orange coalescing like spilled paint on the surface of the Atlantic. I shut my eyes and felt tears because I sensed a breaking down of a barrier, an honesty and complicity between us that had been overshadowed by manifold demons.

The next morning was pitch-perfect. An aquamarine sky, cloud-free, faultless. We awoke from a late carnal sleep to a knock at the door. Glancing at the bedside clock I noticed it was high noon. Damn, damn, damn. Soraya had asked if she could organize the lesson earlier today (it was a Friday—the Sabbath day in Morocco), and if it could last only one hour. She had a day off teaching and was coming into Essaouira earlier than usual to catch a 4:00 bus to Marrakesh and a weekend with a friend from university.

"I had to have my friend's mother phone my mother and vouch that she would keep an eye on me over the weekend. I am twenty-nine years old and am still having to check in like an adolescent," she told me in a low, confessional whisper.

I had agreed to that midday Friday lesson. And now it was . . . 12:02. Soraya was always punctual. Damn. Damn. Damn.

As I jumped out of bed and scrambled for some clothes, Paul groaned awake.

"What time is it?" he asked, half asleep. When I told him, he smiled and said, "I'm glad you're succumbing to my bohemian ways."

Actually it was the first time we'd overslept since arriving here; Paul always wanting to get to the café by eleven to capture the souk at its most manic.

"That's Soraya," I said. "I'll do the lesson downstairs."

"No need. Do it in the front room and I'll slip out in around twenty minutes."

So I quickly dressed and let Soraya in, apologizing for the slight delay. As she set up her books and pens and papers in the small living area, I ran downstairs and asked for coffee and bread and preserves to be brought up. When I returned to the room I could hear the shower going in the adjacent bathroom—and Soraya looking just a little uncomfortable with the notion of a naked man in the immediate proximity.

"Sorry, sorry," I said. "I should have suggested we go elsewhere."

"No problem," she said, clearly relieved to have me back in the room. "Shall we start?"

We began by discussing the verb *vouloir*—*to want*—and variations of its usage, especially in the conditional, *would like*. The great aspirational hope. As in: *Je voudrais un café . . . voudrais-tu un café aussi? . . . il voudrait réussir . . . nous voudrions un enfant . . .*

At which juncture the bedroom door swung open and Paul emerged, dressed, his hair still wet from the shower. He greeted me and Soraya with a big smile.

"*Tout à fait nous voudrions un enfant,*" he said, coming over and kissing me on the lips. *We would absolutely like a child.*

Then, after greeting Soraya, he asked her in rapid-fire French, "And how is my wife progressing?"

"She's doing fantastically. Really gifted with the language. And she works so hard."

"That she does," he said.

"You think too highly of me," I said.

"She doesn't think well enough of herself," Paul said. "Maybe you can help her in that department, Soraya."

"Breakfast should be here in a moment," I told him.

But I saw that he had his satchel over his shoulder, stuffed with his sketchbooks and pencils.

"I'll let Fouad provide that for me. Come find me after the lesson. *Je t'adore.*"

With another kiss on the lips he was gone.

Once the door was closed behind him, Soraya looked away as she said, "*Je voudrais un homme comme votre mari.*"

"*Mais plus jeune?*" I added.

"*L'âge importe moins que la qualité.*"

I would like a man like your husband . . . But younger? . . . Age is less important than the quality.

"I am sure you will find someone of quality," I told her.

"I'm not," she said in a near whisper. "All right: *essayer* in the subjunctive. Give me an example in first person singular."

I considered this for a moment, then said, "*Il faut que je voudrais d être heureuse.*"

Soraya did not look professorially pleased by my answer.

"I must would like happiness," she said, translating my sentence into her excellent English. "You can do better than that."

"Sorry, sorry. The problem is the use of the subjunctive with *would like*. As you noted you can't *must would like* something."

"So if you were talking about wanting happiness . . ."

"*Je voudrais le bonheur.*"

"Fine. And in the subjunctive?"

"I would sidestep *vouloir* and use *essayer*. To try. As in: '*Il faut que j'essaie d'être heureuse.' I must try to be happy.*"

Soraya then had another one of her thoughtful pauses.

"It is all about 'trying,' isn't it?" she said.

The breakfast arrived. She shared the coffee with me. We worked on for another ninety minutes. Then I paid her for the week and wished her well in Marrakesh.

"*Entre nous*, there is a man—French—whom my classmate wants me to meet. A banker working at Société Générale. My parents would half approve—the banker, not the French part. But I am getting ahead of myself here, aren't I?"

Then, telling me she'd see me Monday at five o'clock, she headed off for her weekend and her meeting with the Frenchman who might, or might not, become a conduit into a new life.

When Soraya was gone, I took a long shower and changed into fresh clothes, then checked my watch and thought that, if I moved quickly, I could still join Paul for a late lunch at Chez Fouad. But as Friday was the one day of the week I read my email, I decided to quickly scan this week's dispatches before heading out to the souk.

The first email I saw had been dispatched just twenty minutes earlier from the ever-scrupulous Morton. It read:

Now that we have your husband's audit problems with the IRS out of the way I've been doing his books in an attempt to bring them up to date so we are not in a bind at tax time next year. You know how he throws all his receipts and invoices and credit card statements into that file box you gave him. Well I started working through it on Wednesday and came across this invoice this morning. I debated about whether I should send it to you now or wait until you got back in a few weeks. But I decided that—as this was something of an ethical/moral call—I should err on the side of immediate transparency.

I clicked on the attached file. I found myself staring at an invoice from a Dr. Brian Boyards, MD, Urologist. The invoice was for a patient named Leuen, Paul Edward. His date of birth—04-11-56—was the same as my husband's. So too was the home address. And the Blue Cross/Blue Shield health insurance policy that he used to defray 80 percent of the $2,031.78 charges for the procedure listed on the invoice.

Outpatient Non-Scalpel Deferentectomy.

What is a deferentectomy?

I switched over to Google and typed in that exact word.

And discovered that a deferentectomy is the clinical term for a very common bit of urological surgery . . . also known as a vasectomy.

And the date on which this Outpatient Non-Scalpel Deferentectomy was performed on my husband? September 7, 2014. Around the same time that we both agreed it was time to start trying for a child.

NINE

I SAT IN front of my computer screen, trying to convince myself that what I just read was somehow false. A fabrication, an invention dispatched by a malevolent individual who wanted to see my marriage thrown completely off-course.

The problem with hard-and-fast evidence—and an invoice from a doctor in the wake of a surgical procedure is about as irrefutable as it comes—is that you can't negotiate with its black-and-white verities. It's a bit like a client of mine who had run up around $10K in internet porn charges on his MasterCard one year. All the charges were assigned to Fantasy Promotions Inc. The time code for each of the transactions showed they were all late in the evening. His wife had seen the MasterCard statements and was just a little appalled. My client entreated me to provide him an alibi for these purchases. As I told him at the time, "How do you explain over one hundred and fifty dealings after midnight with an online company called Fantasy Promotions Inc.? There's no wiggle room here. It's the smoking gun."

Strange how that client—who was divorced with extreme prejudice by his wife thereafter—popped into my head as I found myself staring at that document from Dr. Brian Boyards, MD, Urologist. All the facts in front of me. Facts which I must have reread a dozen times, trying to find a way of reinterpreting the irrefutable:

Patient: Leuen, Paul Edward
Date of birth—04-11-56
Home Address: 5165 Albany Avenue, Buffalo, NY 10699
Insurance: Blue Cross/Blue Shield A566902566
Procedure: Outpatient Non-Scalpel Deferentectomy
Date of Procedure: 09-07-14

The seventh of September last year. Around ten months ago. A few days after Labor Day, when we returned from a long weekend in a friend's cottage in the woods fronting Lake Placid. My husband and I making love twice a day. And me, after a candlelit dinner at some nearby inn, stating that, after two years together, and with my fortieth birthday looming in a few months, I wanted to come off the pill effective immediately . . . though it would be, as my gynecologist told me, at least two weeks until I would be moving into a fertile cycle.

Paul did not blanch or talk about joining the merchant marine when I brought this up. On the contrary, he told me that having a child together was "the essential bonding of a couple in love" or some such line. Paul returned from the gym on a Thursday evening, limping slightly, telling me how he pulled a muscle in his groin and was worried that he'd given himself a hernia. With my complete understanding, he absented himself from sex for several days, saying that he'd be going to the university infirmary the next day to get himself a medical opinion. Then, upon returning that night, he informed me that, though it was only "lightly herniated"—I remember his exact words—he was advised not to exacerbate it and refrain from sex for another week. Which we dutifully did.

Now, here I was, all these absurd months later, on the website of Dr. Brian Boyards, MD, reading all about this seemingly simple, no-fault surgical procedure:

Over 500,000 vasectomy procedures are done each year in the United States.

Vasectomy is a simple, safe surgical procedure for permanent male fertility control. The tube (called a "vas") which leads from the testicle is cut and sealed in order to stop sperm from leaving.

The procedure usually takes about 10 to 20 minutes.

Since the procedure simply interrupts the delivery of sperm it does not change hormonal function—leaving sexual drive and potency unaffected.

The no-scalpel vasectomy is a technique used to do the vasectomy through one single puncture. The puncture is made in the scrotum and requires no suturing or stitches.

The primary difference compared to the conventional vasectomy is that the vas deferens is controlled and grasped by the surgeon in a less traumatic manner. This results in less pain and fewer postoperative complications.

This procedure is done with the aid of a local anesthetic called Xylocaine (similar to Novocain).

The actual interruption of the vas which is done with the no-scalpel technique is identical to the interruption used with conventional techniques.

The no-scalpel technique is simply a more elegant and less traumatic way for the surgeon to control the vas and proceed with its interruption.

So my husband murdered my chance at motherhood with him by opting for "elegant and less traumatic" surgery.

I snapped my eyes shut, caught somewhere between desolation and pure unalloyed rage.

Tout à fait, nous voudrions un enfant.

The bastard actually said that just two hours ago. Just as, for months, he kept reassuring me that it was only a matter of time before I got pregnant. I slammed the lid of my computer shut and began to sob. I was in free fall. Beyond stunned. As if the entire foundation of this new life we'd created together was nothing more than a house of cards built on the lies of a man I had been dumb enough to trust. How could I—Ms. Forensic, Ms. Extra-Scrupulous, Ms. Exhaustively Thorough—not have sniffed out the con behind all his declarations of intimate commitment?

I knew the answer to that question.

We only see what we want to see.

I understood from the outset that Paul Leuen was, on certain fundamental levels, incapable of proper adult responsibility. But I chose to sidestep such realizations and embrace the bohemian lure, the romantic effluence, the hallucinogenic sex. I was so desperate for love that I shoved all doubt into that mental basement room and plunged right into the delusion of domestic bliss and child rearing with a man who . . .

Who? Who?

Can I even define him now? If he'd betrayed me in such a fundamental way, if he'd deliberately had himself fixed while assuring me so passionately that he wanted a child with me . . .

I went to the bathroom and threw cold water on my face, avoiding the sight of myself in the mirror. I didn't want to cast a cold eye on myself right now. I returned to the room and went out onto the balcony, staring out at the North African world below. *This could have waited until our return, Morton.* But decent rabbinical Morton had, no doubt, done a considerable amount of ethical soul searching before deciding to send me the urologist's invoice. And he finally decided: cards on the table. Leave it to my disorganized husband to have thrown the doctor's invoice into his box of financial paperwork and forget that I would eventually see it—because I was still his accountant, forever holding him accountable. I clutched the balcony railings, steadying myself, rage trumping sorrow; a certain clinical clarity asserting itself. I returned inside to my laptop. I opened it and wrote a fast email to Morton.

Knowledge, they say, is power. But it's also often a sorrow beyond dreams. Can you please look around his MasterCard statements for

*September 2014 and see if there is a payment for four hundred dollars
to Dr. Brian Boyards. Then scan it to me. I sense I will be back in Buffalo
in a matter of days. Alone.*

As I awaited a reply, I dug out our plane tickets and discovered
(through some further searching on the internet) that Royal Air
Maroc would change my flight before the return date for a charge
of 3,000 DM—around $350. Yes, I did pay for the entire month at
the hotel, but we were already into the third week. Paul could stay
behind and finish his drawings and remind himself what it was like
to be alone once more. I was pretty certain that this was the outcome
he privately desired. When he'd had his secret vasectomy, part of
him must have known that all would eventually be revealed. Surely
he had to figure that after, say, a year of trying with no success, I'd
insist that we go to a fertility clinic for tests. Bing. An email . . . from
Morton.

*Found it. Attached as a scan. I am here for you. Anything I can do,
just ask. Courage . . .*

I started crying again and was interrupted by a light knock at the
door.

"Fuck off!" I shouted, certain it was Paul. But why would Paul
knock when he had a key? Instantly I was on my feet heading into the
other room and opening the main door to the suite. Outside stood
the young girl who cleaned our room and did our laundry. She looked
ashen and cowed.

"*Mes excuses, mes excuses,*" I said, taking her hands. "*Je suis . . .
dévastée.*"

As soon as that last word was out of my mouth I broke away and
went inside, attempting to keep down the new sob that was trying to
escape from the back of my throat. Don't break down, don't break
down. The young girl was gone from view, no doubt running down
the stairs, unnerved by the sight of this crazy woman in the throes of
a nervous collapse.

Back to the bathroom. More water on my face. My eyes were red.

I returned to my desk, put on my sunglasses, grabbed my passport, a pad and paper, the printout of my airplane ticket, my wallet, and credit cards. I stuffed it all into my shoulder bag and headed out the door. On my way downstairs I dug out a 100-dirham note. I saw the young girl hovering at the bottom of the stairs, clearly uncertain by my approaching presence.

"I am so sorry," I told her. "I received some difficult news today. Please forgive me."

I thrust the note into her hand. Her eyes went wide when she saw the sum—what Soraya told me was two days' wages—and she whispered, "*C'est trop . . . Ce n'est pas nécessaire . . .*"

"*Si, c'est nécessaire . . . Et merci pour votre gentillesse.*"

"*J'espère que tout ira bien, madame.*"

"*On verra.*" We'll see.

And I headed out into the blazing afternoon sun.

There was an internet café two alleys away from the hotel. I walked in and asked the clearly bored young man, cigarette screwed in one side of his mouth, scatting along to some local pop song, if he had a printer.

He pointed to a beat-up machine.

"Two dirhams per page, ten dirhams for an hour on the computer. You can pay me afterward."

The hotel had a printer and computer for guests that I could have used. But I was concerned that, somehow, the documents I'd be printing would be seen or duplicated. I sat down at the computer, went online, and printed out the medical invoice, the scan of Paul's credit card statement, and all the details from Dr. Boyard's website about the non-scalpel vasectomy. Then, on the Royal Air Maroc website, I booked myself on the direct flight at noon the next day from Casablanca to New York, charging it to my credit card. The flight would arrive at 2:55 p.m. (with the five-hour time change). I switched over to the JetBlue website and found a seat on the 5:58 p.m. flight from JFK to Buffalo. Finally, an email to Morton:

*Arriving tomorrow at 7:22 p.m. If you could pick me up and get me
home that would be a mitzvah. And if you know the name of a good
divorce lawyer . . . But more on all that when we meet.*

Three minutes later . . . *bing*:
*I'll be there and will bring you to E.B. Green's for a sirloin and sev-
eral needed martinis. Hang tough.*

Not only was Morton a great friend, he was also one of the few
Jewish accountants I knew who liked to drink. He always liked taking
on the role of older brother to me, yet never played the I-told-you-
so card when it came to Paul. I knew from the outset that he didn't
approve of him, once telling me: "As long as you know you're about
to marry Vincent van Gogh, my blessings upon you." But after this
single admonition, he never said another questioning word about my
husband again. Morton knew how desperate I was to have a child.
And Paul had promised.

I felt myself getting shaky again. Snapping my eyes shut, I willed
myself back to the appearance of calm, collected all the documents I
had printed, and settled the bill with the pleasantly spacey guy at the
reception desk, watching him take in my distraught state.

"*Ça va, madame?*"

I just shrugged and said, "*La vie.*"

I checked my watch. Paul would be expecting me at Chez Fouad
for lunch. Steering myself away from the alleys that passed through
the center of the souk, I took a byway that led to a narrow unpaved
thoroughfare and out the main gates. I was bracing myself for the
usual vulturelike swoop of the touts who descend on any unsuspect-
ing foreigner (especially a woman alone). But today when one such
guy—sweaty, overweight, the usual smarmy ingratiating smile on his
face—approached me and said, "A camel ride for the beautiful lady?"
I put my hand up like a traffic cop and barked one word: "*Imshee.*"
Get lost. The man looked startled. I felt like an asshole. I raised my
sunglasses, showing him my red-from-crying eyes.

"*Mes excuses, madame,*" he said.

"*Je m'excuse aussi,*" I said, hurrying off to the bus depot, dodging the women hawking embroidered linen, and the little kids selling strings of cheap candy, and a twelve-year-old on a moped who kept yelling, "Lady, lady . . ." Reaching the bus depot, I stood in line for around twenty minutes, while each person in front of me engaged in an extended conversation with the guy in the ticket window. When I finally got my chance to speak with him, I discovered that there was a bus early the next morning for Casablanca Airport, nonstop, leaving at 6:00 and arriving at 9:45. I bought a one-way ticket for 50 dirhams, and was told by the gentleman that I should be here no later than 5:30 a.m.

"*Entendu,*" I said. *Understood.*

Actually, nothing was now understood. I felt myself drifting into panic again. I glanced at my watch. It was now 2:18. Paul might be wondering where I was and might come back to the room looking for me. Or maybe he'd simply decide that I had drifted off somewhere, as I sometimes did. I was hoping that time was on my side. I would get home, pack my bags, leave him the corroborating evidence, a short note, head off for a long walk on the beach. And then . . .

Part of me wanted to simply jump a cab from the hotel to the bus depot, change my ticket, and hop the next coach to Casablanca. But this expedient part of me was being held back by the need to confront Paul with everything, to demand some sort of explanation, to let him see just how decimated I was, feel the consequences of his actions.

But where would that bring us? Me recriminating, screaming. Him playing the little boy and begging me to give him another chance.

Why is it that we always want some sort of payback, reprisal, a long tearful aria of apology, even when we know it won't change anything? The damage was so comprehensive that there was no way the two of us would ever recover from this. Why even confront him? Just leave.

I got back to the room ten minutes later, handing ten dirhams to an elderly woman out front who wore the full niqab, and had the most haunted pair of eyes beaming out from the narrow black slit.

"*Je vous en supplie . . . je vous en supplie,*" she hissed. *I beg you, I beg you.* I thrust the bank note in her hand.

"*Bonne chance!*" she whispered. And even though she was wishing me luck, she sibilated it so it sounded like a curse.

At the hotel I ran into the cleaning girl in the corridor.

"*Tout va bien, madame?*" she asked me, eyeing me carefully, fearful that I might explode again.

"*Tout va mieux,*" I lied. *All is better.*

"*La chambre est prête, madame.*"

I went upstairs. I walked into the room. I stared long and hard at the bed in which we had made love every day, always with the hope that . . .

I had been wavering for the past ten minutes about what tack I should take. The sight of the bed made me adopt a different strategy. After packing all my bags I then laid out on top of the bed all the documents I had just printed, beginning with the invoice, continuing with his credit card statement showing the excess amount he paid for the procedure, then his doctor's mission statement about the non-scalpel deferentectomy. I wanted Paul to understand that he'd been well and truly found out. Leaving him alone with the evidence of his betrayal would sufficiently unnerve him to make him . . .

Make him what? What do you think he'll do? Fall on his knees and beg forgiveness? Even if that does happen, then what?

Let him cry himself to sleep. Alone. Let him reflect on what life without me will be like.

I reached for a notepad. I scribbled: *You have killed everything and I hate you. You don't deserve to live.* Then I scrawled my name and placed it at the end of the documents I had left fanned across the bed. Grabbing my sunhat and my bag, I headed out. I rushed past the reception desk. Ahmed must have sensed my disquiet. "Is there a problem, *madame*?"

"Ask my husband!" I shouted.

I stormed my way to the beach. Keeping my head down, walking ferociously down to the sand, sidestepping the camel drivers and the elderly men selling roasted corn, remaining on the move until I reached that point when all signs of the external world had disappeared. I sat myself down. I stared out at the ocean over which I would travel the next day, fleeing the worst sort of heartbreak and knowing full well that, even after running back home, the anguish would cling to me like a metastasizing cancer. I could only begin to imagine the emotional blowback ahead. And the realization that I was, for the second time, about to deal with the debris of a collapsed marriage. Only this time the sense of failure and betrayal would be beyond agonizing. Because I had bought into a lie.

I let go, crying wildly for around ten minutes, free from prying eyes, no one around to watch in disconcerted unease. Here my grief was drowned out by oceanic surf. When I subsided I found myself thinking, Now what? I go home. I go back to work. I try to pick up the pieces. I face into the most crippling sort of loneliness. As much as I now hated Paul, another part of me was convulsed at the thought of losing him. How can you feel that way about someone who has so violated your trust? Why was I needy of Paul at the very moment that I wanted to leave him forever? How could I be so torn? Why couldn't this be straightforward?

Guilt began to force its way into my psyche. I knew I had no cause to feel guilty, that I was the one who had been wronged and sold short. I was the one who now had to grapple with the agony of such an act of intimate treason. And it was I sitting here, alone on a North African beach, wondering if I'd been too extreme in the note I'd scribbled in fury and left for Paul to find.

The problem with ongoing guilt—especially the sort that has been clogging up your psyche since childhood—is that you simply cannot rationalize your way out of its chokehold. You find yourself negotiating with it in the manner that a hostage tries to talk terms with the terrorist holding him in a basement cell. *Surely we can be*

reasonable about this . . . can't we talk it through? . . . Yes, yes, even
though you have me chained to a bed and only allow me out to the bath-
room twice a day, I know I am, in part, to blame here.

The light above was beginning to fade. I checked my watch. It was
edging toward five in the afternoon. Had I been out here that long?
Or was one of the reasons that I had stayed so long on the beach the
vain hope that Paul—having discovered all the evidence left for him
and the packed bag indicating I was leaving him—would have, by this
time, rushed off to find me here, knowing that I walked these sands
every afternoon.

But I must have hiked more than an hour to reach this empty
spot. Maybe he only got back to the hotel from his lunch and working afternoon at Fouad's just a few minutes ago . . . perhaps he was
heading this way?

And there you go again, wanting some sort of Hollywood moment: *I have made the mistake of my life! The vasectomy is reversible!*
I've made an appointment with the urologist! I will fly back tomorrow
with you and be unfixed by the weekend!

But the beach was empty. Paul usually returned home from
Fouad's by three for a siesta. Not a sign of anyone on the horizon. I
was totally alone.

The walk back to the hotel took an inordinately long amount of
time. When I reached the front desk Ahmed seemed unnerved by
my arrival.

"Is something wrong?" I asked him.

"*Le patron*, M. Picard . . . he needs to speak to you."

Not *wants* to speak with you. *Needs to.*

"What's happened? Where's my husband?"

"You wait here, please."

Ahmed ducked into the back office. I shut my eyes, wondering,
What fresh hell is this?

M. Picard emerged a few moments later, looking as grim-faced
and bleak as an oncologist about to articulate bad news.

"We've been looking everywhere for you, *madame*. We were deeply worried."

"What's happened? Where's my husband?"

"Your husband has . . . vanished."

I blanched, but in a way that perhaps indicated I was not surprised, as Picard said, "You were expecting this?"

"No, not at all."

"But you left him documents and a note . . ."

"You've been in our room?" I shouted, suddenly angry. "Who gave you the right to—"

"What gave me the right was the fact that the cleaners heard your husband screaming in the room. Screams that followed loud thumps."

Immediately I was dashing up the stairs, Picard calling after me, telling me I shouldn't go in there, that it was a potential crime scene, and the police were—

But I raced ahead, throwing open the door when I reached it. When I stepped inside what I saw was . . .

Chaos.

It did look like a crime scene—in which robbery and violence played prominent roles. Clothes strewn everywhere. Every drawer pulled out, contents dumped. Two of his sketchbooks torn apart, the ripped, decimated paper littering the room like deranged confetti. And on the stone wall in front of our bed, a cascade of blood in the process of drying.

Next to the documents and the note I left for Paul was a piece of paper. On which was scrawled—in his characteristic cramped calligraphy—five words:

You're right. I should die.

TEN

"DON'T TOUCH THE documents," Picard warned me when I reached for Paul's scrawled note.

"But they belong to me," I said.

"The police might think otherwise."

"The police?"

"Your husband was last heard screaming in this room. Then there was silence. Ahmed reported all this to me when I returned to the hotel just ten minutes ago. He said he didn't want to disturb Monsieur Paul, as there had been no further screaming since his initial outburst. I told him to go upstairs and check on him. What Ahmed discovered was that your husband had vanished, but blood was covering the walls. Of course we called the police, as I was initially concerned that it might be your blood. Until I saw the letter you left him. Where were you when all this was going on?"

"I was out hiking along the beach."

"I see."

His tone unsettled me. It sounded studiously neutral—as if he was hinting that he didn't believe me.

"I was back here briefly around four thirty and then went out for my usual walk."

"There's no need to explain this to me. It is the police who will be asking the questions."

"Questions about what? I should be out looking for my husband."

"The police should be here shortly. I had them standing by, waiting for your return."

The cops did arrive two minutes later. A corpulent officer sweating in his blue uniform, and a narrow-shouldered detective in a cheap suit, a white shirt yellowed from overwashing, and a thin paisley tie. He was around forty with a pencil moustache and slicked-back hair. They both saluted me, simultaneously eyeing me with professional interest. Ahmed showed up in the doorway as well. The detective spoke to M. Picard in Arabic. Picard spoke back at an equally high speed. Then the detective questioned Ahmed, who half-gestured toward me several times. Meanwhile the uniformed officer inspected the bed, the documents, and the two scratched notes that we'd left for each other, the disarray of the room, the bloodied stonework. The officer said something to the detective, who came over to inspect the blood, pulling out a small handkerchief to dab at a drop of it, studying it intently. He asked a question of Ahmed, who replied in a torrent of Arabic, again gesturing at me throughout. Then the detective introduced himself to me, in French, as Inspector Moufad.

"When did you last see your husband?" Moufad asked.

"Around twelve fifteen. We'd slept in late. My French teacher, Soraya, woke us up."

"What's her full name and address?"

Picard supplied these immediately, which the officer dutifully wrote down. Moufad continued. "So you slept late . . . your teacher arrived . . . and then?"

"I had my lesson. Soraya saw my husband leave our room. He was heading off to have lunch and work at Chez Fouad."

"Your husband was working at the café?"

"He's an artist . . . and a professor at a university back in the States. He was working on a series of line drawings about life in the souk."

"Where are these drawings?"

I pointed to the cascade of torn paper everywhere, tears coming to my eyes as I took in the debris around me. His exquisite, extraordinary drawings. The best work he'd ever done; the new turning point in his creative career. And now . . . shredded beyond redemption.

"Who tore up these drawings?" Moufad asked.

"I presume it was Paul."

"Do you have your husband's passport?"

"Of course not."

"Why do you think he tore up his artwork?"

"You'd have to ask him that."

"But he's not here, is he, *madame*? M. Picard reports that one of his cleaners heard a commotion in the room around four o'clock. M. Ahmed went upstairs to check—but found the room empty, turned upside down, this fresh blood everywhere."

He brandished his handkerchief with the still-wet sample blotting into its cotton fibers.

"Was someone here with him?" I asked.

"Was that someone you, *madame*?" Moufad countered.

"I was taking a walk on the beach—as I do almost every afternoon."

"Did anyone see you take that walk, *madame*?"

"No, I was on my own, as always."

"So you weren't with somebody then?"

"I just told you I was on my own."

"How do I have proof of that?"

"What you have proof of is an incident in our room when my husband was here and I was out walking the beach. Look at the state of this place! My husband's been robbed and clearly injured."

"But where is your husband now if he was so injured?"

"I am desperate to find that out."

"If it was a robbery, why didn't they take either of your laptops?" Moufad asked, pointing to the pair side by side on the desk. "And there is that very expensive Canon camera by the bed."

The uniformed cop now picked up a mug on the desk, looked inside, and said something to Moufad. He asked him to bring the object over. Once it was handed to him, he pulled out a small wad of dirhams.

"And a thief would have also definitely taken all this cash that you unwisely left out," Moufad said.

Picard seemed offended by this remark.

"In the twenty-three years I have run Les Trois Chameaux," he said, "we have never once had a robbery."

"There's always a first time," I said. Picard and Moufad exchanged a fast knowing look with each other.

"Even if your husband had surprised the thieves," Moufad said, "even if they had slammed his head against the wall, they would have left with the cash and the electronic goods. They would have grabbed what was valuable and in plain sight—as all these items were. So the fact that the computers, the camera, the cash were left behind . . . a little strange for thieves. Then there is the matter of the whereabouts of your husband. Why would thieves smash his head against a wall and then drag him away with them, while leaving all the valuable booty behind? It simply doesn't make sense."

"But surely someone saw my husband leave the hotel."

"One of the young cleaners—Mira—heard the commotion in the room," Picard said. "She came downstairs to the reception and raised the alarm. Ahmed came racing upstairs, found the room in its current state of disorder, and found me. We searched the hotel. No sign of your husband."

"Might he have headed out while Ahmed was upstairs?"

"That is a possibility," Moufad said. "Another possibility is that you and your husband had an altercation."

"We didn't have an altercation."

"There was an angry exchange of notes, wasn't there? I don't read English—but M. Picard, when he called us, translated them for me."

Inspector Moufad reached into the breast pocket of his jacket and pulled out a small black vinyl notebook. He thumbed through it until he found the page he wanted.

"One note—I presume it was yours—reads, 'You have killed everything and I hate you. You don't deserve to live.' You did write this, yes?"

I hung my head, then quietly said: "I wrote that."

"And his reply: 'You're right. I should die.' If, that is, he actually wrote that."

"Who else could have done that?" I asked, sounding angry now.

"Someone who might have wanted to harm him."

"Let me get this straight, Inspector. Are you actually thinking that I had an altercation with my husband that saw me—a woman around half his physical size—slam his head against the wall, smuggle his unconscious body out when nobody was looking, but before doing that, write a note in his handwriting, indicating that he was planning to kill himself?"

The inspector thought this one through for a few moments, then said, "Who's to say that you haven't hidden the body somewhere in the hotel?"

"But I wasn't here."

"Nobody saw you leave for your alleged beach walk."

"I did no harm whatsoever to my husband," I said, the anger again flashing. "After he headed out to Chez Fouad I didn't see him again."

"But you nonetheless left all these documents behind for him to discover, along with a note wishing him dead. M. Picard translated all the medical transcripts for me. They too make interesting reading. A record of your husband having undergone a vasectomy."

Silence. I could see the three men quietly relishing my immense discomfort at discovering that they knew everything about this grubby business. I motioned to a chair, indicating that I would like to sit down. Moufad gave me his okay. I positioned myself on the armchair for several moments, trying to figure a way out of this. I decided the only way forward was to tell the truth.

"I am an accountant back in the States. My firm also does my husband's accounts. One of my associates contacted me today with the information you discovered on the bed. Information that my husband, having agreed with me that we would try for a child—and knowing full well that, at the age of forty, time was no longer on my side—went ahead and got himself . . . sterilized. As you can imagine, the discovery of this . . . betrayal . . . well, it was shattering. My husband was out at Chez Fouad when these documents arrived. I printed them up and left them on our bed with an angry note in an attempt to prick his conscience. Then I left for my beach walk—and returned to find all this."

Silence. A quick glance between the inspector and Picard. The inspector then approached me.

"As sympathetic as I am to what has befallen you, *madame*, you have left out a key part of your story: the fact that, earlier this afternoon, you booked a flight back to the States tomorrow at twelve ten from Casablanca."

I felt myself tense.

"You work fast, *monsieur*," I said.

"My job," he replied.

"But . . . the decision to fly back tomorrow . . . that was my determination to leave him there and then. I had decided that, in the wake of what I had discovered, it was over."

"And you left him a note saying he should die for what he did."

"That was anger," I explained. "Pure rage. I certainly wouldn't want any harm to come to my husband."

"Even though there is written evidence that you wanted him dead. Perhaps with good reason—as he did something so cunning, so calculated, so treasonous."

Moufad had me locked in his line of vision—to the point where I was beginning to feel my hands go clammy and beads of sweat cascading down my face. As far as he was concerned I was the person of interest in this case.

"Monsieur," I said, trying to calm myself, "why would I leave a note like that if I was planning to do my husband harm? Why would he leave me his reply if he didn't feel horrendous about being caught out in this terrible lie?"

A little shrug from the inspector.

"Perhaps you wrote his note yourself."

I stood up and walked over to the desk where Paul kept the large black hardcover Moleskine notebook that was his journal—and which I never dared touch, as I do believe that privacy is sacrosanct (especially after experiencing my mother's habit of going through my own journal back when I was in the throes of adolescence). The uniformed officer tried to stop me from collecting it, but the inspector said something that made him back off. I opened the journal and found page after page of Paul's spindly penmanship. Followed by pages of sketches, doodles. And several bulky items in the inside pocket on the back cover. I came over to the bed and placed a page of the handwritten journal next to the note Paul left on the bed. Even if you weren't a trained forensic penmanship specialist, it was blindingly evident that the writing belonged to the same person. The inspector, the uniformed officer, and Picard all took turns staring down at the comparative scrawls. The inspector pursed his lips.

"And who's to say this isn't your journal?" he asked.

I felt myself getting very defiant. I stormed back over to the desk and picked up my own diary, flinging it down on the bed next to the enraged note that had landed me in such deep trouble.

"This is my journal—and, as you will note, the handwriting matches my own."

Another shrug from the inspector.

"I will need to take all this evidence with me, along with your passport."

"Are you charging me with a crime?"

"Not yet. But there is clear evidence here that—"

"What?" I said, now emboldened and angry. "The way I see it, my husband realized that I had found out about his lie and that I was planning to leave him, and went berserk. Tearing up his drawings, slamming his head against the wall. We have to find him. *Now*."

My delivery of this statement was so vehement that it rendered Moufad and Picard wide-eyed. Moufad finally replied, "I am still taking the journals, the documents, the notes, and your passport as—"

"You will do no such thing," I said, "unless you want to formally charge me with my husband's disappearance . . . if, that is, he disappeared."

"*Madame*, you do not know the law here."

"I know that the United States has an embassy in Rabat and a consulate in Casablanca. If you try to seize my passport or any of my possessions—and that includes my husband's effects—I will make a phone call. You will then have to deal with the consequences."

Just to prove that I meant business, I started to reach for my journal. The uniformed officer instinctively reached out and grabbed me roughly by the arm. I broke away and screamed at him:

"*Comment osez-vous? Je connais mes droits!*"

The officer backed off immediately.

"There is no need for drama, *madame*," Moufad said.

"Yes there is. My husband is in distress, perhaps terribly injured. And probably wandering around Essaouira, bleeding badly and disoriented. We are wasting precious time here. I suggest that we all rush to Chez Fouad to see if he might be there now, or if Fouad has taken him to a doctor."

Silence. I could see that the inspector was calculating his next move.

"Okay," he said. "We will go to Chez Fouad. But everything remains here."

"No way," I said. "Because we could return from Fouad's and find that, in my absence, your men cleared the place out."

"You have my word, *madame*."

"With respect . . . that's not enough, *monsieur*."

Another silence. Then an idea dropped into my head.

"I will, however, allow you to photograph everything—just as it is now. Before we leave. But the documents, the notebooks, remain with me."

The inspector bit on his lower lip, not completely disliking this idea . . . but not at all pleased with the way I was setting the agenda.

"I will agree to that—on two conditions. The room is sealed after we photograph it. I am certain M. Picard can find you another room for the night. And I will assign one of my men to watch guard over you."

"That is not at all necessary."

"Yes, *madame*, it is. Though you have not been charged with any crime so far, there is the fact that some sort of potentially criminal activity took place in this room. Perhaps you are right. Perhaps your husband has indeed attempted to harm himself, as he is burdened by guilt and the realization that he has lost you; that you are leaving him. Which, no doubt, must be something very hard to bear. But who's to say he might not come back and try to harm you? We must rest assured that you are safe here tonight. Would you not agree?"

I felt myself about to flinch again.

"I am certain that Paul will not do me harm."

"But if he's left blood on the walls from self-inflicted wounds, and has ripped up his precious artwork . . ."

I didn't have a retort to that, so I said nothing. The inspector asked M. Picard if there was any access from the roof or a back door into the hotel. Picard informed him that only a cat could find a way from the roof into one of the rooms, and that the rear entrance was always padlocked from the inside.

"There is no way for a guest to leave the hotel except by the front door," Picard noted.

"Then I will, with your permission, have one of my men stationed in front of the hotel all night to ensure that no harm comes to *madame—*"

"If I choose to go for a walk tonight?" I asked.

"The officer will accompany you. By the way, *madame*, I will be approaching a judge tomorrow morning to obtain a warrant to seize the evidence we've photographed and also to force you to turn your passport over to us until the investigation into your husband's disappearance has been concluded."

"Then I will be contacting my embassy first thing tomorrow morning as well."

"That is your prerogative, *madame*. Meanwhile"—he turned to M. Picard—"with your permission I will have several of my men search your hotel to see if *madame*'s husband might still be here, hidden away somewhere."

Picard nodded his assent. But then I said, "Could it be that my husband went out when someone wasn't standing watch on the front door?"

Now all eyes were on Ahmed. He looked uneasy with all the attention.

"I was at the desk all afternoon—and never saw M. Paul leave," he said.

"So he must still be here," the inspector noted.

"But surely if M. Ahmed had to pick up the phone, or deal with a guest, or answer a call to nature, my husband could have slipped by undetected."

Again all eyes were on Ahmed. He just shrugged. And said, "Of course the nature of my job means that I am not at the front desk one hundred percent of the time."

"So he could easily have gone out," I said.

"Someone would have seen him," Picard interjected. "We have our own man out front most of the time. Karim. He is our informal security person during the day—and is always outside, sweeping, tending to the plants, ensuring no one loiters near the entrance. We have another man there at night—as *madame* knows, since he helped rescue her on her first night when she made the dangerous mistake of wandering off on her own."

Trumped again. I could see the inspector, in the wake of hearing this little tale, deciding I was trouble.

Just to twist the knife deeper, Picard added, "I spoke to Karim in the hours after we heard the commotion in your room. He was out front all afternoon and never saw your husband go out."

"But I did not see Karim when I left for my walk," I said.

Picard narrowed me in his sights.

"Yes, he saw you leave—and he told me you had murder in your eyes."

"That's not true," I said . . . though, of course, I knew that, after leaving all that self-implicating evidence on the bed, I did storm off, looking frenzied. But that line about Karim seeing me . . .

"Does it matter if he thought I looked angry?" I said. "The fact that he saw me leave the hotel before my husband got back—"

"He never saw your husband come back," Picard retorted. "Nor did he see him leave. Neither did Ahmed. Isn't that right, Ahmed?"

Ahmed nodded his head several times. Who wants to bite the hand that pays him? Especially when the hand belongs to such a cold calculating operator as Picard, who wants to keep the police on his side and will happily see me framed for all this if it wins him points with the cops. In a place like this, having the police in your corner is a serious necessity.

"I will say this once more. My husband left the hotel around twelve ten. I left around two o'clock. I came back an hour later. I went and took a walk on the beach. In my absence something happened in our room which left blood on the wall and my husband . . ."

I felt myself tear up, but I held down the sob and managed to say, ". . . he's somewhere out there, injured, in desperate need of help. So can we please get out of here and over to Chez Fouad?"

The inspector studied his fingernails for several moments, then said, "We will leave for Chez Fouad when we have photographed everything in the room and when we have searched the hotel and are satisfied that your husband's body hasn't been secreted here. And no, you may not go to Fouad's alone. I may not as yet be able to take your passport away from you. But I can have you escorted and followed everywhere in Essaouira. Which is exactly what I am planning to do."

ELEVEN

IT TOOK THEM more than two hours to search the hotel. Every room was opened—and several guests disturbed—as the police, all led by Inspector Moufad, looked under every bed and in every bathtub and insisted on opening every wardrobe. All storage closets were inspected on each of the four floors. The meat locker and the big freezer in the kitchen. The extralarge garbage bins in the rear alley. The staff rooms in the basement.

On and on the inspection went, despite my entreaties to let me go, accompanied by an officer, to Fouad's. The inspector was informing me that, from this juncture on, we'd be playing by his rules. He insisted on sending for the "official police photographer" to take detailed pictures of the two telltale notes, the two journals, the shredded drawings, the broken chest of drawers, the crimson splatter on the stonework. At one juncture the young cleaner, Mira, came in with a tray of mint tea for the policemen, but Ahmed, accompanying her, insisted on pouring it himself. I could tell immediately that Mira found the sight of the destroyed room more than a little unnerving. She looked at me with silent trepidation, as if she wanted to tell me something but clearly couldn't with all the officialdom around. When I caught her eye and motioned that we should talk in the corridor, she shook her head and hurried off. I checked my watch. It was now 8:10 p.m. The inspector came back into the room.

I said, "We could have spent the last two hours searching for my husband. Instead we—"

"Are you telling me how to run this investigation, *madame*?"

"I just want to find Paul. I'm scared, *monsieur*. Scared for him."

"You will be pleased to hear that I had two of my men scouring the beach. They had our four-by-four, so they were able to drive around ten kilometers down its sands. No sign of your husband . . . unless, of course, he decided to go into the water. Or was pushed."

Again the inspector was studying me, trying to fathom how I was dealing with that unveiled accusation, or the thought that perhaps Paul threw himself into the Atlantic with his head hemorrhaging blood. Again I felt the anguish welling up. But I managed to push it away as I met his accusing stare straight on and said:

"*Vous êtes un homme très sympathique. Un mec très class.*"

I could see him flinch. Just as I could also see him quickly recover and shoot back, "*Vous allez regretter cette parole.*"

A moment later the same uniformed officer who'd arrived with the inspector showed up in the room to inform him that the search of the hotel was completed and nothing had been found.

"Can we now go to Fouad's?" I demanded.

"We first need to make an inventory of all the goods you are taking with you."

This process took another half hour. Every object I was moving into the new room that Picard found for me down the corridor had to be first registered in a police log. After documenting the journals, the papers and notes, the laptops, our respective clothes and toiletries, I was allowed to put the crucial items in a backpack. Picard called back Mira and told her that she should pack up all our clothes and move them with our suitcases to Room 212, and also deal with anything left in the bathroom or elsewhere. Again I sensed she wanted to make contact with me. Again the presence of others thwarted her.

"All right, *madame*, we will now go to Chez Fouad," the inspector announced.

I hoisted the backpack onto my shoulders.

"Surely you should leave that behind in your new room," Picard said.

"And discover it all not here, but with the police when I return?"

"I appreciate your confidence, *madame*," the inspector said.

"*Je vous en prie*," I replied.

As we were leaving, Picard asked to speak to me for a moment.

"I will have to charge you for the new room in which I am putting you until the police allow me to redecorate the one that you and your husband destroyed."

"I had nothing to do with—"

"I must inform you that, in addition to the five hundred dirhams per night for the new room, I estimate that, to replace the chest of drawers, repaint and repair everything in your old suite . . . it will be around eight thousand dirhams."

That was almost one thousand dollars. Absurd. Especially as just three of the drawers were smashed, and the hand-painted chest itself remained undamaged. There were only three long blotches of blood on the wall, most of which would come off with soap and hot water. But I was too stressed to argue with this oily little man. So I told him, "I will pay for the extra room tonight. We have paid the entire month for the suite in advance. So your lawyer can speak to my lawyer about the cost of the alleged damages."

"That is not satisfactory, *madame*."

"Nor is your attempt to gouge me for money at a terrible moment like this."

I walked off down the stairs to the foyer, the hefty backpack strapped across my shoulders.

When I reached the front desk, part of me wanted to make a break for it; to dash out into the now dark alleys and byways of Essaouira and run to Fouad and find my husband sitting there, his head bandaged, nursing a glass of red wine, sketching mournfully, a sad smile crossing his face; me rushing into his arms, so relieved to find him alive, willing for the next few days to push aside the terrible things that resulted in all this madness, and simply be happy that he was out of danger . . . even though another part of me seriously doubted if I could stay in this marriage much longer. But that gut feeling was overshadowed by the culpability I felt about springing that trap on him, one I knew would send him into a downward spiral. That was the worst part of all this. Had I simply confronted him, face-to-face, with the urologist's bill, we could have yelled at each other and worked out some sort of resolution, even if it meant the end of us as a couple. But instead I took the cruel option. Leaving those documents out . . . accompanied by my note suggesting he should die . . . that was a vindictive impulse. As with most attempts at revenge, the blowback had now badly singed me.

A tap on the shoulder. The inspector was by my side.

"Okay, we can go now," he said.

"If it turns out he isn't there . . ."

"Then he isn't there."

I checked my watch. Now nearly eight thirty. Hours since he fled the room, unseen by anyone. As we walked down the back alleys toward the souk, my gaze was fixed on everyone who came toward us, who lurked in a doorway, or was slumped against a wall. Is this how the parents of a missing child must feel? The desperate horror of knowing that the center of their lives had disappeared, and hoping against hope that, by accident, he or she would suddenly stumble out in front of them, ending the nightmare from which there was absolutely no release?

It took less than ten minutes to reach Chez Fouad. The six tables on the little verandah out front were all packed. Fouad was taking an order when he caught sight of me. From the way he tensed—and then tried to quickly mask his distress—I sensed that he must know something about Paul's whereabouts. But when the inspector approached him—flashing his badge, giving him the suspicious once-over—Fouad played dumb.

"Of course I know Monsieur Paul," he told him. "One of my best customers. Always sits at the corner table over there. We have a collection of his drawings behind the bar."

"And the last time you saw him here?" Moufad asked.

"When he left at four p.m."

"You're certain he didn't return?" I asked.

"*Madame*, it is I who poses the questions," the inspector said.

"And it's my husband who's missing. I also know Fouad, so—"

"When Monsieur Paul said goodbye to me at four that was the last time I saw him today," Fouad said.

"Surely someone saw him since then," I said.

"I've been on duty here since three. Had Monsieur Paul shown up again I would have seen him."

"Could you ask any of the other waiters?"

"I am the waiter, as you well know, *madame*. Had he been here I would tell you."

As he said this I glanced down and saw him rubbing his right thumb manically against his forefinger. The inspector was looking elsewhere when I caught visual manifestation of Fouad's nervousness. When the inspector informed Fouad that he wanted to "look around the kitchen and any storage room," Fouad told him he had carte blanche to search wherever he wanted. As soon as the inspector went inside the café, I turned to Fouad and said, "I know you know where Paul is. You need to tell me: Is he all right?"

"Can you come back later?"

"That's going to be hard. They have a cop positioned at the door of the hotel under orders to follow me everywhere. They think I hurt Paul."

"Find a way of getting back here before midnight."

"Please, please let me know if my husband is okay."

The inspector emerged from inside, asking Fouad to come with him.

"Be back before midnight," Fouad whispered to me, then disappeared. I was momentarily free of my police escort, but knew if I vanished now it would just raise more suspicion. But how would I be able to get out of the hotel later on and find my way to the café?

There was a moment when I considered dashing off into the night, hiding somewhere for an hour, then creeping back here to learn the truth from Fouad. But as soon as I took a few steps away from the café, a uniformed police officer emerged from the shadows opposite the hotel. He saluted me, then said, "*Madame*, I have been instructed to ensure that you don't leave this immediate area. So please return to your table and await the inspector."

I had no choice but to do as ordered. When the inspector returned a few minutes later with Fouad, he told me that he had thoroughly searched the café, and there was no sign whatsoever of my husband's presence.

"I will now have you escorted back to the hotel," he told me. "I will be sending my men to the bus station and the taxi rank to see if he tried to leave town. We have our contacts there, so if he did board a bus or arrange a car to take him elsewhere we will know. Now you must return to the hotel."

"And if I want to go again?"

"Then one of my men will accompany you."

The officer who stopped me from leaving the café brought me back to Les Trois Chameaux. At the front desk, Ahmed informed me that Mira had moved all our clothes and personal effects to the new room and that M. Picard was demanding 500 dirhams now before I could be allowed to go upstairs.

I handed over the cash, telling Ahmed, "Please inform M. Picard that I consider him to be nothing less than *un connard*."

I could see that Ahmed was shocked by my choice of insults and struggling not to grin in agreement. Insisting that he carry the heavy backpack upstairs, I followed him to Room 212, a tiny cell with a narrow single bed, a sink, a view of the wall in a nearby alleyway, and an elderly bathroom with peeling paint.

"Could you find me something else?"

"M. Picard told me that you have to sleep here tonight. When the boss returns tomorrow—"

"I will call him *un connard* to his face. Please ask Mira to bring me some mint tea."

"*Très bien, madame.*"

As soon as he closed the door, I sat down on the bed, threw open the backpack, and dumped out its contents. I reached immediately for Paul's journal. Its rear pocket revealed a shock: my husband's passport. So he ran off without this crucial travel document. On one level this was a relief, as it indicated that he wasn't planning to leave town or country. But, like me, Paul went nowhere in Essaouira without this important piece of documentation. Why did he dash off without it? Unless, in the anguish of discovering that I had learned his nasty little secret, he simply ran out, not knowing what to do next. Which made my sense of guilt augment tenfold.

But then another discovery in the back pocket of his journal hit me like a donkey kick. A photograph. A small three-by-five photograph of a young woman, no more than twenty-two. Moroccan, yet with certain features that hinted at someone who might be of mixed parentage. A rather beautiful young woman with jet-black hair that was a cascade of curls. Slim, perfect skin, lightly rouged lips, stylish: a tight black T-shirt and tight black jeans that managed to highlight her long-leggedness. Moroccan-French, I decided—and could easily be labeled a heartbreaker.

I stared at the photo in quiet shock for several moments. It deepened further when I turned it over and saw the inscription:

From your Samira
Absence makes the heart grow fonder.
With all my love,
S xxx

She now had a name. Samira. A young woman—almost four decades his junior—who had sent a photograph of herself to my husband, expressing her love for him—*L'absence rend le coeur plus affectueux*—and not just her love for Paul, but that being apart from him increased her yearning.

Samira. *La belle Samira*. Whose handwriting was highly calligraphic—as if she'd used a special italics pen to write this declaration, signing it with a little heart next to her name. I tossed the photograph onto the bed, away from me, my head reeling.

I grabbed his journal. Page after page of his tortured penmanship. With Mira arriving any moment with the tea, I didn't have time to try to decipher them. Instead I whisked through the entire journal, looking for some sort of indicator of where this Samira might be found.

A stroke of good luck. On a page creased in half, and half decorated with sketches of . . . oh, God, this was too hard to bear . . . her face . . . I opened the fold to read, *I have to find a way of getting Samira back in my life. Robin will freak—to put it mildly. But she has to know the truth sometime . . . though if she found out all the truth I would lose her forever.*

So there it was: a second secret he'd been harboring for some time now. The other woman. How could I have been so naive, so guileless? How could I have fathomed so little? How did I not see this life in parallel that he was leading? And how did he meet this Moroccan beauty whom he was desperate to get back into his life?

The other woman. The stuff of cliché.

And a younger woman, who lives at 2350 rue Taha Hussein, Casablanca 4e.

No phone number. Damn. No email. I flipped open Paul's computer. The strangest feeling hit me, unease about violating his privacy, yet another part of me simultaneously castigating myself for even allowing guilt to enter the current equation. I didn't know Paul's password for his computer—and it was very much locked. I tried several combinations of possible passwords—I knew that our joint bank account was robinpaultogether. That was Paul's suggestion. Simply typing it got me tearing up again.

A knock at the door had me scrambling to put everything away, ensuring that the photograph of Paul's beloved was slipped back into the inside pocket of his journal. When I opened the door I found Mira there, holding a tray of mint tea, looking like she wanted to be anywhere but here. I ushered her inside. As soon as I shut the door she asked in French where I would like the tea. I pointed to the chest of drawers.

"You know something, don't you?" I asked.

She looked at me, wide-eyed, as if I had caught her in the act of theft. She shook her head several times. I saw that her eyes were awash in tears.

"It's all right, it's all right," I told her.

That's when a shudder ran through her body. Reaching into the pocket of her djellaba, she pulled out a hundred-dollar bill.

"I'm sorry, I'm so sorry. I should have never taken this," she stammered in broken English.

"Did my husband give this to you?" I asked.

More tears. "I told him I didn't want it. But he pushed it into my hand. 'This is what I make in two weeks!' I told him. He just shrugged and said it was a little thank-you if he could—"

Again she broke off and seemed on the verge of breaking down.

"You didn't do anything wrong," I said, motioning for her to put the money back into her pocket.

"Yes I did. Because I took his money in exchange for showing him a way out of here that avoided going by the front desk."

"Did he say why he wanted to sneak off without anyone knowing?"

"Of course not. He just said that he needed to 'vanish without a trace'—his exact words. He gave me all this money after asking me if I knew a hidden passage out of the hotel."

"Do you know of such a passage?"

Mira now looked even more distraught by this question. "I should never have helped him," she said.

"Did he say he was running off?"

"All he said was, 'Can you find a way for me to disappear without being seen by anyone . . . and can you keep a secret and not tell anyone that I left?'"

"Why are you telling me now, then?"

"Because you're not 'anyone.' You're his wife. He's done something bad, hasn't he?"

"Nothing criminal—just hurtful."

"I let him escape."

"All he was doing was running away from himself."

Silence. I could see that thought taking up residence in her consciousness, and leading to more confusion.

"Did my husband say where he was going?"

She shook her head. "I insisted on bandaging his head before he left."

"What had he done to himself?"

Pointing to the bed—and asking my permission to sit down—she positioned herself on the edge of the mattress, grasping its thin edges as if it was keeping her afloat.

"I heard a lot of noise before I came into the room. It sounded like he was throwing himself against the wall. Deliberately smashing his head. When I opened his door I saw him run towards the wall and take the entire blow against his head. The room was madness, as if it had been torn apart. When he collapsed on the ground and I started running out the door to get help, he shouted at me not to find anyone. Then he apologized for yelling, and asked if I could find a bandage for his head, again begging me not to mention all this to Ahmed or anyone else. So I ran and found a bandage and some hot water. When I got back Monsieur Paul was sitting on the bed, looking very much as if he might pass out. I cleaned up the wound. I wrapped his head in a bandage, as there was considerable blood. I told him that he had a very large lump on his forehead—already blue-black in color—and that he should really see a doctor. I worried he might have a concussion. They can be dangerous, *n'est-ce pas?*"

"Yes, they can be dangerous. What happened next?"

"He asked me if there was a way out of the building that would permit him to avoid passing the front desk."

"Did he say why he wanted to sneak out the back door?"

"No."

"I suppose he didn't want anyone to see what he'd done to himself."

"I wouldn't know. He seemed very . . . unstable. I was worried that, after injuring himself, it mightn't be a good idea for him to go out. But he said he had to see a friend."

"Did he tell you the name of the friend?"

"The man who runs the café. He asked me again if I knew a way out the back of the hotel. When I told him I didn't want to get into any trouble he gave me this"—reaching into the pocket of her apron she brought out the crumpled $100 bill—"I was shocked when he insisted on giving me so much money. I told him I didn't want his money and that M. Picard would be furious with me if he discovered that I had helped him sneak away . . . especially with the state of the room. But he told me that M. Picard would get money from you to pay for it—and the one hundred dollars was a gift to me for helping him out and not saying anything. But I really can't keep it."

She proffered the creased portrait of Benjamin Franklin, making me wonder if Paul had a stash of American dollars he wasn't telling me about.

"Of course you're keeping the money. I will give you an additional three hundred dirhams if you show me the back way out of here."

"But the police . . . they will get very angry with me . . . maybe get me into trouble . . . if they find out that I have helped you."

"They didn't know you helped Paul. They won't know that you helped me. Anyway, I will be back in an hour or so. You are absolutely sure that Paul didn't tell you where he might be going?"

She shook her head many times.

"What did he take with him?"

"Take with him? Nothing. Once I bandaged his head he stood up and said he could walk, and gave me the money. I asked him to wait in the room for several minutes, then returned when I was certain it was safe for him to go."

"Where's that secret way out of here? Will I be able to get back in myself?"

"Please, *madame*, if they catch me aiding you—"

"I will take the blame," I said, reaching into my pocket for the cash and thrusting it upon her.

"You and monsieur are being too generous," she said.

No, what we are being is very American, I thought. Thinking that money can buy our way out anything. Mira looked at the cash. A week's wages for opening a door. I could see her hesitating.

"I will come back in twenty minutes," she finally said. "Ahmed is on a break right now, and he often goes out the back for a cigarette. When he returns on duty to the front desk I will come for you. We won't have much in the way of time, because he could call for me. But as long as you are ready when I return . . ."

"I'll be ready," I said.

Mira nodded and left. I went over and poured out a glass of Moroccan whisky. The mint tea not a balm tonight. I quickly repacked the backpack with things I didn't want left behind in the room: my laptop, my passport and journal, Paul's diary. I recounted all the remaining cash that had been kept in the mug on the desk in our other room. There was close to 8,000 dirhams—around one thousand dollars. My great hope was that, once I got over to Chez Fouad, I would find Paul, hiding in some corner of the café that Inspector Moufad hadn't discovered. With some coaxing and kindness (and me pushing aside my considerably maimed pride for a day or so), I could get us back to the States and Paul into the hands of a good shrink—who would help him negotiate the aftermath of my leaving him.

I finished the mint tea. I resisted the temptation to look further through Paul's diary. I tried to control the hurt and anxiety coursing through me. A light knock on the door. I opened it. Mira put her

finger to her lips and motioned for me to follow her. I hoisted the
backpack. We both scanned the corridor. It was clear. We crept along
like cats. At the end of the hallway was a small door. I had to take
off my backpack to follow Mira and squeeze through it. There was a
narrow stairway, the steps crumbling, the walls here reeking of damp.
Down and down we went, entering some subterranean warren. We
reached another door. Opening it the stench of sewage hit my nostrils. It was vile, overpowering. Reaching into her apron pocket Mira
brought out a candle and a disposable lighter. Holding a flame to the
wick she whispered:

"Don't say a word, don't make any unnecessary noise."

We were in a tunnel, with wet muddy walls and a damp dirt floor.
The height of this burrow couldn't have been more than six feet. Paul
must have been forced to painfully crouch down all the way along
its moist, odorous passageway—further pain after the self-inflicted
pain. I sucked in my breath. I put my hand over my mouth and used
my thumb and forefinger to pinch my nostrils shut. I followed the
candle being held in Mira's hand. It took us a very long and unsettling
five minutes to reach its far end. The walls seemed to be sweating,
as trickles of liquefied dirt commingled with insects, worms, and . . .
oh, God, no . . . a rat that ran right out in front of us and made me
gasp. Mira—who was completely unfazed by the sudden emergence
of this filthy rodent—put her finger to her lips. I kept wondering if
one wrong move, an accidental bump into its delicate substructure,
would cause the entire tunnel to collapse, burying us alive. That's
always been a recurring nightmare of mine—to wake up and find
myself suffocating after having been entombed in an avalanche of
snow or mud. My horror at being in this tiny passage was magnified
many times over by the thought that I had endangered a young girl,
who couldn't have been any older than fourteen, by insisting she
bring me along the same escape route that Paul had convinced her
to also guide him through.

We reached a metal door. Mira tried to open it. It wouldn't budge.

She rapped on it harshly with her tiny knuckles. After a moment it creaked open. A small hand reached in and pulled Mira through. Then the same hand reappeared. I took it and was hoisted around the door's rusted frame and found myself face-to-face with the owner of the hand: a young man around fifteen, with a sly, challenging look on his face. He said something to Mira in Arabic. She answered back in a way that made it clear to him that she wasn't impressed with his wiseass comment. Switching to French she told me:

"This is Mohammed. He thinks he is my boyfriend. He is not. He wants one hundred dirhams for opening the door and guiding you up to the street. I have told him thirty dirhams. We've agreed fifty. You pay him half now, half when you return."

Then she barked something at Mohammed, which made him tense for a moment before that flirtatious look returned to his face. Mira saw this and rolled her eyes—and then raised her finger close to his face and said something that, from its tone, sounded half like a warning, half a threat.

"I've told him if he plays any games with you—like asking for more money—he will have to answer to me," Mira said. "Now I have to go back. You must assure me that if anyone finds out you disappeared for a few hours . . ."

"I will never tell them of your involvement in my disappearance. That is a promise."

"*Merci, madame,*" she said, sounding very formal.

"I can't thank you enough."

"There is no need to thank me, *madame*. You and your husband paid me well for my silence."

With a formal nod—and a last withering glance at Mohammed— she pulled open the rusted door and disappeared back into the underworld. Mohammed motioned for me to follow him. We were in a basement, above which was loud music and the sound of rhythmic chopping. When I looked quizzically at this sound, he said in very rudimentary French:

"*Mon père est boucher.*" *My father is a butcher.*

His establishment was evidently right above us. And he was dismembering something as Mohammed held out his hand for the first installment of his payment. The twenty-five dirhams turned over to him, Mohammed then guided me through a basement that looked like a makeshift abattoir. Garbage pails and industrial-size Dumpsters filled with the remains of carcasses. Dried congealed blood on the concrete floor. All the associated stenches that accompany the left-behinds of dead animals. Mohammed smiled when he saw the effect that the aroma of his father's basement had on me. I clamped my hand over my face as we went up the stone steps into the back of the shop. When I emerged from behind the counter, Mohammed's dad—a man around forty with a hangdog face, bad teeth, a bloody hatchet in one hand—looked bemused to see me coming up from the lower depths of his basement. He nodded a polite hello, then barked something at Mohammed. When Mohammed barked back—and also rubbed his thumb and forefinger together—his father seemed placated. He even offered me mint tea.

"*Mille mercis, mais j'ai un rendez-vous,*" I said.

But where was I now? Though I knew the souk well after more than two weeks here, the fact remained that it was so densely structured, so labyrinthine in design, that you inevitably found yourself down a dark lane which you had never encountered before. Much like the alley I now was ushered out into. It was full of ominous shadows and no markings to tell me where I might exactly be. Mohammed pointed to his father's shop and said, "*Je reste ici.*"

"*Mais où suis-je?*"

"*Essaouira.*"

"*Mais où?*"

"*Vous cherchez où?*"

I told him that I was trying to find a café owned by a man named Fouad. Mohammed looked at me blankly.

"*Vous ne connaissez pas Chez Fouad?*" I asked.

Mohammed gave me another bemused shrug.

"*Aidez-moi,*" I implored, getting worried that Fouad might think I wasn't returning and would vanish before the midnight deadline he set.

Mohammed held out his hand again, indicating more money was being demanded. I decided not to argue—and started reaching into my pocket for another ten dirhams. But before I could hand him the ten-dirham note, his father emerged from his shop, running toward him with one of those mallets (soaked in blood) that is used to tenderize meat, shouting loudly, clearly terrifying his son, who ducked behind me. When his dad reached us he grabbed his son by the shoulder and shook him furiously, castigating him in a free flow of Arabic. I sensed he had caught sight of him demanding further money from me—and took offense at his boy's shilling for more cash. I tried to intervene on Mohammed's behalf, explaining that I had asked him for directions to a certain café, that it was I who offered to pay for his service to guide me. Mohammed, now in tears and sobbing, translated my words into Arabic. Though it took a few very tense moments for his father's anger to subside, he seemed to buy into this story, shaking Mohammed once more and telling him something that Mohammed then translated into broken French.

"My father he says . . . you lie to protect me."

"Tell him I'm not lying."

And then, all but acting out my words, I pointed to myself as I explained:

"I asked your son to bring me here"—I gestured to the alley ahead—"to a café owned by a man named Fouad." I mimicked handing him money. "I offered to pay him for his service. Your son never asked me for money"—again gesticulating between myself and Mohammed and pointing to my pocket and back to him and shaking my head to emphasize he never insisted on payment.

It was quite a pantomime performance. But the butcher finally believed me. Gripping his son by his shoulder he pointed to the far distance and barked another order to him. Mohammed translated. "My father tells me to bring you to Fouad's café."

"But where is it?"

Mohammed posed that question to his dad. Another angry torrent of Arabic poured forth—but halfway through this tirade I started to realize this was this gentleman's way of giving directions. At the end of this rant—replete with gesticulations indicating right and left turns—the butcher then looked at me and became unfailingly polite, touching his heart with his right hand, executing a little bow, and (from what I could glean by his countenance) begging apology for his son's behavior.

I shook my head and touched Mohammed on his right shoulder in a manner that was both maternal and protective, then asked him to tell his father, "Your son was most respectful and courteous. A great credit to you, *monsieur*."

That seemed to finally placate the butcher. He bowed gravely to me, then swiped his hand forward to indicate that Mohammed should get a move on with me.

We headed down the darkened alley. As soon as we turned a corner Mohammed stopped and started to cry. The cocky kid had been reduced to a sad little boy with an unforgiving dictator of a father. I tentatively put my arm around him, wanting to comfort him, but assumed he might just push me away. To my surprise he buried his face in my shoulder and sobbed. How I wished I could have lifted him out of his life and brought him to a place that was happier and less threatening. How I wished I could have lifted myself out of my own life.

When Mohammed subsided he said one word, "*Merci.*" Then he led me down several other byways until we reached Chez Fouad. I knew full well that I would not be able to find my way back without his help, so I handed Mohammed fifty dirhams and asked if he could wait here until I was finished.

"*Mon père sera fâché.*" My father will be angry.

"*Je vais parler avec ton papa. Je vais tout régler.*" I will talk with your dad. I will make everything all right.

Mohammed nodded and found a stone step on which to sit as I approached the café. When I looked back in his direction he was perched on this stoop, looking forlorn, not knowing what to do with his time. I could not help but think of men I'd seen everywhere in Essaouira, sitting on brick walls or by carts stuffed with goods, quietly despondent, inert in the midst of life's chaotic flow. I didn't want Mohammed to end up like one of those men, yet sensed he was facing a future in his father's butcher shop and a lifetime of animal carcasses in the basement.

As I walked onto the terrace of the café, Fouad looked at me as if Typhoid Mary had just come a-calling. It was clear I was the last person he wanted to see but, with a grimace of resignation, he motioned for me to take a table in the far corner. Then he disappeared inside for several minutes, returning with a plastic shopping bag in one hand. Mint tea arrived. Fouad poured us two glasses. We sat there in silence for several moments. It was clear he was expecting me to initiate the conversation . . . or, more to the point, the questioning.

"Do you know where my husband is?"

"Perhaps."

Fouad was not going to be immediately forthcoming. I chose my next words with care.

"I am concerned—not just about the fact that my husband has gone missing, but also that he injured himself."

"He told me you did that to him."

"He what?" I yelled. Immediately all eyes in the café were on us. This displeased Fouad even more. He raised his finger to his lips.

"You do not want to draw attention to yourself," he whispered.

"I did not hurt my husband."

"That is your story."

"That, *monsieur*, is the truth. My husband is in a very unstable state, and one of the maids at the hotel saw him slam his head against the wall—"

"Which you made him do."

Oh, God, I was lost now.

"I did not force him to hurt himself."

"He said you rejected him."

"I caught him out in a lie. A terrible lie."

"Then you left him a note, telling him to kill himself. Which is what he tried to do."

"I was angry," I said. "Desperately angry."

"He took you at your word. And now . . . why should I help you?"

"Because he needs my help. Because he is fragile and in a bad place."

Fouad looked away.

"I am begging you . . . just tell me where he is."

Another shrug.

I reached into the backpack and pulled out Paul's journal. I opened it and showed him the photograph of the young woman named Samira.

"Do you know her?" I asked.

Silence.

"Do you know if he was heading to Casablanca to see her?"

Silence.

"You have to help me, Fouad."

"No I do not."

"I will give you one hundred dirhams if you tell me."

"Five hundred."

"Two-fifty," I said.

"Three hundred."

I nodded assent. He motioned for me to hand over the money. I did as demanded. He counted the small pile of dirhams, then said, "Yes, Monsieur Paul had gone to see this woman."

"Did he explain why he was seeing her, why he had her photograph in his journal?"

"You have to ask him that."

"But how am I going to ask him that?"

"Go to Casablanca."

"He met her at the university where he teaches," I heard myself saying, articulating a scenario that had become clearer to me in the hour since I'd made the discovery of her photograph. She was one of his students, and he'd become intoxicated with her during the course of their affair over the past year. When she said she was going back to Morocco for the summer, he felt the compulsion to follow her across the Atlantic to North Africa. But as he couldn't disappear without me, he convinced me to join him. However, he was always looking for that decisive moment when he could run off into her arms. Did he use the head-butting incident to give him an excuse to vanish—and to land me with the guilt of believing I had tipped him over the edge? Did the discovery that I had found him out make him play the self-destructive card, then push him to realize that the only future now open to him was with her in Casablanca?

"Tell me, please," I said, "did he meet her back in Buffalo?"

Another of his infuriating shrugs. Then: "Ask him yourself."

I held open a page of his notebook and pointed to the place where he'd marked down her residence.

"Here's her address. Can you get me there?"

"What would the police think?"

"I can make it worth your while."

"If I take you to Casablanca there will be questions, many questions from the inspector. He might even consider closing my café down. So . . ."

"Then find somebody else to drive me."

"Ten thousand dirhams."

Over one thousand two hundred dollars.

"That's absurd," I said.

"That's the price. You don't like the price, take the bus. There is one that leaves at midnight. Of course, the police always have men stationed there to see who is coming or going out of town. We are a police state, Morocco. A very polite police state. But everyone is, in some way, under surveillance."

"So how did Paul get away undetected?"

"He had help."

"Now I am asking for your help."

"I have given you a price."

"All I can give you is four thousand dirhams cash."

"You wait here," he said, and disappeared into the interior of the café. I glanced over in the direction of Mohammed. He gave me a shy wave. I waved back, wondering simultaneously if Fouad was going to return with the police, telling them how I had snuck out of the hotel and was trying to bribe him to get me out of town.

But after a minute or so, Fouad returned alone.

"Okay," he whispered. "Four thousand dirhams one-way to Casablanca. You pay me in advance."

"When do we leave?"

"Now."

TWELVE

THE CAR WAS an ancient Peugeot with bad suspension and a tendency to emit an automotive burp every few minutes. We'd be driving along at fifty miles an hour, and out of nowhere would come a loud glottal belch from the engine that was evidently on the verge of cardiac arrest. These eruptive internal combustion noises didn't seem to faze the driver, a man named Simo: wiry, edgy, around fifty, with a pronounced hack cough courtesy of a ferocious cigarette habit. In the four hours it took us to reach Casablanca, he always had a cigarette on the go. When one was burned almost down to the filter, he reached for the packet on the seat next to him and lit a fresh one off the remnants of the one that was about to expire.

Simo insisted that I sit in the backseat, where I had both windows wide open to rid the car of his incessant cloud of smoke, and to provide some ventilation on a torpid night when the humidity and the actual mercury level made the air seem as glutinous as maple syrup. Simo also made it very clear that, outside of driving me, he wanted absolutely nothing to do with me. When I asked him if he knew the address that Fouad had given him, he nodded. When I asked him if he thought we might encounter police checkpoints on route, he shrugged.

Fouad had warned me while we were still in the café that Simo was the wrong side of taciturn. Before we got up to leave and meet him, I went over to where Mohammed was sitting. I told him that

I needed to head off somewhere, and asked him to not say a word about this to anyone.

"But Mira might be concerned if you don't come back."

"You can tell Mira I had to go find my husband. She won't tell anybody. She assured me of that. Please assure me that you will keep this secret."

I pressed two 100-dirham notes into his hand. His eyes grew wide.

"*Shokran, shokran,*" he said.

"That money is for you, not your father. Do you think he'll wonder where I've gone to?"

"I will give him the fifty dirhams you gave me. That will keep him quiet."

"I wish you well, Mohammed."

"Bless you, *madame.*"

Then I hurried back to the café. Fouad escorted me through the kitchen—a small, cramped, hellishly steamy place where two men in stained, sodden white T-shirts were frying falafel and scooping hummus on plates. They glanced up at me. Fouad favored them with a scowl. Their eyes returned to the task at hand.

Within a moment we were in the back alley, in which had been squeezed the ancient Peugeot, with a man standing in the shadow, smoking a cigarette. Fouad introduced us and explained that Simo would be driving me to Casablanca. He asked me for the address. I opened Paul's notebook and showed him the spot where the address of Samira's apartment was marked down. He, in turn, took out a small crumpled notebook from his back pocket, pulled a pencil out from behind his ear, licked the lead, and wrote, in Arabic, the address. Handing it to Simo he barked several instructions to him, then motioned with his hand for him to get lost for a few moments. Simo walked deeper into the shadows of the alley.

"I didn't want him to see you handing over the money," Fouad explained. "I will pay him later. I chose him because, although he doesn't say much, he's not the sort who will try to hit you up for money. He knows that he'll have to answer to me should anything go wrong, or if he tries anything—which he won't."

I reached into my pocket and counted out four thousand dirhams. My crazed hope was that, on arrival in Casablanca, I would find Paul at the apartment of his mistress, verify that he was all right, give him the chance to get on that midday flight with me to New York, and, at worst, have the door slammed in my face, ending a marriage that was, in my mind, already finished.

Fouad counted his way through the money. When he was satisfied that he had the complete amount, he called the driver over and spoke to him in a low, firm voice, showing him the address, gesticulating toward me several times, then making a point of writing out a series of numbers on another scrap of paper, tearing it along its perforated edge, and handing it to me.

"If there is any problem, you phone me on this number," Fouad said. "But there should be no problem whatsoever. Simo . . . he is okay."

Then he handed me a plastic bag. "Your husband left this behind when he showed up late this afternoon. I'm not saying he wanted you to have it, but I'd rather that you keep it safe for him."

"You still won't tell me where your other driver dropped him?"

"I cannot . . . because I gave him my word I would not."

"Can you at least tell me if I am right to be going to this address?"

Fouad considered his response for a moment, then answered, "Inshallah."

Allah willing.

Five minutes out of Essaouira I discovered that the reading light in the back of the car was not working. When I asked Simo if there was a problem with the light he just shrugged. I asked if he could pull over and get it fixed—as I was completely in the dark and very much wanted to see what was in the shopping bag that Fouad had given me. I also wanted to use the four or so hours on the road to read through Paul's journal—though the prospect of delving into the inner sanctum of his mind made me uneasy. Maybe the blown light was a hint that I'd best not pry into his private world. But the very fact that I was in this broken-down car, fleeing our hotel in search of this lost man . . .

"*J'ai besoin de lire, monsieur,*" I told Simo when he reported that he could do nothing about the busted light. In response, he reached into his pocket and tossed a disposable lighter into the backseat.

"*Ce n'est pas suffisant. Vous n'avez pas une lampe-torche?*"

He shook his head and accelerated the engine, causing the first of many belches to exude from the exhaust pipe. I sank back into the vinyl seat, aware of springs sticking up through the upholstery. I had to shift around until I could find a spot that didn't feel like acupuncture. Then I reached into the plastic bag. I felt something close to massive relief when I pulled out one of his large sketchbooks. Flicking on the lighter—its flame meager—I opened its hard black cover and felt myself tearing up when I found page after page of his Essaouira line drawings. Whatever agony or fury or self-destructive rage made him rip up several of his notebooks back in our room, some sliver of self-preservation clearly kicked in, for this book contained his best work by far. Over fifty drawings, so innovative and daring in his use of line, in his mingling of the abstract and the representational, in the heat-and-dust authenticity he brought to the souk, yet all underscored by Paul's absolute need to draw these market scenes in an original way. At one point I had to shut the album and put down the lighter and sit silently in the dark, absorbing the sense of loss that was careening through me like a fast-acting toxin. I looked out at the scrubby dusty landscape we were traversing, the beclouded sky that blocked all celestial light. The sheer immense stress of the past few hours, the fear and anguish of what I would find in Casablanca . . . all of it suddenly sideswiped me. I found myself overcome by the realization that the entire terrain of my life had changed.

I began to cry. Weeping in the dark of this shabby car, being watched in the rearview mirror by a silent man uncomfortable with this show of emotion. He lit another cigarette. When I stopped crying he reached into a bag on the front seat and handed me several cubes of baklava wrapped in paper.

"My wife . . . she makes these," he said in basic French. "You eat them."

"*Shokran*," I said.

He nodded acknowledgment. Not another word passed between us until we reached Casablanca several hours later.

I closed my eyes, hoping sleep might overtake me. It didn't—so I snapped them open again. I reached into my backpack and pulled out Paul's journal. Holding the lighter so close to its pages I was afraid that a bump might set it all aflame, I began to go through its contents. Most of them were taken up with fast sketches, doodles, visual improvisations on the life he was incessantly observing. Then there were interspersed jottings, musings, confessions—never more than a line or two at most. The flame from the plastic lighter threw strange, spectral shadows as I read page after page of my husband's frequently epigrammatic confessions. The fact that they were all undated . . . that was so Paul, wasn't it? Numbers, deadlines . . . he eschewed them all. There was no definitive chronology to this cavalcade of self-doubt and self-reproach and . . .

Robin looked so shocked and disappointed when I told her, on arrival in Casa, that I wanted to run back home. I don't blame her for being disappointed. She married a man who shouldn't be married . . . and who knows that his wife is far too good for such a two-faced loser like himself.

Then, a few pages later, a sketch of me nude in our hotel bed.

Amazing sex, as always. My ambivalence to her, to all this, ebbs away when I am deep inside her.

I snapped my eyes shut. This is why you should never read your significant other's journal.

Robin sometimes looks at me like I am a five-year-old who has just thrown all his toys out of the crib. Which is not far from the truth.

Close the book now.

She overpraised the new drawings today. I felt humbled by her kudos. Why does her reassurance about my alleged talent make me feel so small?

There was another fast-rendered sketch of me, standing on the balcony of our room, staring out into the great distance.

She'll leave me when she finds out. She'd be an idiot to stay with me. I will mourn her. Then I'll turn the page. And tell myself it's better this way. Because I don't deserve happiness. I can't even begin to fathom what it would mean to be responsible for a new life.

So he knew that, by having the vasectomy in secret, he'd loaded a gun that was eventually going to go off in his face.

I can't ever say what I want. No, the real problem is: I can't say what I don't want.

Like assuring me he wanted a child when he clearly didn't want a child.

This place is full of too many shadows for me. And reminders of all that promise squandered. I must get Samira back in my life. Can Romain B.H. aid my cause?

Who is Romain B.H.? I had an answer to that question a few moments later when I came across a page in his book, with the name Romain Ben Hassan scrawled across the bottom of a page, followed by an address. I searched my memory for several key moments, trying to remember where I had heard that name before. Then the penny dropped. Ben Hassan had been his fellow artist friend during Paul's Casablanca year. French-Moroccan and something of a louche character who kept Paul endlessly amused and frequently drunk. Luck was on my side; there was a phone number below the address. But turning back to Samira's address I noticed that she lived in the same arrondissement. Was there some sort of connection between them? Didn't Paul tell me that he had fallen out of contact with Ben Hassan when his name came up a few weeks ago? Another of his lies to commingle with all the other falsehoods he had been feeding me.

One thing still puzzled me. Why did Paul take his last remaining sketchbook when he vanished but not his passport or any clothes or personal effects whatsoever? The fact that he left without even his all-crucial pencils and charcoals unnerved me. Paul never went anywhere without a notebook and his beloved French pencils—meticulously curated from several key art supply stores in Manhattan. The trauma of all that self-harm . . . perhaps the fact that he was concussed or, at the very least, disorientated after slamming his head against the wall . . . was that the reason he left the hotel, carrying nothing? Or did he already have clothes and toiletries at his girlfriend's house? But how would he have gotten them there? Unless he gave her a suitcase to bring back to Casablanca when they were having their assignations in Buffalo, and he was just looking for an excuse to stalk out of the marriage, which I certainly gave him today.

Will you listen to yourself, engaging in crazed speculation . . .

But how could he have otherwise gotten involved with this Moroccan woman? In the three years we'd been together he'd never traveled anywhere without me . . . except for three quick two-day trips to New York to see his gallerist. We'd done a few days in Montreal when he was in a group show there at the Musée des Beaux-Arts. Beyond that we'd never been outside the country alone or together. So he couldn't have met his mistress anywhere but Buffalo. Which must mean that he got to know her at the university where he taught. The photograph of her in her journal indicated she was only in her early twenties. Did he get the vasectomy to ensure that she didn't get pregnant as well?

Stop, stop, stop. This is getting you nowhere.

But the problem with discovering a lie—especially when you cannot yet confront the liar—is that it leads to further hypothetical scenarios.

When I said earlier that Simo didn't say another word to me all the way to Casablanca, that wasn't quite true. He actually said one: "Police."

Up ahead there was a roadblock and two cops standing in the middle of the road, one of them using a powerful flashlight to indicate that we should pull over. Oh God, they've found out somehow that I've fled the hotel and am on the run. Now I am going to be brought back to Essaouira and be made to face Inspector Moufad, whose suspicions about me have trebled since I disobeyed his order and fled town. Now he's going to have someone guarding my door until he gets a judge to sign an order allowing him to relieve me of my passport. Now I am definitely going to be his prime suspect. And he will argue in court that only a guilty person would have tried to run.

But another part of me knew that Mira wouldn't have betrayed me like that. Because by doing so she would simultaneously land herself in immense trouble. And also because she was, I could tell, someone who believed in keeping her word.

Still, here we were, being pulled over by the cops. I could see Simo's lips tighten. He finished sucking down his cigarette as his back and shoulders noticeably stiffened. The beam from the blinding police flashlight filled the windshield of the car, forcing Simo to slow right down.

He pulled up in front of the parked police vehicle, stubbing out the cigarette in the brimming dashboard ashtray. The window was already rolled down. I could hear the static of a police radio in the near background. I could make out, as the flashlight beamed around the car, two youngish policemen in ill-fitting uniforms; the novelty of the late-night hour in the absolute middle of nowhere was augmented by their immediate curiosity in discovering a woman—correction, a Western woman—in the backseat. There was a lot of fast talk in Arabic. Simo handed over his identity papers and his driver's license. One of the officers disappeared for what felt like a long time, then returned and talked at length with his colleague. Then this officer turned his attention to me: "*Vos papiers, madame.*" I already had my passport in my hand and turned it over. Now the two cops spent far too long studying it, going through it page by page. There was so much blank space on those pages, evidence of how little I knew

of the world outside my own country. I saw them reach the page
on which my Moroccan entry visa had been stamped. They studied
this intently. They talked among themselves. Then the more senior
of the two officers asked me if I spoke French. I nodded affirmation.
He asked, "The driver says you hired him as a taxi to take you to
Casablanca. Is this true?"

"Yes, I have paid him to do exactly that."

"Why are you traveling in the middle of the night?"

I had already reasoned that this was a question they just might
pose, and I had an answer already prepared.

"My husband is arriving in Casablanca off an early flight tomorrow—and I am meeting him at the airport."

They then disappeared with my passport. I watched as they
walked over to their vehicle, lighting up cigarettes, passing my travel
document back and forth. Meanwhile Simo had fired up another
smoke—and I could see that he was sweating out the outcome of
their deliberations as much as I was. I knew if one of them reached
for a phone—or the handset attached to the crackling police band
radio in their car—to verify my identity, I would be screwed. A good
five minutes passed. The older of the cops opened the door of their
vehicle. Here it comes—the beginning of the end. But then he pulled
out a bottle of water. More talk between them. Then the senior officer approached us. He knocked on the back window. I rolled it down.

"*Donc, madame . . .*" He handed me back my passport. "*Bon voyage à Casa.*"

With a nod to Simo, he saluted us as we drove off into the night.

Two minutes after we'd passed the police checkpoint Simo let
out a pronounced sigh. Even when you're guilty of nothing, an inter-
action with the law is always a source of internal agitation. Did Simo
sense I was on the run? The stress of those past few minutes hit me
sideways. So too the lateness of the hour, the immense strain of the
day. Stretching out along the backseat of the car, again manipulating
my body in such a way as to avoid the protruding springs, I passed

out. Though the lack of suspension in the car, and the roughness of
the road, jolted me awake several times, my exhaustion was such
that I vanished instantly again into the underworld. Until there was a
massive jolt, followed by the loud braying of an animal and the even
louder braying of a car horn. We were on a city street, tall apartment
blocks defining the horizon, no traffic except a cart with a donkey
parked right in front of us. A man in a djellaba was attempting to
move the donkey and its attendant cart, but the animal was refusing
to budge and was blocking the road. Its driver was using a whip to
get it to move, but the beast was obstinate even in the face of pain.
Simo—who could not get around the donkey and the cart, given
the narrowness of the street—was blasting his horn. Snapped back
into consciousness, but still fogged in, I glanced at my watch. It was
just a few minutes before six. Light was beginning to claw back the
night sky. It took me a moment to work out that, indeed, we were
in Casablanca.

"*Arrêtez, s'il vous plaît,*" I told Simo, indicating that honking the
horn was doing no good. Simo's reply was to point to a building
across the street; a semi-crumbling apartment block, art deco in style,
with a shop on the ground floor that was already open and seemed to
function as an all-purpose neighborhood store. There was a café with
a terrace directly across the street. I also took in an optician's and a
boutique displaying white and maroon leather jackets in its window,
along with stone-washed jeans and paisley silk shirts. A cavalcade
of expensive bad taste, playing visual games with my psyche after a
night of brief, fitful sleep in the backseat of a rusted car. The donkey
cart driver finally got his beast moving, clearing the road. Simo pulled
the car over, pointing again to the building across the way.

"*Votre adresse,*" he said, motioning for me to leave. I reached into
my pocket and dug out a 100-dirham note. When I proffered it to
him, he just shrugged and accepted it with a fast nod. As I slid off the
backseat, my pants suffering a slight tear from one of the springs, he
uttered, "*Bonne chance.*"

Myself and my backpack having been deposited on the street, the car engine belched one last time in my presence before disappearing into the already congealing traffic. I checked my watch again and wondered if I should go up to Samira's apartment now, bang on the door, confront her, and force my husband to leave her bed and come with me.

All my instincts told me to walk away. Cut my losses. Accept the sad finality of it all. Not try to save him—as much as I still wanted to; as frightened and worried as I was that my husband was heading toward some sort of point of no return.

I knew I was now negotiating with myself, talking myself into some sort of compromised position from which nothing good would arise.

Go to the café. Order a coffee. Ask them to call you a cab. Immediately. Get to the airport. Get on the plane. Hit the portal marked *I'm out of here . . . permanently.*

Instead I hoisted my backpack and crossed the street to her building. I scanned the list of names accompanying the apartment numbers and buzzers that were banked on a wall to the left of the entranceway. They all listed the tenants by last name, with no *Samira* or even an *S* in sight. Damn. Six thirty in the morning. The shop next door was open. I considered going inside and showing the picture of Samira to the man behind the counter to see if he knew her. Then I reasoned that she was probably a regular there. Which probably would mean that if some sleep-starved, stressed-out, middle-aged Anglophone woman held up her snapshot and demanded to know her last name and apartment number, the guy in the shop would undoubtedly give her a ring to warn her. He might also call the cops. Best to be prudent and wait across the street.

What I discovered within surprised me. It was well stocked with upscale prepared foods, largely French in origin. It had a considerable amount of local produce—hummus, tahini, couscous, assorted Moroccan pastries—but it also sold teas from Hédiard in Paris and

Nespresso coffee capsules, Belgian chocolate, and Italian extra-virgin olive oil. This was the sort of local deli that would have fit into any cosmopolitan city, and clearly catered to an educated clientele. There was also a rack of foreign newspapers in French, English, German, Spanish, Italian—all that day's editions. I grabbed a copy of the *New York Times* International Edition and the *Financial Times*, paid for them, then crossed back across the street and found a table on the café terrace with a direct view of the apartment building's entrance. A waiter arrived. I ordered breakfast, realizing that, in addition to dealing with virtually no sleep, I also hadn't eaten anything except a piece of baklava since breakfast the previous day, fear and stress supplanting hunger. I started to properly take in my surroundings. The buildings here all were largely art deco, with a few new structures dotting what was otherwise a rather intact architectural quarter. There was an interesting-looking bookshop next to one of those places that specializes in exquisitely packaged soaps and bath oils. There were advertisement posters showing young, vibrant professional couples looking dreamily at each other while holding the latest in mobile phones. There was a high-tech electronics store, hawking the latest in laptops and cellular communications. A woman in a tight track suit came jogging by. An impressive number of high-end Audis and Mercedes and Porsches were parked on the road. There was not a niqab in sight. I was in a Morocco divorced from the realm behind the walls in Essaouira; a world familiar, yet utterly foreign.

Two more men with donkey carts came trudging down the road. One of the animals stopped to pee and simultaneously splashed the fender of a Mercedes SUV. Its owner—a portly business type in a black suit, white shirt, smoking a cigarette, a cell phone in each hand—arose from his café table and came waddling over, shouting reproaches and abuse. The donkey driver tried to ameliorate the situation by rubbing the wet fender with a corner of his djellaba. This infuriated its owner even more. My orange juice and croissants arrived just as a policeman showed up on the scene, telling the businessman to calm down and also instructing the driver to stop rubbing more donkey urine into the Mercedes's paintwork.

I bit into my croissant, relieved to be eating something. I stared down at the international *New York Times*, thinking that during our weeks in Essaouira never once did I think about buying a newspaper. Now I was learning about a Wall Street downturn, and another wave of bombings in Beirut, and the death of a onetime dictator in the Caucasus, and . . .

The yelling across the street rose in volume. The businessman was now so frustrated with the donkey driver's mild-mannered reaction to the bestial baptism of his car that he actually pushed him, causing the policeman to restrain him. Then, in a moment beyond stupid, the businessman shoved the cop so hard that he tumbled into the street. Regaining his balance, the officer dodged an oncoming car. It braked wildly, front-ending the Mercedes.

Chaos ensued, as the businessman became nearly deranged, yanking open the door of the car that had just flattened the front of his own, clawing at the driver.

I was grateful to the donkey for having peed on the businessman's German fender. Because it made me look directly across the street at a crucial moment—just when the door to the apartment building opened and a young woman with long, richly curled black hair walked out. She was exceptionally tall—over six feet, long-legged, absurdly thin, dressed in tight blue jeans, chic sandals, a loose white linen shirt. I had Paul's notebook out on the table. I pulled out the photo of Samira. It must have been taken a few years ago, as the woman before me was more mature, but still unbearably beautiful. I threw some money down on the table and raced over. She was standing not far away from the scuffle still in progress—the businessman now being handcuffed— watching the drama unfold. I approached her.

"Are you Samira?" I asked.

She seemed thrown by the question, but still asked me in flawless English, "Who wants to know?"

"Paul's wife."

Her face tightened.

"I have nothing to say to you."

She turned and started walking off. I followed her, shouting, "Please, I need to know—"

"Did you just hear what I said to you?"

She kept walking, with me alongside her.

"Is he here, with you?" I asked.

"I am not talking to you."

"You have to talk to me."

As I said this I made the mistake of touching her on her arm. She shrugged me off, hissing, "You put a hand on me again . . ."

She stalked off. But I kept pace with her.

"You know where he is," I said.

"No idea. Now leave me."

"Don't lie to me."

Now she stopped and turned on me.

"Lie? Lie? You dare—"

"Tell me where he is."

"Let him tell you that."

"So he's upstairs? In your place?"

"I wouldn't let him through the front door."

"So he came here?"

"I am getting into my car now."

"You have to help me," I pleaded.

"No I don't."

She reached into her bag, pulled out a set of keys, and clicked open the door to a small Citroën parked on the street. As she went to open the driver's door I blocked her path.

"I know who you are. I know that you're involved with him. And if you want him, that's actually fine by me. But I just need to know—"

I was all but yelling. But her voice rose louder than mine.

"Involved with him? I *want* him? Do you know who I am?"

"Yes, I do."

"I doubt that," she said, suddenly very cold and quiet. "Because if you did know, you wouldn't dare make accusations like that at me."

"Who are you then?" I demanded.

She met my gaze with a look of ferocious contempt.

"I'm his daughter."

THIRTEEN

I STOOD ON the curb for a long time after she drove off. I was stunned by the revelation just rendered, stopped dead in my tracks. When I glanced up I caught a final glimpse of her face, staring back at me with hardened contempt. Yet her eyes also radiated the saddest sort of despair.

Then she accelerated and the car shot off down the street.

I remained motionless for several moments, not knowing what to do next. Eventually I retreated back to the café. The waiter was keeping an eye on my table, my newspapers, my croissants, my *jus d'orange*. As I approached he handed me the 100-dirham note I had thrown on the table before I got up to pursue Samira.

"You left all this behind, *madame*."

"I had to speak to someone."

A small nod of acknowledgment from the waiter. Had he watched that scene unfold? Had he put two and two together and reasoned it was a wife confronting the woman she thought was her husband's mistress? If only he knew the truth. If only I knew the truth.

I sat back down at my table. I shut my eyes, exhausted and confused and flattened by a disclosure that I simply never saw coming.

He has a child. He has a child who is at least thirty years old. Maybe older. He has a daughter. A beautiful daughter. Evidently conceived with a Moroccan woman. Judging by her age, the point of conception was all those decades ago—and the photo Paul kept of her in his notebook must have been ten years old. A secret he kept from me always. A secret that made his other great deceit—promising me a child and then having a vasectomy—even more heartbreaking.

"Would you like your coffee now, *madame*?"

I indicated that would be fine. Hunger forced me to eat the croissants, drink the very good orange juice. I tried reading one of the newspapers. The words swam in front of me. I pushed the newspaper away. In front of me the businessman was now being forcibly pushed into the back of a police car, struggling against the cuffs that were restraining his hands behind his back. Now he was going to be arrested for assaulting a police officer and would have to spend serious money on a lawyer. We really are the architects of our own miseries, aren't we?

I checked my watch. Six forty-three. My flight was in just under five hours. I drank my coffee. Having been turned away by his daughter, seeking refuge in the city he once called home, Paul would surely turn to friends. Or to one specific friend. Someone whose name he dropped in both conversation and in the pages of his notebook. Opening Paul's journal I found the entry I was looking for. The entry where he wrote about wanting to reestablish contact with Samira.

Can Romain B.H. aid my cause?

Romain Ben Hassan. Whose address was written just below.

I called the waiter over. I showed him the scrawled address and asked where it might be.

"Two streets from here," he said, then insisted on drawing me a map on the back of a bar coaster, explaining that I could make it to his front door in around five minutes.

A manic plan began to form in my head. I would leave here in fifteen minutes and walk over to Ben Hassan's place—where, no doubt, my husband was sleeping off the events of last night, which must have involved some sort of confrontation with his daughter. Knowing Paul, the last thing he would have done is try to find a hotel and recuperate alone. Which is why I was pretty sure that he had taken refuge at his friend's apartment. The idea of now crossing the Atlantic, uncertain of his whereabouts or his injuries, would be a refutation of all the responsible rules I lived by. If he was at Ben Hassan's, I could, at least, verify that he was in one physical piece (whatever his mental state), and have a face-to-face with him. Then hit the street. Jump a cab to the airport. And fly out of all this sadness.

The coffee arrived. I drank it quickly, the caffeine a fast antidote to my fatigue. I ordered a second and threw it back. I settled the bill, counted out my remaining dirhams, and asked the waiter how much a taxi would cost from here to the airport.

"You will need to negotiate, but don't pay more than two hundred dirhams. Make sure you agree on the price before he starts driving."

I thanked him for his kindness and his advice, as well as his impromptu map, which I now used to guide me to 3450 rue Tahia. Though I was too preoccupied to take in much of my immediate surroundings, I did note that this *quartier*—which the waiter told me was known as Gaulthier, after the French architect who designed the layout and many of the 1920s apartment buildings in the area—still evoked the Jazz Era, albeit in a slightly crumbling way.

3450 rue Tahia was a building that looked as if it had seen happier days. Chipped masonry. A broken sequence of pavements in front of its main entrance. A huge water stain above its front doorway. Electrical wires dangling down from a broken entrance light. I scanned the list of names by the front door, spied *Ben Hassan, R., 3ème étage, gauche*. I knew that by ringing his bell, I would be alerting him and Paul of my arrival. To hell with the fact that it was now 7:12 a.m. I had to see my husband. So I loitered in the lobby until a woman around fifty—dressed in a black business suit and big Chanel sunglasses—came out the door. She looked at me askance when I walked in past her, holding the door for her as she exited. I was about to invent some excuse—"I forgot the door code"—but thought better of it and simply headed to the staircase, probably once grand and marbled, now showing signs of the same water damage that marked the ceiling, with wood banisters that bent when I grabbed hold of them.

The spiral staircase tilted upward at a dangerous angle, and—as I noticed when I reached the first and second landings—the space between an apartment doorway and the deteriorating banister was minimal. A misstep or two and over you could go. The lack of sleep, the pressing sense of anxiety, the thought *What am I doing here?* and the sheer dizzy incline all conspired to make me hug the wall on the way up, terrified of losing my balance and encountering what would certainly be a horrifying plunge.

I reached the fourth floor. I turned left. The door in front of me was painted an insane shade of purple, its outer frame glossed black. The choice of color immediately threw me. Too hallucinatory, too out there. I rang the bell. No answer. I waited thirty seconds. I rang it again. No answer. I checked my watch. Almost 7:30. Everybody inside—my husband included—must be asleep.

I leaned on the bell, holding it down for a good thirty seconds. Eventually the door cracked open. I was facing a very short man in his early thirties, a bald head, immaculate skin. He looked like he'd just gotten out of bed. He stared out at me with tired, leery eyes.

"I need to speak with Monsieur Ben Hassan," I said in French.

"He's sleeping," the man said in a voice that defined tonelessness.

"It's urgent."

"Come back later."

He started to close the door, but I inched my foot into its path.

"I can't come back later. I must see him now."

"Not now."

He tried to close the door, but my foot stopped him.

"You see him some other time," he said.

"No, I am seeing Monsieur Ben Hassan now."

I barked that last word. I could see the man's eyes grow wide. I grabbed the knob and pushed my left knee up against the door just as he tried to force it closed.

"You go away," he now hissed.

"I am Monsieur Paul's wife. I know he's inside. I have to talk to him."

Shoving against his shoves, I began to shout: "Paul? Paul? You have to see me—"

Suddenly the door swung open and I found myself face-to-face with a man who must have weighed at least three hundred pounds. He was in his early sixties, with thin hair that he brushed across his bowling ball of a head. His face was corpulent and treble-chinned. His eyes—vampiric blue—hinted that my entreaties had just roused him into consciousness. But it was his girth that threw me. Encased in a sweaty white caftan, he had the appearance of a monumental block of Camembert cheese that had been left out in the sun and was now oozing. He studied me through squinting, tired eyes.

"Your husband is not here."

I was thrown by this comment.

"You know who I am."

A shrug. "Of course I know who you are, Robin. I am Ben Hassan. And, alas, your husband is gone."

"Gone where?"

As I said this I felt my equilibrium giving way. I leaned against the wall for support. Putting my right hand over my face I wondered if I was about to pass out. I heard Monsieur Ben Hassan say something to his friend in Arabic. That's when he put his hand on my arm. I flinched, pulling away.

"Omar simply wants to help you inside—before you faint."

Wooziness was overtaking me.

"He's gone where?" I asked.

Ben Hassan looked directly at me. And said, "He's gone to see his wife."

Now I was in free fall.

"His wife?" I heard myself saying. "I'm his wife."

That's when I felt myself pitch forward. Omar caught me. I remember mumbling something about needing to sit down. What happened next? I remember little, except being led into a large room that appeared to also be painted purple and furnished with a surfeit of heavily embroidered velvet cushions. I was led to what seemed to be a mattress on the floor covered by some sort of velvet blanket. Words were being spoken to me in French. They wafted over me, sounding as garbled as my brain. I kept telling myself, Get up, you have a plane to catch. Just as that declaration, *He's gone to see his wife,* kept ricocheting around my head. Surely I didn't hear that correctly.

And then, having been settled by Omar on the mattress, I promptly blacked out.

When I woke again I was in a world of shadows. It took a moment or two to work out where I was and then another nanosecond for me to descend into panic as I glanced at my watch and saw that it was 4:12. I jolted upright. After four in the afternoon. I had been asleep for hours. I had missed my flight.

I was in a large living room with dark purple walls. Floorboards painted black gloss. Heavy red velvet drapes. Red velvet cushions. The red sheet covering the mattress on which I'd crashed for the last . . . had I been asleep almost nine hours? Strange bad abstract art on the walls, depicting boxes within boxes, or gyrating circles that seemed to spin inward and had been painted in bloodied tones against a black background.

I had an urgent need to pee. I also had a terrifying thought: Where was my backpack, within which was my laptop, the printout of my airplane ticket, my wallet with all my credit cards, and, most crucially, my passport? I was on my feet, scrambling around the room in search of it. When there was no sign of it in this velvet whorehouse of a room, I started shouting, "*Monsieur, monsieur, monsieur,*" and ran down a corridor, throwing open doors. The first one led into a room, bare except for several wooden folding tables, on which were several piles of passports in a variety of official colors, a photocopier, assorted embossing stamps, and a machine that, on closer inspection, seemed to provide a plastic covering for documents.

What the hell was this all about?

I charged down the hall, entering a kitchen that had several days of dirty dishes and brimming ashtrays scattered everywhere, not to mention a stench that I associated with rotting vegetables. I kept shouting, "Monsieur!" Again no answer. Another charge down the long corridor. Another door thrown open. Only this time I found myself staring in at a huge carved bed, on which Omar and Monsieur Ben Hassan were sleeping naked. They were on separate corners of the expansive mattress, Omar looking so diminutive and compact compared to the fleshy enormity of Ben Hassan. As soon as I threw open the door, Omar snapped awake. Seeing me he scrambled for a sheet to cover himself, then started hissing at me in Arabic. At which point Ben Hassan opened his eyes slowly, took me in, then said, "You interrupted our siesta."

"I can't find my backpack."

"And you immediately thought that the dirty Moroccans had stolen it."

"You let me sleep through my flight. Where have you put my bag?"

"In the closet by the front door. You will find that nothing has been touched. If you need the bathroom, it's the door next to the closet. There is a shower there as well. Fresh towels have been laid out for you. Please excuse the state of the kitchen. We have been working flat out on a project for several days, and housekeeping, alas, has taken a backseat. But we'll eat out tonight."

"I need to get going."

"Get going where?"

"To find Paul. You know where he's gone, don't you?"

"Go have a shower. I will have Omar make some tea, and then we will discuss your husband and his whereabouts."

"I left Essaouira in a hurry yesterday when I learned that Paul had come to Casablanca. So I have nothing to change into, and nothing with which to brush my teeth."

"I could supply you with a toothbrush, but I sense we are in two different worlds when it comes to size or taste. However, there is a big French clothing store just five minutes' walk from here. Omar would be happy to guide you."

"I'll think about it," I said. "Could I use a phone, please?"

"Are you wanting to call Royal Air Maroc?"

"Perhaps."

"I've taken care of that for you."

"You what?"

"When you passed out I tried waking you many times. When you wouldn't arise I took the liberty of going into your bag and finding your travel documents and the printout of your airline ticket. I saw it was for midday today. Given your exhaustion I knew you simply wouldn't be making the flight. So I called a friend who runs everything at Royal Air Maroc. You are booked on the same flight at midday tomorrow. May I now extend the invitation for you to take advantage of our guest bed tonight and allow me to take you out for dinner?"

I was completely dumbfounded.

"Now, if you will give us ten minutes to wash and dress . . ." Ben Hassan said.

Still in shock, I simply nodded and headed down the corridor. In the closet near the front door there, indeed, was my bag. My passport was in place. So too my computer. And my wallet with assorted credit cards. And a fresh printout of the changed airplane ticket with the old ticket stapled behind it. The new ticket also reflected the fact that the flight change had been made without cost to me.

I reproached myself for assuming that my host and his assistant-lover had robbed me. I was having that knee-jerk Western reaction to things North African; a belief that, with few exceptions, no one here was to be trusted. But if the past few weeks had proven anything, it was that, outside of a few hassled moments, I had been treated with considerable respect and propriety. And Monsieur Ben Hassan, rather than turning me away from his door, took me in, allowed me to pass out and sleep unencumbered for many hours, changed my ticket to the following day, and was now offering me the chance to stay here tonight. I owed him thanks for that, although I couldn't help but be a little suspicious about his going through my bag just to see if I had an airplane ticket in need of changing. Was there some hidden motive there? The man was up to something in what I presumed was the false passports industry. And I wondered what he might have on Paul in the way of information that my husband might not want shared with others. Then there was the way that, like a ruthlessly cool bridge player, he trumped me with that little bombshell: "He's gone to see his wife," a revelation that landed like a kick to the head.

Still, I couldn't fault his hospitality, while I could certainly fault my hyperanxiety and paranoia for coming across as wildly suspicious and distrustful. I returned to the living room and began making up the bed.

"There is no need to assuage your guilt by tidying up."

I turned around and saw that he was in a white djellaba, already marked with sweat, as the ceiling fans did little to temper the heat of the late afternoon.

"But I do feel guilty—especially for the way I immediately assumed . . ."

"We all have our prejudices—even when we tell ourselves that we are not prejudiced."

"I apologize."

"*Ego te absolvo*," he said with a smile.

I smiled back. "You're Catholic?"

"My mother was. My father kicked with the Muslim foot. *Moi* . . . I am somewhere in between. But the Catholic in me likes the instant redemption of confession. There is no need to be apologetic about before. You will join me for dinner tonight?"

"That is most generous of you. But I need to find clothes first. I left Essaouira with nothing at all."

"Being on the run from the police usually means exigent departures."

"How did you know I was running away from the cops?"

"I have my sources. But fear not, none of them know you are here. I am *complètement discret*. But bravo for eluding them the way you did. Of course they think that you beat up Paul with some heavy object. Perhaps he deserved your wrath. A brilliantly talented man, Paul. One of the most gifted artists I've yet to encounter, yet someone who cannot face any sort of grounded reality. Instead of simply saying what he does not want, he plays the game of agreeing to something that he knows he cannot follow through on, thus creating an entire substructure of lies as an exit strategy."

I looked at Monsieur Ben Hassan with even greater respect. Never before had I heard someone nail Paul's manifold psychological complexities. Of course, when you are in the midst of a crisis with somebody else, you are more than receptive to anyone who confirms your own dark thoughts. I sensed that if I hung around today and accepted Mr. Ben Hassan's hospitality, I would learn much more about the man I once thought I knew and understood.

"If you can put up with me for another few hours," I told Ben Hassan, "I'd very much like to stay."

"I think I can put up with you," he said.

FOURTEEN

THERE WAS, INDEED, a large chain department store just five minutes from Monsieur Ben Hassan's apartment. Ben Hassan explained how to find the H&M outpost, and said there was a café next door—The Parisian—that had Wi-Fi. I took what few worldly goods I had with me, knowing that a passport is something you never leave anywhere in Morocco, especially with a man who dealt in travel documents of an illegal variety.

Ten minutes later I found myself back in a monocultural world of consumerist goods and fashion, an air-conditioned environment with a low hum of poppy Muzak which, some marketing guru no doubt reasoned, provides the right sonic smoothness to encourage you to buy more. As I filled my basket with several pairs of underwear, T-shirts, a pair of tan cotton pants, khaki shorts, two white linen shirts, and a pair of sandals, I felt another stab of desperate sadness. A fantasy Paul and I concocted just days earlier came back to me. Standing out on the balcony of our room, the sun declining into the Atlantic, a glass of wine in hand, still intoxicated with the love we had just made, the heat of the day diminishing, the light bathing the cityscape in a cognac glow . . .

We'd talked excitedly about how we should consider a new way of dealing with the shallow consumer world and how we might live our lives with more purpose. How, perhaps, in four or five more years, Paul could take early retirement from the university; I could sell my accounting firm; our house in Buffalo would be paid off and could be sold and exchanged for a smaller house on the Maine coast, with a barn we could transform into a studio for Paul, and maybe with a large attic that we could convert into an office for me, where I could finally try to pound out the novel that had been gestating within me for years (but which, given my creative self-doubt, I'd never gotten around to starting): the story of my dad's life, and the sadness inherent at the heart of the American dream.

"You'll be able to write and I'll be able to draw without encumbrance," he said. "If I manage to shift a few drawings a year, we can easily afford a couple of months here in Essaouira, or maybe somewhere in the South of France where I've heard you can rent cottages in the Pyrenees for three hundred euros a month."

"A life of ongoing adventure," I added.

"That will be us," he said. "It's all there for the asking. Even when we have our son or daughter with us."

I felt myself going rigid with fury again. Hurt and rage and . . .

He has a daughter . . . and he has a wife.

Another wife.

"*Madame*, are you all right?"

It was one of the shop assistants—a very pretty young woman, her hand on my arm, trying to steady me. Did I need steadying?

"Fine, fine," I heard myself saying, even though I knew that was anything but the truth.

"My apologies. I shouldn't have intruded. Can I help you find anything?"

"Toiletries. I need toiletries."

"And makeup?"

"Do I need makeup?"

"*Madame*, I am not trying to interfere. My apologies again."

"No, it's me who's sorry," I said. This kind young woman informed me that the toiletries were on the second floor, near the café. I thanked her and went upstairs and bought deodorant and talcum powder and shampoo and conditioner and a hairbrush and a tooth-brush and toothpaste and a face cream that ludicrously promised to reduce all noticeable wrinkles in two weeks. I paid for all my pur-chases (close to two thousand dirhams . . . prices were hardly bargain basement here), and asked the woman behind the register where I could find the nearest post office. She said there was one opposite a café called The Parisian. Now there was a bit of synchronicity. It was the café that Monsieur Ben Hassan told me had reasonable Wi-Fi. Leaving the department store I walked the block to the local outpost of Poste Maroc. I bought an extralarge padded envelope, reached into my backpack, and withdrew Paul's one intact sketchbook, contain-ing over fifty of his Essaouira drawings. I resisted the temptation to look through them again, certain that the sight of his artwork might toss me into further tumult. Instead I sealed the notepad into the envelope, wrote the name and address of my accounting firm on the front, then had it airmailed by registered post back to the States. I wanted to get Paul's recent work home right away. I figured that, whatever was to become of us, he would be relieved to know that I had ensured his drawings had not been lost.

Post office business concluded, I adjourned to the café across the street.

The Parisian was very much a facsimile of one of those big bras-series in Paris—like La Coupole or the Terminus Nord—which I had read about in guidebooks and had vowed to loiter in someday. I found a table. I ordered *un express* and also asked the waiter if he could find me some bread and jam. I was ravenous. Seeing my com-puter, he told me the name of the network and the password that I needed to get online.

I hadn't checked email since the day before, so there were over forty emails awaiting me. Mostly spam or "Buy this!" commercial mail shots. A few professional matters to do with clients, all of which I answered while simultaneously forwarding them on to Morton.

The coffee and sliced baguette arrived. I thanked the waiter and layered the bread with strawberry jam, eating it quickly, hunger and disorientation making me feel lightheaded. I drained the coffee in one go, then asked the waiter if he could get me another, along with *un citron pressé*.

"*Le petit déj' est à 17h00*," he said with a smile. I managed to smile back.

I switched over to a new screen, calling up the joint MasterCard that Paul and I shared; a credit card with a severely enforced credit limit, over which neither of us could spend. I checked the balance—and was horrified (but not surprised) to see that the $3,000 limit was maxed out. When I had last looked at the balance three days ago, it had only $300 we had run up on a week's worth of eating out and small incidentals in Essaouira. Since yesterday, there had been two large cash withdrawals of ten thousand dirhams apiece, and a plane ticket on Royal Air Maroc this morning to Ouarzazate, plus a one-thousand-dirham charge for the Oasis Hotel in that same city. I googled the hotel and was directed to their website, where I discovered it was a two-star establishment with rooms at this low-season time of year costing four hundred dirhams a night. Which meant that he must have booked himself in for at least four nights. I wanted to call and find out if he was there right now, to confront him on the phone, to demand . . .

His "wife"—his other wife—must live in Ouarzazate. So why did he drag us to Essaouira instead of going to that city where he could have snuck between the two of us? Why run here—to Casablanca—to see his daughter after I had exposed his deceptions? Why did his daughter reject him, and why did he feel the need to run off to his wife? And how did he get on an airplane without some piece of identification . . . like the passport he left behind, and which I was now carrying?

Ouarzazate. I googled it and discovered that it was a city of around sixty thousand in the southeast of the country, that it was considered "the gateway to the Sahara," that it had a film studio and was often used by foreign film companies as a location for anything with a desert setting, that the city prided itself on its "modern infrastructure and historic Saharan architecture," that it was home to an international airport with daily flights to Casablanca and Marrakesh, and twice-weekly direct service to Paris Orly.

It was now 5:12 in coastal North Africa and 12:12 in Buffalo. I found the printout of my changed Royal Air Maroc reservation. I went to their website. I tapped in my locator number. I switched over to the JetBlue website and changed my internal JFK to Buffalo flight to the same time tomorrow. The *citron pressé* arrived. I felt improved by this late-afternoon breakfast. I paid the waiter. On my way back to Ben Hassan's I passed a florist and purchased a gift for my host: twelve long-stemmed lilies. Yes, I smelled my host's deviousness. But he was also being hospitable—and I needed hospitality right now. And my mother would have climbed out of her grave to haunt me if I hadn't followed one of her key social directives: always bring a gift.

"Lilies!" Ben Hassan said when I returned to his apartment. "How did you know I so love this flower?"

"Just a guess."

"Perhaps you think me death-obsessed?"

"Are you?" I asked.

"When you weigh two hundred kilos and cannot walk more than two blocks without chest pains, yes, lilies do remind you that the River Styx is just a few streets away. But thank you for the gesture."

"Speaking of death wishes . . . I know that my husband is now in Ouarzazate. That's where she lives, doesn't she?"

Monsieur Ben Hassan pursed his lips.

"Paul told me that you were a dangerously thorough woman, as befits your profession. We will talk more over dinner. The guest bathroom, as you may remember, is two doors down on the right. If you throw your dirty clothes out into the corridor, Omar will have them washed and ironed by the time we return tonight. We don't want to send you back to the United States with dirty laundry, now, do we?"

"Don't we all have dirty laundry, *monsieur?*" I asked.

"Ah, you are an accountant with soul."

The bathroom was cramped; the shower a tiny stall with a hand-held hose. But the water pressure was reasonable, the temperature hot. And it was good to strip out of clothes in which I had traveled and slept for the past twenty-four hours.

Getting dressed in the new clothes, I caught sight of myself in the mirror and saw that the eight-hour snooze had lightened the dark circles below my eyes. The seismic disturbances within had hardly dissipated. But the upending of a life—*your life*—is so far better handled when you've had proper sleep and a very hot shower.

"Don't you look radiant," Ben Hassan said when I wandered down the corridor and found him and Omar at work in the office in which multicolored passports were stacked high.

"Thank you for all your kindnesses," I said.

"You deserve nothing less than that, *madame*. Especially with all that you have discovered in the past few hours. Not that Paul himself would ever stare directly into the wrecked ship that is his life. Who on earth wants to do that?"

A pause, as Monsieur Ben Hassan let that last comment hang between us. Then he whispered something in Arabic to Omar, who got up from the laminating press at which he was at work on a Belgian passport. He brushed by me.

"Time for a kir," he said, "if that is agreeable with you."

"Yes, I could use a drink."

"Glad to hear it. I am a good Muslim who believes in Allah and the inevitable gates of paradise from which I can finally cast off this corpulent worldly shell and spend the rest of eternity floating capriciously in the celestial vapors. But I am a bad Muslim who also believes that it is very hard to get through the day without having a drink, or two, or three. In fact, I am rather suspicious of anyone who doesn't drink. Paul doesn't overindulge . . . unless the world is crowding in on him."

"So he was drinking heavily when he was here the other night?"

"Of course. Especially after his daughter slammed the door in his face. But more on that anon. May I ask how you figured out that he went to Ouarzazate?"

I explained how we shared the same credit card and we could track all purchases online.

"You really are Big Brother," he said.

"Hardly. Had I been watching him closely I would have known long ago about his secret."

"You mean, his *secrets*."

"Yes, as I have discovered, they are plural. But let me ask you something—considering that Paul ran off without his passport, how did he get onto that Royal Air Maroc flight without any identification?"

Ben Hassan smiled wryly, then fanned his hand out to indicate our immediate surroundings.

"Surely you know the answer to that question already," he said.

"So he's now traveling on what passport?"

"British."

"How much did you charge him for the false document?"

"My usual price is ten thousand dirhams."

"Which is why he withdrew that sum yesterday."

"Your powers of deduction are exceptional. But ten thousand dirhams is, I should point out, my 'Friends and Family' price. If you are someone in need of false documents owing to problems with the authorities the price does head considerably northward."

"You were benevolent toward your old friend."

"That's one way of looking at it."

"Did Paul tell you why he showed up in Casablanca, without papers and in what I gather was an extreme mental state?"

"The business with his daughter, of course—but how much exactly do you know of all that?"

"Only that he has a daughter named Samira and a wife named . . . ?"

"Faiza."

"What does Faiza do?"

"She teaches English language and French literature in a *lycée* in Ouarzazate."

"How long were they married?"

The drinks arrived.

"We'll get to that matter—and many other matters—over dinner. Meanwhile . . ."

Omar handed me a glass of cassis-colored wine.

"The basis of this kir is a white from the Meknès region . . . which is the Moroccan Bordeaux when it comes to our *vignobles*," Ben Hassan explained, also accepting a glass from Omar. "Your very good health, Robin—and a good flight tomorrow out of all this unfortunate mess."

We clinked glasses. Ben Hassan whispered something again to Omar, who withdrew from the room, closing the door behind him. Once he was out of audible reach, Ben Hassan said, "It was rather unfortunate, attacking poor Paul with a bottle."

"I never did that," I said, stunned by this accusation.

"So you say."

"I'm telling the truth. Paul threw himself against the wall of our hotel room after—"

I cut myself off, not wanting to go further.

"After what?" Ben Hassan asked.

I chose my next words with care.

"After I caught him out in an enormous lie."

"But if you caught him deceiving you . . . I presume it was another woman . . ."

"It wasn't another woman."

"Then what was it?"

"That's my business," I said.

"And it's also your business why you attacked him with a bottle."

"Why won't you believe me?"

"Why should I? Paul is my friend. He arrived on my doorstep late last night in a state of emotional disarray, telling me that he fled Essaouira when his wife attacked him with a bottle, and showing all the physical side effects of this attack. Had the person I shared my bed with attacked me with a bottle . . ."

Ben Hassan maintained a light, almost jovial tone throughout this banter—as if this was all a rather amusing turn of events.

"Why did Samira turn him away?" I asked.

"Because he was a very bad father who hadn't bothered to show any interest in his daughter until just a few months ago."

"How do you know this?"

"Samira considers me her surrogate father." He looked straight at me as he said this.

"Where was her mother?" I asked.

"Here in Casablanca until Samira entered university—and they began to have all sorts of problems. Then Faiza, who was also having a variety of professional difficulties, lost her job. And lost her home, owing to many debts and a man in her life who was not honorable, let alone honest."

"Not Paul?"

"No—Paul cut complete contact with his wife and his daughter when he left for the States some months before Samira's birth."

"Then why did he feel the need to reconnect if he hadn't been in contact for decades?"

"You would have to ask Paul that."

He raised his glass again, downing it all in one long draft. After a small, discreet belch, he raised his eyebrows as he told me, "Of course, the fact that he discovered he was a grandfather might have had something to do with it."

"Samira has a child?"

"Yes, an eighteen-month-old son named Claude. The father is a French lawyer from Marseille. Married. Highly intelligent. Highly complex. But Samira has always liked her men intelligent and complex. Which is why she was always intrigued from afar by her absentee father—and also desperately hurt that he refused all contact. But it's the strangest damn thing. Not a word to Faiza or Samira for decades. And he never once sent them anything in the way of money. He'd vanished across the Atlantic, out of sight, clearly uninterested. Then, a few months ago, he suddenly gets in touch with me, asking for news of his daughter. Not just news, but recent photographs and her email address. And he began to write to her, wanting to know everything about her life. Samira came to me, upset and confused."

"Why would he contact her after all this time?" I asked. "Why now?"

"I told Samira she should ask that question of Paul in an email. His response was: 'I have just discovered that I cannot have children with my new wife.'"

I was so thrown by this statement that my glass of wine went flying to the floor.

"He wrote that?" I whispered. "He *actually* wrote that?"

Ben Hassan pursed his lips, suppressing a smile.

"Yes, he wrote that he could not have children with you . . . that you were not fertile."

"That is beyond a lie," I said, starting to sob. "And the reason he came fleeing up here to Casablanca is because I found out that he'd had a vasectomy behind my back."

He received this information with a momentary shocked stare—which quickly morphed into what I had now begun to discern to be his default state of wry passivity.

"That is quite an accusation," he said.

I was now digging into my backpack, manically searching for the clutch of documents I had brought with me.

"It's not an accusation," I cried, "it's the truth!"

I slammed the documents down on the worktable in front of Ben Hassan.

"There it is, in black and white."

In a hurried, manic stream of words I told how the invoice for the surgery had found its way to me, and everything that had happened from that point on, leading to my being here now. Ben Hassan listened to me in silence. When I was finished he picked up a small bell nearby and rang it twice. Omar was back in the room within seconds. A fast interchange in Arabic. Omar disappeared and returned immediately with a new glass of kir for me. He also began to pick up the shards of glass that were scattered everywhere on the floor. When I tried to apologize for my angry clumsiness, Ben Hassan held up his hand and told me to go easy on myself.

"You have been subject to far too many shocks in the past twenty-four hours. Happily the glass in question is not Rosenthal crystal, just *un verre ordinaire*, so no damage done."

More whispered words to Omar, who dumped the broken glass into a nearby trash can and left us alone again. As soon as the door was closed, Ben Hassan reached for the surgery invoice and held it up.

"Here is the proverbial smoking gun; further proof that you did attack him with a bottle upon discovering the nature of his treachery."

I snapped my eyes shut, now cognizant of the fact that I should have never uttered a word of any of this to the crafty operator seated opposite me. I finally said, "You need to know that I am telling you the absolute truth when it comes to Paul's head injury. And that I am desperately worried about him. I have to find him."

Ben Hassan fell silent for a moment, sipping his wine. Then he said, "I hope you will take solace in the fact that your husband has worked very hard at making amends with his daughter."

"By which you mean . . . ?"

"He helped buy her an apartment."

Now I really was lost.

"He what?"

"He helped buy Samira the apartment she lives in now; the apartment in front of which you verbally attacked her this morning."

"I was not verbally attacking her. I was simply . . ."

". . . letting it be known that you believed she was your husband's other woman. Samira called me while you were asleep, just a little aggrieved at such an accusation and the way you accosted her in public."

"I did not accost her."

"As before, *madame*, you are, I know, telling the truth."

"Paul couldn't have bought her an apartment."

"He only paid for half of it. The other half came from her French lover."

"How much did my husband give his daughter?"

"One million dirhams."

Ben Hassan watched me absorb that little detail.

"I can't believe that," I said.

"Why can't you?"

"Because that's, what?"—I did some rapid calculations—"something in the neighborhood of more than a hundred thousand dollars."

"You are the human abacus, *madame*."

"There is no way he could have borrowed that money in the States without my knowing about it."

"Which is why Paul borrowed the money here in Casablanca."

"But he has no credit rating here, no equity that he could have put up as collateral against a loan of that size."

"Again you have hit the bull's-eye. Which is why your husband didn't turn to a bank or some other financial institution to loan him the funds."

The penny (actually an ocean of pennies) dropped.

"Are you telling me he turned to a loan shark?" I demanded.

"*Loan shark* is a rather pejorative word, is it not? A *financial facilitator* is a far more elegant turn of phrase and not as derogatory."

"Do you think I care about verbal niceties right now, Monsieur Ben Hassan? He borrowed money from a loan shark. Which also means he's in even more trouble than I had imagined. I suppose you know the name of the gangster to whom he's now probably paying three times the hundred thousand borrowed?"

"The man is no gangster. He's just a businessman."

"And his name is . . . ?"

A long pause as my host drained his glass, belching loudly and pointedly. Finally he spoke.

"His name is . . . Monsieur Romain Ben Hassan."

FIFTEEN

BY THE TIME the second bottle of wine was emptied, Monsieur Ben Hassan was trying to insist that he was my new best friend.

At the start of the meal, however, he wasn't oozing bonhomie and easy camaraderie. On the contrary, he was showing me his more menacing hand.

"When Paul heard from me that Samira might talk with him again if he helped her buy an apartment for herself and her son, his immediate response was 'Get her the money.' I told him that if he was actually serious about borrowing one million dirhams from me, he would have to take the consequences if he did not meet his monthly payments."

"What sort of consequences might these be?"

"Unpleasant ones."

"Surely you weren't planning to send somebody over to Buffalo to rough him up . . . or worse."

"Had that become necessary, of course there were ways and means—contacts, so to speak, in that corner of the world—who could have been called upon to intervene on my behalf. For a price, *naturellement*. A price which would have been tagged onto the monthly repayment."

"I think the actual term in loan-shark-speak is *vig*. The monthly *vig*—which you had to meet or else contend with grievous bodily harm."

"I presume you picked that term up from some sort of crime novel, *un polar*, yes?"

"In my business you occasionally run into a client who has made the mistake of borrowing money from a thug like you."

Ben Hassan put his fingers together in front of his face, as if creating his very own cathedral, into which he now stared. I could see his lips twitch. Was he trying to contain his anger? Had I crossed a line of no return? If my husband had signed something quasilegal and binding, had he fled to Ouarzazate because he simply could not pay the vig, leaving me behind to clean up his financial mess, per usual? The sum involved—one million dirhams—was a vertiginous one; I certainly didn't have that sort of cash in a bank account, let alone my back pocket.

Ben Hassan stopped looking through the lattice web of his thick sausagelike fingers. Then, favoring me with a paternal smile, he said, "There's no need to be holding on to your bag, as if I am going to snatch it away. I know you still don't trust me. But you have my word that I would not dream of harming you in any way."

"My husband, on the other hand . . ."

"He will hopefully work out a way to honor our little arrangement."

"You know he doesn't have that kind of money."

Ben Hassan covered my hand with his own—actually burying it under this soft mound of flesh.

"Let us discuss such matters later on."

With that he insisted on ordering dinner for us, the waiter immediately at our table, treating Ben Hassan as if he were some godfatherly pasha, telling him that the patron wanted him to have a bottle of the Cuvée Hassan II "on the house," and informing him that the chef had prepared a lamb tagine with preserved lemons "especially for Monsieur Ben Hassan and his lovely guest."

Part of me wanted to ask my host, "So do they owe you money as well?" As if anticipating my question, Ben Hassan told me, "I made a small investment in this establishment some years ago—and the management remains exceptionally grateful for my aid at a particular moment when they sorely needed assistance."

"You are quite the businessman, *monsieur*."

"Such flattery," he said. "But I find myself a less-than-interesting subject. Especially when seated opposite such a lovely, fascinating woman like yourself."

He got me talking about myself—and I gave him the abbreviated version of my life, sidestepping much in the way of any telling detail about my father, my first marriage, the way I fled a journalistic career for the surer waters of accounting. But Ben Hassan turned out to be a master of subtext, immediately deducing much and using it to make me feel even more uneasy. The man was ruthlessly clever when it came to taking an inference ("Dad never could really settle down") and turning it into a psychological revelation ("So you have always been attracted to unstable, unsound men"). I cottoned on to his game rather quickly. Instead of getting defensive, I started asking him about his own background, discovering that his French father had run a vineyard in the Meknès-Tafilalet region, had married a Moroccan woman from a bourgeois Rabat family, but abandoned her and his young son when an opportunity arose for him to return to Bourgogne; how his father refused to see his son thereafter, "excising me from his life as if I was a nasty boil"; how Ben Hassan had studied business in Paris and tried repeatedly to maintain contact with his father; how his "attempts to enter the world of international business in Paris came a little unstuck"; how he returned to Casablanca and began to make his fortune here . . .

"Did you get into some sort of trouble in France?" I asked, the exceptional food and wine emboldening me.

"Why do you immediately assume that the discrimination I encountered in France was, in fact, due to some sort of scandal?" he demanded.

"Aren't there plenty of North Africans who have successfully integrated into French society?"

"It is still the country of Le Front National."

"I think I read that one of Sarkozy's senior ministers was a woman of Moroccan origin."

"I couldn't stay there."

"But you must have a French passport, thanks to your French father. When were you last there?"

"My girth has mitigated against my ability to travel."

The second bottle of wine arrived. The waiter opened it and, with great ceremony, placed two fresh glasses on the table and delicately poured a fingerful for Ben Hassan. My host again made great theater of sampling it, swirling it around the glass, sniffing in with such great force that I feared he might just inhale it, then taking a sizable sip and rolling it around his mouth like a gargle before gulping it straight down. Nodding his approval, the waiter poured out two glasses, then left us. As soon as he was out of earshot I posed a question that I had been wanting to raise for several hours: "How serious was Paul's relationship with Faiza?"

Ben Hassan used his finger to encircle the top of his wineglass several times. The man loved creating a sense of drama before making a statement. Finally he spoke.

"We were all part of a bohemian circle in Casablanca: writers, poets, visual artists. I may have studied commerce in Paris, but that was to please my mother. As I sense you know, one can never please one's mother. Still, before Paris, after Paris, abstract painting was my métier. I even had a gallery here in Casablanca that sold my work. Was I considered a serious painter? Quasiserious, but not a major artist like your husband. And Faiza—well, she was teaching in a *lycée* here and trying to write the great Moroccan feminist novel, seeing herself as a sort of North African Simone de Beauvoir. Truth be told, she had little in the way of literary talent. But she was rather fetching all those years ago, before disappointment and cigarettes began to work their toxic magic. Paul back then was the young American bohemian of every artistic girl's dreams. Faiza comes from a good family in Rabat. Her father worked for the Moroccan Central Bank as an economist, and they were hardly rigorous Muslims. But even if you are a secular Muslim—as so many Moroccans still are—you are also the by-product of a conservative society, especially when it comes to sex. Paul was Faiza's first lover. They were quite the handsome couple. She wanted Paul to whisk her off to New York and make her his wife and fund her writing while he became the famous artist.

"We all have our flaws. Faiza's was her need to control at all costs. Within two months of their involvement she was already starting to make demands, to criticize Paul's lack of order, to argue with him regarding just about everything. On the two or so occasions that he posited the idea of ending things, Faiza turned all teary and apologetic. From what I also ascertained, though she was not experienced in the world of sex, she'd become a very fast learner. And Paul, being a man who likes sex . . ."

"You think I'm not aware of that?"

"I've spoken out of turn."

"I was just making a point. An exceedingly defensive point."

"I like a woman who can laugh at herself."

"Now . . . let me guess. Paul being Paul, he couldn't face her emotional meltdowns in the face of him trying to leave her, and was too cowardly to walk away. Given the way she was making him feel like a sex god . . . he trusted her when it came to little matters like contraception."

Ben Hassan emitted a curious giggle, reminiscent of a little boy who'd just heard something naughty.

"It's you who should be telling this story," he said. "Yes, Paul believed Faiza when she told him she was on the pill. So when she announced, '*Mon chéri, j'ai une grande nouvelle à t'annoncer. Je suis enceinte*'—well, Paul was stunned by the news. When he didn't exactly sweep up Faiza in his arms and proclaim that she was the love of his life and that, *bien sûr*, a child together would be the ultimate expression of their *amour éternel*, she began to hector him, insisting that they get married. When he hesitated, she told her family. Her father showed up with her two rather violent brothers at the École des Beaux-Arts just a kilometer or so from here, threatening to castrate Paul if he didn't marry Faiza on the spot. They also raised so much stink with the head of the college that Paul was suspended, but told by our enlightened principal that he could have his job back if he married Faiza and made her an honest woman. For around twenty-four hours the two brothers actually had Paul trapped in his flat. Then their father showed up with Faiza, an imam, and a lawyer. They insisted on being let in, Faiza crying wildly, telling Paul that she was going to die if he didn't marry her. Paul panicked. Paul let them in. He went through with the shotgun service there and then. Said the vows, signed the legal document, tried to kiss the bride, who then began to insult him and stormed off with her father, saying she'd see him tomorrow when her brothers returned to move him into their new home in Rabat. 'I have found you a job teaching English there,' his new father-in-law announced to him. The two brothers informed Paul that they would be downstairs, guarding the front and back doors—so there was no way he was going to be able to do a run for the airport. As soon as they were gone, Paul phoned me in a total panic. I told him he'd been insane to have gone through with the marriage, but that I would find him a way out of this nightmare. Which is what I did. Around three hours later I called Paul back and told him to get his passport and a small bag and head to the roof of the building at precisely midnight. I put on a djellaba with a hood. I didn't know if Faiza had alerted her brothers about Paul's fat gay artist friend who might try to rescue him, but I was taking no chances. Dressed in my djellaba—my face hidden within its hood—I drove down to his *quartier*. He lived in an area where the buildings were so packed together that it was a three-foot jump from one roof to the next. But you had to do the jump right, as it was a ten-story fall if you made a misstep. I had to bribe the superintendent of the adjoining building to give me access to the roof. It cost seven hundred dirhams—a small fortune back then, but I had just sold a painting

and also I knew that if I didn't get Paul out of the country he would
be throwing his future away on a woman who, for all her bohemian,
'second sex' cant, was a future harridan in waiting.

"Now, Faiza's brothers were not stupid. I discovered that they
had hired some stooge to guard the rear of the apartment building
where Paul lived. That rear entrance was located next to the building
onto which he was going to jump. Anyway, I left the area, returning around a quarter hour before midnight. One of Faiza's brothers
was positioned outside Paul's building. When I entered the adjoining
building—still wearing the djellaba with its hood tied close across
my face—the superintendent told me that their stooge was still out
guarding the back door. Up I went to the roof. Even thirty years ago,
walking up ten flights was torture for me. Still, there was Paul—on
the other roof, looking down with fear at the gap between the two
buildings, terrified of making the jump, rooted to the spot. I had to
signal him with a cigarette lighter. When he wouldn't move, I remember hissing at him, 'If you don't jump you are sentencing yourself to a lifetime of marital servitude with a woman who will grind
your talent, your gift, into the ground. Stand still and die. Or jump
and live.'

"Of course he jumped—and managed to twist his ankle on landing, which made things just a little complicated when it came to
getting him down ten floors. But we eventually made it. The superintendent brought us down a series of corridors to the rear exit. Before
Paul set foot outside he changed into the hooded djellaba I'd brought
for him. He hobbled out the back door, leaning on my shoulder for
support, walking right past the stooge who'd been posted by the
brothers to look out for their sister's fleeing American lover. When
the guy saw Paul limping, he actually took his other arm and helped
him to where I'd parked the beat-up Peugeot I drove back then. To
his credit, despite being in terrible pain, Paul kept his mouth shut.
And he'd tied the djellaba so tightly across his face that his very Caucasian identity remained hidden from view. The stooge had Paul by

the other arm, asking me why he was limping. I informed him that he was deaf and dumb and had been set upon by bandits. Fortunately for us the man was so stupid, and also had a certain shred of kindness in him for an apparently disabled cripple, that he never once questioned the absurdity of the story I was spinning. He even wished us both luck as we drove off.

"I knew that Faiza's father—having certain connections, owing to his position at the Moroccan Central Bank—was probably having the airport watched, or at least had made certain that Paul wouldn't be able to board a flight back to the States. Which is why I drove him the six hours—no *autoroutes* in those days—up to Tangier, and got him on the six a.m. ferry to Malaga. I even gave him enough pesetas to get himself a doctor for his ankle, a hotel room for the night, and a train ticket up to Madrid. And then"—Ben Hassan snapped his fingers—"whoosh! Paul Leuen vanished from my life."

"Surely he contacted you when he got back to the States?" I asked.

Ben Hassan shook his head.

"Did he ever repay you?"

Again he shook his head.

"What happened when the baby was born?"

"What happened? Faiza endured the shame of being a single mother. She wasn't allowed to work at the *lycée* for several years, and struggled to make ends meet through tutoring and even cleaning other people's apartments, as her family largely disowned her."

"Surely she tried to contact Paul."

"She tried. She failed. She went to the US Embassy with her father, demanding some sort of action, actually seeing if they could get him extradited back to Morocco and force him to play house with her. The US counsel said that, outside of finding an American lawyer who could try to chase Paul for child support, there was nothing they could do to get him back here. Though Faiza wrote him several times, showing him pictures of their baby daughter, he maintained his veil of silence. Even when I wrote him after—"

He broke off, reaching for his glass of wine, drained it in one go, poured himself another substantial slug, and polished off most of it immediately.

"After what?" I asked.

Ben Hassan hesitated before speaking.

"Faiza's father was furious to discover that Paul had managed to slip out of the building undetected. He vented his rage at his sons who, in turn, beat up the sad little stooge who'd been guarding the back door. Beat him up so badly that he was hospitalized for months. Then, on their father's orders, they strong-armed the superintendent of the building next door and found out who had whisked their now vanished brother-in-law away. The superintendent gave them my name. The two brothers cornered me leaving the École that evening. They dragged me into an alley. And used a hammer to smash all my fingers."

"You're serious?" I asked, my voice a stunned whisper. "They did that?"

He held out his hands.

"Every finger. Smashed to a pulp. All bones broken. The pain was so overwhelming I passed out. I was found hours later by a street cleaner. Thank God he ran into the École and found two of my colleagues still on duty, teaching night classes. They called the police and the *pompiers*, and both came with me to the hospital. Thank God as well they were there, as the doctor on duty was so appalled by the catastrophic state of my fingers that he wanted to have them amputated. My colleagues—both artists—insisted that he do nothing so rash. But the fingers were so pulverized that I was in a pair of casts for over a year. I got lucky. There was a French orthopedic surgeon who had decided on a change of scene and was on a three-year secondment to the big hospital here in Casablanca. He took an interest in my case—and convinced me to undergo a series of experimental bone reconstruction operations. Ten in total, followed by around three years of physiotherapy. It took those pathetic little men just two or three minutes to destroy my hands, and for me, over thirty-six months of agonizing surgery and reconstruction to be able to hold a pen again."

I truly didn't know what to say. Except: "Was Paul aware of the price you paid for helping him escape?"

"I wrote him . . . correction: I dictated a letter to him, as it was around two months after the attack. I explained what had befallen me in the wake of driving him to Tangier. I didn't ask for any money or recompense. I just wanted him to know what had gone down, what those bastards did to me."

"What was Paul's reply?"

As Ben Hassan reached for his wine, I noticed for the first time just how much work it took him to grasp the stem of his glass, and how his large fingers were more misshapen than corpulent.

Ben Hassan took another long sip of wine, and I could see that he was steadying himself, tamping down some of the anger within.

"Paul's reply was . . . silence. Even when I wrote him back another eight weeks after my first letter . . . nothing but silence."

"I'm truly shocked that the brothers and father were never prosecuted for what they had perpetrated."

"The police arrested the three of them. But Papa had connections. And the two boys said in court—yes, there was a hearing in front of a judge—that they had attacked me after I attempted to come on to one of them. This being the nineteen eighties they accepted gay-bashing as a defense. They reached an out-of-court settlement with me for one hundred thousand dirhams."

"But that's just twelve thousand dollars."

"Back then it was enough to buy an apartment . . . which is what I did with the money. The apartment in which you will be staying tonight."

"What happened to your hands?"

"The French surgeon was a miracle worker. He reconstructed the bones, and he reconnected certain nerve endings so I could have some feeling in them. But not an exceptional amount of feeling. Even today . . ."

He reached into his jacket pocket and brought out a disposable lighter, ignited the flame, and held it directly under his left pinky—and didn't flinch once as the flame came into direct contact with his flesh.

"As you can see," he said, "there is considerable permanent numbness. And my ability to hold a paintbrush, even after the ten operations and all that physiotherapy . . . well, to be blunt about it, my career as a painter was decimated after what Faiza's brothers did. Those paintings you see in my apartment . . . *à la recherche du temps perdu*. Ancient history."

"I don't know what to say . . . what a terrible story."

"That it is. Still, in Chinese calligraphy, the symbol for 'crisis' has two meanings: danger and opportunity. My opportunity in the wake of the attack on my hands was to become . . . how shall I put this? . . . a facilitator. Someone who could pull strings, grease palms, work wonders with travel documents, settle scores."

I had a question I didn't dare pose. Ben Hassan did it for me.

"I sense you want to know what happened to Faiza's father and brothers, after they bought me my apartment. Faiza, wanting to repay me in kindness for the cruelty her family had inflicted upon me, regularly visited me in the hospital and insisted on hiring people to do the initial decorative work on the new apartment. I can't say that we were ever friends. She's quite the bitter, disappointed woman. She never truly got over losing Paul, especially as the next man in her life was a stockbroker who was, in my opinion, Prince Not So Bright, though I gather he could play a decent round of golf. By the time Samira was an adolescent, their mother-daughter relationship was like something out of a bad Joan Crawford film. Then the stockbroker lost everything, including their home. Samira lived in my guest room for several months, then went to France for a spell, but didn't have a *carte de séjour* so she couldn't find work. Even though she could have gotten an American passport through her father, the fact that he never claimed paternity and refused all letters from Samira to meet her, or at least tell the US authorities that, yes, she was his daughter . . . that made it administratively difficult for her. And her bitterness just grew.

"Faiza, meanwhile, managed to alienate the director of the *lycée* where she taught. But then, at a cocktail thing here in town, she met a man named Hamsad who was the director of the film studios in Ouarzazate. Within months she was living down there on the edge of the Sahara—a place which, though somewhat picturesque, has always struck me as a recipe for despair after seventy-two hours. Still, with her daughter estranged from her, with another relatively well-heeled man willing to look out for her, and even a job opening at a language school there . . . off she went to the desert. That was five years ago. The relationship fell apart after around eighteen months. Hamsad showed her the door. I gather that she's still teaching at the language institute, and she was rather supportive of Samira when she fell pregnant and her foreign lover returned to France."

"So history repeats itself."

"Only, in this instance, the gentleman—his name is Philippe—acted reasonably. He's paying close to the equivalent of five hundred euros a month in child support, and also offering to part-finance an apartment for Samira and her child."

"With my husband paying the other half."

"As I said earlier, when Paul contacted me out of the blue seven months ago—clearly in the wake of his little surgical procedure to secretly deny his new wife a child—I was flabbergasted. When I heard him sounding sad and guilty about being such a bad father to Samira . . . well, how can I put this? I saw an opportunity . . ."

"For revenge?"

"For payback."

"By which you mean?"

"We communicated for several weeks by email and spoke twice on the phone. He sounded increasingly unstable and just a little haunted. Especially as he'd written twice to Samira who informed him by return email that she wanted absolutely nothing to do with him; that he couldn't simply drop back into her life after thirty years and think there was any chance whatsoever of a relationship. He had ignored her time and again when she'd needed him most. Whatever it was he now wanted from her—forgiveness, absolution—she was unwilling and unable to give.

"But Paul refused to give up. That's when he asked me directly if there was something he could do for his daughter. At which point . . . a plan fell into my head."

My mind was racing. As someone who had spent much of her accounting career second-guessing malevolent tax inspectors and certain fraudulent clients, I did have an intuitive nose for a scam, a subterfuge, an ambush.

"You decided to set him a trap," I said.

"I decided to give the man what he wanted . . . which, on a certain existential level, might be interpreted as being what Monsieur Paul also subconsciously thought he deserved. Payback for abandoning his daughter and not once offering assistance or even basic compassion and decency for his great friend whose life was, on a certain level, ruined by his thoughtlessness and callous disregard. I told him that his daughter needed an additional one million dirhams to buy her apartment . . . and that she couldn't afford a mortgage of that magnitude."

"Was that the truth?"

"Put it this way—she wasn't asking for the money and her lover had given her enough to put down a deposit on a small two-bedroom apartment in this *quartier*."

"Did you lead him to believe that, having given her essentially half of her apartment, he would repair his relationship with her?"

"Perhaps."

"And let me guess—you also told him that, in order to borrow the money from you, he would have to come back to Morocco to sign the papers and give you the first payment?"

He laced his fingers together again, and gazed into its cathedral-like structure.

"Absolutely."

"Since he never spent any time away from me while here, where did you meet him to sign the documents and get his first payment?"

"I had Omar drive me to Essaouira. We had a very pleasant lunch at Chez Fouad while you were off improving your French and walking the beach, if my memory serves me well. He signed the papers, and he paid over the first month's repayment. As you strike me as somewhat legally minded, I took the liberty of bringing along the loan agreement—which was notarized by a local notary whom I also arranged to meet us at Chez Fouad."

He reached into his jacket pocket and brought out a three-page document in French and Arabic. I scanned it briefly, turning to the back page to see my husband's telltale cramped signature, right next to a notary's seal and corroborating signature. On the second page I found the piece of information I also needed: the terms of the loan. I could see that the 1 million dirhams would be paid back over five years, at an annual rate of 320,000 dirhams, in payments of 26,660 dirhams per month—around $2,700, or close to $32,000 per annum. As Paul only earned $100K gross from the university and maybe another $15K, tops, for his artwork, by the time he'd finished paying taxes, Social Security, and his share of the mortgage, he had around $40K to cover his car costs, his share of utilities and groceries, his cell phone, his health club, and contribute to the month away on the Maine coast we allowed ourselves every summer. That gave him very little left over from the five hundred a week he had to meet all these not extravagant expenses. And then to take on a loan that was going to cost him $2,700 every month . . . and all for nothing . . . it was madness.

I tossed the document back in front of Ben Hassan.

"You are certainly getting your revenge on your friend. And you will be making six hundred thousand dirhams out of this little loan."

"*Madame*, I am not Société Générale or Chase Manhattan Bank. I am a businessman, and one who had to dig into his resources to finance his friend."

"Now I know why Paul was so insistent that we spend these weeks in Morocco. You wouldn't give him the money unless he was in the country. Because that would mean you'd have him here, potentially ensnared. I bet you didn't even tell Samira that her father gave her the one million dirhams."

"She just closed on the apartment last week, and won't move in for another month. Perhaps it was an oversight on my part not to mention that Paul had helped her."

He was barely containing a smile as he said this.

"Bullshit," I said. "You wanted him to confront her on her doorstep and let her slam the door in his face."

"Perhaps. But do remember, *madame*, that the only reason he came running up to Casablanca was because you caught him out in his little lie."

"And then he probably called you in a panic, asking you to smooth the way for him to see Samira. You gave him her address, and didn't warn her he'd be showing up, knowing what her reaction would be."

"Revenge is a dish best served cold," he said.

"How did you revenge yourself on Faiza's father and brothers?"

"That's for you to find out. But, again, Madame Robin, I must say that I am most taken and impressed by you. And my advice to you is very straightforward: Get up tomorrow, head for the airport, cut your losses, leave your husband to whatever destiny brings his way."

"And if Paul doesn't pay you the monthly vig?"

Ben Hassan unlocked his fingers and stared directly at me, a stare as arctic as it was menacing.

"What will happen to your dear husband if he doesn't meet his legally binding commitment to me? I will have the great pleasure of watching Omar use a hammer to smash every one of his fingers."

SIXTEEN

AS SOON AS Ben Hassan uttered his threat, the temptation arose to toss the contents of my wineglass in his face. For several edgy moments I had to keep the glass fixed to the table and under control. Ben Hassan worked out what I was stopping myself from doing. He raised a finger, saying, "If you create havoc here—and shame me in public—there will be ramifications."

"You're a gangster."

"That is an interpretation. As is the fact that I am your only friend here."

"A 'friend' who tricked my husband."

"Your husband is the architect of his own despair. He approached me. He begged for a way back to his daughter. I gave it to him."

"While achieving payback at the same time."

"He knew how much I would be charging him for the money. He accepted the sum. He knew that he would have to return to Morocco to sign the papers—and yes, now you know the real reason why you came to Morocco this summer. He accepted that too. I did warn him that finding a way back into Samira's heart would be challenging; that she grew up haunted by the absence of her father and the way he never once contacted her. She herself must have written Paul at least once a year until she was twenty-five. Even after that terrible rupture with her mother, she still held on to the naive hope that, somehow, he was going to be the good father and rescue her from her immense loneliness. In short, he was fully aware that, by trying to reengage with his exceptionally messy past, he was walking right back into a compromised and precarious situation. But he still chose to head across the Atlantic and into my open arms. And you, innocent you, who knows all about absentee fathers and men who are in endless negotiation with their various conflicted selves . . . you should now lose the maternal protectiveness that you cloak Paul in and let him play the adult for a change. But you can't do that, can you? Which is why you want to dash that glass in my face—and, in doing so, earn my displeasure . . . which, as I think you can sense by now, is not a wise thing to court."

"Because you might smash my fingers? Or maybe I'll suffer the same fate meted out to Faiza's father and brothers?"

"I don't remember alluding to any fate being 'meted' out to them."

"But they are no longer with us, right?"

"I never said that."

"Because I didn't ask it before. But I'm asking it now."

"Why don't you ask Faiza about all that? Because that's where you're heading now, aren't you? In fact, let me expedite matters for you and give you her address in Ouarzazate."

"Oh, you're a mind reader, are you?"

"Actually I am. I know you are simply someone who can't walk away, even if it means following the man who betrayed you into the vortex."

He pulled out a notebook and an elegant silver pen, then scribbled away for a few moments before tearing the page out and handing it to me.

"Here is Madame Faiza's phone number and address. Of course, you already know the name of the hotel where Paul is staying."

"Why haven't you dispatched Omar there to drag him back?"

"Because the next payment isn't due for another ten days. Of course, if you prefer to pay that now . . ."

"I don't have sixteen thousand dirhams on me in cash."

"And I don't accept credit cards. Anyway he has ten days of grace. Meanwhile, you are still more than welcome to avail yourself of our extra bed tonight."

"You can't be serious."

"Just trying to be generous. The other option is an all-night bus that leaves the Central Station at eleven p.m. I know this because that is the bus which Paul boarded last night. It is a monstrous journey, via Marrakesh, of around ten hours. Or there is a flight at six fifty tomorrow morning on Royal Air Maroc. But a last-minute ticket is something on the expensive side. Around five thousand dirhams one way. The bus, on the other hand, is one hundred and fifty dirhams. Your call, *madame*."

"You're going to call Faiza as soon as I've left the restaurant, warn her I'm on my way."

"Actually, you're wrong there. I'm going to make no such call. I'm going to let the element of surprise guide things from now on. Like the look on Monsieur Paul's face when you surprise him at his hotel room. Or perhaps finding him in Madame Faiza's bed."

"Whatever I discover, I am ready for it."

"I love a forward-thinking realist. But before you dash off into the night . . . surely you will want to try one of the celebrated desserts they make here. The baklava is especially sublime. And the patron will no doubt offer us a very good *digestif* to accompany *le thé à la menthe*. You still have almost forty-five minutes before the bus leaves. It is a mere ten minutes by taxi from here to—"

I stood up, hoisting the backpack, uncertain what my next move should be.

"Going so soon?" he asked. "A pity."

"Are you going to keep your word about not contacting anybody in Ouarzazate?"

"*Madame*, if I give my word I always keep it. Which is why, when I lend money, I always remind the client that they have my word that all will run smoothly as long as the money is paid back on time. If you do catch up with your husband, do tell him I will expect to see him on the first of August. Without fail. And if you think you can spirit him out of the country and somehow elude me . . . do please think again."

Then, slowly pushing back his chair and gingerly elevating his mountain of a body to its feet, he executed a small, very formal bow and uttered two words: "*Bon voyage.*"

I stared at him, long and hard, trying to communicate the fact that he didn't frighten me. Truth be told, he terrified me.

"Until next time."

Out on the street I didn't know what to do next. I needed to think cleanly, logically. I had forty minutes to make the bus. Finding a taxi seemed to be no problem. There were plenty around here. But the thought of ten hours on a bus heading south over the Atlas Mountains—and an all-night bus at that—filled me with dread. Yet my budget needed to be managed with care. So I decided, in the first instance, to hurry back to The Parisian and go online and find out whether a flight was available tomorrow at dawn and whether there was a way of ensuring that it wouldn't break the bank.

The café was a three-minute walk. I ordered a Perrier and told the waiter that I might have to leave within ten minutes. Then I opened up my laptop and, using assorted travel sites, discovered that, yes, the actual price of the ticket was 5,400 dirhams, but one last-minute site was offering it for 2,600 dirhams—just over $300. Not a bargain, but still cheaper than the official price. I booked myself onto it. The Perrier arrived. I informed the waiter I was no longer in a rush. I drank the fizzy water, allowing its soothing properties to act as an antidote to all the food consumed, and to momentarily balm my considerable distress.

Another search engine led to me a hotel—The Select—located just three streets away from here. One star, very basic, but the photos of the spartan rooms indicated a degree of cleanliness, and it was cheap. They didn't have an online booking service, but I asked the waiter if I could borrow a phone. He offered his own, and turned down my offer of ten dirhams for its use, "As long as you are calling locally." I assured him that I was just phoning down the street, and quickly punched in the hotel's number, which connected immediately. I explained I needed a room until four this morning.

"No problem," the man at the front desk told me.

Five minutes later I was at the reception desk of the hotel. There was an elderly man in a shiny suit behind the counter. I paid cash and told him I needed a wake-up call at 4:00 a.m. and a taxi here promptly at 4:30.

"I'll handle it," he said.

"And please, I am counting on you to bang on my door loudly at four."

The room was Early Nothing. Basic drab furniture. A hard double bed with much-laundered, stiff sheets and a floral bedspread. A sink, a toilet, a tiny shower stall with a meager hose. I undressed and brushed my teeth. I rubbed some of the miracle face cream into my face. I noted that I would be having to get up again in five hours and cursed myself for not having found a bookshop in the shopping center late this afternoon and choosing something there in the English-language section.

Then my mind began to race. How would Paul react to my arrival in Ouarzazate, how would he deal with the realization that I knew all about Ben Hassan, and that we were going to have to figure out some way of getting out of Morocco undetected? Didn't I read somewhere that the border with Algeria had been closed by the Moroccan authorities since that very bloody and frightening civil war in the 1990s? Could we get into Mauritania on US passports without a visa? Would Ben Hassan have people watching for us at the port at Tangier?

But these logistical questions were overshadowed by a flashback I had of my father. I was eighteen and had just arrived at the University of Minnesota. My second day there, Dad called me from Las Vegas (of course) to tell me that the professional windfall he'd been waiting for had finally come his way.

"Here's the thing, kiddo," he said. "Just had this big interview for a senior job in casino management out here. A VP for Human Resources at Caesar's Palace. The guy who interviewed me today told me I was head and shoulders above all candidates. So looks like me and your Mom will be singing 'Viva Las Vegas' before too long. And as soon as my John Hancock is on that employment contract, I am organizing that big Christmas trip I've been promising you and your mom for years to Hawaii."

"No rush, Dad. I mean, Hawaii has never been on my list of priorities."

"Well, if you want to transfer next semester to Columbia . . ."

"Minnesota offered me the full scholarship, Dad."

"You're being too nice here, Robin. My little girl gets admitted to an Ivy League university and has to go to State U because her deadbeat father can't afford to pay the tuition."

"Don't think that. You're a wonderful dad."

"I don't deserve such kindness."

Then the line went dead. As this conversation took place in 1993, well before everyone had cell phones, I had no way of knowing the number from which he had been calling me. Nor did he call me back—though I waited by the phone in my dorm for an hour, hoping he and I might finish the conversation.

But no call ever came.

Until six the next morning. Only the person on the phone was my mother. And her voice was so hushed that she could hardly get out the words.

"Your father died last night."

I remember the world going so quiet that all peripheral noise seemed to have been smothered.

"He had a heart attack after losing five thousand at the craps table."

She'd heard this from the cops in Vegas. He'd been winning all night, then put all his chips on one throw of the dice. Which didn't go his way. This time he didn't weather the impact of another act of self-sabotage. This time it proved overwhelming to his psyche . . . and the cardiac incident that followed killed him. How I've assembled and reassembled this scene in my mind since then—and all based on those few tough, terse details that my angry mother supplied. How part of the overwhelming grief that followed—the sense that I was now very much alone in a difficult world—was also wracked with the incessant reproach that kept ringing in my ears for months, years afterward, a lament that, truth be told, has never faded away: *you should have been able to save him.*

Was that what was at work now? Was that what I was chasing here: a chance at redemption? Was I somehow convincing myself that—despite the desperate betrayal, despite the realization that I had been truly shammed—I still needed to rescue my husband from harm as a way of appeasing the guilt about my tragically affection-ate wreck of a father, the man who gave me the only actual love I'd ever encountered until Paul Leuen walked into my life? Might I claw back a little final peace if I could do what I was too young and too unschooled in life's harsh contours to do at the time? Was that why I was sitting alone in this sad cheap hotel room, my brain on overdrive, so desperate to find Paul and bring some resolution to all this?

I can fix this. I must fix this. I will fix this.

Heaviness clouded my eyes. Then came darkness. And several hours of mental void before the loud knock on the door. I had a fast shower and was in the taxi to the airport at the agreed time of 4:30. Casablanca in the middle of the night was still the strange faceless metropolis I'd briefly passed through, in which the sense of ugly modern sprawl was omnipresent.

At the airport I picked up my boarding pass and then proceeded on to the Royal Air Maroc ticket counter, where I was told that, if I didn't fly to New York today on the scheduled flight onto which I had been rebooked, I would lose the ticket.

"But I changed it once already," I said. "Can't I please change it again?"

"That was an exceptional change, clearly made by someone in authority," the clerk told me. "If you can get back in touch with him before your flight departs at midday, then perhaps he can make a second exceptional change. But I cannot do anything, *madame*. My apologies."

The flight south was on a small turboprop with just thirty seats. The sun was ascending as we took off. After twenty minutes, we passed over Marrakesh and the Atlas Mountains came into crisp silhouette. These were no mere hills but proper stern alpine peaks: craggy, with switchback roads frequently defining their vertical terrain. There were dazzling valleys. There were impossibly positioned villages clinging to mountainsides. There was even a hint of snow atop one summit.

Then, out of nowhere, the sand began. It was as if someone had flipped a topological switch, transporting us out of high rugged terrain and into a world of endless aridity. Sand that was not white, but actually bathed in a bleached red ocher. Sand that was full of strange undulations and irregularities. Sand that was duned and, in the emerging sunlight, crimson. Sand that stretched into an absolute infinity. Sand that could bury you with ruthless disinterest. Sand on a scale and a dimension that I had never glimpsed before; a realm so well known by mythic repute, yet so unseen by most of the planet's habitants. That ultimate empty quarter. The Sahara.

We were coming into land, passing buildings that had a 1930s French Foreign Legion look about them. The sand was just beyond; the encroaching reality abutting the city's frontiers. As apprehensive and tense as I was—as much as I dreaded the confrontation that was ahead of me—there was still something extraordinary about my first sighting of the Sahara. The airport also seemed 1940s desert military—hot and fly-blown. Inside the arrivals hall was an information desk, manned by a young woman in a hajib. I told her the name of the hotel I was seeking. She knew it immediately and said it was a short taxi ride from here. I also showed her the scrap of paper on which Ben Hassan had scribbled Faiza's address. She got out a map of Ouarzazate and marked the location of the hotel, then used a yellow highlighter to trace a route to Faiza's front door. It was, she said, about five minutes by foot.

"Don't pay the taxi driver more than thirty dirhams," she said. "If he says no, tell him that you are going to report him to me—Fatima. He'll know who I am. They all do."

Actually the cabbie accepted the offer of thirty dirhams without the usual bartering. The Oasis Hotel was just off the very wide main drag that, at eight in the morning, still seemed half awake. I took in the desert deco architecture, the languid men loitering in cafés, the blast-furnace heat. The cab had no air-conditioning. According to the gauge on the dashboard the temperature was 43 degrees Celsius— an astonishing 109 degrees Fahrenheit. By the time we reached the hotel—all of two minutes later—my lightweight clothes were sodden.

The Oasis was, at first glance, a slightly shabbier version of our hotel in Essaouira. At least the lobby was air-conditioned—and the heavyset woman behind the desk was welcoming. When I explained that I was Paul Leuen's wife, I could see her lips tighten.

"Monsieur Leuen just went out for a walk," she said.

"Really?"

"You seem surprised."

"It's a bit early for a walk, that's all."

"Monsieur Leuen . . . he was out walking until three a.m., so my night man told me. And he came in very intoxicated. I am sorry to report this, *madame*."

"I'm sorry to hear it."

"He was also shouting in his room late last night. The night man had to go up and tell him to be quiet. He found Monsieur Leuen in a very bad place. Drinking wine and crying. He was very apologetic when he was told he was waking the other guests."

I shut my eyes, trying to keep my emotions in check. I was furious at Paul. I was terrified for Paul—and the crazed trajectory down which he was traveling.

"Do you have any idea where he headed to just now?" I asked.

"None at all. But Ouarzazate is not a big place. And he just left five minutes ago. Try the cafés on the avenue Muhammed V."

"I apologize for all the trouble he's caused you."

"I am simply happy to see you here, *madame*. If you can assure me that he will be quiet tonight, I will let you both stay here. Had you not arrived I would have shown him the door."

I wanted to go upstairs and drop my bag and have a shower before facing the heat again. But part of me also knew that time was of the essence, that I needed to find Paul now.

"A question, *madame*," I said. "Besides the flights to Casablanca, isn't there a direct service from Ouarzazate to Paris?"

"Every Tuesday and Thursday at five o'clock. So yes, as it is Thursday today . . ."

"Could you please find out if there are any seats on this afternoon's flight while I go look for my husband?"

"With pleasure, *madame*. If you would like to leave your bag here, I will make certain it is kept safe for you."

"Thank you for your kindness and decency."

"I wish you luck, *madame*."

I wished myself that too.

Before I left I dug out Paul's passport from my bag, and slipped it into the button-down pocket on my pants.

I headed out into the back street, turning up a dusty alleyway in which a young boy—he couldn't have been more than seven—was milking a goat, the white liquid being sprayed into an empty tin can. He looked up and smiled at me, saying, "Fresh milk—just ten dirhams."

I smiled back and moved on, dodging two elderly women on canes, their faces hidden by black niqabs. They moved slowly in the maniacal sun. How in the world were they able to cope with the hefty black Islamic garb in this inferno? One of the women held out a hand. I stopped, reached into my pocket, found a five-dirham coin, and placed it in her palm. Out of nowhere her fingers closed against mine. In a croaky whisper she uttered, "*Faites attention, madame.*"

Be careful.

What did she know that I didn't?

I turned down another spindly street before reaching the city's main drag, avenue Muhammed V. Adobe-shaded sandstone in a colonial fortress style defined the architecture. The sun was, after just two minutes outside, beginning to play games with my equilibrium. So I stopped at a small stall and bought a replacement green khaki field hat and a liter of bottled water, drinking almost half of it in one go. Then, over the next twenty minutes, I went from café to café, scanning all terraces and interiors for any sign of my husband. I approached every waiter I saw, Paul's passport in hand, showing them his photograph, asking them if they'd perhaps seen this man in the past few minutes, indicating that finding him was an urgent matter. All the waiters were polite. All said that, alas, they hadn't seen him.

One man at a café—midfifties, a little portly, but still relatively well preserved and dressed in Moroccan merchant casual (cream slacks, a gray polo shirt, Italianate loafers)—overheard me inquiring about Paul and stood up.

"Perhaps I can help you," he said in excellent English, motioning me over to his table. He introduced himself as Mr. Rashid and offered me a coffee.

"You think you've seen this man?" I asked, holding up the passport photo.

"Indeed I have. But you first need something to drink, I think."

"Where did you see him exactly?"

"On this street a few minutes ago."

"Can you tell me exactly where?"

"I'd love to know your name first."

I told him.

"Well, Robin, let me offer you a *citron pressé* and then we can get into my car—I have a very large and comfortable Mercedes—and we can start looking for him. And if we don't find him, maybe you can have lunch with me."

I stood up.

"Thank you for wasting several valuable minutes of my time."

The man looked shocked at this rebuff.

"Now, there's no need to talk to me that way."

"You never saw him, did you? You were just hoping to take advantage of a woman in distress."

"Are you always so aggressive?"

"Are you always so disrespectful?"

"Now I know why your husband went missing."

He said this with a smirk on his face, quickly translating his comment into Arabic for the men who were seated nearby and watching the scene with amusement.

That's when I lost it. "What the fuck did you say?" I hissed.

"*Madame* has an ugly way with words."

"Only when being hustled by a little man with a small penis."

Now he looked as if I had kicked him directly in the crotch.

"Go on, translate what I just said to your friends," I said, hurrying off down the street, trying to contain my considerable fury.

But then I suddenly stopped dead in my tracks.

There, on the far side of the street, was my husband.

He was wearing the same white shirt and shorts he'd left the hotel room in over two days ago. He was seriously unshaven, his long gray hair askew across his head. Even in the white light of the Saharan morning I could see that he was exhausted, lost.

"Paul! Paul!" I yelled. But as soon as the words were out of my mouth a vast truck—the length of a city block—came rattling down the avenue. Paul didn't seem to hear my cries, or maybe they were drowned out by the approaching truck. Not thinking, I tried to dash across the street, but was thrown by the deafening blast of the truck's horn, the driver gesticulating to me wildly. I had to jump backward, and found myself now almost in the path of a Renault van coming in the opposite direction. The driver slammed on the brakes and started shouting things at me through his rolled-down window, while men in the nearby cafés stood up to watch.

When the truck pulled away fifteen seconds later, I prepared to dash across the street and take my husband in my arms and assure him that, despite everything, I still loved him; that we would be out of this craziness and be in Paris tonight.

But when the truck pulled away . . .

Paul was no longer there.

It took me a dazed moment to register this fact. Paul had vanished.

I dashed across to where I'd seen him standing. I looked north. I looked south. I ran into the little patisserie directly behind the place where he was momentarily rooted. There were only two people in the shop, along with the baker behind the counter.

"Anyone seen an American?" I shouted. "Very tall, long gray hair?"

They all looked startled by my outburst. When the baker shook his head, I ran back into the street, scanning all corners of the immediate horizon, certain he was there somewhere. There were two cafés nearby. I charged up the street toward them. No Paul. A fast dash back to the exact place I saw him, thinking maybe there was a rear alley directly behind this spot into which he had disappeared. No alley. No Paul. Up the street I hurried, turning left into the first side street I could find. It was open and spacious, with blocks of modern apartments on either side. No Paul. And no shops or restaurants or cafés into which he could have ducked. Back to the avenue Muhammed V, my head increasingly stricken by all this running in one-hundred-degree heat. No Paul. Again I stood in the spot where I'd just seen him, less than three minutes ago, beyond perplexed as to how I could have lost him moments after finding him.

I still had the half liter of water in hand. Standing under the shade of the patisserie's awning, I leaned against the wall and downed it all in moments, wooziness overtaking me. Suddenly I felt a hand on my shoulder. Paul!

But no, it was the baker from inside, who'd come out with a small folding stool and a small pastry and a bottle of lemonade. He insisted on helping me onto the stool.

After ensuring that I was eating and also getting some necessary sugar into my bloodstream, he went back inside and returned with a linen cloth soaked in cold water. He placed it around my neck—evidently a fast desert remedy for anyone suffering from dehydration. It worked. I felt somewhat better within a few minutes. Refusing my offer of money, he asked again if I was certain that I was all right, that he could get one of his assistants to help me back to my hotel. I thanked him repeatedly, telling him how truly touched I was by his kindness.

"I wish you luck, *madame*."

Could he too read the despair and worry in my eyes?

I stood up, gauging just how rubbery or resilient my legs were. Their present status was somewhere between those two extremes. I headed out across the boulevard with the intention of returning to the hotel and seeing if Paul had returned there in my absence, and was cursing myself for forgetting to tell the woman at the reception desk not to mention that I'd been out looking for him. But as I made it to the other side of the avenue and cut down the same narrow alley where I'd seen the boy milking the goat, a figure maybe fifteen feet in front of me veered to the right, taking an even narrower bypath. The man's height and free-flowing gray hair left me in no doubt that it was Paul. When I shouted his name, he seemed oblivious to my voice. I started to sprint, determined to catch up with him. But when I reached the alley—a tiny passage no more than four feet wide—no Paul. There were no immediate doorways into which he could have disappeared. Even when I reached, after around a hundred feet, an archway, all I saw inside were two elderly men brewing tea on a little gas stove. Again I showed them the passport photo. They looked at me, puzzled. I returned to the alley—so attenuated and confined— trying to figure where he could have vanished. Or did he clear out of this byway further on? I hurried to the end of the alley, only to discover it dead-ended into a wall. The wall had some rusted barbed wire on it, which made the idea of getting over it just a little daunting. When I touched it I discovered that it had the density and grip of damp chalk. There was no way whatsoever that even a particularly adept cat could have scaled it.

I shut my eyes, wanting to be anywhere but here and also knowing that I had to get out of this blind alley now. So back I went, retracing my steps until I found the main alleyway again, glancing frantically everywhere as I made my way back to the hotel.

The woman who greeted me earlier was back at the front desk.

"No luck?" she asked.

I shook my head.

"Maybe he'll come back soon. If you want to go upstairs . . ."

"I would like that."

"Housekeeping hasn't been in to clean the room yet."

"I'm sure it will be fine. Just one small request: when my husband does come back, please don't tell him I'm upstairs. He's in a delicate place and might run off if he finds out I'm here. My hope is that, when he does come upstairs, I will be able to talk him into leaving this afternoon."

"I have good news on that front. There are still seven seats open on the Paris flight. They are expensive, being last-minute—five thousand two hundred dirhams apiece. Still, if you want them you should let me know no later than three o'clock. *D'accord?*"

"*D'accord.*"

The room was air-conditioned. And reasonably spacious, though given the narrowness of these back streets, its balcony only afforded a view of a wall some ten feet away. What was more noticeable was the absolute chaos of the place. Twisted sheets, streaked with blood-stains on the pillows (was his head wound still bleeding?). Crumpled paper everywhere. An ashtray brimming with cigarette butts (he gave up nicotine around the same time we got together). The remnants of two bottles of wine. And in the bathroom . . . no, this was too grim . . . an unflushed toilet.

I pulled the cistern chain. I picked up the house phone and rang downstairs, asking if the maid could be sent up now. I then returned and dumped the ashtray into the toilet and flushed it all away. I found a box of matches and lit two of them, walking between the bathroom and the bedroom in an attempt to mask the fecal smell and the lingering aroma of sweaty sheets that permeated two rooms. I emptied the remnants of the wine bottles. I began to uncrumble the many pieces of paper that had been balled up and tossed everywhere. Tortured line drawings of a lone man in an empty space that seemed to be a desert. The drawings were half finished. In each one of them it was evident that Paul was having trouble finishing the figure's face; a figure so tall that he seemed to be towering over a sand dune. But this self-portraiture was underscored by a face that had turned grotesque. Drawing after drawing showed this representation of Paul with his face half melting away, or being scorched beyond recognition by the sun. Amidst these discarded, unhinged sketches, there were several half-started letters. *My love . . . Dearest Robin . . . You have married a catastrophe* . . . Most chillingly, there were two notes, already half burned, with the same word repeated on both balled-up scraps of paper: *Finished*.

The last of these notes unnerved me—because the word appeared to have been scratched on the page with blood.

The maid knocked on the door. I told her to give me a minute and quickly finished dumping all the paper into a dustbin, then pulled off the bloodied pillowcase and gathered up the soiled towels and shoved them into a pillowcase so she wouldn't be exposed to such extremity. Yet again I was cleaning up after my husband—and even slipped the very young cheery maid thirty dirhams, apologizing for the state of the room.

"*Mon mari est bordélique,*" I told her. My husband is out of control.

The maid seemed nonplussed by the state of things, yet graciously replied, "I've seen worse."

She told me to come back in a half hour—"when everything will be all fine again." Would that a magic wand could be waved.

All I could think of now was that one word—*finished*—interspersed with those wildly destructive self-portraits. And my fear that unless rescued . . .

No, don't enter that terrain. He's still here in Ouarzazate. It's only a matter of time before he shows up back at the hotel. I glanced at my watch. It was just a little after 9:00 a.m. As long as he returned here within four hours, we could secure those seats on the Paris flight and be out of all this.

I went down to the lobby. The woman behind the desk asked me if she could get me anything. She also told me her name was Yasmina. I suddenly needed to confide in someone—not about the grubbier aspects of the story, but about the fact that my husband had suffered a breakdown, had disappeared from our hotel in Essaouira, and, through the wonders of the internet, I had traced him here.

"Anything you can do to help me find him—or, at the very least, hold him here and get us on that plane to Paris . . ."

"I don't have a pair of handcuffs," she said with a half-smile. "But I do have a man who runs things here at night. His name is Yusuf, and he usually sleeps until eleven a.m. But if you would agree to give him, say, three hundred dirhams, I sense he wouldn't object to me ringing him now and getting him out of bed and searching Ouarzazate for your husband. He knows every corner of this town. He knows everybody here. If he can't find him, then he is lost to the sand."

I handed over the three hundred dirhams, thinking this was a small price to pay for someone who might be able to root out Paul.

The maid came downstairs to tell me that the room was cleaned, and that she had lit a jasmine incense stick there to purify the place. Again I thanked her and Yasmina for their benevolence.

"If you leave your clothes outside the door we'll have them washed and dried in less than two hours."

I felt absurdly tired—the short night, the climatic adjustment to the ferocious Saharan heat, the fruitless hundred-yard dashes all morning in search of Paul . . . all I could think of now was a cool shower and then a spell in cool sheets. I headed back upstairs. Once inside I stripped everything off and dropped it outside the door. Then I stood in the shower for a good ten minutes. Before climbing into the freshly laundered bed, I called downstairs and asked Yasmina to give me a wake-up call at three . . . unless Paul arrived before then.

I fell asleep instantly. Then, out of nowhere, the phone rang. The little alarm clock on the bedside table glowed in the dark, 15:02. And here I was, alone. No sign of Paul. I reached for the phone.

"Your three o'clock wake-up call, *madame*," Yasmina intoned in the phone.

"And my husband?"

"No sighting of him so far. But Yusuf is still out looking, and he is phoning in regularly. Alas, not a trace so far."

"I'll be down in a few minutes. Might you be able to call me a taxi?"

"But the Paris flight isn't until five o'clock."

"I'm not going to Paris. I'm going to . . ."

Reaching over to a pile of paper I dug out of my pocket before tossing my dirty clothes outside the door, I found the scrap on which Ben Hassan had given me Faiza's address. I read the details into the phone. Yasmina told me that the address given was a five-minute drive, tops—and that my clean clothes were now on the way upstairs with the maid.

A quarter of an hour later I was in a taxi headed to an apartment complex not far from the entrance to the Atlas Film Studios. The complex was semimodern in a 1970s reinforced concrete style. There were three separate blocks, all no more than seven or eight floors tall. I asked the driver to drop me in front of Block B. I paid him and headed up four concrete flights of stairs to Apartment 402. I took a long steadying breath before pressing the doorbell, expecting either no answer or an angry woman refusing to see me and telling me to go away and never come back.

But on the third ring the door opened. There stood a woman who was surprisingly tall and still stylish, albeit wildly thin, with a face probably once beautiful. She had a lit cigarette in one hand, a glass of pink wine in the other. When she spoke, her voice sounded nicotine cured.

"So . . . you finally got here."

"You know who I am?" I asked.

"Of course I do," she said. "You're the other wife."

SEVENTEEN

"I PRESUME YOU drink a bit," Faiza said.

"A bit, yes," I said.

"I drink a lot."

She motioned for me to seat myself on a brown corduroy sofa.
I was in a one-bedroom apartment of around eight hundred square
feet. Concrete walls painted white. A bentwood rocking chair. Splat-
ter-paint abstract canvases. An elderly rug. A few framed photographs
of Samira at varying stages of life. An air conditioner that, though effective, emitted a low wheeze. A couple of old lamps that, like the
rest of the decor, seemed around twenty years out of date. A balcony
that overlooked the encroaching desert.

Seeing me take everything in, noting many empty wineglasses
and brimming ashtrays and the aura of dustiness, she let out a serious
smoker's cough and said, "I didn't invite you here, so I'm not going to
apologize for this place. Except to say that I had a change of personal
circumstances in April and had to find a new apartment in a hurry.
Life, sometimes, is an ongoing series of letdowns. Especially when it
comes to men, wouldn't you agree?"

She began to cough wildly.

"Are you all right?" I asked.

"Of course not," she said.

She was as thin as a stalk of celery, dressed in black linen pants
and a black linen shirt, with around nine gold and copper bangles on

her spindly wrists. Her hair—long, very straight—was still jet-black. But her skin was leathery, and her teeth were tobacco-stained.

She disappeared into the kitchen for a moment, returning with a chilled bottle of rosé and a second glass.

"It's Moroccan, but good," she said.

"Like most of the wines I've had here."

"So Little Boy Paul married himself a much younger woman," she said, lighting up another cigarette.

"I'm not that young."

"But you are at least twenty years younger than me . . . which, in my book, makes you a kid. More to the point, you are his wife."

"So are you."

"Actually, the marriage only lasted about ten minutes . . . and then was annulled."

"Annulled? Really?"

"You seem surprised."

"I'd been told that you were still his wife."

"Whoever told you that—and I have my suspicions—simply wanted to play head games with you. I am—*definitely*—Paul's ex-wife."

She splashed some wine in a glass and handed it to me. When I raised it she just nodded curtly.

"No need to get friendly," she said. "Anyway, I have a class to teach—Conversational English—in around forty minutes. Though speaking conversational English with you might have its professional benefits, it honestly doesn't please me being here with you."

I apologized for showing up on her doorstep, unannounced, uninvited. "But I am genuinely worried about Paul."

"Poor you for being so involved with the fool. Because that is what he is: a fool. And one who has to shoot himself in the foot with a Kalashnikov, pausing twice to reload."

Faiza was suddenly hit with another horrendous coughing fit. When she brought it under control she used some wine to clear her throat, then said, "Well, they always told me smoking was a

stupid habit. But one without which life might be even more intol-
erable. Not that you've probably ever smoked a cigarette in your
life. I bet you're one of those Americans who work out six days a
week."

"I know Paul came here to see you," I said, refusing to take the bait.

"Correction: Paul came here to plead with me. To ask that I intervene with our daughter and get her to have contact with him. Of
course I refused to do any such thing."

I took another sip of wine, choosing my next words with care.
"I can understand why you turned him away," I said. "Please understand: until yesterday I didn't know that you and Samira existed.
Nevertheless, Paul has had a major breakdown and he has gone
missing."

"And perhaps this time the disappearance will be a permanent
one. I can handle self-destruction. It's a personal choice. Like my
smoking forty cigarettes a day. The difference is that mine is self-
directed. Paul is someone whose self-destructiveness ends up de-
stroying everyone else in his immediate path. When I kicked him
out last night I told him to do the world a favor and kill himself."

"Your capacity for hate is impressive."

"And who are you, Mother Teresa?"

"I am probably going to divorce Paul as soon as I get him back
to the States. But first I am going to get him home. And away from
Ben Hassan."

"That fat fuck: he can be your best friend and your ultimate
nightmare."

"Are you still in contact with him?"

"You mean, considering that he might have killed my father and
two brothers . . . not that I totally blame him for having done that."

"They're all dead?"

"Well, they are all planted in the earth now. So that should answer your question. Was Ben Hassan behind all this? That's the great
ongoing question."

She splashed some more wine into our two glasses and continued.

"Not that I would blame Ben Hassan for having killed them. After he helped Paul escape his shotgun marriage to me—that's the term you use in the States, isn't it?—they destroyed his hands, his future as a painter. The police and the judiciary let my father and brothers off with a small cash payment. But Ben Hassan was never able to hold a paintbrush again."

"Didn't you feel guilty about that? According to the story Ben Hassan told me last night, you were pounding on Paul's door, telling him you'd be killed if he didn't marry you."

She stabbed her cigarette into the ashtray.

"Do you have any idea whatsoever what it means to be a woman in this culture? Even though the situation has somewhat improved over the past thirty-five years, there was no possibility of negotiating with my family once they knew I was going to have a child. Did I deliberately fall pregnant by Paul? Put it this way: we were careless. And no, I wasn't on the pill. And yes, it was my hope that Paul would marry me and get me out of Morocco and to the States. So yes, I was being completely mercenary. But Paul and I loved each other back then . . . for a while, anyway. I even told him: 'Marry me, get me my green card, and once we're in the States I'll make my own way.' But when he balked I made a fatal error. I told my father that I was pregnant. From that moment on we were, on a certain level, doomed. Because Papa could never do anything subtly or cleverly. He had to always bring out the heavy artillery. He had to get his way, and punish anyone who blocked him—which was poor Ben Hassan's fate."

"Did he eventually kill your father and brothers?"

"As I said before, that is the ongoing question. My father died in a car accident, driving alone between Casablanca and Marrakesh. According to the police report, the brakes of his Mercedes failed. They couldn't establish if they had been tampered with or not, but it seems that someone had so significantly stripped back the brake pads that when a motorcycle swerved in front of him and my father tried to hit the brakes, the result was catastrophic. He lost control of the car. It flipped over three times and then ignited. The chassis was so badly burned that they couldn't really establish if maliciousness had been behind it. Of course the driver of the motorcycle was nowhere to be found. The fact that it happened late at night on an otherwise empty road . . . it all seemed to me and many others to have been carefully planned. So carefully planned that the police could not hold anyone accountable, or even justify an investigation.

"Then around seven years later, my brother Abdullah was found hanged at his condo on the Costa del Sol. Abdullah had done very well in the wall-to-wall carpet and linoleum business. He'd married a very beautiful, very stupid woman quite late in life—he was over forty—and had two little girls whom he doted over whenever he was at home, which wasn't very often. He'd expanded his business into Spain, bought a *petit bourgeois* seaside condo, and was showing no signs of depression or any other signs of psychological instability. It was his mistress—a local bar girl—who found him. She was considered the prime suspect for a while. The thing was, Abdullah had grown almost as large as Ben Hassan, and ended up weighing at least three hundred pounds. So it was very unlikely that she could have strung him up herself. The fact that he seemed to have taken three too many sleeping pills that evening raised all sorts of suspicions. She was held along with her actual boyfriend, for many months under suspicion of conspiracy to commit murder. But I was always convinced that the hand of Ben Hassan was behind it all."

"Why didn't you alert the authorities?"

"To what? To the fact that, fifteen years previously, my father had ordered his two sons to carry out an appalling act of violence on a man who, in the intervening years, had become, in his own ingratiatingly corrupt way, a sort of Mr. Fixit in Casa and Rabat . . . and who had so many connections in so many echelons of the establishment here? Not that anyone high up in government administration or the world of finance would ever admit to calling a sleaze like Ben Hassan a friend. He knew this too. It didn't bother him. He had 'connections.' Tainted, blemished connections. But it kept him and whatever younger man he was sodomizing that month in a level of modest comfort . . . and yes, I am getting nasty. Talking too much. But after kicking our husband out of here last night, I found myself unable to sleep. As I had two classes to teach this morning, I popped a Dexedrine to keep myself up. I took another Dexedrine just fifteen minutes before you came, and the wine works wonders with its speedy properties. A sort of yin-yang effect."

I put down my glass of wine, suddenly too buzzed from the alcohol and the desert afternoon, which the wheezing, consumptive air conditioner was almost keeping at bay.

"You didn't tell me about your other brother," I finally said.

"Driss? Even a bigger fool than Abdullah. Never married. Never succeeded at much. Worked for his brother running inventory in Casa. After Abdullah was 'suicided'—because I know that is what happened—the man who bought up the company let Driss go. As there wasn't much in the way of family money—what little Driss had inherited from our father he spent at the roulette table and on prostitutes—he ended up as a limousine driver for a company ferrying somewhat important people from the airport to one of Casablanca's five-star hotels. Every summer he had a week off down in dreadful Agadir: the Moroccan package holiday resort. He went out swimming one evening, maybe fifty meters from the shoreline. A speedboat ran over him. Split his skull in two. Being a speedboat, it sped away. Not a trace of who was commandeering it, or even a glimpse of its registration. The thing is, Driss loved swimming at night—and it was his fifth night in Agadir, so I am pretty damn certain that someone had been watching him, figuring out his habits."

A shrug. Another slug of wine. Another cigarette.

"I don't think I like your silence," she finally said. "It feels very fucking judgmental."

"Your English is impressive," I said.

"So is your sense of irony."

"I am hardly being ironic. I am just trying to figure out your story."

"What's to figure out? I have never asked Ben Hassan directly if he was behind all that befell my family. Because he has been, on a certain level, a very good friend to me and my daughter. When Samira pushed me away over a decade ago—after I moved down here, but also as a result of a lot of built-up anguish—he acted as a surrogate parent for her in Casa, and also gradually brought her around to establishing some sort of détente with her mother, for which I will always be grateful. You know she got pregnant by a French business-man. But Ben Hassan negotiated with him on Samira's behalf. He may have headed back to his wife and children, but he does give her three hundred euros a month . . ."

"Ben Hassan told me it was five hundred."

"Maybe he pays Ben Hassan five and he gives her three. Who cares?"

"But that means Ben Hassan is pocketing twenty-four hundred euros a year."

"Yes, Little Boy Paul did tell me you were an accountant. What was a highly rational, competent woman like yourself thinking when you hooked up with such a disaster zone?"

I met her gaze straight on.

"I was thinking about the sex—which was pretty spectacular. I was thinking about the sexiness of being with an actual artist—and one with real talent. I was thinking how wonderful it would be for our child to have an artist for a father."

As I spoke these words I felt myself slipping into a haze, my boldness succumbing to fatigue. Perhaps it was the wine, or the ab-solute despair of the bitter, strange woman sitting opposite me, or my naive wish to connect with someone who once wanted everything with Paul and, like me, was betrayed by him. I took a deep steadying breath before continuing.

"With Paul I believed I could think about adventure and culture and freedom. Freedom from all the trappings of modern American life. But Paul wanted all those trappings—the nice home, the gym membership, the summers in Maine, good food, fine wine—even as he bemoaned our materialist culture. And he knew I would deliver all that to him, because I had what he lacked—which was a sense of responsibility. And a real belief in *us*. Our life, our future together. Of course, I also made that pathetic mistake of thinking I could change him. So, yes, you're right. I hooked up with a disaster zone. Guilty on all charges. Despite all that, despite everything he's done, I still don't want to see Paul come to harm."

She reached for what must have been her fifth cigarette.

"Do you want me to congratulate you on your directness, your openness?"

"I just want to know two things."

"Go on."

"Did you know about Ben Hassan talking Paul into taking out this loan for your daughter's apartment?"

"What loan?"

"Ben Hassan told me that Philippe gave Samira one million dirhams for an apartment in Casablanca."

"Oh, please. The Frenchie has been reasonable about giving her a degree of child support. But . . . one million dirhams? That is beyond absurd. Samira lives in a fifty-square-meter apartment that she rents for two thousand dirhams a month—which is quite a bargain for the Gauthier neighborhood of Casa. You know she is a professor at the university there. Literature. Her specialty is Romantic melancholy. How apt. She did get her doctorate in France. At Aix-en-Provence. Her thesis was even published. So yes, I am very proud of her. And I so love being a grandmother to her wonderful son. But the fanciful idea that her Frenchman gave her a million dirhams for an apartment . . ."

I felt myself getting hyperstressed, because I was beginning to figure out the actual game that Ben Hassan was playing. I said, "But

Ben Hassan also told me that when Paul contacted him, begging that he put him back in touch with Samira, he informed Paul that a quick way back into her life was by giving her the matching one million dirhams for the apartment she was buying."

"And Paul naturally bought into this?"

"I'm afraid so. Ben Hassan showed me the loan agreement he signed. He's repaying one-point-six million on a one-million-dirham loan."

"The first I've heard of it. If he had given that money to Samira—or went and bought an apartment for her . . . well, Samira and I are reasonably close now, so she would have told me. I mean, one million dirhams would buy her close to one hundred square meters in the Gauthier district. She'd be over the moon. So . . . it is clear that your husband allowed himself to be scammed."

I picked up the glass of wine I had put aside. I took a long sip, trying to absorb what I just heard.

"So Paul going missing . . . ," I said.

"That is largely due to you. I heard all about the secret vasectomy."

"Paul told you that?"

"Hardly. It was Ben Hassan."

"That bastard. And let me guess—he also called you last night or this morning, telling you I was on my way to Ouarzazate."

"Indeed he did. I am sure he promised you that he wouldn't phone me. Just as I am certain you regret now letting him in on that little betrayal that Paul perpetrated on you. Again I am dazzled by how a bright woman like you—"

"Yes, I was naive. Naive because I was also so hopeful. Never a good combination, apparently. Just as I now know that Ben Hassan has deceived Paul. Lending him money on the basis of giving it to your daughter, and then not passing it on to her. Isn't that known as embezzlement?"

"That's a matter of conjecture. Did you read the loan agreement? Did Paul? I tend to doubt it. Do you know what I now think—having heard about Ben Hassan's newest vengeance game? Even though this is all speculation, I'd bet that after Samira gave birth to my grandson, Ben Hassan got in touch with Paul, informing him that he was a grandfather and that Samira desperately needed his help. He probably played up the fact that, having never answered any of her letters or emails over the years, Samira had written him off as a terrible man; a nonexistent father. But Ben Hassan told Paul that, if he would find her the money needed for her apartment, he would be able to reestablish his relationship with her and play a role in his grandson's life—and that he would also right the wrong that he perpetrated on Ben Hassan all those years ago. Of course, Ben Hassan being Ben Hassan, he probably sent that email as a way of seeing if he could play on Paul's guilt after all these years. Knowing my 'friend' as I do, I am certain he felt that the account would not be closed until he found a way of ensnaring Paul. What he couldn't have known—until you told him last night—was that his email arrived right after Paul promised you a baby and had himself fixed in secret; an act that Paul knew, when revealed, would destroy everything between you. Ben Hassan's email allowed Paul to think: here was his chance at making good on past wrongs; here was a chance to reconnect with the only child he would now ever have.

"So maybe that's why Paul showed up on Samira's doorstep two days ago, thoroughly expecting her to greet him as the man who finally redeemed himself in her eyes. Instead she rebuffed him. Which had him running back to Ben Hassan—who comforted him and put it into his head that maybe if he headed south to Ouarzazate, I would be able to help him find a way back to Samira."

"Ben Hassan did all this to break him. He got your father, your brothers. Now Paul. He was the last member of the quartet who cost him his career. And he has certainly revenged himself."

"But he is still an obese man with a sad life. And someone who was denied his life's dream—to become a great painter. How does revenge fix that?"

I drained my glass. Faiza glanced at her watch.

"I really don't feel like talking much more," she said. "I have a class to teach . . . not that I really want to be doing that either. Still, it is my work. And my work, as minor and inconsequential as it is, tucked away in the mouth of the Sahara, does give some form and shape to the day. So . . . I'd like you to leave now."

"I just need to know one last thing."

"Which is what?"

"Did Paul give you any indication he was suicidal?"

"Or would follow my advice and kill himself? Put it this way: I told him that he had ruined my life, that he had ruined his daughter's life, that he had ruined Ben Hassan's life. Then I let him know that I knew all about how he tricked you into believing he wanted a child with you. That really sent him into a spin."

"And he said what . . . ?"

"He said: 'I've fucked up everything.' Then I told him he had to leave. He started to cry. He begged for my forgiveness. I told him, 'I'm kicking you out. Just as you kicked me out of your life years ago.'"

"So you too had your revenge. Has it changed anything?"

She lit another cigarette.

"It's changed nothing. Nothing at all."

She walked to the front door and opened it. "Leave," she said.

"I'm sorry you're so bitter."

"And you're not?"

Outside I found myself frantically searching for a taxi, the mid-afternoon heat now even more frightening in its intensity. My brain was spinning like the wheels on a slot machine—and turning up zero in the way of solutions. Except the absolute need to find Paul immediately—and to at least alleviate one of his fears by telling him he owed Ben Hassan nothing.

Did he keep a copy of the loan agreement? Was there a lawyer in Casa I could bring into the picture to break the contract and also sue Ben Hassan for fraud, while also pursuing the authorities to prosecute him for embezzlement?

Absurd thoughts. If, as Faiza indicated, Ben Hassan really had all those high-up connections, I knew that the best I could hope for was that, once Paul was back home, he never came near us.

A taxi passed by and halted when the driver saw my frantic waving.

I was back at the hotel five minutes later, scanning every passing corner of the city for a sighting of Paul. When I walked in Yasmina stared at me wide-eyed.

"Why aren't you with Monsieur Paul?"

"Paul! You found him?"

"He came back to the hotel."

"He what?"

"He came back. Maybe three or four minutes ago. Left this here for you."

She handed me an envelope with the letter *R* written in Paul's characteristic penmanship.

"Surely you saw him as you were pulling up in the taxi," she said.

"Had he been there I would have seen him, I was looking everywhere."

"But he just wandered out a minute ago. Maybe even less than that. Heading to the bus station. Carrying no bags, but telling me he was going south. You can't have missed him."

"But I did," I said, now frantic. "Was he on foot?"

She nodded.

I turned around. My taxi had pulled away.

"How do I get there?" I cried.

"It's a five-minute walk. Head to the main street, turn left, keep going until you see the station. It is opposite the Q8 petrol station. But hurry—the bus he's taking . . . I think it leaves very soon."

Envelope in hand, I charged down the maze of alleyways, then bounded along the avenue Muhammed V, oblivious to the scorching afternoon, the pavements burning through my sandals, certain that up ahead I could see Paul's six-foot-four frame, his long gray hair bobbing with his bouncing gait. I was running faster than I have ever run, my eyes suddenly going foggy, the bus station up ahead, the bus there, me pushing myself against a heat so dense, so viscous, my equilibrium going sideways, but, oh, God, no . . . there he is getting on the bus, and I start to scream, "Wait, wait, wait . . . ," and, no this cannot be, the bus door closes and it pulls away, and I am seeing people on the street in nearby cafés, hearing myself scream, signaling to the driver to stop, and the bus is now turning out of the depot and down the main drag of Ouarzazate. I reached the bus station around thirty seconds later, fell into the dirt, and blacked out for a moment, and people rushed over, and two men helped me to a nearby café table, and one of them rushed inside while the other kept my head between my legs, and the second man returned with a sodden cloth that he put around my neck. As he helped me back into an upright position, a flash flood of sweat rolled down my face. I was handed a chilled bottle of water, which I drained in moments.

The men kept asking if I was all right, if they could get anyone to help me, why was I running like that?

I still had the envelope in my left hand. I asked for more water. I opened the letter. Though my eyes were still having trouble focusing, I still was able to make out the following lines in Paul's even more tortured scrawl:

I have hit the wall. I am now heading to the end of the line. Don't pursue me. Let me do what I have to do.

I am beyond sorry. But forgiveness is not merited in this instance. Which is why I am now disappearing. Permanently.

You were the love of my life. I only see that now.

Farewell.

P.

I looked up from the letter and into the faces of the men all huddled around me, their concern and worry at my mental and physical state evident.

"Where was that bus heading?" I asked.

A voice said:

"Tata."

"What's Tata?" I asked.

"A town six hours south of here."

I shut my eyes.

"What time is the next bus to Tata?"

EİGHTEEN

ONE OF THE men who came to my aid was a taxi driver. He insisted on driving me back to the hotel and refused my offer of money for the ride. When I reached the front door, Yasmina came racing out and helped me into the lobby. She found me more water. She sent one of the cleaners for another wet cloth to put around my neck. She told me I should go upstairs and lie down. She would check on the flight to Paris, as there was still time to catch it.

"He left on the bus to Tata," I said. "The next bus to Tata leaves in ninety minutes. I'm getting on it."

"But Tata is a six-hour journey from here. And it is absolutely in the middle of nowhere."

"He's threatening to kill himself," I said, brandishing the letter. "If I get there tonight there is a good chance I can find him before—"

"*Madame*, one simple call from me to the gendarmes will see the bus stopped somewhere between here and Tata, and your husband taken into protective custody."

What she said made sense. But I was operating according to a different sort of logic, in which I had convinced myself that if he fell into the hands of the authorities Ben Hassan was certain to be contacted. Given that he was still so set on revenge, who's to know what horror he would instruct them to concoct for Paul. Two days in a Moroccan jail would break him. No. Two hours would be enough to upend what little equilibrium he had left. Especially with Ben Has-

219

san's ability to pull all sorts of evil strings. The stories about Faiza's father and brothers were still fresh in my mind. I could easily see Paul being "suicided" while in protective custody—and the officials (along with everyone else, from Ben Hassan to Samira to Faiza to the very kind woman behind this hotel desk) all corroborating the fact that he was in troubled mental health in the days leading up to his death by hanging in his padded cell; a suicide that Ben Hassan could easily effectuate for one thousand euros.

"I'm getting on that bus," I told Yasmina. "Because it's me and me alone who can get him out of trouble."

"I beg you—"

"No discussion! None!"

I could see Yasmina recoil at the way I snapped at her.

"I'm sorry," I whispered.

She put a restraining hand on my arm. "I implore you. Go to your room, have a shower, lie down, let me call the gendarmes."

"My decision is made. And I am going to say this: if, when I get to Tata, I find that he has been taken off the bus by the police—"

"You have my word. I will not make that call. But as you have a little time, I ask that you go upstairs and stand under the shower and drink at least another liter of water. You are in danger of dehydrating."

I did as ordered, asking her to have a taxi here in just under an hour.

After my shower I dried off and got dressed, constantly pushing out of my head any conflicting thoughts about the wisdom of chasing Paul to Tata. *There is no choice*, I told myself. *I told Paul he was better off dead. He may have betrayed me, but my initial fury set this entire nightmare in motion. And now he seems determined to kill himself. And yes, I know I am beyond panic, beyond confused. But the only end to this panic is to get to him before he falls off the edge.*

Downstairs I offered Yasmina money for letting me stay in the room long after the checkout hour. She refused.

"You have been too kind to me," I said.

"I wish I could convince you to stay."

"I have to see this through."

Her reply was a look that said, *No, you don't . . . and you know that.* Then she handed me the hotel card with her cell phone number on the back of it.

"If I can help you in any way, you now know where to find me."

Ten minutes later I was on the bus heading south. To call this vehicle old would be an understatement. It looked to be a relic of the 1980s, with half-stripped paintwork, chewed up seats, grimy windows, no air-conditioning, no ventilation.

Thankfully there were only ten of us boarding it at Ouarzazate. Which meant that I had two seats to myself all the way to Tata. The other passengers were four elderly women in full niqabs, three men of equally advanced years, a young mother with two babies, a shy adolescent girl who glanced back at me on several occasions, clearly curious as to why I was on this bus. I managed to smile back, but drifted back into my preoccupied reverie. Outside we were traveling through a terrain that was part oasis—trees, patches of arable land—part encroaching sand. There was the occasional change in the topography—a vista in which stern mountains could be seen on the horizon; a densely populated village, its souk in full late-afternoon swing; the tents of Bedouin families pitched alongside the road; the sense that, with every kilometer, we were traveling deeper into a geographic void. I had read online the day before that, in Berber Arabic, *ouarzazate* means "without noise, without confusion." Gazing out at the darkening terrain—the sand turning copperish in the declining sun—I could understand just why, when compared to the noisy jumble that was other Moroccan cities, Ouarzazate wasn't simply the doorway to the desert but also to the immense silence into which I was now further venturing. When I stared at the ever-expanding Sahara, I could understand why it was something akin to a blank canvas, divorced from the disarray and chaos of life beyond. But I began to wonder if that too was an illusion. You look at a sea of empty sand, two Bedouin parents crossing this terrain with their children, and marvel at the timeless simplicity of it all. The truth is more complex. The necessity of survival. The need to find water. To find money for food and other essentials. Their place in a harsh, unforgiving universe.

Without noise . . . without confusion.

Life is noise, confusion. We can run to the ends of the earth, and it will still impinge on us. Because the demons within us never vanish—even in a landscape as planed and silenced as the Sahara.

The bus stopped in a tiny village built next to a small stream. I bought a cup of mint tea from a sad-faced man. There was a toilet in a nearby shed: a hole in the ground over which had been constructed a wooden box with a makeshift seat. The smell was overpowering. I emerged choking, desperate for fresh air. But even at sunset, the heat stifled everything.

I reboarded the bus. I attempted to nap. But the bus's lack of suspension and my own preoccupations mitigated sleep. I attempted to strategize. Tata couldn't be that big a place. A handful of hotels at best. I'd stop in each one until I found Paul. I'd soothe and comfort him. I'd call Yasmina back in Ouarzazate and get her to book us tickets on the next flight to Paris. I'd get us back to her hotel by midday tomorrow. I'd . . .

Make plans, as usual. In the hope of regularizing someone for whom regularization was more than a stretch. And yes, Faiza—as angry and vindictive and toxic as she was—did get one thing right: Paul brought chaos into everybody's life. But there was a difference between the Paul I met three years ago—who feigned obliviousness to the mess he frequently engendered—and the man who left me what was a suicide note. He could no longer run from himself. But he could run into the Sahara.

The hours on the bus went by slowly, the vanished sun lowering the temperature somewhat, but not acting as a palliative against the grubbiness of the journey. I nodded off for a spell, waking with a jolt when the bus screeched to a halt, a horn was honked, and the driver shouted one word, "Tata."

We were in a parking area, outside of a walled town. I had been sleeping against my backpack. Getting off the bus, I was immediately confronted by two young men—both in their early twenties, both trying to grow beards with not much luck, both wearing baseball caps, both eyeing me over.

"Hello, pretty lady," one of them said in French.

"You need some help to guide you around?" the second one asked.

I held up the photo page of Paul's passport.

"I'm looking for this man—my husband."

"I know where he is," the first guy said.

"You do?" I asked. "Honestly?"

"You come with us, we show you," the second one said, but he was interrupted by the bus driver, who began to shout at them in Arabic, using the word *imshee* several times. These two operators were not so intimidated, however, and began to sass him back, until another man—in his late fifties, wearing a dark suit, also weighed in on the argument. The two guys were clearly enjoying the confrontation. The older of the two was being bold and arrogant, eyeing me up and down, making flip comments ("Don't you want a date with me?" . . . "I love American women" . . . "You don't need your husband, you need a younger man") amidst this ever-heated interchange with my two protectors. Eventually the older man—he was tall, heavily lined, a cigarette clutched between his teeth, ash dropping on his brown suit jacket—mentioned police and the two operators backed off, but not before Mr. Arrogant winked at me and said, "Maybe some other time." Once they were gone, the older man handed me a card and explained in French that he worked for a small hotel within the walls, and he could offer me a very clean, safe room for three hundred dirhams . . . discounted from the usual five hundred. If I was hungry he could convince the cook to stay on to make dinner for me. I pulled out Paul's passport and showed him the photograph, asking at what hotel I might find my husband.

"When did he arrive?" asked the man.

"On the bus before mine," I said.

"That's impossible," he said.

"How can it be impossible? I saw him leave on the earlier bus."

"But I met that bus—as I meet all buses here. And there was only one Westerner on the bus: a man around seventy, traveling alone, German."

"Couldn't he have gotten off when you weren't looking?"

"*Madame*, I promise you . . . I see everyone who arrives by bus in Tata. You can check the other hotels in town, if you wish."

"I'll give you fifty dirhams if you take me to every hotel in town."

"But I assure you . . ."

"One hundred dirhams."

The man shrugged, then nodded for me to follow him.

We went through the archway that led into the center of Tata. The town was something of a maze. Dark, twisting streets. Little in the way of streetlight. We stopped by a dive of a place, which from the outside looked like a flophouse. A haunted-looking man—his face sallow, his eyes sunken, endlessly forlorn—was behind the desk. He came out and greeted the man escorting me. They embraced. Words were exchanged. I was asked to show Paul's passport. The desk clerk shook his head, pointing out into the darkness of the night. I asked him to study the photo again to make absolutely certain that he didn't see him. Again he shook his head.

Ten minutes and three hotels later we had come to the end of the line for all places of accommodation outside the one to which I was now being brought to spend the night. At each of these establishments it was the same routine: the passport photo, the question if this man was staying there, the shake of the head.

As we left the last hotel, I asked my escort his name.

"It's Naguib, *madame*."

"What time is the first bus back to Ouarzazate?"

"There's one at five a.m."

"So I should leave my hotel when?"

"Four forty-five will be fine. It's all downhill and just a ten-minute walk."

From the shadows a voice began to intone, "Downhill, downhill," the tone mocking, amused.

Out stepped those two young tough guys who had harassed me upon my arrival. They lit up cigarettes and the flirtatious one even tipped his baseball cap in mock salute. When Naguib snapped at them—hissing something angry in their direction—Mr. Arrogant said to me in French, "We were not trying to be disrespectful, *madame*."

They disappeared back into the shadows.

"Do you know them?" I asked.

"I'm afraid so. They come from Marrakesh. They work on the crew that is repaving part of the road near here. They've been here for two weeks and think they're big men from the big city. They're stupid, but harmless. Shall we head to my hotel now?"

We began to ascend the narrow pathway that led up a Babel-like hill. It was a steep climb, but the moon was full, so we weren't stumbling in the dark. When we reached the summit I was panting and feeling parched. It had been quite the ascent. Immediately an elderly woman in a hajib insisted that I sit down and found me a bottle of water. Naguib took my passport and three hundred dirhams, saying he would fill in all the necessary registration forms. The woman asked if I liked lamb couscous. I indicated that would be just fine, as I had hardly eaten all day and was now famished. Naguib returned and led me through an extraordinary structure: castellated, with great open spaces and an outside walkway that looked down on the village below. The sky was dominated by a very full, spectral moon.

My room was under the eaves: simple, well furnished, clean. There was a double bed and a decent shower. I handed Naguib one hundred dirhams and thanked him.

"I am back on duty here at six thirty tomorrow morning," he said. "There is a bus that leaves at eight. You could sleep in a bit and have breakfast and still be back in Ouarzazate by four."

"Is there any chance whatsoever that my husband could have gotten off somewhere between Ouarzazate and here?"

"The bus can stop at assorted villages—but only if a passenger requests a stop. So, yes, he could have possibly requested a stop—but these places have little in the way of hotels or restaurants."

"Might the driver of the earlier bus be here now?"

"No—because he returned as a passenger on the eight o'clock bus back to Ouarzazate. He won't be back until tomorrow. I don't have his cell phone number, so I cannot get in touch with him until I actually see him. You could wait until he returns tomorrow, and we could ask him together."

"I think I am going to head back on the early bus," I said.

"As you wish, *madame*. But here's my phone number if you need me."

Drawing a notebook and a pen from his pocket, he wrote it down and handed it to me.

"Thank you so much, Naguib."

"How long will you need before dinner?"

"Fifteen minutes at most. I just want to shower and freshen up."

"I'll tell the cook to expect you shortly."

A quarter of an hour later, I arrived at the outdoor terrace that served as a dining room. It was a wonderful open area on which six or seven tables were situated. There was only one other guest—a lean gray-haired man, with round wire-rimmed spectacles, a blue short-sleeved shirt, tan shorts, a pair of orthopedic sandals on his feet, a book propped up against his wine bottle: *Der Zauberberg* by Thomas Mann. This must have been the German who'd arrived on the earlier bus. Someone who rode the bus with Paul! Someone who could confirm his whereabouts. Immediately I approached his table. He looked up, his face somewhat lined but still strong, with deep blue eyes that seemed to be harboring some quiet sadness . . . or was that just me projecting my own sadness on everyone?

"Sorry, but I don't speak German."

He smiled at me. I continued, "But I am very competent in English and not bad in French . . . and my apologies for interrupting your dinner."

"My dinner is finished," he said in English, pointing to his empty plates. "But if you are about to eat and would like company . . ."

He pointed to the empty seat opposite his own.

"That's really kind of you," I said. "But before I sit down I have a rather urgent question."

"By all means."

"Were you on the bus that left Ouarzazate at four o'clock?"

"Indeed I was."

"Did you see this man?"

I reached into my pants pocket and pulled out Paul's passport, flipping it open to the photo page. The gentleman studied it carefully for several moments.

"I'm afraid there was no one at all like this individual on the bus."

"Are you absolutely certain of that?"

"When I got on the bus in Ouarzazate I took a seat right in the back, so I walked by everyone who had already boarded."

"But he got on right when the bus was leaving."

"I remember looking up when the last person came onto the bus, but that was the driver."

"Sir, please, I saw him get on the bus."

"Who is he?" he asked, pointing to the photo.

"My husband."

That got his attention.

"Sit, sit," he said, motioning to the empty chair. "My name is Dietrich."

I told him my own. We shook hands.

"Germany is one of around fifty countries that I keep telling myself I should visit," I said.

"If you come, besides Berlin and Hamburg and Munich, you should drive along the Romantische Strasse—and stop at Rothenburg ob der Tauber. A medieval city between Würzburg and Nürnberg. Completely restored after much bombing in the war. *Sehr gemütlich*, as we say. A very quiet, beautiful town—and the place I've called home for thirty years. I had a very faithful congregation in Rothenburg until I stepped down last year."

"You're a priest?"

"A pastor. Lutheran. And recently retired."

"And, if I may ask, what brings you to the Sahara in mid-July?" I asked.

He paused for a moment, collecting his thoughts.

"I remember once reading in an English novel about a man traversing this corner of the world after suffering a terrible grief, and the writer noted, 'He crossed North Africa, trying to empty his mind.' I came here, at an absurd time in the calendar, trying to empty my mind."

"Because of a terrible grief?"

"My wife of forty-four years died at Christmas."

"Oh, God, that is awful. Was it sudden?"

"Completely out of nowhere. A brain aneurysm. She got up from the dinner table at home to get something in the fridge. Suddenly she looked startled, then in terrible pain, then she fell to the floor. When I raced over to her she was no more. You know that line, 'In the midst of life we are in death.' "

Immediately I heard myself saying, " 'Earth to earth, ashes to ashes, dust to dust.' It's from the *Book of Common Prayer*. One of the side benefits of being raised an Episcopalian."

"And it was also a Latin antiphon: *Media vita in morte sumus*. And it has appeared often in poetry. Rilke used it in a poem once."

I let his words wash over me. "It is good to be speaking with you."

"Were you hoping to be speaking with your husband?"

"Of course," I said, finding myself tearing up.

"I apologize for intruding."

"You're hardly intruding."

"Would you like a glass of wine?" he said.

"I think I'd like that very much."

He reached for the still-full bottle and poured me a glass. At that juncture the couscous arrived. I thanked the diminutive woman for bringing it, apologizing for keeping her up so late.

"*Pas de problème,*" she said in a near whisper, disappearing back into the kitchen.

To his infinite credit, Dietrich steered us into more neutral waters, asking me about my work, fascinated to learn how I shifted from journalism to accounting, and I asked him about his student years at Heidelberg. I learned that he had two sons, a lawyer and a tax inspector ("We'd have much to talk about," I noted), living in Nürnberg and Munich respectively.

Then the couscous was finished and I'd drunk a second glass of wine and was feeling considerably less shaky. But I now had a desperate need to talk; to sit and speak calmly about my life with Paul— beginning with my doubts and concerns about him before we were married, ending with the discovery of his appalling betrayal and all the crazed uproar since then.

"Truth be told," I said at the end of this monologue, "I cannot say for certain that it was Paul whom I saw on the avenue Muhammed V at two this afternoon. I kept thinking I saw him everywhere before that. But when I shouted at him in the streets of Ouarzazate he never turned around, even though we were only a few feet away from each other. And I'm haunted by the letter he left for me; a letter which let it be known that he was considering taking his own life. In my darkest moments, I cannot help but wonder if I was seeing a ghost."

"But there is no reason to think he is dead. You told me the woman at the hotel confirmed that he'd left just before you'd arrived back from seeing his ex-wife."

I nodded. Dietrich sipped his wine, cogitating.

"I'd like to posit two thoughts here," he finally said. "The first is that one of the reasons why his former wife, and his rather dangerous friend, Ben Hassan, were so furious at him was that, on a certain level, he behaved just like an old-fashioned colonialist. He came into a fragile country. He took advantage of many of the people he encountered. He wreaked a degree of havoc. Then he packed up and left, accepting no responsibility at all for the mess he left behind.

"But the other thing that strikes me about this story is your desperate sense of guilt. He betrayed you terribly. All you did was confront him with his betrayal. That story you told—about his assurances that he wanted a baby with you, and then to do what he did—is nothing less than horrible. The fact that you have been desperately trying to track him down since his disappearance from Essaouira, the fact that you are here in the middle of a great sandy nowhere, on your own, still trying to save him from himself . . . Robin, you have my admiration."

I felt my eyes welling up. I lowered my head, fighting back tears. Dietrich reached over and took my hand, squeezing it in a way that implied one word: *courage.*

"You will get through this," he said. "Think of it as a maze, a labyrinth. But you haven't lost your cartographic skills, let alone your ability to negotiate your way out of its ensnaring contours. The biggest devastation, in my experience, is the loss of hope—and the revelation that there was so much you just didn't see."

"Oh, I saw a great deal about him . . . but I also chose to ignore all the early warning signs; all the telltale indications that he truly couldn't handle the responsibility implicit in building a life with another person."

"Sometimes the need for hope blinds us to other more evident verities. What else can we do but keep trying to see things a little more clearly?"

"As you do."

"Don't be certain of that. I have my limitations and flaws like everyone else. My marriage was hardly perfect."

"But it did last forty-four years."

"That it did. But we did separate for six years, during which time we both had relationships with other people. It was my initial weakness—an involvement with a woman who also happened to be a parishioner—that sparked the separation. It caused many problems and hindered my clerical career. Finding our way back to each other . . . that was a remarkable journey. And not without considerable pain. But the result was twenty more extraordinary years together. Then, out of nowhere, she died. Herta was only sixty-eight. As I used to tell parishioners who had suffered a tragedy, we never can completely fathom God's plan for us."

"But do you truly believe that it was His hand who 'smote' your wife down?"

Dietrich smiled. "I appreciate your use of Old Testament language. The answer to your question is that I have no answer to whether He is an all-seeing, all-controlling God who decides the fate of us. God for me is a more complex idea. You know it was Montaigne who stated that the unknowingness of life is something that we all must embrace."

"I do believe you can have religious faith and be thinking at the same time."

"But you yourself have never been able to embrace the idea of faith?" he asked.

"Oh, I have plenty of faith . . . in the need to fight forward. And though I would, on a certain level, like to fall on my knees right now and beg Him to somehow deliver my husband to me, I sense I would be talking to myself."

"I will nonetheless pray for you tonight . . . and for your lonely journey into this *Niemandsland*. A no-man's-land. Like the terrain just beyond Tata. I just returned after two days out on the dunes. I drove myself—which everyone here said was very risky, as once you leave the road you are driving directly on the sand. So I had to rent a four-by-four. The owner of the hotel wanted me to hire a driver, a guide. But I had to do it alone. Solo."

"What were you trying to prove by heading out on unpaved Saharan tracks, alone? Was it about communicating with God?"

He pulled off his glasses and rubbed his eyes. "It was about confronting my loneliness."

"Loneliness in the face of grief?"

"Of course. But also loneliness in the face of God. And the fact that I finally know now that He cannot provide me with the answers I so need."

"Yet you still believe?"

"Indeed I do. I do so not out of habit or the need for ritual—though I do love so much about ecclesiastic ritual. I think I also still believe because I need to allow myself to be open to the inherent enigma of life. What is real to us? What is a mirage? Why do we spend a lifetime trying to somehow discern between the two? And when we die, when this corporeal self is no more, if it is simply the end of consciousness . . . then what?"

"That is the great mystery," I said.

He glanced at his watch. "I promised my son Horst that I would Skype him at one o'clock his time; midnight here. He is going through a divorce now and isn't sleeping much and is having difficulty coming to terms with the fact that his wife recently announced she no longer loves him. He's just thirty-two with a little daughter—my granddaughter—and he is devastated, even though he's been unhappy in the marriage for years. But he is choosing immense sadness at the moment. I can appreciate that. I chose that myself at certain difficult junctures in life."

"You're a very good father, calling him so late."

"Being a parent—it is a lifetime job. They are always your children. And you are always engaged with their vulnerability and their own struggles to try to carve out something happy . . . or not."

"Being a parent . . . that dream is dead for me."

"Don't say that."

"I turned forty last October."

"The way medicine works today, you still have time."

"I wish I could believe that."

"I must say this was not a conversation I was expecting to have in Tata," he said. "The man of faith in me might even posit the idea that we were brought together tonight for a reason. Even when you are stricken by the most desperate solitariness or doubt, someone can come along and remind you that no one is alone."

"Beautifully said. One final question. Did God speak to you when you were all alone—and so severely vulnerable—in the Sahara?"

"Of course he did."

"May I ask: What did he tell you?"

"He told me: get back to a place of safety."

"Good advice," I said.

He stood up.

"I will be taking the eight a.m. bus tomorrow—so if you'd like a travel companion back to Ouarzazate . . ."

"I need to take the five a.m. bus."

"But you'll have no sleep."

"True—but there's a two p.m. direct flight to Paris. I am going to see if I can get a place on it. And the five a.m. bus will get me back to Ouarzazate in time for it."

Now it was my turn to stand up. As I took Dietrich's hand he executed a small, almost formal bow—a hint of old-worldliness in the midst of the Sahara.

Five minutes later, back in my room, the air conditioner cranked up against the heat beyond, I could not help but keep reflecting on that sage piece of advice that Dietrich received from the Almighty while facing the void of the Sahara.

Get back to a place of safety.

I dug out my laptop. I went online. I found a travel website. I booked myself on three flights for the next day: Ouarzazate to Paris at 4:00. Paris to Boston at 7:00, arriving at 8:30 with the time change. And a tight but still possible connection—Boston to Buffalo at 9:45.

The cost of this last-minute ticket was absurd: seventeen hundred dollars in Economy. But it was also just money. I needed to finally call time on this madness and return home.

After paying for the ticket with my credit card, I sent an urgent email to Morton:

I hope you have your BlackBerry in hand, as I know you are due to meet me at Buffalo airport tonight at 9 p.m. I am still in Morocco, so don't bother. I will explain all when I see you at the office in two days. I fly tomorrow and arrive late. And yes, I have a story or two to tell.

I set the little alarm clock for 4:15 a.m. It had been, on every level, a vast, difficult day—and I had to remind myself that this time last night, I was having a short sleep in a Casablanca hotel. Amazing how the narrative of one's life can become so skewed in such a short space of time.

Now, in a less frantic, more reflective moment—and after that truly interesting dinner with the German man of God—I saw that the "essential" clarification that came out of the last frenzied few days was the decision to abandon ship and head back to the States. I had made a crucial decision. I could now surrender to sleep without hesitation—for just four hours.

When I was jolted awake at 4:15 I forced myself into the shower. I dressed and washed my face. I loaded up my small backpack with everything I had taken out for the night and I left the hotel.

Outside it was still moonlit. I had to watch my step on the walkway down into the main town. The descent took five minutes. As the bus depot was just a minute beyond the city walls, I'd be there easily with ten minutes to spare.

When I reached the end of the descending pathway I spied two figures leaning against a wall, smoking. As I came into their field of vision, they both tossed away their cigarettes. Suddenly I noticed the two matching baseball caps and realized these were the two guys who flirted with me last night.

"Hello there, pretty lady," the talkative, arrogant one said. He and his friend were now positioned directly in front of me. A red warning light went off in my brain.

"You're up early," I said, trying to keep my tone light while simultaneously glancing frantically from side to side, desperate to find a way to squeeze by them. But this was a narrow pathway and they had comprehensively blocked the way forward.

"We wanted to say goodbye," Mr. Arrogant said.

"Goodbye, then," I said.

I immediately tried to dash past the other guy, who had a jar of some liquid and a rag in one hand. As I made a break for it, Mr. Arrogant caught me by the arms and pinned them behind me. I tried to scream but his friend had the rag over my nose and mouth within a nanosecond. The rag was sodden in a liquid that gave off a high chemical aroma. Kicking out with my feet, connecting with nothing, I tried not to inhale its toxic fumes. But the rag was forced down on my face with such force, while my hair was simultaneously being yanked backward, that I could no longer hold my breath.

When I exhaled the chemicals hit me like a sucker punch to the head. *This is not happening, this is not happening.*

And then the world went black.

NİNETEEN

WHEN THE WORLD came back into focus, I wanted to jump back into the darkness again. Because to be conscious meant facing my imminent death.

I was nowhere. I was being bounced up and down. Tossed from side to side. My head felt as if it had been split in two. Nausea was consuming me. But even if I wanted to be sick, that was impossible, as a rag had been tied tightly around my mouth. To vomit would be to risk suffocation. My hands had been bound to my feet. Movement was impossible.

I had been thrown into the cargo area of an open-back truck. It was still night outside, though a small hint of dawn was beginning to cleave the sky. I forced myself up for a moment and spied nothing but emptiness around me. Until another bump in the terrain slammed me back down against the floor of the truck.

I was being driven into the Sahara. Once they had me at a place far away from any hint of civilization, I knew what they would try to do with me. I also knew that two against one meant that, once they had raped me, they would then have to kill me. And bury my body deep within the desert. And return to their road gang job by sunrise and act as if nothing had happened. When my absence was eventually reported, what trace would there be of me? I saw my backpack out of a corner of my eye. It had been thrown into a corner of the cargo area, near a plastic jerry can that had slid down and was bumping against my face. From the fumes emitting from its cap I could tell that it was filled with spare gas.

They are going to rape me. They are going to then strangle me. Then they'll use the gas to burn my body and bury its charred remains deep in the drifting sand.

I began to scream. I screamed through the gag. I screamed like a lunatic. I screamed in the desperate absurd hope that someone would hear me. I screamed with rage and fury and disbelief. I screamed with hatred. I screamed with terror.

I tugged at the ropes that were binding me. My hands had been so fiercely tied to my feet, the knot pulled so tightly, that there was absolutely no way of loosening it, let alone undoing it without a knife. I pulled and yanked and desperately tried to get my fingers— gone numb owing to the pressure on my wrists—to deal with the knot. But it was impossible. Every time I yanked my hands, the ropes seemed to apply more pressure, increasing the numbness, making me wonder if the lack of circulation would . . .

This is not happening . . . this is not happening.

But this was definitely happening. With the sky beginning to lighten, I was pretty certain it was going to happen very soon. That would be their logic: fuck and strangle her before sunup. Cremate the body, bury the remains, be back on the road with the new day dawning.

I struggled and struggled and struggled. My muzzled screams turned into hysterical crying as I began to realize there was no way out of this. *I am doing to die. Before that happens I am going to suffer the worst sort of degradation imaginable. A monstrous death by strangulation.* There was nothing I could do to stop them.

The truck began to slow down, then came to a halt. The motor was cut. I heard both front doors being opened, then slammed shut. Footsteps. Then a voice.

"Sleep well, pretty lady?"

He climbed into the back of the truck and began to stroke my hair. When I began to struggle, he slapped me hard across the left ear. The effect was like being instantly concussed, ferocious pain coupled with a profound echo effect. I screamed in agony, and was rewarded this time with a fist to my cheekbone. I blacked out for a moment. When I came to again, it felt as if the cheekbone had been fractured. The little shit now was brandishing a knife in front of my eyes and yanking my hair at the same time.

"You fight me again I will cut you," he hissed. "Cut off your tits, maybe gouge your eyes. You want that, cunt?"

I shook my head many times, fear making me whimper. Now his fury turned into a broad frightening smile.

"You fight me, you will get hurt. You no fight me, everything will be very nice. Understand?"

To give emphasis to the last word, he yanked back hard on my hair. I whimpered again, nodding many times.

"Good girl," he said, stroking my cheek. Then he shouted something in Arabic and his accomplice came over, a knife in hand.

"My friend is going to cut off the ropes," the little shit said. "You going to struggle?"

I shook my head many times.

"Good girl," he said.

More shouts back and forth in Arabic as the cords were cut. Immediately the restoration of blood flow to my hands made me shudder. A hard clip across the ear was the punishment for that involuntary movement.

"I fucking told you: no movement," the little shit hissed.

"Sorry, sorry," I whispered through the gag.

"Tell me you want this," he whispered.

I tensed and was hit again.

"Tell me you want this," he repeated.

"I want this," I muttered through the gag.

"You move you get cut."

He threw my now untied hands behind me as he slid off the

truck and, with his accomplice helping him, cut the remaining rope off my ankles, pulled off the gag, then proceeded to lift my buttocks up and unzip my pants, pulling them down with my panties at the same time. As he did so my free right hand quickly darted around the immediate vicinity of the cab, trying to find something I could use as a weapon. I knew I only had seconds—and nothing came to hand. Until my fingers connected with the jerry can. I managed to get my hand around its cap when I felt my legs being spread wide and I looked up and saw the little shit above me, his pants pulled down, his penis erect.

"You going to fight me?" he asked as he climbed on top of me.

I shook my head, seeing out of the corner of my eye his goon standing on the ground by him, folding up his knife, lighting a cigarette, frightened and scared and also waiting his turn. With my hand still on the cap of the jerry can I reached over with my left hand and touched the little shit's arm, actually stroking it in a come-on way. A huge smile came on his face.

"You want me, yes?"

I nodded. Another big smile from the little shit. I could now feel the head of his penis rubbing against my vulva, trying to gain entrance, but being defeated by the absolute dryness within.

"Open wider," he ordered, and heard him spit into his hand then rub it against the lips of my vagina and force his way in. I felt as if I was being ripped apart; an agony beyond agony. But as I glanced upward at him I could see that he had his eyes snapped shut as he began to thrust wildly within me. My left hand tightened around his arm, and I deliberately began to match his thrusts with my own as a way of letting him think I was into it. Meanwhile, my right fingers were manically unscrewing the cap of the jerry can. As I could hear his moans rising, and feel his penis beginning to stiffen even further as ejaculation approached, the cap finally came loose enough that a small trickle of gas came spilling out. That's when I reached up with my free hand and stroked his face. He opened his eyes and I dug my nails directly into them, digging down, blood spurting forth, his screams deafening. I let go with the jerry can, drenching him with the gas. He jumped back, falling to the ground, his face in his hands, blood now gushing from his eye sockets. In a nanosecond I jumped off the truck, grabbed the Zippo lighter from the hand of his startled accomplice, ignited it, and tossed its flame directly at my rapist. All this took maybe three seconds. There was a huge conflagrating whoosh. The cigarette had ignited the gas. The little shit burst into flames.

His cries of agony were mirrored by a scream from his accomplice, especially as I was now gunning for him with my claws. As I sideswiped his cheeks, he caught me with a punch to the face. I fell to my knees. He kicked me with full force in the head.

And the world went black again.

TWENTY

THE HEAT BROUGHT me back to life. Then it threatened to finish the job and kill me.

When I snapped back into murky consciousness, the pain was beyond ferocious. My head battered, my cheek fractured, my lips split, a reverberating echo in one ear, the throbbing in my skull unbearable.

I'd collapsed facedown in the sand. I knew this because when my eyes finally opened, sand cascaded into them, making me jump upright and then nearly fall over again as the pain hit. I held my head for several moments, eyes snapped shut. I became aware of the boiler-room heat. And the fact that I had no pants on. The entire exposed lower half of my body felt as if it was charred.

I tried to stand up. I failed. I sank to my knees, but the sand was so fiery that it forced me to somehow become vertical. That's when I doubled over. Because that's when I saw him. Or what was left of him. Still on his knees. Charred everywhere. Most of his features burned beyond recognition, but half his face still intact. The upper half, where his two eyeballs had been gouged so fiercely that one of them had dislodged and was dangling by his cheek.

I turned away, pulling off the gag. I was sick, the vomit disgorging from me with a ferocity and a vehemence that had me collapsing again. Until the scorching sand forced me back on my feet.

It all came flooding back now. Every appalling detail. From the moment they grabbed me. Everything that transpired. Everything they did. Everything I did. Evidence of which was right there in front of me. And the punch in the face and the kick to the head that blacked out the world. Blacked out everything. Until now.

All the vomiting left me with a ravenous thirst—though I was already severely parched from all the time unconscious under that pitiless sun. How long had I been left here? I instinctively glanced at my wrist, thinking they must have snatched my watch. But my father's Rolex was still there. So too were my engagement and wedding rings. The watch told me it was 8:23 a.m., the hands on the dial blurring before me, as my vision felt as if it had been knocked out of kilter with that final boot to the head. The vehement sun blanched the landscape. As I tried a step forward, my foot felt something soft underfoot. I stared down, almost crumbling again. The blurriness in my vision was alarming. But I could discern white pants in front of me. My white pants and underwear, stripped off me by the little shit before he forced his way inside me. Before I tore out his ability to see the world. Before I set him ablaze.

It took considerable work to reach down and pick up these discarded garments. Trying to put them on was torture. When I finally got the underwear and the pants back on, and also located the pair of sandals pulled off my feet, I then noticed the tire track right by me. A tire track that continued forward for a few feet before turning into a circle and then . . .

He'd driven off. After kicking me in the head, the punk had clearly jumped into the truck and driven off into the dawn. Leaving his accomplice on fire and his victim unconscious in the sand, exposed to the monstrous elements that would kill her in a manner that might have made strangulation preferable. Because as I looked up from the encircling tire track what I saw was . . .

Nothing.

Nothing but sand.

Stretching to infinity. Burned beige in color. Lunar, with craters and fossilized dunes. A boundless, evaporated void on the far side of the moon.

And nothing hinting at human life in any direction.

Nothing but the tire track. When the punk raced off in the truck, he took with him everything that gave me an identity and a means of contacting the outside world. My passport, my credit cards, what cash I had left, my airplane ticket, my laptop. He'd also taken the few clothes I had, including a hat to shield my head. I was alone in the Sahara with nothing. No water. No protection from the fireball above. No papers indicating who I was.

I glanced back at the blackened corpse of my attacker. This would be my fate. I would not last more than a few hours out here. I would fall over somewhere, succumbing to sunstroke, dehydration, ravenous thirst. I would slowly die. If I was ever found—and that was unlikely, given that they had brought me to a place no one dared to venture—my body would be so burned by the sun that . . .

No, no, don't think that. You can't think that. You must somehow try to find help. Or a water hole. Or . . .

I scanned all corners of the horizon again. Nothing. Not even a speck in the distance of some outpost of civilization. Nothing but the tire tracks.

That's it! The punk did a U-turn and headed back to civilization. Just follow his tire tracks and you will eventually . . .

Die. For you are miles and miles away from anything resembling life.

I stared down at the tracks. I started following them, my gait hesitant, unstable. My head was throbbing, my vision obscured, the need for water desperate. I could now feel the sun smoldering the top of my head.

But I forced myself to walk, to let the tracks be my guide. I had no choice. To stand still was to accept death.

My sense of balance began to leave me. I must have been walking a good quarter of an hour, each step a small agony, my mouth desiccated with dried vomit, my saliva in increasingly short supply, the back of my throat beginning to tighten. Is this how death by thirst begins? The esophagus slowly contracting due to the lack of hydration, eventually strangling you mercilessly?

My death.

I felt myself beginning to stumble.

My death.

Who would notice my passing? Who would care that I was no longer walking the planet? Would Paul—were he still alive—feel some sort of guilt? Beyond him? A few friends and work colleagues might mourn my absence. Otherwise . . . my forty years on this planet wiped clean. My footprint on life as insubstantial and impermanent as the marks that my sandals were now making in all this Saharan sand.

I stumbled, collapsing onto one knee. The sand singed it. But I didn't have the strength to somehow lift myself up. I so wanted to ask for some sort of celestial help, for God to save me. But how could I call out to an Almighty whose existence I still doubted? How could I cry out, *Don't forsake me . . . show me a way out of this wilderness, this hell.*

My other knee sank into the sand. I tried to swallow. I shut my eyes. My head felt near to implosion. This was it. Endgame. The final moments of my sorry little life. Throwing my head back I reopened my eyes and looked straight up at that fiery object that was about to kill me.

Thy kingdom come.

The sun burned right into me.

Thy will be done.

I pitched forward. Gone from this world.

No white light greeted me. No heavenly way station. No cognizance of anything. Just blackness. I remained there until . . .

Until I felt a hand touching me. And whispering to me in a language foreign to me. The whispering became louder, as if the voice was right up against my ear.

"*Salaam, salaam . . .*"

I opened one eye. Vision was clouded, indistinct.

"*Salaam, salaam . . .*"

I tried to open my mouth. It was seared closed. I had no energy. I had no will to do anything, let alone respond to the hand shoving my shoulder, her little voice louder:

"*Salaam, salaam . . .*"

Her little voice.

What I could discern from my one befogged eye was a small figure, in a robe, her face obscured by a flowing head scarf that covered everything but her eyes and mouth. From the sound of the voice emitting those words, and the lack of force behind the hand trying to rouse me, it was a young girl crouching beside me.

Was she some intermediary figure sent to guide me to the next afterlife passage?

But why was she speaking in Arabic?

"*Salaam, salaam . . .*"

Hello, hello.

And I knew what *es-hy* meant because one of the cleaners in Essaouira used it when trying to rouse the man always asleep behind the hotel front desk.

Wake up, wake up.

But I couldn't do anything beyond halfway open that one eye. And wish myself back into the darkness again.

Suddenly I felt liquid against my lips.

The little voice intoned, "*Ma'a . . . ma'a . . . shreb.*"

More liquid against my lips. I opened my mouth wide and let her pour in . . .

Ma'a . . . ma'a . . .

Water.

Within moments my throat opened again.

Water.

With it came the knowledge that I was still here. Prostrated in the Sahara. Alive, albeit barely. But still here. With water flowing into my mouth. And the little voice then saying:

"*Bellati . . . bellati . . .*"

Then I felt a cloth being put over my face.

And I was alone again.

Within moments, the darkness enveloped me once more.

Until I heard the little voice again. Accompanied by two other voices. Older. Male. Shouting to each other. Then to me.

"*Shreb . . . shreb.*"

Now someone pulled the cloth off my face and was holding up my head, while someone else was filling my mouth with water. At first I gagged it up. The man holding my head gripped me tightly as I heaved, then used something to clean my mouth, then gently pushed the bottle back between my lips. This time I could hold it down. And drank and drank and drank, the water surging through me. At another point I started choking on it again. The man cleaned me off, then made me drink more. He was not going to stop feeding me water until he was certain I was somewhat hydrated again. I have no idea how long this process took. What I do know is that the water brought back enough consciousness that I could see two men—both with hard, wizened faces—engaged in the act of saving my life. I also heard the one who seemed to be doing all the talking shouting orders. Then I was being lifted and put on a mattress. The smell of animal dung nearby. Then someone climbing in beside me. Opening one eye I saw the young girl who had found me now seated beside me, smiling shyly at me before covering my head again with a cloth, then taking my hand and holding it. I felt some movement in front of us, and the slope on which I had been placed righting itself out, and the crack of a whip and the bray of a donkey.

I have no idea how long I descended back into darkness. When I awoke I was in a very different place. As my eyes opened, I saw candles and two gas lanterns illuminating what seemed to be the walls of a tent. The fact that I could open both eyes was surprising. So too was the fact that there was an elderly woman—her face like a bas-relief, with only four or five teeth—gazing down at me, and exclaiming as I stared up at her:

"*Allahu Akbar!*"

I tried to sit up. I was too weak, too enervated, to do so. The elderly woman spoke quietly to me, gently pressing my head down on what seemed to be a cot of some sort. Another woman came over, far younger, pretty, all smiles.

"*Hamdilli-la!*"

She touched my face with her fingers. I flinched. Even the light pressure she'd placed on my cheeks touched off wild nerve endings of pain. She was immediately contrite, especially as the elderly woman shouted at her to do something. Moments later, some sort of balm or oil was being lightly rubbed into my face. It was then that I realized I was virtually naked from the waist down. Lain out on this bierdlike cot, my legs and thighs covered with assorted cloths; my crotch encased in a white bandage that was covered in now dried blood.

As soon as I saw the blood I was back in that truck, my assailant thrusting into me, tearing me apart.

I began to shudder. Immediately the young woman was holding me, whispering to me in Arabic, calming me, once even gesticulating to the bloodied bandage, then spouting out a long array of reassuring words, as if to say, *I know what happened, and it is horrible. But you will be better*.

Meanwhile the elderly woman approached us holding a mug of something steaming and strangely aromatic. She motioned for the young woman to help me up, and then encouraged me to drink this highly herbal, bittersweet brew. It had an immediate, soporific effect. Within moments I was asleep again.

When I woke it was daylight. I still felt desperately weak, concussed, with a ringing in my ear that wouldn't go away. I also urgently needed to pee. But as soon as I tried to sit up I lost my equilibrium, and fell back against the cot. At which point I saw the young girl who'd found me, until now asleep on a mattress in a corner of the tent, scramble up and run over to me. Though still half awake she smiled broadly at me. I managed a fogged smile back.

"*Parlez-vous français?*" I asked.

She shook her head, then raised her finger, telling me to wait, and ran outside. I could hear her shouting to someone. Within a few minutes she returned with the very pretty young woman whom I'd seen . . . When? . . . Was it yesterday? I only knew it was that same young woman when she removed her niqab once inside the tent.

"*Salaam Alaikum,*" the young woman said to me. The little girl was by her side, holding onto her djellaba.

"*Mema,*" she said.

"Your mother?" I asked. A baffled look from them both. I tried a more phonetic word: "Mama?"

That worked. They both smiled and nodded.

I asked the young woman if she spoke French. She seemed a little embarrassed by this and shook her head.

"No problem," I said, trying to smile back, but suddenly feeling woozy. The young woman told her daughter to run outside. My need to pee was now immense. From my French lessons with Soraya I remembered that she would occasionally drop an Arabic word into our conversation to help me negotiate the Essaouira streets. She taught me a few phrases.

"*Ayn al-hammam?*" Where is the toilet?

The young woman's beautiful face lit up at the sound of Arabic. She answered back in a stream of words, none of which I managed to follow. But she did indicate to me that I should wait a moment then raced over to the far side of the tent and returned with a long black djellaba. As she started helping me into it the elderly woman returned, shouting orders to the young woman, who explained that I needed the toilet (or, at least, I heard the word *al-hammam* in her onslaught of words).

With the elderly woman in charge of things, I was helped into the djellaba. The weakness I'd felt lying down on the cot was exacerbated when I tried to stand up. But the elderly woman had hands as rough and reinforced as a vise. She forced me up vertically. When I attempted to look down at the condition of my crotch and legs she had her hand under my chin and moved my gaze away, while the young woman and her daughter removed all the bandages and dressings. Then they helped me slowly into the djellaba, keeping me upright throughout. The elderly woman then held up a niqab and started explaining—with a lot of hand gestures—that I needed to put it on, as she pointed to the flap in the tent, letting me know that the *hammam* was outside. I nodded understanding. With the help of the young woman, I organized the niqab around my face. Within moments I felt like a horse with blinders. I was looking at the world from a narrow horizontal slit. I was very conscious that my legs felt raw and my face seemed somewhat out of place. Walking was an arduous business. All three women had to support me as I took my first tentative steps forward.

Once outside the tent the heat and the harshness of the light made me snap my eyes shut. From what I could take in, we were in some sort of encampment—several tents, shaded by a few sparse trees. Was this an oasis? All I could see were the meager trees, the tents, the sand beyond.

The women led me to a small tent. As the little girl opened the flap, the elderly woman told the others to halt for a moment. Disappearing inside, she returned moments later, tucking a mirror into the folds of her djellaba. That got my attention and heightened my sense of fear. She didn't want me to see myself.

When I motioned to the mirror the elderly woman became very maternal, shaking her finger at me as if I were a child who had been caught seeing something she shouldn't. Then she motioned for the mother and daughter to bring me inside, giving instructions along the way.

The toilet was a bucket, with a pail of water nearby. The young girl pulled up my djellaba. But when I attempted to inspect what I suspected was severe sun damage to my legs, her mother repeated the same procedure as the elderly woman. She placed her hand under my chin to keep my gaze upward.

They settled me on the bucket, and I let go. The stinging that accompanied the urination was frightful. The young woman gripped my shoulder, helping me through it. When I finished, the little girl went over to the pail, dipped a rag into the water, and handed it to me. I cleaned myself with it, noticing that when I touched my vulva it was instant agony. The mother saw this and gripped my shoulder, her hand gestures indicating that I needed to be patient, to not be afraid, to give it time.

They got me back to the tent. The elderly woman helped me off with the niqab and the djellaba. Once I was naked they laid me down again on the cot, the little girl keeping my gaze upward by standing over me and touching my chin with her index finger anytime my gaze wandered away from hers. I felt oils being rubbed into my legs and thighs, and some sort of balm being applied to my cheekbones and the areas around my eyes. Then I smelled that strange herbal beverage being brewed again—the one that ensured a deep slumber. They were knocking me out again. The elderly woman raised my head and put the mug beneath my lips, and I drank down the brew in several gulps. Moments later, as the darkness recaptured me, I wondered: Will I ever leave this place . . . and do I even care?

TWENTY-ONE

I SLOWLY BECAME cognizant of minutes, hours, days—whenever I was awake. Which wasn't very often, as my rehabilitation involved drinking that herbal dram twice a day and sleeping almost nine hours each time.

The curious thing about this tisane was that it was ferociously potent, but also left me feeling peculiarly clearheaded when I re-emerged into the world.

Not that I was in any way "clearheaded." On the contrary, the battering that my head and eardrum had received meant that I was suffering from some sort of serious concussion and inner ear damage. Only sometime later did I realize why the elderly woman who took charge of my recovery had insisted on having me knocked out. This was her way of keeping me sedated and allowing the brain to heal.

The elderly woman was named Maika. Her daughter—the beautiful young woman who had been at my side throughout—was Aicha. And the little girl who came upon me and saved my life . . . that was Naima.

I discovered their names on the day that Maika decided I was ready to come off the eighteen-hour sleep cure. Before then the herbal medicine had kept me so drugged that only the basic sort of information seeped through. But on the morning when Maika did not give me another dose of the tisane, a certain fog lifted by the early afternoon. Gesturing to myself I explained that my name was Robin.

"And your names?"

Naima understood immediately—and pointed to her grand-mother and mother, informing me of their names before pointing to herself and saying, in a wonderfully bold and forthright voice, "Naima!"

Her grandmother rolled her eyes, as if to indicate that such exuberance would be tolerated only for a certain number of years. But when I gave Naima the thumbs-up she mimicked the gesture, delighting in it, showing her mother and grandmother with amused pride how well she could do it. Though Aicha encouraged her, clapping and laughing as her daughter marched around, Maika called time on this little escapade when she gestured for me to stand up, indicating I should walk toward her, unaided. For the first time since Naima had found me in the desert I was being permitted to take steps without the three women being there to help me. I was uncertain at first, wondering if I could actually make it across the floor of the tent—which wasn't more than four feet—without stumbling. When I tried to rush at first, Maika held up her hands and indicated that slowness was key. I followed her advice, carefully putting one foot in front of the other, testing my balance, so conscious of my fragile state. But I did make it over to the far side of the tent, and was rewarded with applause from Aicha and Naima and a curt nod from Maika.

The tent. There was the cot on which I had spent so much time sleeping. There was a dirt floor. There was a gas lamp. Two buckets. One for washing, one for drinking water. There were two stools for guests to sit on. That had been my world for at least a week, maybe ten days, perhaps longer.

When I reached the other side I had to sit down on one of the little stools for a few moments, as I had started to feel woozy. Maika touched my head, made a flapping gesture with one hand, then held both up. I took this to mean that I was still not completely recovered. Then she got me to stand up and ordered Aicha and Naima to help me out of the simple white nightgown Aicha had brought to me several nights before and in which I had been recently sleeping. My legs and thighs were still wrapped in white cloths, prepared with oils that gave off an herbal, medicinal aroma. The bloodied bandage covering my vulva had been changed daily. Though the bleeding had long since stopped, Maika had insisted on using what seemed to be a salve on both lips and deep into the vagina itself, administering this on a twice-daily basis.

Maika decided the moment had arrived for me to inspect the damage done to me . . . or perhaps to see how its recovery was progressing. As they began to undress me, and to remove the cloths from my legs, I instinctively looked away. Whereas earlier on I had been curious, now that I was finding my way back to some sort of skewed norm, the last thing I wanted to contemplate was how badly disfigured I was. I knew that would raise the question of my life beyond this tent—and whether I could ever get back to it. Or, if the injuries were so severe, whether I would ever want to.

Maika—shrewd old bird that she was—worked out my fear on the spot. Being someone who clearly did not believe in the art of mollycoddling, she disappeared outside for a moment as Aicha and Naima undressed me, returning with a mirror in hand. She began to remove all the cloth bandages around my legs and thighs. Having been left for dead, half naked in the sun, meant my lower extremities had been exposed unprotected for several hours. So too my face. When the bandages were finally off—and I refused to look down—she gently but firmly forced my head south. My thighs had long red welts on them, some truly virulent, others already starting to fade. My legs also displayed several nasty burned blotches. But what was most alarming were the clusters of tiny off-white and red welts everywhere, up and down both legs and very much concentrated around my right thigh.

"What are these?" I said, pointing to these dozens of microblisters. Immediately Maika began to lecture me in a reassuring way, explaining (by tapping her thumb rapidly against her middle finger and then diving with it against my thigh) that while unconscious I had been attacked by some sort of insect. She tried in French: "*Des puces.*"

Fleas. Sand fleas. Which I had read about in one of the many Moroccan guides I'd devoured prior to my trip. They were prevalent in the desert. They came out at sunrise and were merciless whenever any sort of human or animal flesh was in their immediate vicinity. The density of blistering welts was shocking. Maika saw my distress. Through the usual elaborate pantomime of hand gestures, she indicated that, in time, they would diminish.

"And the burns," I said, pointing to the deep red welts, some still blistering. Maika motioned downward with her hands, as if to say, *They will lessen.* Then she touched my shoulder in a firm but comforting way, and said one word: "*Shaja'a.*"

When I looked baffled as to its meaning she tapped my heart, my head, and then forced my chin up with her index finger. The penny dropped.

"Courage?" I asked, trying to give it a French pronunciation. Aicha immediately nodded her head several times, saying something to Maika who also concurred. Waving her finger in my face, like a corrective Mother Superior, she repeated, "*Shaja'a.*"

Immediately Naima was imitating her grandmother, wagging her finger at me, saying several times over: "*Shaja'a, shaja'a, shaja'a,*" even causing her usually grim-faced grandmother to smile for a moment or so.

Maika now moved the mirror directly in front of my vulva, making me see that the lips were mostly healed. She then asked Aicha to bring over the tin of homemade salve with which she had been treating my ripped insides. Then, indicating that I should spread my legs a bit, she dipped her fingers into the salve and began to explore within me. The way these women treated me in such a kind, knowing, and direct way was both surprising and necessary for my still-fragile state of mind. The fact that they were involving Naima in all this—without, I'm certain, going into the reasons why I had been injured—

struck me as canny and demystifying. Here, the young girl watched while her grandmother prodded and probed within me. That I wasn't going insane with pain—just a small amount of discomfort—I took to be a positive sign. Withdrawing her fingers, Maika put her thumb up (she too had adopted this gesture). She made assorted hand movements to indicate that, in her expert opinion, all was repaired within.

Now it was time for the revelation I was most dreading: the state of my face. What's that old line about it being the mirror of the soul? If that was the truth, then my soul was still battered and scarred. As Maika presented me with the mirror I could see her daughter looking distinctly uneasy, as if expecting me to fall apart at first glimpse of the lingering impairments. I closed my eyes, took a deep steadying breath, and opened them.

What I first noticed were the sunburned red patches on my forehead and cheeks, and a plethora of small bites. All those hours with my face in the sand had allowed the fleas to run riot. Again Maika signaled that, in time, they would diminish. So too the blistering welt that covered my chin. But what shocked me even more was the deeply discolored bruise that covered my right cheek, spreading up to the blackened ring beneath my eye. My left ear was slightly cauliflowered from the punch that the little shit had landed on me, a punch that left me with an ongoing echo. And my lips were still severely chapped. I lowered the mirror. I tried to stifle a sob and failed. I was a disfigured freak show. Seeing my battered self brought back the monstrosity wreaked on me—and the insanity of the pursuit of a man whom I should have simply cast aside as soon as the nature of his treachery had become clear.

When I started to break down, Aicha immediately put her arms around me, letting me bury my head in her shoulder. But Maika wouldn't stand for such a show of self-pity. Literally pulling me away from her daughter, she bore down on me with that bony exclamation point of a finger, almost shouting at me as she gave me a fast and furious lecture in a language completely beyond my comprehension, but which, by this point, I could somehow understand. Following her broad gestures I intuited the central gist of her sermon:

"Don't you dare feel sorry for yourself. What has happened has happened. You have survived. You are not dead. You will be able to walk. You will be able to have babies. Your face will heal. So too your legs. There may be scars, but they will not be disfiguring ones. We all have scars. But now your duty to yourself is to get back to your life when you are ready. But no more self-pity. That is not allowed here. I will not accept it. Understand?"

Maika's vehemence was so forthright (and loud) that Naima hid in her mother's skirts. I stood there with my head lowered, fighting back tears, feeling very much like a censured child, while also knowing that everything she had just told me made complete sense, that I had no choice but to somehow get beyond the horror of it all.

But Maika also made it clear that there was no way I was able to travel yet. She held up ten fingers, then four, indicating that she might consider letting me go in two weeks. That's when I had—courtesy of my hands and gestures—the conversation that I had been dreading. I explained that the men who had raped me had also robbed me. I had no money, nothing. Maika shrugged as if to say, *Why do you need money here? You are our guest.*

I acted out and said at the same time, "But I feel bad about taking your hospitality and giving you nothing for it."

Maika understood immediately what I was saying and got even more vehement, telling me (or, at least, this is what I was thinking she was telling me), "There is absolutely no need to consider money. You are our guest. We will look after you. We will continue to help you get better. When you are ready we will figure out a way for you to get home."

I thanked her profusely. She held up her hand, as if to indicate *You're welcome . . . now stop.* Then she ordered me back on the cot, and got Aicha and Naima to begin readministering the cold compresses and the oils and balms to my injuries and scars.

The next ten days marked a time when, on so many levels, a certain clarity descended upon me. I was still being given the soporific tisane every evening around eight o'clock. Though she was not knocking me out twice a day, Maika had upped the nightly dose so that I was sleeping twelve hours a night. I understood that this was her ongoing induced-coma cure for head injuries. I was largely restricted to my little tent and had nothing in the way of reading material or writing paper and pen to fill up my waking hours (let alone any of those modern distractions—the internet, nine-hundred-channel television, a humble radio). For the most part I was being kept separate from the life of this encampment. So I found myself very much thrown back onto my own thoughts, my own reflections. What's that line from Pascal about all of man's problems owing to the fact that he cannot abide sitting alone by himself in a room? As the concussive fog began to lift, as I became ambulatory again, as the terrible shock in which I had been living transformed into a functional numbness, I found myself alone for nine hours a day with little to do except try to sort through the inventory of my life.

Maika—having taken charge of my recovery—was also insisting that I begin to eat normally again. I had lost a shocking amount of weight since the attack. One day I tried on the white linen pants which I'd been wearing when the two men grabbed me, and which Aicha had laundered for me. I wasn't more than 120 pounds when I arrived in Morocco. Even trying to tie the drawstring as tightly as possible, the pants still all but fell off me. All that time in a semicomatose state, existing on small amounts of bread and couscous and vegetables, had resulted in my losing many pounds, and Aicha—who was slightly wide-hipped and clearly liked her food—indicated that I needed to be fattened up.

It was now August. The heat outside was maniacal. I was finally able to leave my tent on my own to use the toilet. I was also invited to join the family for group meals. Maika made it clear that, as their guest, I needed to abide by their customs. Wearing the niqab when outside was obligatory, and I was certainly not going to express my feminist distaste for this practice. These people had saved my life. They had taken me in. They had nursed me back to health. They were demanding not a penny for all the immense kindness and generosity shown to me. How could I question their request?

Once inside, however, I was allowed to be as unmasked as all the other women in this little village.

I was, I came to understand, among Berbers. Jabalah—Aicha's husband, Naima's father—was one of the men who'd returned with Naima to rescue me. I so wanted to ask her what she had been doing out in the desert alone. I could only surmise that she was allowed to roam the Sahara, and that I hadn't seen the oasis—which, I came to discover, was behind a stone wall that, when seen from any distance in the desert, blended in with the dusty horizon. Jabalah was somewhat older than Aicha—his heavily grooved face and bad teeth made him look like he was in his early fifties, though I sensed that the hardness of life here had aged him considerably. From the freshness of her outlook and the flawlessness of her skin I guessed that Aicha was, at most, in her early thirties. Jabalah wasn't a great conversationalist— but it turned out he did speak a smattering of French, enough for the two of us to understand each other. He explained that the Berbers weren't a "tribe," but rather, a people; theirs was a pan-Maghrebian population, with Berbers in Algeria, Tunisia, even Egypt. But the greatest concentration of Berbers was here in Morocco, specifically south of Ouarzazate.

"Here you are in our country," he explained. "We may be officially governed by Rabat, by the king . . . but we see this as our own kingdom."

The other man in the encampment was Immeldine. He was Maika's husband and, like his wife, showed the wear and tear of a life lived under a fierce Saharan sun. He was a compulsive smoker—he always had a cigarette on the go. In the two weeks during which I ate with the family nightly, he spoke very little. I often wondered if he considered me an imposition. I discovered that he and Jabalah farmed a bit in the oasis, growing herbs and a few vegetables that they sold at a market once a month in Tata. They also raised a few goats, which provided milk. The women had a loom on which they made simple rugs of traditional design. And small lace items. And knitted skullcaps of the type worn by Jabalah and Immeldine.

"They do very good work," Jabalah told me in his basic French. "Every month we have a friend—Aatif—he drives a van to Marrakesh. He takes everything our women make and sells them to a dealer. Last month he returned with two thousand dirhams for us! Most money ever! A fortune!"

I thought of my husband, spending the equivalent of two hundred and thirty dollars on a bottle of wine he could hardly afford. Or how I took a potential corporate client out to dinner a few weeks before I'd left for Morocco and insisted on picking up the three-hundred-dollar tab at Buffalo's best steakhouse. And how two thousand dirhams (at best) was keeping these five people alive for a month. From what Jabalah had indicated, this had been more than twice what they were used to. I could see Aicha and Naima beaming with pride as he said this. With Maika, they were the labor force at the loom.

It was exactly that—an old-style loom, located beneath a sheet of canvas that had been attached to four poles embedded in the ground. I wandered over one morning to see the women at work. The niqab and the djellaba in which I was dressed was like being encased in a sauna. Watching Maika work the loom, barking orders, stitching with fiendish precision, I couldn't help but wonder how she managed this in the long garment and severe mask that hid all but her eyes. Aicha favored lighter materials in cream or off-white—but she too was imprisoned in fabrics that covered every inch of her body. Only Naima—still too young to wear the niqab—got away with a head scarf and djellaba. Like her mother and grandmother, she never seemed to succumb to the ocean of perspiration that overtook me every time I stepped outside, hidden from worldly view, my eyes and hands the only parts of my anatomy visible.

When I offered to help, Maika tried to teach me some basic techniques. But the heat overcame me after a few minutes and I was ordered inside.

Water was an issue out here. There was, I discovered, a small water hole within the oasis—and an old-style pump garnered this essential fluid of survival up from the ground. It was rationed by Maika. I was handed an old plastic liter bottle four times a day—and had to make do with that. Which also meant that spending much time outdoors before nightfall was tricky. I was given a large pail of water twice a day to wash myself. There was a bucket and a rag in the toilet tent to clean myself.

I discovered that Aicha was homeschooling Naima. Every afternoon they spent several hours on reading and writing and basic mathematics. One morning, Naima came into my tent hugely excited, as her father and grandfather had returned from selling their produce at the market and Papa had brought her back a large book. *Tintin*. In Arabic. She showed me its large glossy cover, a little battered in places. I too had read Hergé's books when I was Naima's age, and tried to explain to her that, yes, I knew all about the intrepid Belgian journalist Tintin and his faithful fox terrier, Snowy. I asked Naima to read to me. She climbed up on my lap and proceeded to read me the entire book, even sometimes acting out the voices of Tintin, his dog, and the highly egoistic Captain Haddock. Having Naima on my lap, listening to her wondrous singsong voice, feeling the way she snuggled in against me, made me long for a child like never before—and feel the pain and sadness that this was never to be for me, especially with all that had happened in the past few weeks.

I was so engrossed in listening to Naima read to me that I didn't notice Aicha enter the tent, watching us with a smile. When I caught sight of her I was just a little thrown, thinking that she might not like me having her daughter in my lap. Seeing my concern she indicated that this was hardly a problem—and in fact said something to Naima that made her return to her reading.

Later that day, when she returned alone to change my bandages, she touched my engagement and wedding rings on my finger and made a hugging gesture, followed by a touch to her head. It was her way of posing the question *Where is your husband?* In reply I made an outward flapping motion with my hands, saying, "He's gone." She looked at me with great pity. Then touching my stomach and making a curving motion with her hand, she indicated pregnancy. I shook my head. "I want a baby. But . . ."

Even though she might not have understood English, she clearly grasped what I was saying. Her reply was "Inshallah." Allah willing.

The days passed slowly. I was still unsteady both physically and psychically, but the languidness of my current existence didn't bother me. Outside of the nightly meals with the family, and the arrival of breakfast and lunch in the tent, and Maika and Aicha spending a good hour on my wounds each day, the highlight of the day was the hour or so I had every late afternoon with Naima. After a morning spent helping her mother and grandmother on the loom, and then several hours of tutoring by her mother, she would race over to my tent and we would hang out. Early on, Naima said to me, while pointing to her mouth, "English."

In reply I said, while pointing to mine, "*Arabia*," which, I knew from Essaouira, was the Arabic word for *Arabic*.

We spent the next ten days or so teaching each other words, expressions, numbers. I learned how to count to ten in Arabic. Naima got very proficient at English pronouns: *I, me, you, he, she, it*. I picked up phrases like *Shokran min fadlik* (Thank you for dinner), *Min fir shreb* (I need water), and *Nti sahabti* (You are my friend). Naima delighted in being able to do the ABCs as far as *M*—with my promise that we would add two more letters a day.

When the hour was up, Aicha would arrive, Naima would give me a kiss goodbye, and I would have another two hours alone until dinner. I wish I could report that, during the many hours a day I was alone with nothing but my thoughts, I achieved some sort of resolution about the state of my life; resolving to somehow follow Maika's directive and move forward. But what happened frequently was a panic attack on a major level. A desperate sense of falling into a vortex. The agonizing replay of everything that went down in the desert. The barbarous image of my assailant after I had fought back. My sense of horror at what I had been forced to perpetrate. Had I truly killed someone? The accompanying terror of discovering that ability within me.

I knew I was still in shock. Whenever I thought of the world outside this nowhere place to which I had been transported . . . I knew I couldn't stay here indefinitely. But returning to life beyond this oasis seemed out of reach.

I could see that, though Jabalah could communicate with me in the basic French we both shared, he kept his distance from me. He never indicated that I was a burden to him or his family. But I was a woman. Except for the evening meal, I was being kept out of his life. I accepted this polite isolation, just as I accepted the niqab when outside. He spoke little to me during dinner . . . though I must admit that was probably due to the small television, which captured everyone's attention including my own. It had a wire antenna that brought in one Moroccan channel. The fact that our encampment had no electricity meant the television was powered by a car battery that they charged using jumper cables from the small ancient truck on which they brought their produce to market.

On the eleventh or so day of my convalescence I came in for dinner to discover the five members of the family huddled around the glowing set, watching the evening news. Out of nowhere a photograph appeared behind the news anchor. A photograph of a Western woman. As the broadcast was in Arabic, as the reception wasn't exactly brilliant, it took me a moment to realize that the photo on-screen was of . . .

But Naima beat me there. Craning her neck toward me, she pointed to the screen and mouthed one of the English pronouns I'd taught her. "You."

TWENTY-TWO

THE NEWS REPORT: a mug shot of me. A mug shot of Paul. Footage of a crime scene in the desert, with police tape around an area showing scorched earth. And then—oh, God, this was beyond bad—Police Inspector Moufad from Essaouira, giving a news conference, holding up the same photograph of me, shaking it vehemently, as if to say, *Here is our prime suspect.*

You.

Me. Now wanted by the police.

Me. Now revealed to these Good Samaritans as someone who was on the run. Wanted not just for the disappearance of her husband, but the death of another man in the desert.

My mind began to race. How were they tying the burned corpse in the desert to me? Did the goon who'd assisted in my rape drive back to Tata? In his panic did he concoct a story that he fed to the police? He was worried about the welfare of his friend who'd met an American woman the night before and invited her on a romantic drive at dawn into the Sahara in her rented car. The discovery by the cops of his pal's charred body—and no sign of me—would lead them to presume that I had turned on him, things got out of hand, and I immolated his body before driving off into . . .

No, that's ridiculous. You arrived by bus. You didn't rent a car in Tata. The man who'd escorted me from the bus depot in my search for Paul would remember, under police questioning, that the two little shits had been loitering by the stairs as we headed up to the hotel. So how, why, were they bringing the desert corpse into Paul's disappearance . . . and the fact that I too had vanished? What incriminated me even further was that I had fled virtual house arrest in Essaouira, much to the fury of Inspector Moufad. On television he was stabbing my photograph with his index finger, as if I were a public health hazard or an escaped war criminal. Apparently they had some sort of evidence to link me to the incinerated body in the Sahara.

Another possibility: the goon got back to Tata, tried to work all day, was in a state of escalating panic, as he had my backpack hidden away somewhere, and then suddenly came up with an ingenious solution to his problem. He drove back out to the desert, tossed my backpack out near the corpse, returned to Tata, reported his friend missing, said he had met an American woman . . . and didn't fill in any further details. How we ended up in that spot in the Sahara . . . would that matter when compared to the smoking-gun evidence of my backpack near the corpse? It would directly link me to the events that culminated with a young man being torched alive.

"What are they saying?" I asked Jabalah. He waved away my question, keeping his attention riveted on the screen. This was worrying. So were the even more hardened looks of Maika and her husband. Aicha, meanwhile, was betraying all emotions, appearing both shocked and distressed. When she actually put her hands over Naima's ears, so she could hear nothing more of the broadcast, I sensed trouble.

The news item ended. There was an immediate heated exchange between Immeldine and Jabalah. When Aicha tried to interject something, she was shouted down both by her husband and her mother. Naima began to cry.

"Please tell me what they said," I asked Jabalah.

Out of nowhere Immeldine barked something at me so fierce that Naima hid herself behind her mother.

Then Jabalah said to me, "You go. We bring the food to you."

"If I could just explain . . ."

"Go!"

I wrapped my face in the niqab and crossed the few steps back into my tent. Once inside the fear turned into a crazed panic attack. I found myself pacing manically around the tiny space, all sorts of extreme scenarios playing out, including Jabalah and Immeldine deciding that they had to turn me over to the police, and the cops picking me up, and my being thrown into a squalid cell in which I would be repeatedly abused by the guards. And Inspector Moufad from Essaouira conducting an all-night interrogation designed to break me, and my signing a confession that, yes, I had killed Paul in a fit of rage on the beach and dumped his body in the Atlantic. And yes, I had agreed to go on an all-night joyride with those two monsters, and when the little shit got a bit fresh with me I lashed out and . . .

Stop this insanity, I hissed at myself. But my brain was on overload. In moments of lucidity I told myself that all the repressed mental trauma of the rape was now finally coming to the surface. But those nanoseconds of clarity were soon subsumed by full-scale sobbing. All those terrible childhood moments of our family being evicted from a series of houses and apartments came flooding back. With it the realization: *It's happening again. I am being forced out from a place of safety, a family who had given me more love and acceptance and a sense of shelter than I'd ever had. Now this new family is about to reject me, turning me out into a malevolent world that will engulf me as soon as I am beyond this little oasis.*

My sobs became convulsive, so out of control that I felt as if I was about to become unhinged. I was literally crashing into corners of the tent, endangering its stability. Suddenly Maika and Aicha rushed in. Aicha had me in her arms in a moment, firmly settling me down on the cot, cradling me, whispering consoling words that had no meaning for me except that they were soothing. She held me as I buried my head in her shoulder and fell apart. Maika kept her distance as the grief came cascading forth. Perhaps she knew—given what I had been put through—that this was long overdue. Perhaps she also understood my fear of the world beyond. Whatever the reason, she let me cry myself into exhaustion. When I briefly subsided she stepped in, helped Aicha to undress me and get me into the white nightshirt I'd been sleeping in. Laying me down on the cot, she rubbed a different kind of balm (it smelled of patchouli and chamomile) across my forehead and into my temples, then massaged the same substance deep into my feet before sitting me up and making me drink an extralarge dosage of the nightly tisane.

Just before I surrendered to the night I grasped Maika and Aicha's hands and said, *"Shokran."*

I came to and was shocked to discover it was almost 11:00 a.m. When I got off the cot and changed out of the nightshirt and back into the djellaba and niqab, I noticed a certain physical stability that had been absent for so long. Then I started considering again what might happen if Jabalah turned me over to the cops and the shakiness began to reassert itself. But I managed to get dressed, wrap the niqab around my face, and make it to the toilet without succumbing to another panic attack.

When I returned I found Jabalah standing outside. "I would like to speak to you," he said.

"Of course." I motioned that we should go inside. He shook his head. I instantly regretted my faux pas, as there was absolutely no way he would enter a tent alone with a woman who wasn't his wife, mother, or daughter. He pointed to the tent where we ate dinner. I followed him over, removing my niqab once inside. He bent down in front of a little gas stove and illuminated it, boiling a small kettle of water, then opening a tin and throwing a large handful of mint into a pot, filling it with hot water, and waiting several minutes for it to steep. Nothing was said during the tea making. After pouring us out two glasses, he handed me one and nodded gravely as I thanked him. He motioned for me to sit down on one of the two stools. Then, in his hesitant French, he said, "I know what happened to you. I am very sorry for what happened to you. I do not want to judge you. But . . .

the police are looking for you. If they find you here, they will accuse us of hiding you. This will be bad for us. So you have to leave."

I acknowledged his decision with a nod of my head.

"I know all your money and papers were stolen."

"I don't know what I should do next," I told him. "I was so unwell after the attack that I hadn't really thought about how I would proceed once I left here. All I know is that I will never forget for the rest of my life what you and your family have shown me."

He scrunched up his lips.

"The man who drives the rugs and things that the women make . . . he will be here late this afternoon. I will ask him to take him with you. He will be going to Marrakesh, but usually makes many stops along the way."

"You have to tell him I am wanted by the police."

"Of course I will tell him that. He is my friend. Go back to your tent now. Think how you will get money and papers—because you will need both. I will have my wife fetch you when the driver arrives. His name is Aatif."

With a final nod he left the tent.

A few minutes later, back in the tiny space I was going to be vacating in just a few hours, I tried thinking through a solution to my rather large problem. I had no easy answers. The accountant in me reasserted herself for an hour or so, weighing up all the checks and balances available to me. They were virtually nonexistent. Say I found a phone and called Morton in the US, and told him he needed to wire money to me. Say that my disappearance had been picked up by international news services, and was also being monitored on the internet (no doubt, a small item—but a husband and a wife separately missing in a North African country, with overtones of foul play, would cause interest). Even if Morton wired the funds there I would have to show ID to collect them at a bank or some outpost of Thomas Cook, and I had no ID. Then there was the little problem of the previous night's television news bulletin. It is a strange experience, watching a missing persons report in which you are not only the individual the police are trying to track down, but also the chief suspect as well. Remembering Inspector Moufad stabbing that photograph of me, I was in no doubt that if I simply went and turned myself in I would be burying myself alive.

So wiring money from overseas was out of the question, especially as the Moroccan version of the FBI and Interpol were probably now monitoring any potential emails or wire transfers in the name of Robin Danvers. As they had broadcast my mug shot last night on Moroccan television, there was a good chance that it was going to be a regular feature on future news broadcasts until I was apprehended. Would the Moroccan police also put a Wanted poster up in post offices and banks and, indeed, places where foreigners would collect money? Were they sophisticated enough in their surveillance techniques to have flagged any emails sent or received from rdanvers@buffalomoney.com? When Paul had first proposed this trip I quietly googled "Moroccan terrorism" just to reassure myself that the security situation was as good as Paul had said. Bar a terrible bombing of a Marrakesh tourist café in 2005, and certain warnings about travel in the extreme south, all the reports I read noted that the country was a highly stable one. But like every other place on which the specter of terrorism had fallen, Morocco had a very sophisticated intelligence and antiterrorism apparatus at work—which surely meant the monitoring of telecommunications and the internet. The fact that a national manhunt was under way for me . . . I was absolutely convinced that the moment I sent or received an email, the alarm bells would go off, and the geographic location from which it was read or dispatched would be flagged. Yes, I could borrow somebody's cell phone to call the States, but if I couldn't physically collect the money without photo ID, why would I risk a call? Especially if the Moroccan Sûreté and the US Embassy here had alerted the NSA and the feds to my disappearance, and they too were monitoring calls to my office, my home, my professional colleagues.

As I kept pondering the lack of options open to me, I kept twisting the two rings on my left index finger. Which is when the penny dropped. When Paul proposed to me three years ago—it was during a romantic weekend in Manhattan—he brought me to Tiffany's to choose an engagement ring and wedding band. He'd just sold a few lithographs and insisted that I choose a very beautiful single diamond ring and white gold wedding band, which cost together thirteen thousand dollars. When I worried out loud that this was far too much money to be spending on rings he made an amused comment to the very gracious, very formal saleswoman about "my wife-to-be understanding the bottom line far more than I do." I could see the saleswoman smiling politely and taking in Paul's long gray hair and his leather jacket and black jeans, and telling him the two rings were an elegant choice, and him slapping down his credit card, and me thinking how wonderfully romantic and impetuous my man was, and how I hoped he'd have the funds to clear the credit card debt the following month.

But now . . . now I had on my left index finger the one negotiable piece of currency on me. Surely, if this driver was heading to Marrakesh, there were several serious jewelers there who would be willing to buy my rings. I wouldn't raise anything close to their original value, but I would, at the very least, come out with around thirty, forty thousand dirhams. Maybe I could then find another driver to get me up to Casablanca. I would barge in on Ben Hassan. I would wave the money in his corrupt face and get him to issue me one of his false passports. I would then find another driver to get me to Tangier and the boat to Spain. Once I was on the other side of the Mediterranean—and out of the shadow of the Moroccan Sûreté—then I could call Morton and a lawyer and see about getting the US Embassy in Madrid to issue me a new passport to get me home.

So there it was. A plan, of sorts. Getting from here to Marrakesh might not be the simplest of journeys, but I didn't want to consider any of that until I met the driver and sized him up, and found out his price. But first . . .

There was a terrible moment when Aicha and Naima paid me a midmorning visit, bringing me an early lunch of pita and couscous. Naima ran to me and threw her arms around my legs and started to sob, putting together three of the English words I'd taught her: "You no go."

When I crouched down beside her she buried her head in my shoulder. I looked up and saw Aicha also in tears. I held Naima for several moments before loosening myself from her embrace. Keeping my arms around her, I said, "I don't want to go. I don't want to leave you. But I must go home."

I touched my head and my heart. "You will always be here and here."

Naima smiled sadly as she too touched her head and heart. "Here and here," she repeated, pronouncing each word beautifully. Now I felt tears. Aicha also choked back a sob. I reached beneath my djellaba and unfastened the silver chain around my neck. Bringing it out, I showed Naima the sterling silver horseshoe that had been a gift to me from my great friend Ruth only nine months ago on a weekend visit to Brooklyn, just after Paul and I decided to try to have a child. When I announced this to Ruth, she couldn't have been more thrilled for me. She returned that evening with this gift—a small, elegant luck charm. No charm has much luck against an operation guaranteed to render pregnancy impossible. But maybe, just maybe, it brought me the good fortune to survive the ordeal in the desert and land me here.

I put the charm around Naima's neck, explaining that my best friend had given it to me, and since we were best friends—I signaled this by pointing to the two of us and then touching my heart—I wanted her to have it. Naima had the horseshoe in her little fingers, looking at it with wonderment. When her grandmother entered the tent a few moments later, holding some of my clothes in her hands, Naima ran over to her and proudly showed off her gift. Maika smiled gravely at her granddaughter. Approaching me she handed me my freshly laundered pants and underwear. She also brought a fresh djellaba and a niqab, indicating that I was to keep them as a gift . . . and through more of her gestures, also letting it be known that I might need them en route to Marrakesh. Then she did something completely uncharacteristic. Out of nowhere she embraced me. Taking me by both shoulders, she touched one of her leathery hands to my face and said, *"Allah ybarek feek wal 'ayyam al-kadima."*

It was a phrase I had heard regularly in Morocco. But here it was a benediction, a maternal prayer: "May Allah bestow his blessings on you . . ."

Outside I heard the sound of a vehicle pulling up into the oasis. We all stiffened as the engine idled, then cut. Because we all knew: my driver had arrived.

TWENTY-THREE

HIS NAME WAS Aatif. At first sight he did not inspire confidence. A short man, with a small but pronounced paunch, thinning hair, a handful of brown teeth left in his mouth, world-weary eyes. I judged him around my age, but the victim of a hardscrabble life. His vehicle was a Citroën 4x4, at least fifteen years old, once white, now scuffed and dented, with two front seats and a reasonable cargo area in the back. It looked like it was being run into the ground.

What struck me immediately about Aatif was his immense shyness. Unlike Immeldine, he wasn't taciturn or distanced. Nor did he exude the sort of detached authority that Jabalah displayed. Rather he seemed almost ill at ease around others. An innocent. And an unsure, timid one at that.

There was a rather strange, awkward moment when Jabalah called me over. I removed the niqab. I could see Aatif flinch. Was this due to the fact that he wasn't expecting a Western woman (but surely Jabalah had explained I was American), or owing to my still-battered face? I couldn't tell. Without thinking, I extended my hand in greeting. He looked horrified, as if I had exposed a breast to him. When he took my hand in return his was cold and clammy.

One positive detail: Aatif spoke French. A somewhat simple French, but with more fluency than Jabalah. When we started to talk it was clear that we could make ourselves understand each other.

Jabalah explained that he had informed Aatif about the circumstances that landed me in the oasis. He also understood that I had been robbed of everything, that I had no papers or money, and that I would settle up with him when we reached Marrakesh.

"Do you understand that the police are looking for me?" I asked him.

He nodded.

"Does this worry you?" I asked.

He shrugged.

"As long as you are willing to take the risk," I said. "I don't want to put you in any jeopardy."

Another shrug. Then he said, "Two thousand dirhams to take you to Marrakesh. *D'accord?*"

It seemed a very reasonable price, considering the potential hazard for him.

"That's fine—but I am going to need to sell some jewelry in Marrakesh to be able to pay you. I promise that I will pay you."

A shrug, then, *"D'accord."*

"How long do you think it will take to get to Marrakesh?"

He thought about this for a moment. "Three days," he said.

"Three days! But it's only maybe six hours by car from Ouarzazate, and Ouarzazate is perhaps seven hours from here."

"I have many goods to pick up before I go to the souk in Marrakesh and deliver them to the merchant who will buy them. Many stops to make, many people dependent on me. Like your friends here."

"But . . . if we are going to be three days on the road, where will we sleep? I have no money for hotels or food."

"I have no money for hotels either. I have two bedrolls in the back. We will sleep by the van at night."

I didn't like the sound of this at all. I gave Jabalah a telling look, asking with my eyes if I could trust this man. Jabalah gave me a quick nod. Aatif noticed this visual exchange. Looking half away from me he said, "You will be safe."

"All right," I said.

With that, Jabalah and Immeldine spent the next ten minutes fill-

ing up a portion of the cargo area of the Citroën with rugs, lace napkins, lace doilies, and skullcaps. I could see Jabalah negotiating with
Aatif, clearly hopeful that he could return in ten days with a good sum
for them. From the way he was indicating his pockets and the sparse
garden that was tended beneath one of the trees, I sensed that money
here was urgently needed. How I wished I could have reached into my
pocket and handed them five thousand dirhams right now.

"When I get to Marrakesh and sell my ring," I told Jabalah, holding up my hand, "I will ask Aatif to bring some money back for you."

Immediately Jabalah waved his hands. "We took you in because
you were in need," he said. "There is no need to repay us."

"I cannot begin to thank you . . ."

Again Jabalah waved his hands, but then thought about it for a
moment and made the smallest of bows in my direction. Naima was
standing near him. He touched the horseshoe pendant, which she was
now proudly wearing around her neck, and bowed again toward me.

Aatif closed the cargo door of his vehicle. It was time. Aicha
started to weep again and held me for several moments. Maika also
seemed to be fighting tears but was absolutely determined not to
cry. As she squeezed my shoulder I noticed she had made a fist with
her right hand and was, I sensed, demonstrably making it clear that
she approved of the way I'd hit back at the men who'd attacked
me Naima glanced up at her father for approval before going over
to me. I kneeled down. She kissed me with great delicacy on both
cheeks. Intriguingly there were no tears, none of the sense of impend-
ing loss that we both shared alone with the other women in the tent
that had been my refuge. Here, in front of her father and grandfather
and a visiting man, she was conscious that she was under a paternal
gaze and needed to act with restraint. After a moment she went running back to her father, looking up at him for approval—which he
gave with another of his characteristic nods.

Immeldine's goodbye was also a nod. So too was Jabalah's.

"Okay?" Aatif asked. Now it was my turn to nod. Moments later, the niqab veiling my face once again, I was inside the cab of the vehicle. The three women gathered by my window as Aatif slammed the driver's door behind him, placed the key in the ignition, put the van into gear. With a lurch we began to drive off. My eyes met Naima's. She raised a hand and tried to look brave. Behind the niqab I began to weep. The daughter I always wanted. The daughter I would never have. The wondrous little girl whom I would never see again.

Aatif drove the hundred or so yards to the edge of the oasis. I looked back once more at the small plot of quasiarable land in the great sandy vacuum. Their entire world. My entire world for a spell. And now I was going to have to negotiate the world beyond.

With a bump we crossed through the stone archway that separated the oasis from the sand. Aatif pulled out a lever and said, "Four-by-four. We will need it now."

We started traversing the desert, following a track that was discernable by the grooves of past tires. After a minute I craned my neck and tried to spy the oasis. But it had vanished, its pale wall melding invisibly into the bleached horizon.

The cab of the vehicle was a mess—torn seats, trash strewn on the floor, the windscreen streaked with sand and dead flies, the ashtray brimming. And the heat was ferocious. I rolled down my window. This was a serious error. As the vehicle gained momentum, sand blew in everywhere. Immediately Aatif slowed down.

"You do not have to wear the niqab here," he said.

"Are you sure of that?"

"It is fine with me. Especially as I do not have air-conditioning. So if you also want to get out of the djellaba . . ."

Immediately I was posttraumatic defensive.

"What do you mean by that?" I asked.

He looked startled.

"I meant no offense," he said. "I just thought you might be more comfortable in your own clothes."

"Where am I going to change out here?"

He stopped the vehicle. He got out. He went to the back and pulled out the bag that contained my laundered clothes, the garments I'd been found in all those weeks ago. He brought it over to the passenger door.

"You can get out and change behind the van. I will take a walk and have a smoke. When you are dressed call me."

He said this all in his quiet, shy, matter-of-fact way.

"Thank you," I said, getting out of the van.

Aatif walked out quite a distance in the desert, lighting up a cigarette. He was dressed in a loose shirt, loose brown-colored trousers, sandals, a skullcap on his head. I watched him walk for around a minute, then stop and not turn around once in my direction. Quickly I pulled off the djellaba, the relief of being free of its entombing weight countered by the immediate exposure of all my still-scarred flesh to the Saharan sun. Within a moment I had slipped on the linen pants and simple white shirt I had bought in Casablanca, then shouted that I was ready. Aatif turned and walked back slowly toward me. At that instant I began to feel shaky. For the first time since I had woken up violated and battered and near death, I was back within the Sahara's terrifying enormity. I felt as if it was about to swallow me whole. I suddenly slumped against the door of the jeep, a full-scale panic attack blindsiding me again. At which point Aatif—walking toward me—saw what was happening and came running. When he reached me, out of breath and drenched in sweat, I was clinging on to the door handle as if it were a life preserver in treacherous seas.

"Can I help you?" he asked.

I nodded.

"May I take your arm?"

I nodded again.

He put one hand on the hand that was gripping the door handle. The other supported my right arm.

"Let go, please," he said. "I will get you inside."

I did as ordered, all but collapsing against him. He may have appeared short and squat, but when it came to disengaging me from the van door and settling me into the passenger seat, he had surprising, forceful strength.

Once I was safely inside he went to the cargo area, fished something out, and returned with a bottle of water, still dripping wet, making me wonder if he had some sort of basic cooler in the back. He handed me the bottle.

"Drink."

I drank half the liter before handing back it to him. He took several judicious sips, then gave it back to me.

"You need to keep drinking water."

"Thank you," I said. "Thank you so much. I am sorry I snapped at you before. I had a terrible experience out here."

"I know. Jabalah told me. Terrible. I am so very sorry for you. But . . ."

He turned the ignition on. The Citroën reassuringly fired back into life. He put it into gear. We set off. And he finished the sentence.

"I will get you to Marrakesh."

I fell back against the seat, agitation and anguish still coursing through me. Aatif lit up a cigarette and said nothing as we drove for almost an hour along the desert track, the sun beginning to dip, bathing the Sahara in a blue-hour glow. How I wanted to be dazzled and exalted by its frightening beauty. But all I could do was try to stop myself from sinking into a chasm in which all the recent horrors loomed large.

To his credit Aatif said not a word during the hour that we barreled across the sands. He just smoked one cigarette after another, occasionally glancing over at me to make certain I wasn't going into meltdown mode again. I appreciated him giving me the space to somehow push the nightmare away . . . for an hour or two, anyway.

That's the problem with the worst sort of trauma. You can will it elsewhere. You can tell yourself you will somehow "manage" it. But you also begin to realize very quickly that you will be living with it for the rest of your life. Even if, somewhere down the line, you might come to terms with it, reach some sort of accommodation with its abhorrence, it will be with you forever. Your world has been inexorably changed.

With a bump we left the sand and returned to a paved road. Seeing a road sign ahead for Tata, I shuddered.

"Do not worry," Aatif said. "We are not going there. But I am going to pull over in a moment and you are going to have to change back into the djellaba and niqab."

"Why?"

"Because two, three kilometers ahead of us, there is a police checkpoint."

"How do you know that?"

"I passed through it a few hours ago."

He slowed down the van. We were on an empty stretch of the road that, if followed, would bring us to Ouarzazate. He pulled over, telling me that, thanks to nightfall, I could change outside without being seen. But if a van came down the road, headlights blazing . . .

"I'll be fast," I said, and was out of the van and grabbing my backpack, changing into the djellaba and niqab in under a minute. As soon as I got back in the van a truck came up behind, its high beams illuminating us.

"You did well," Aatif said as the truck passed us by.

"What happens if the police demand to see my papers?" I asked.

He reached over into the glove compartment and drew out a Moroccan identity card of a woman around my age—attractive in a severe sort of way. But mug shots—my own included—always seem to capture life's cramped disappointments in grainy, institutional close-up.

"Is that your wife?" I asked.

"My sister." he said.

"Doesn't she need her papers?"

"Not anymore," he said. "She's dead."

"She was so young."

"Cancer doesn't care how young or old you are."

He lit another cigarette.

"Anyway, when the police stop us, I will tell them that you are my sister."

"And if they ask me questions?"

"They won't. Because you are behind the niqab, and they would have to think us terrorists to ask you to remove your veil. I drive these roads frequently. I can't say I know all the policemen, or that they know me—"

"But if you are from around here—"

"I live in a village many hours from Ouarzazate. If we were going through that *département* I wouldn't dream of passing you off as my sister. Everyone knew her. Everyone knows she's dead. But here . . . no problem."

"But say they still question me?"

"Say nothing, I will tell them you are deaf and dumb."

Five minutes later we were at the checkpoint. Two uniformed cops had their squad car half blocking the road. They greeted Aatif. They asked to see identification. He handed over the two sets of papers. One of the cops shined a flashlight in on me. I kept my eyes—barely visible through the slit of the niqab—fixed on the road ahead. The beam of the light snapped off after a moment. They asked Aatif to step outside the van. The next thing I heard he was answering their many questions, then opening the cargo door and letting them search within. The mounting terror I felt during these nervy minutes was immense. If the flashlight beam was turned on me again I knew I would go under. And reveal very quickly that I was the woman all of Morocco was looking for.

But within moments Aatif was back in the van, the officer was wishing him a good night, and we were driving off.

A fresh cigarette lit, Aatif exhaled a huge cloud of smoke, his relief tangible. Finally he said, "The first checkpoint behind us."

TWENTY-FOUR

WE SLEPT ON the outskirts of a small village, around thirty minutes down the road from Tata. It was called Bou Tazart, a nowhere place, off a semipaved track from the main thoroughfare on which we were traveling. It was en route to the first stop Aatif would need to make early tomorrow morning. I didn't want to stay anywhere near Tata, so Aatif suggested we camp outside the village.

"I know a little area that is quiet and where no one will see us," he said.

This area turned out to be a small plot of arable ground, shaded by a single meager tree. A few cows and goats grazed nearby. As before, Aatif wanted to reassure me of our sleeping arrangements. He took out the two bedrolls and lay one down on either side of the van. The bedroll was a thin cotton mattress, two light sheets, and some netting that he suggested I put over my face when I slept in case the sand fleas came out early. When I'd been in the oasis sand fleas had been an ongoing problem during the daylight hours. At night they vanished into the ether. But come sunrise they were out on the attack again. Which is why, as Aatif explained, it was essential to get to bed early and rise just before sunup.

"You don't need an alarm clock out here," he said. "The sand fleas provide that."

With light fading he moved to his own bedroll, positioned himself in what I presume was the direction toward Mecca, prostrated himself on his knees, and with his head touching the mattress, spent several moments saying his evening prayers. When finished he opened the back of the van and retrieved a small Styrofoam box, out of which came a small gas burner, a pot, two plates, two forks—and made us a simple dinner of bread and couscous with a few carrots. Over dinner—which we had on my side of the van—I asked him about himself. He told me he came from a village called M'hamid, around four or five hours from where we were by car. It was at the end of a paved road that started at Ouarzazate, then passed through an important Berber town called Zagora, before dead-ending at his village, beyond which was the Sahara. He also considered himself very much a Berber and therefore had decidedly mixed feelings about the government in Rabat.

"I deal with the police politely," he said. "I deal with the functionaries who regulate our *département*. But I also like being able to sneak around them, not to let them run me. I am not alone in this sentiment. Which is one of the reasons why I said yes to getting you to Marrakesh. If you are on the run from them—"

"They think I did harm to my husband," I said.

"That is not my business, whether you did or didn't."

"I promise you, I didn't."

"If you say that I believe you."

"But what you need to also understand . . ."

Out came the entire story in one exhalation. I kept it short, and didn't get into the reason why Paul vanished—except to say that I had discovered a betrayal on his part. I also explained about Inspector Moufad in Essaouira who was determined to frame me at all costs. And the friend of my husband in Casablanca who had cheated him. And then the events in Tata and beyond.

Aatif listened in silence. When I finished he lit one cigarette off the other.

"That policeman in Essaouira . . . I've known people who have been persecuted by men like that. They decide you are guilty. They will run you to the ground and will change evidence and everything else to ensure they can win the conviction. They are not Berbers."

I then explained my plan—to get to Marrakesh and sell these rings and get to Casablanca and use the cash to bribe that shady former friend of my husband to give me a false passport and get me out of the country.

"I want to be direct with you," I said. "I don't want to hide anything. I want you to understand exactly all the risks here."

"I saw your face on television before I came out to the oasis," he said. "So when Jabalah told me it was you I was to bring to Marrakesh . . ."

A pause, then the smallest of smiles crossed his face.

"Now that I know we need to outsmart that police inspector . . . well, a game is a game, *n'est-ce pas?*"

The night sky was above us. It was astonishing. In the oasis I was being put to bed most nights at sunset. Here I got my first proper glimpse of the celestial show on display. The clarity in the desert was dazzling. Such density of constellations. Such a sense of heavenly potentiality. Even deep in the country, just ten miles from Buffalo, on a perfectly clear night, you still never could discern even thirty percent of what was apparent tonight. It was like discovering an entirely new component to the universe. And the realization that so much of this light might already be extinguished. My dad always said that looking up at a constellation underscored your insignificance. But tonight, seeing such immense radiance—in the light of recent events—was galvanizing. I looked to the stars and the stars told me: since nothing in the great cosmic scheme of things is important, everything that defines you is absolutely important. What else do you have but your life, your story?

"It is an amazing sky," I told Aatif.

"Nice, yes," he said, sounding less than overwhelmed.

"I wish I could believe in heaven, in some sort of eternal paradise. I thought about that when I saw you praying earlier."

"It is important to believe in paradise. Especially when life is hard."

"Faith is a complex thing."

He thought about that for a moment. "No, faith is simple. And good."

"Do you have children?"

I saw him tense.

"Sorry, have I asked the wrong question?"

He lit another cigarette. After several long drags he asked me if I would like tea—and told me that Maika had given him several days' supply of the tisane that had repeatedly knocked me out. This was most welcome news, as I'd wondered how well I'd sleep out here.

"A mug of that tea would be wonderful."

He went off to fetch water from a big plastic container he also had in the back, then boiled it in a pot on top of the stove. Knowing how quickly the tea induced sleep, I told Aatif I was going to change into my nightshirt before drinking it down. Immediately he stood up and walked a good distance away. I retrieved the bag and quickly got into the freshly laundered nightshirt, then hiked away from Aatif, lifted up my nightdress, and baptised the sand. How strange to think that everything I had once taken for granted—like an actual toilet or the internet or even a phone—had been out of my reach for so long. And how I had adapted—because I had no choice but to do so.

As soon as I finished the mug of tea I wished Aatif good night. Crawling in between the two sheets, I placed the netting over my head and stared up at the luminescent heavens above. Just before sleep overtook me, I glanced over at Aatif. He had walked out into the middle of the nearby unpaved road to smoke another cigarette. He too was looking up into the great lustrous unknown. I saw him wipe his eyes. Was he crying?

But then the tea did its magic. The world vanished for a spell.

Aatif was right. The sand fleas were an automatic outdoor desert alarm clock. With first light came their pernicious arrival. At least ten of the wretched creatures were dancing on the net covering my face. It was just before 7:00. Aatif was already awake, making tea. He wanly waved hello.

"Sleep well?" I asked.

"Okay."

"Where are we headed today?"

"We go back to the main road. I have stops in several villages. You will need to wear the djellaba and the niqab. There may be roadblocks."

I did as I was instructed. I changed into them. By the time we hit the road I was already awash in sweat.

"First stop is Tissint—about an hour from here," Aatif said.

We headed back to the main road. The sun seemed even more ferocious this morning. When I pulled down the visor to try to mitigate the blinding effects of the sun, Aatif reached over and opened the glove compartment, pulling out a pair of sunglasses in a plastic red frame.

"You can use these," he said, handing them to me.

"Thank you so much."

But when I pulled off the niqab to put them on, Aatif hissed at me, "Get the niqab on now!"

I looked up and saw why. We'd hit a bend in the road. Right up in front of us was a police roadblock. Fortunately there was a big truck in front of us, but I saw one of the cops glancing in our direction just as I got the niqab back in place. Did he see me? If so, was this the beginning of the end?

The police were being very thorough with the truck in front of us, demanding to see the driver's papers, opening up the rear of his vehicle, searching inside.

"If he asks you a question, say nothing," Aatif whispered to me.

"If he makes me take off the niqab?"

"Say nothing."

The inspection of the previous vehicle completed, we pulled up to the police car that had been parked across the road to allow only one vehicle through in each direction. Taped to one of the rear passenger windows was a poster in Arabic and French with my mug shot adorning it. The French words needed no translation:

Personne disparue—Recherchée par la police.

Aatif also saw the poster and gripped the steering wheel tightly as the young policeman—he couldn't have been more than twenty-two—stuck his head into the van and demanded identity papers. Aatif had them at hand. Meanwhile his older colleague was at the rear of the vehicle, opening it up and pulling out all the neatly stacked rugs and lace goods. The young cop seemed supervigilant, asking considerable questions, demanding the registration papers—which Aatif supplied—then also being thrown questions from the other officer about the goods in the back. Aatif answered these politely. But when the young cop got tetchy, Aatif's voice also rose and got just a little defensive. Then the older cop sidled up to my window and began to ask me some questions in Arabic. The fear coursing within me was massive. It was a good thing he couldn't see how much I was sweating right now. But I kept my eyes fixed on the road ahead and, as instructed by Aatif, said nothing. The older officer now got cross with me, reaching in and tapping me on the arm. I turned to face him, but remained silent. Aatif now got heated, saying something angrily to the older officer. Whatever he told him, the cop backed away from me. Aatif continued on, gesturing to the back of the van, tapping himself on the chest, pointing to me. The young officer exchanged a glance with his older colleague, then they both disappeared over to the squad car with our papers. I quickly glanced at Aatif. He refused to look at me but was gripping the steering wheel, trying to remain calm. He looked over at the police car again and saw the poster with my photo on it. Now he closed his eyes, clearly regretting that I was here with him. I wanted to say something apologetic, but knew I had to stay silent. After an exceedingly long amount of time—and I could see the older officer on a police radio, reading in the ID card details (would the centralized system have noted that the woman whose name and personal details I had co-opted was actually dead?)—he finished his call and came marching toward us.

But instead of ordering me out of the van and demasking me, the officer handed back the two cards to Aatif. With a dismissive flick of the wrist, he informed him that we were free to go.

Aatif muttered thanks, put the van into gear, and we drove off.

Five minutes later, with the checkpoint far behind us and the road empty of cars, I turned to Aatif and said, "I am smothering in here. I have to take this off."

Aatif said nothing. But from the look on his face I could see he was not pleased. Pulling off the niqab I caught sight of myself in the rearview mirror. My hair drenched, my face beet-red, terror in my eyes. Aatif handed me the bottle of water.

"Finish it," he said. "You need it. We'll get more in the next village."

"I am so sorry."

"For what? You did exactly what I told you to do. The police . . . they were just being difficult. When the officer asked about you I explained that you were mentally disabled, and could not understand language. The cop challenged me, saying he needed proof. I told him to pull off your niqab and interrogate you—but that he would face serious consequences afterward. He got scared and backed off. But you saw the posters. These roadblocks are normal, but there are not usually so many. The police are looking for you. That makes the main roads difficult. There will be no further checkpoints between here and Tazenakht. All the villages where I pick up goods are between here and Tazenakht. We will have to find a back route for tomorrow, away from the main roads."

"We got lucky with your sister's ID."

"We only buried her two weeks ago," he said. "They probably haven't registered her death as yet on their computers in Rabat."

"Only two weeks ago? That's terrible. Shouldn't you be having some time off?"

"I have to work. My sister has two children. Their father is in the

Royal Moroccan Army and stationed in the Western Sahara, near Mauritania. He sends back little money. My mother is looking after them, but she is a widow and elderly. So I have to work."

"Listen, that was a close call back there. I don't want you to get into trouble, lose your livelihood."

"I said I would get you to Marrakesh. I will get you to Marrakesh."

Ten minutes later we pulled into the village of Tissint. A row of low-lying buildings, dusty, fly-festooned. A butcher shop with bleeding carcasses of meat, a few cafés, a mechanic, idle young men everywhere, the stench of rotting sewage amidst the blast-furnace heat. Aatif's client was a large cheery woman who lived in a tiny lean-to on the outskirts of the village. She insisted on serving us tea. I could hear Aatif offering an explanation about me, using, I presumed, the mentally deficient excuse. She smiled sheepishly at me as she helped Aatif load up the intricately decorated velvet bedspreads and cushion covers that she'd made. Before we left she clutched his right hand with two of her own and seemed to be making a plea to Aatif.

When we were back in the van and heading to the next village I asked him what her entreaty was all about.

"She was telling me that her husband has been unwell. They have two young children. Because he is in the hospital—and isn't expected to live—they are dependent on the sales of the things she makes, which I will sell to my merchant in Marrakesh."

"Do you have to negotiate hard with your merchant on behalf of your clients?"

"Of course. He is a businessman and he wants to buy at as low a price as possible."

"So you fight hard on their behalf?"

"It is on my behalf too. I get thirty-five percent of all their sales. The more I get for my clients the more I get for me."

"How much did that woman back there ask you to get for her?"

"She told me she needs fifteen hundred dirhams. That will get her and her two children through this month. Which means I need to sell her items for around two thousand dirhams. This is not easy, as the merchant tells me the market is very bad right now. Not as many tourists as before—even though there is little trouble in Morocco. Still I do argue hard for them."

"Can you make a living out of this?"

He seemed a little taken aback by the directness of my question. But then he said, "I can support myself. Trying to support a family . . ."

"Do you have a family? A wife or children of your own?"

"Not yet. But . . . I have met a woman I like very much. Hafeza. She is a bit younger than me. Twenty-eight. A seamstress. Very kind. A good heart. And she would like many children, like me. She's also from my village—which means I know her family. I know that several men before me asked for her hand. But she is very choosy! So, alas, is her father. He has told me that, though Hafeza wishes to be my wife, I cannot have her hand unless I can buy a house."

"He wants you to buy a whole house outright?"

"Not outright—but he wants me to make . . . how do you say it? . . . a payment up front?"

"A down payment?"

"That's right."

"And how much would that cost?"

"I've found a little place. Four rooms. Simple, but enough space. The price . . . one hundred thousand dirhams. I have saved over the last year maybe ten thousand dirhams. But the bank wants me to put down forty thousand dirhams before they give me a loan."

"And Hafeza's father is adamant?"

"Until I can move us into that house she will not be my wife."

"That's a little rigid of him."

"I wish I could make more money faster. When I am back in my village I repair bicycles, a second trade. But it maybe brings in three, four hundred dirhams a month."

Forty thousand dirhams. That was just under five thousand dollars. Which meant the house itself cost around twelve thousand four hundred dollars. Less than a very basic car back home. The sum standing between Aatif and his dream of a wife, a family.

"You've never been married?" I asked.

He shook his head.

"That's surprising," I said.

"Why?"

"You are an extremely nice and honorable man—and there are few of that species out there."

His reaction to this was a touching mixture of embarrassment and pride.

"You shouldn't tell me such things," he finally said.

"Why not?"

"It will give me a big head," he said, all smiles.

He lit up a cigarette. The smile quickly faded.

"Ten years ago," he said, "I proposed marriage to another woman from my village. Amina. She said yes. Then a man came through one day from Ouarzazate. A baker named Abdul. He owns three bakeries there. He meets Amina. One week later he returns and sees her father and proposes marriage. Of course the father says yes. Because he has money and I have none."

"I can see why trying to find that forty thousand dirhams is so important."

"I will never get it. Her father has given me a year to do it, no more."

"And the bank won't loan you more?"

"The bank . . . I have a cousin who works at the bank in Zagora, which is why I am getting the loan. But I make so little . . ."

From the look on his face I could see that Aatif wanted to get off this subject quickly, that even speaking about all this was foreign . . . especially with a woman.

We stopped at a village called Melimna, where an elderly woman loaded up the van with several dozen white linen tablecloths and napkins. She also insisted on cooking us a wonderful chicken tagine.

I got to use a proper flush toilet for the first time in weeks. There were additional stops in Foum Zhguid and Alougoum—tiny, sand-struck villages, with a few local shops, a café or two, and many young and old men loitering without much intent. At each stop Aatif was greeted in such a warm and welcoming manner that it was clear that the women for whom he delivered their goods to market regarded him as an honest broker, someone they could trust. Again I could see everyone's interest in the woman traveling with him, someone who clearly needed a lot of water behind her niqab. At every stop I entreated him to score us an additional two liters, as I was seriously dehydrating encased in all those clothes. Aatif was most adept at explaining away my presence, and also telling everyone that a defect at birth had robbed me of speech or reason.

By the time we left Alougoum on a sandy half-paved side road, it was late afternoon and I could no longer stand being imprisoned in this strict Islamic dress.

"Surely we can risk me getting out of these clothes for a while," I said.

Aatif thought about this for a moment.

"We are going to pull into Tazenakht—which is a town, not a vil-lage—by nightfall. I know a place beyond there where we can sleep for the night. Until then . . . this road is not very traveled, because it is not paved. The police rarely set up checkpoints here. So, if you must change out of those clothes . . ."

He pulled over and went for another smoke as I got out of the niqab and the djellaba, slipping back into the linen pants and shirt that were still sweat-stained from yesterday, but were a complete liberation after the confinement in which I had been living for the past ten hours.

Back in the van Aatif had a question for me: "You have no chil-dren. Is this your choice?"

I paused before replying, explaining that I had discovered that my first husband was not someone with whom I could have had children, and that my second husband professed to want them, but then changed his mind. I was certain that Aatif would think I was clearly damaged goods, having been with two men who didn't want children with me. But what he said instead surprised and disarmed me: "So you've had bad luck with men."

"Or maybe my choice of men—"

"—was not worthy of you."

I was about to tell him that he was being far too kind—and to thank him for such a lovely comment—when, out of nowhere, we both heard the sound of a motorcycle approaching us from behind. Aatif immediately tensed, as did I.

"Pull over," I said urgently, thinking I could jump out and hide behind the vehicle until the person commandeering the bike passed us by.

"Too late," Aatif answered, as the motorcycle sidled right up by our vehicle in the process of passing us by. As it drew level I saw that there were two passengers—both with helmets, both in jeans and denim shirts, both Caucasian. Up close I saw it was a man and woman. The woman smiled as they drove by us. But seeing me she poked the guy—who was driving the motorcycle—and said something urgently to him.

"Accelerate," I told Aatif.

But the bike had stopped directly in front of us, the man and woman had dismounted, and were pulling off their helmets. They both appeared young, superfit, well heeled. They waved at us to stop. Aatif looked at me, wondering what he should do.

"I'll deal with this," I said.

Aatif slowed the van down. I got out. The couple approached me.

"*Parlez-vous français?*" the man asked in an accent that made it clear he was definitely French.

I nodded.

"Are you all right?" the woman now asked.

"Yes, fine. Why?"

"Aren't you the American woman everyone's been looking for?"

"We've seen your picture everywhere," the man said.

I had a decision to make—deny this truth and arouse their suspicion. Or . . .

"Yes, I'm that woman. And yes, this man is driving me to the nearest police station to let everyone know I am all right."

"What happened?"

"That's a long story."

"Are you sure you're all right? We could come with you."

"That's very kind . . . but no need."

I could see them glancing regularly at Aatif, trying to size up if he was dangerous or holding me against my will.

"I would feel better if we accompanied you to Tazenakht," the man said.

"Again, my thanks for such a generous offer. But I can assure you—I am not in any danger here. On the contrary, this man has gotten me out of a great deal of danger."

They exchanged a glance with each other. I could sense that they were wondering if I was in a reasonable mental state, especially as I was clearly trying not to act nervous.

"I can talk to your driver if you like," the man said.

It was time to end this.

"Sir, your kindness is noted. But . . ."

"Will you agree to meet us at the police station in Tazenakht?"

Damn these Good Samaritans. Damn myself for taking off the niqab. I had to think fast.

"I'll tell you what: I'm sure there's a café on the main drag of the town. Say I met you there in an hour? Then you'll have the reassurance that I am all right."

"We should follow them," the woman said in rapid-fire French that was not meant for my ears, but which I still discerned.

"And I have to call Martin in Paris in thirty minutes. So we'll go to the police station, tell them that we've seen her en route to Tazenakht, and put it in their hands."

"By all means tell the police," I said. "The thing is, as I will be seeing them as soon as I pull into town . . ."

The couple exchanged a look, and another telling glance at Aatif.

"Okay," the man finally said. "See you in Tazenakht."

"The café's on the main drag," I said, having no idea if this was true. "We can have a beer."

The man checked his watch. He clearly had a schedule to meet. Looking hesitant about leaving me they walked back to their motorcycle, donned their helmets, shot off into the horizon.

As soon as they were out of sight I rushed back to the van, climbing back in, Aatif immediately discerning that the conversation with the French couple didn't go brilliantly.

"We have to get off this road," I said. "Now."

TWENTY-FIVE

AATIF THOUGHT FAST. If we headed south back to the main road at Foum Zguid, we would hit something of a dead end, as the road east was nonexistent there. He knew this because his own village, M'hamid, was about thirty miles in a straight line from here. But the desert track passed through serious sand dunes that were treacherous. Vehicles got bogged down in them—and at this time of year, with temperatures around 110 degrees Fahrenheit, a horrible death was not out of the question.

"Anyway, even if there was a direct road to M'hamid, it would be very hard to bring you to my village."

"Understood."

"But if we go west for Foum Zguid, the road brings us very far south. Then we would have to head north through Agadir. Big tourist town. Many police."

His solution: he had one more pickup of goods to make in the tiny village of Asaka, a few miles inland from here down a narrow desert track. He had a client there whom he was planning to visit in two weeks' time. But she always had goods on hand. "I'll tell her that I have a little extra room in my van. There is another track near to her house. We can sleep there tonight."

"Won't the police perhaps come looking for us there?"

"They will have been told by the French tourists that you were in a van with a Moroccan. If we are lucky they won't mention the make of the van. But there are many vehicles like this in Morocco. You will have to go back behind the niqab. It's the only way we can make it to Marrakesh. If we leave early tomorrow, the police in Tazenakht will probably figure we headed south. There may still be a roadblock, but my hope is if they see me driving a woman in a niqab it will fool them again."

Stepping behind the van I changed back into the niqab and djellaba. Then, with light receding, we drove slightly north before turning right down a desert track. Unlike some of the other unpaved roads on which I had traveled, this one was a treacherous uneven surface featuring many ruts and the sandy equivalent of potholes. We bumped along, our progress torturously slow. The landscape here was a return to the absolute remoteness of the oasis, only there was not the same sense of wide, open space. Rather, it felt as if we were traveling toward some cul-de-sac, from which there was no way out. There was a narrow barrenness to this route; a sense of heading to the end of the line.

"I can see why the cops wouldn't want to follow us out here," I said.

"Which is why we need to stay here until sunrise."

It took us almost an hour to reach the village of Asaka and its four houses. The one at which we stopped had a man in his fifties with a young wife and four children, all of whom seemed to be under the age of six. The wife was still pretty, but clearly beaten down by life. She barked at her children. She barked at her husband, who sat on a stool, smoking and looking quietly disconsolate. She barked at Aatif, berating him for something while getting her two oldest kids to load up his van with the djellabas she had made. When her husband offered tea, Aatif declined, pointing to the road and making some excuse about needing to get north soon.

As soon as Asaka was behind us, Aatif steered the vehicle down a track so narrow, so hemmed in by sand on either side, that it was just wide enough for our one vehicle. We bumped along for around a quarter of an hour until we reached a small clearing by which there was a pump. We parked and set up camp for the night.

"The water, it is not good for drinking," Aatif said as he got one of the jerry cans of water out of the rear, a cargo area now so jammed with goods that there was little room for the spare cans of gas and water that he wisely carried with him. He used the clean water to make tea and couscous. I asked him if I could wash at the pump. He told me that I shouldn't use more than four or five pulls, as water was so scarce out here that we had to be honorable and not use much of it. Especially as the next person coming along might be in desperate need.

He put the couscous on to boil, then walked off. I stripped down and pumped the water. The first dispatch of liquid was revoltingly brown. The second a little more neutral. The third looked relatively clear. I had no soap, no toothbrush (I hadn't brushed my teeth since that last night in Tata), no basin. Still, the feel of water against my bare skin was restorative. I got into my nightdress, my skin still wet.

"That woman, she is always complaining, always bitter," Aatif said as we ate. "But that is not my Hafeza. She is far too kind to turn into such an angry woman."

Trying to raise four kids in the middle of nowhere, and in poverty, would make anyone bitter.

Instead I said, "I am happy for you that you have found someone nice."

"I will be happy if I can give her father what he wants. You have dowries in America?"

"No, not exactly. But trust me, when it comes to the end of love in the United States, it's all about money."

"Money is not everything," he said. "But without it . . ."

"What else would you like, besides a house for you and Hafeza?"

"A cell phone. It would be very useful for my business. I had one for a while, but it was expensive. Then I had to start saving for a house. So I could not afford the cell phone anymore. Beyond that, a new television maybe. Mine is fifteen years old, and the picture is very bad. And, of course, Hafeza will want to furnish the house."

The hope in that man's face was so touching. I feared for him if he could not find the money necessary to win her hand. Not that he would fall apart, but that he would know further disappointment.

Night fell. Aatif prepared my evening dosage of knockout tea. I drank it down. I opened my bedroll, but found the ground near the van far too uneven. So I told Aatif I was going to move behind a small dune that was just eight or so feet from the vehicle. He said that, with a full load in the van, we could cut short the trip by two days and get to Marrakesh late tomorrow evening, but only if we left before dawn. I told him that was fine by me. The sooner I could get to Marrakesh the sooner I could sell my jewelry.

I wished Aatif a good night, carrying the bedroll behind the low dune, rolling it out, crawling between the sheets, placing the mosquito net over my head, staring up at the stars, thinking, Tomorrow I will be in a city. Will I ever see a night sky so vast as this one again?

Sleep arrived quickly. But then, out of nowhere, I heard voices. Angry, threatening voices. I stirred awake as they grew louder. It was still night, 4:12 a.m. Aatif was being spoken to by some man who sounded gruff and unpleasant. I crawled out of my bedroll and crept to the edge of the dune. Poking my head around it I saw four men surrounding Aatif. Two of them were holding him while the other two were emptying his van of all its goods. When Aatif pleaded with the men, one of them came over and slapped him hard across the face. I ducked back behind the dune. Manically digging a hole in the sand, I pulled off my two rings and my father's Rolex and buried them, finding a stick on the ground to mark the spot. Then I sat very still, terrified of what could happen next.

More voices, more entreaties from Aatif. The sound of a punch and Aatif crying. Then vehicle doors opening and slamming, Aatif issuing one last plea, a car engine rumbling into life, wheels moving along sand. I waited a good five minutes just to be certain that those men weren't coming back. Then I dug up my rings and watch and dashed over. I found Aatif lying in the sand, holding his stomach, crying loudly.

"Thieves, thieves . . . they took everything."

I tried to put my arms around him in order to help him up, but he recoiled at my touch.

"Are you okay?" I asked.

"They slapped my face, they punched me in the stomach, they took everything out of the van, they found my wallet and took the four hundred dirhams I had there. The only money I had . . ."

He got himself to his knees, put his face in his hands, and started to weep. "I have no luck," he sobbed. "No luck at all. Life . . . it is too hard."

I reached out and dared to put a steadying hand on his shoulder. "You're alive," I said. "And there is always a solution."

"A solution? A solution? I'm ruined."

"You're not ruined."

"Those thieves . . . they have wiped me out. All the goods in the van, gone. I have no money to get us to Marrakesh—"

"You filled the tank today. And you also filled the two jerry cans you keep in the back. Did they steal those?"

"I don't know."

I scrambled over to the van, praying to some almighty force in that brilliantly lit sky above to let me find those two full jerry cans in the cargo area. I threw open the back door. Bingo! They were there, along with two full cans of water.

"We've got gas," I said, returning to Aatif. "Two full jerry cans, plus the near-full tank still in the van. Will that be enough to get us to Marrakesh?"

He nodded.

"Well, that's one good piece of news. How much were the goods you were transporting worth?"

He did some quick calculations in his head.

"If I was to get them the best price . . . maybe eight thousand dirhams."

"And you would be getting thirty-five percent of the total price, which means that you would have needed to sell them all for twelve thousand dirhams."

Aatif looked at me, astonished. "How are you so good with numbers?"

"It's my job. Anyway, if we get on the road for Marrakesh now, how long will it take us to drive there?"

"Maybe ten, twelve hours."

"Do you know a good jeweler there?"

"I know people who know people who know jewelers."

"So here's the solution. We give those bastards a half hour to get out of the area, then we'll get on the road. I'll wear the niqab all the way to Marrakesh to get us through the checkpoints. When we get to the city we'll find a jeweler who will give me the price I want, and I will give you the two thousand dirhams I owe you for driving me . . . and twelve thousand as well for the goods stolen from you. So all your clients who are so dependent on you will get paid. And you'll get paid too."

"I can't accept this," he said.

"You're going to accept this. Because it was my stupidity that led me to take off the niqab on the road to Tazenakht and let the French couple see me. Which led us down the back path. Which led you to being robbed. So, yes, you have no choice but to accept the money. Are we clear about that?"

He stifled a sob, rubbing his eyes with his hardened hands. "I don't deserve such kindness."

"Yes you do. We all deserve kindness. And bad luck, *monsieur*, can change."

He stood up, taking several deep steadying breaths.

"*Thé à la menthe?*" he finally asked.

"Moroccan whisky would be very good right now," I said, my adrenaline only beginning to subside now after that chilling wake-up call—and the terrifying thought that history might have repeated itself had I not been hidden behind that dune. I felt a shudder coming on and hugged myself. Aatif saw this attack of nerves—and did something unexpected. He reached out and put a steadying hand on my shoulder.

"Okay, *le whisky marocain*," he said, trying to smile. "And then . . . Marrakesh."

TWENTY-SİX

IT TOOK US almost thirteen hours to reach Marrakesh, a hellish drive. When Aatif first got behind the wheel after the robbery, his hands began to shake. I took hold of his right arm until his sobs subsided. I could see him wanting to push these instances of his vulnerability out of the picture. We bumped along the sand crevasses for almost an hour. The relief at eventually feeling paved road beneath our wheels was massive. So too was the fact that there was no police blockade awaiting us. When we started to head north up the thoroughfare to Tazenakht, I asked Aatif if he was going to report the robbery to the police.

"To do that would be to invite even more trouble. There aren't many roaming thieves in Morocco, though I'd always been warned never to take back roads. But if I let the police know what happened, even if they apprehended these men, then what? They'll do a year in jail. Then they'll come out, looking for me. It's not worth the risk."

"I feel very guilty about making you take that back road."

"Don't be. I've slept near that village several times and never had any trouble. We were unlucky."

We got lucky, however, in Tazenakht. Yes, there was a police roadblock, but we got through it in minutes. The cops looked at our identity papers, glanced at the empty cargo area, asked a few questions, and sent us on our way.

Four hours of nonstop desert followed. We stopped once to funnel one of the jerry cans of gas into the vehicle. We drank a little water and ate what pita bread we had left. I ducked behind an abandoned house to relieve myself. We were both very conscious of the fact that we had no money whatsoever and simply had to get to Marrakesh by tonight.

At the checkpoint before Ouarzazate, the young police officer started asking me a few questions. Aatif had to do his spiel about my mental challenges. Even so, the cop continued to pose direct queries to me. I stared blankly ahead, willing the interrogation to be over. When I didn't answer, he got impatient until Aatif again explained that I was deaf. The young cop seemed suspicious and called over an older officer, motioning to my niqab, clearly indicating that he wanted me to remove it. The older cop sidled over and had a chat with Aatif. Whatever he said to him seemed to do the trick, as the older cop motioned to his young colleague that there was no need to further continue the interrogation. He waved us on.

As soon as we were clear of the checkpoint I could see Aatif gripping the wheel and trying to forestall another panic attack.

"That was close," I said.

He nodded agreement and noted that, with any luck, the next checkpoint would be in Marrakesh.

As we negotiated the avenue Muhammed V in Ouarzazate, our eyes told two different stories. I kept scanning the streets in some vain hope that Paul would suddenly materialize on the spot where he was last sighted. Aatif, meanwhile, seemed pained to be in this city. He spent much of our time on the main boulevard with his eyes focused downward. Just as I was still desperate to lay eyes on my missing spouse, so he was desperate not to make visual contact with the woman who broke his heart and ran off with the bakery czar of Ouarzazate.

"The road ahead . . . it is complicated," Aatif said, snapping me back to the present. "Are you afraid of heights?"

An hour or so later I certainly was, as we had gained almost six thousand feet in altitude and were driving on a single-lane switch-back road, hugging the edge of the Atlas Mountains.

Every hundred yards or so there was a blind corner, behind which lurked assorted obstacles: an oncoming truck, a shepherd with a flock of about two dozen goats, and a young Moroccan daredevil on a motorcycle who nearly plowed into us and shouted abuse before speeding off along another hairpin turn.

But what made this drive across a mountain pass called the Tizi n'Tichka even more terrifying was the fact that one small mistake would send us into vertiginous free fall. On the passenger side, I had a dizzying view of the deep ravine that began around a foot away from our vehicle's tires on the right side. There was no wall, no guardrail, nothing to stop you from going over the side.

"In winter, with snow, it is terrible," Aatif said.

In high summer, it was still something of a roller coaster ride, each turn presenting a new navigational challenge, or some potential oncoming onslaught. Aatif smoked nonstop during the most taxing stages of the drive, humming to himself at the same time. As his humming increased, I was transported back to a drive with my father when I was fifteen and we were moving from Chicago to Minneapolis. We got caught in a huge blizzard on the interstate. Despite the fact that the visibility was zero, Dad kept driving at sixty miles per hour and hummed to himself throughout ("Fly Me to the Moon," of all things), ignoring my mother's entreaties to slow down. Aatif wasn't driving dangerously. But he did tell me that, even though he drove this road twice a month, it never ceased to spook him.

"There is at least one terrible accident here every week," he said.

"But we're not going to be this week's tragedy."

"Inshallah."

There was an awful moment when, passing through a mountain village, a young boy chased a ball into the road, right in the path of our vehicle. Aatif slammed on the brakes. We skidded frighteningly toward the precipice on which the village rested. I screamed and had my hands over my eyes as Aatif somehow managed to stop us just before our front wheels went over. The boy ran off, frightened after almost being run over and almost sending us over the edge into the valley below (a fall of at least one thousand feet). There was a moment of terrible silence. Aatif did what he always did when stressed: he gripped the steering wheel tightly for several moments, trying to regain his equilibrium. Then he lit up a cigarette.

After several inhalations of smoke, he backed up the vehicle and got us back on our way.

"That was nearly the fatal accident of the week," he said.

Happily the road began to improve as we lost altitude. The woozy verticality—and the potential for grievous bodily harm—diminished as we started heading through flatter ground. Night fell. We filled the gas tank with the final jerry can of gas and ate the last of our bread.

"Where's your jeweler?" I asked.

"We first have to go to my merchant in the souk because he is expecting a delivery from me and will be disappointed to see my vehicle empty. But he might know someone."

"The way we're going now we should reach Marrakesh at what time?"

"Just before eight . . . if there are no roadblocks."

But there was a huge one on the outskirts of the city. It took us over forty minutes to edge our way to the front.

"They are not just looking for you," Aatif explained before we reached the officers. "They're also looking for terrorists."

The police were so clogged up with cars that, after a cursory glance at our ID cards, they waved us through.

Marrakesh. I was expecting something mythic. I wasn't ready for all the new housing developments. Or the malls with big international chain stores. Or the chain hotels. Or the congealed traffic. Or the hyper tourist economy. We parked near the famed souk—that amazing open square on which snake charmers frightened visitors with their vipers. Monkeys were running wild. A camel stood forlornly as tourists climbed atop it for a photograph. Men were bothering every foreign woman who was out walking alone. Tour guides were offering an exclusive tour of the souk. I saw a fellow American—late forties, preppy businessman clothes, very button-down with a twin khakis-and-blue-oxford-shirt wife—losing it with a man who was not leaving him alone, blocking his path, hassling him into submission.

"Leave me the fuck alone!" he shouted.

His wife glared at me as I walked by, shrouded in the djellaba and niqab, so disapproving of this encasement of women.

We dodged all the tourist stands, the rug shops, the carved goods and leather store, and entered a back passageway, whereupon we came into a bazaar within a bazaar. Besuited men, elderly gentlemen in immaculate djellabas, venerable establishments dealing in gold, the smell of old established Marrakesh money hidden away from the bleating, cheap commerce of the mercantile arena that Westerners saw.

Aatif steered us into a warehouse in which a young guy around thirty—dressed in a black sweatshirt and sweatpants adorned with the Armani label, Versace sunglasses, a lot of bling on his wrists, including a big Breitling—greeted him with a curt nod. He had a cell phone in one hand, and another on the table in front of him, on which was a calculator, a packet of Marlboros, and a lighter that looked like it was made of solid gold. He eyed me warily, pointing and asking Aatif why I was there. Or, at least, I presumed that's what he was saying, as Aatif began to recite the sad story that had now become so familiar—of a mentally challenged girl behind the veil. Aatif got rather plaintive in tone, as I sensed (from the gestures and the sadness in his voice) that he was recounting the robbery and the reason why he had arrived empty-handed. The guy lit up a cigarette, made a point of not offering Aatif one, and blew smoke in my friend's face. I loathe arrogance—especially that of a preening little man who uses the small amount of power he has in the world to lord it over people like Aatif, whose struggle to survive is seen as a sign of weakness. I could only begin to imagine what he was like around women, how he treated them as contemptuous objects, and how perhaps (wishful thinking) he was inadequate with them. How I wanted to pull off my niqab and call him on his petty cruelty. But I knew that would be disastrous. So I sat there silently as he berated Aatif and, with a dismissive hand motion, as if swatting a fly away, told him to leave his office.

Aatif looked broken and slinked out, his head down, tears in his eyes. I followed but turned and simply stared directly at the guy. I could see him making contact with the accusatory eyes, showing contempt through the veil. He shouted something at me in Arabic. I continued to stare at him. He pointed to the door and seemed to be telling me to get lost. I continued to stare at him. He became nervous, stammering a bit as he stubbed out a cigarette and lit up another, then barking at me again to leave, but in a manner that betrayed his jitteriness. I continued to stare. He picked up his phone and marched to other end of the room, trying to engross himself in the emails on his screen. Still I stared. He turned back at me, now looking spooked. I raised my hand and pointed at him, using my index finger as a weapon of accusation. He stood there, not knowing what to do. Except to do what all bullies do when confronted. He turned and fled out a back door.

I left his office and found Aatif outside, his eyes red, a cigarette alight.

"What did he tell you?" I asked.

"He said he thought I was stupid to get robbed, that I had left him short of goods and didn't care that I could come back next week with a full van of new ones. He also said if I wanted to do business with him again, I would have to pay him five thousand dirhams as an apology."

"Well, you don't have to do business with him again."

"But he and his father have been my contact here in Marrakesh for the past five years."

"I'm sure you can find a better contact—and one who doesn't behave like a spoiled little boy."

"But he has been reliable."

"I bet he's argued over every dirham."

"He is not a nice man. But—"

"No buts. You can ask around here and find another merchant who will gladly take your clients' goods and will treat you with respect. Which you certainly deserve."

He thought about this for a moment, then pointed to a small shop across the alley.

"There is a jeweler there."

His way of changing the subject.

Aatif had to accompany me into the jeweler's, as I feared removing the niqab and causing unwanted interest. The man in charge was hefty, brusque. Aatif explained what I wanted to sell. The fellow held out his fleshy paw. I handed over the two rings. He screwed a loupe into his eye and gave the rings perhaps ten seconds of his attention. Then he announced a price in Arabic to Aatif—who leaned over and whispered it in my ear, "Five thousand dirhams."

I held out my open hand. The fellow dropped the rings back into it. We left.

There was another jeweler adjacent. This gentleman was more polite—a man in a shiny brown suit, with equally brown teeth. But he was also taking me again for a sucker. When Aatif whispered his offer—ten thousand dirhams (I presume he told the man that I had limited hearing)—and I shook my head, he upped it immediately to fifteen. A second shake of the head, and he told Aatif, "Twenty thousand, final price."

I shook my head and held out my hand for the rings. Slipping them back on, I nodded goodbye and we left.

I was beginning to despair of having to let these rings go at an absurdly low price. But then I saw a small, upscale shop at the corner of the alley where we were now standing. Over the front was the name *Abbou Joaillier*. I'd read somewhere, during my pre-trip research, that there was a small Jewish community in Morocco. Abbou Jewelry—with its mosaic tiled décor, its mahogany counter, and a large mahogany desk behind which a well-dressed man in his sixties was weighing diamonds on a small scale—had a Star of David featured in the tiling above its entranceway. When I entered the shop the gentleman immediately stood up. He wore an old-school pinstriped double-breasted suit with a well-pressed blue shirt and black tie. He had a most paternal face. Bifocals were perched on the end of his nose. I noticed immediately photographs of his younger self in front of a jewelry store on West Forty-Seventh Street in New York (he was standing under the actual street sign). He addressed me in Arabic. I decided to take a risk; a potentially huge risk, but one that might just get me a good price for my rings. I reached up and pulled off the niqab. I could see him just a little stunned to discover that behind the veil was this Western woman.

"I presume, from the photographs, that you speak English," I said.

"Indeed I do, *madame*."

He motioned for me to sit down. Aatif was standing in a corner, nervous that I had shown my actual face. I turned to him and said that if he wanted to go outside for a smoke, that was no problem with me. He was happy to comply, bowing to the jeweler before leaving. Once he was out the door the man handed me his card: Ismael Abbou.

"And you once worked in New York?" I asked.

"I lived there for fifteen years. I still have an interest in my former shop there, and get back once a year."

"What made you return to Morocco?"

"Family," he said with just the slightest roll of the eyes. But then he studied me for a moment. I sensed what was coming next.

"Excuse me for asking, *madame*, but haven't I seen your face before?"

I chose my next words with care. "You may have . . . but does that matter?"

He considered this for a second. "May I offer you some tea?"

"That's very kind, but I would rather get down to business. Might

I ask if you wouldn't mind lowering your window shades while we discuss my proposed transaction?"

I could tell that he was deciding whether I was worth the risk. I also saw him glancing at the diamond engagement ring and gold-encrusted wedding band on my left hand.

"As you wish, *madame*."

He stood up and went to the door, putting out a sign that read *Back in Thirty Minutes*. He lowered the shades that covered the door and his shopwindow, turning on several lights at the same time. Then he sat down opposite me again.

"How may I help, *madame*?"

I took off the two rings and placed them in front of him.

"I need to sell these, and I need a good price. They were purchased for me by my husband at Tiffany's."

"Fifth Avenue and Fifty-Seventh Street," he noted with a smile.

"The engagement ring is platinum. The diamond is one-point-one carats. And as I see you have a computer over there, you can check the list price on the Tiffany's website, which I did recently when I got it reinsured. The engagement ring retails now at thirteen thousand dollars. The wedding band is an étoile style in platinum with seven diamonds, carat weight of point-seven-five. List price—"

He interrupted me. "I would surmise four thousand dollars on East Fifty-Seventh Street."

"I'm impressed," I said.

"It's my métier. And I am impressed with your knowledge of such things. Are you in the business as well?"

"Actually, I am an accountant."

Pause. He put his fingertips together. Then said, "Yes, I did read that somewhere."

So there we were. He knew exactly who I was, and he was still going to do business with me. Or, at least, that was my hope.

"Might I inspect the rings?" he asked.

"Of course."

He spent the next ten minutes examining them minutely with his jeweler's eyeglass, weighing them both on his scales, going to his computer and onto the Tiffany's website, then excusing himself as he picked up a cell phone and had a hushed conversation for several minutes. Oh, God, he's calling the cops, I thought. But, as if reading my mind, he smiled reassuringly at me. Concluding the call he explained that he needed to speak to his business partner before making an offer.

"So, indeed, those are Tiffany diamonds on platinum. And yes, the actual retail value in the United States for the two combined would be seventeen thousand dollars. But we are here in Marrakesh, and there is no possibility whatsoever that I could offer you anywhere near that."

"So what could you offer?"

"Forty-five thousand dirhams."

"Seventy thousand."

"Impossible. Fifty thousand. That is close to six thousand dollars."

"And if I went to one of those jewelry exchanges in New York I would get at least twelve thousand dollars."

"But you are in Marrakesh. Fifty-two thousand five hundred."

"And I know you will sell these rings for at least one hundred thousand dirhams in the next few days. Sixty-five thousand."

"Sixty thousand—final offer."

"Sold," I said, holding out my hand. Mr. Abbou took it and made a small bow in my direction. I could also see him eyeing the watch on my wrist.

"Might that be a vintage Rolex Explorer from the nineteen sixties?" he asked.

"It's the nineteen sixty-five edition. It was my late father's. I had it valued recently at fifteen thousand dollars."

"Might I please see it?" he asked. I slipped it off and handed it to him. He studied it, then explained that he was going to open the case and inspect its workings. This he did expertly, using his magnifying glass to study its mechanism. Again he went over to his computer to run a check on current market value. Again he excused himself to make a second hushed call. When he got off the phone he told me, "The most I can offer is fifty thousand dirhams."

"Eighty."

"That is impossible. Sixty."

"And I am certain you have a rich client somewhere who has just been waiting for a watch like this and will pay you at least one hundred and thirty thousand."

"Sixty-five."

"Seventy thousand," I said, adding, "and that is my final price."

Now it was his turn to offer his hand.

"We are agreed, *madame*. And now I insist that we have tea."

I nodded agreement. He stood up and opened a door, speaking to someone in the rear of his establishment. As we waited for the tea he asked me if I needed help with anything else.

"I need to get to Casablanca—but I need to get there without being seen."

"Do you have any ID papers?"

"The man who drove me . . . he has been using the papers of someone else. And because I have been behind the niqab . . ."

"Understood. But why not ask this man to drive you to Casa?"

"Because I don't want him further involved in any of this."

He tapped his fingers on the counter, thinking, thinking. "I may be able to help you."

The tea arrived, carried by a studious-looking young man, also dressed in a double-breasted suit. He too did a double take, seeing this Western woman in a djellaba with a niqab on the table in front of me. Mr. Abbou spoke in Arabic to him, explaining several matters. They exchanged a few more words, tea was poured, glasses raised.

"I wish you a safe return home," Mr. Abbou said. "How, may I ask, are you planning to actually leave Morocco?"

"I need to find a new passport. I don't suppose you would know somebody who specializes in that sort of thing."

Mr. Abbou smiled sympathetically.

"I am happy to send my assistant Mahmoud here with you to Casa, and he will drive you in one of my Mercedes, so you will have a comfortable ride up to the big city. And if the price of three thousand dirhams is reasonable for you . . ."

"I bet I could get a taxi around here to do it for half the price."

"Indeed you could, *madame*. But in my Mercedes, sitting in the rear, looking like a well-heeled woman with a driver—you will fly through whatever checkpoints may be in force tonight. With a normal taxi driver—"

"Okay, fine, three thousand."

"We will, of course, need to speak with your own driver and see if he will be willing to entrust you with the ID card for another day or so."

"Yes, that will be crucial. But before we go any further, might you be able to show me the one hundred and thirty thousand dirhams? I am sorry to be so direct about this, but—"

"No need to apologize. Business is business. And your rings and your Rolex will be left here in front of you while I go to my safe and retrieve the funds."

As he disappeared into a back room, Mahmoud not only kept an eye on the merchandise, but also on the front door. I asked him if he spoke French. He nodded.

"How long is the ride from here to Casablanca?"

"What *quartier* are you going to?"

The quartier where Ben Hassan lives, as he was my only option right now when it came to buying a false passport.

"It's called Gauthier," I said.

"I know it. Very nice. At this time of the evening, it will be two and a half hours. There's an *autoroute* that is almost direct most of the way."

Mr. Abbou returned with several large bundles of bills, all with bank wrappers still around them. He placed them in front of me. I counted them thoroughly, separating them into two distinct piles, putting one of the piles in the pocket of my djellaba. Then I asked Mr. Abbou if he would mind if I used his shop for a fast meeting.

"No problem," he said. "Would you like me to call your driver inside?"

"Yes—his name is Aatif."

"A very good name. Do you know what it means in Arabic?"

I shook my head.

"Compassionate."

Mahmoud stepped outside, calling Aatif in. Mr. Abbou asked if we'd like to be alone. Aatif waved away that privilege. I motioned for him to sit down in the chair next to mine near the desk. I could see Aatif taking in the considerable pile of money in front of him.

"That is for you," I said.

He looked beyond astonished.

"That can't be right. We agreed on two thousand dirhams to get you to Marrakesh."

"Yes, and I also promised you twelve thousand for the goods that were stolen from your van. But I have decided that you deserve a bonus. So the total there is one hundred thousand dirhams."

He stared at me.

"But . . . why?"

"Because, once you pay off your clients, it should give you enough—along with the money you've saved—to buy the house and marry Hafeza."

Silence. Aatif put his face in his hands.

"This is too kind," he finally said.

"As I said before, you deserve kindness."

"But . . ."

Mr. Abbou reached over and put a hand on Aatif's shoulder, whispering something in Arabic. Then, suddenly, Aatif took my two hands in his own and said, "I finally got lucky."

I laughed. "So did I."

Turning to Mr. Abbou and using French for Aatif's sake I told him,

"Aatif needs a new merchant in Marrakesh to sell goods that he brings north from the south. The man he's been dealing with is awful."

Mr. Abbou asked Aatif for the merchant's name. When Aatif mentioned it, Mr. Abbou rolled his eyes.

"A nasty, stupid child," he said. "Will you be around here tomorrow?"

"I could be," Aatif said. "We got little sleep last night, we've been on the road for hours . . ."

"Where are you sleeping tonight?" Mr. Abbou asked.

Aatif shrugged.

"We have a small guest room in the back. It's very simple, but clean. You are most welcome to stay. And I would be honored if you were to eat with me. There is a nice restaurant just two minutes from here. Then, tomorrow morning, I can introduce you to one or two merchants I know. We can discuss all this over dinner. *D'accord?*"

Aatif gave his trademark shy smile.

"D'accord."

I asked Aatif if I could borrow his sister's ID card for a few more days, but said I would mail it back to him if he gave me his address.

"Please keep the card. My sister would have been pleased to know that her identity was put to such good use."

I glanced at the watch on my wrist and realized it was no longer there. The last vestige of my father. My sole inheritance. Gone now for good. But being someone who appreciated life's manifold ups and downs—"You gotta play the hand you're dealt," as he so often told me—he would, I was certain, agree that the money raised on his one and only asset had ended up in the right hands.

"It's eleven minutes past nine," Mr. Abbou said.

That would mean Casablanca by midnight. I reached for a pad on the desk and wrote out my email, handing it to Aatif.

"Here's how to contact me," I said. "Send me the wedding photographs."

He stood up and again took both my hands in his own, saying, *"Allah ybarek feek wal 'ayyam al-kadima."*

I smiled and repeated the benediction back to him.

May Allah bestow his blessings on you in the days to come.

Mr. Abbou insisted on walking me to the Mercedes that Mahmoud would drive. As we reached this venerable black vehicle—it dated from the early 1980s, I was told—I handed Mahmoud the slip of paper on which Ben Hassan had scribbled his address.

"No problem," Mahmoud said. "We have GPS."

Mr. Abbou handed me his card, telling me his cell phone number was written on the back. "If there is any problem whatsoever, you call me," he said. "I can't get you a passport, but I have connections should difficulties arise. And, by the way, the drive to Casablanca is on me."

"That's very kind of you."

"Consider it a mitzvah," he said.

I laughed. "I never thought I'd ever hear Hebrew being spoken in Marrakesh," I said.

"Life is surprising."

"Yes, I am somewhat aware of that."

"And a mitzvah should always be rewarded with a mitzvah."

"How true . . . and how rare."

Now I took his hands in my own. "Very good doing business with you, *monsieur*."

"And you, *madame*."

He opened the passenger door of the Mercedes and ushered me out of his life.

Fifteen minutes later we had cleared Marrakesh and were on the *autoroute* heading north. It was agreed that I would take the backseat and, if stopped by the police or questioned at a checkpoint, Mahmoud would explain that he was my father's driver, and that I had mental challenges, and so on.

But in the two and a half hours I was in the vehicle, we were never stopped. Sitting in the back, drinking in the air-conditioning, I fell into a subdued daze. There was one checkpoint on the outskirts of Casa. But the officer simply looked in, saw a besuited driver and a veiled woman in the backseat, and waved us on.

Ten minutes later we pulled up in front of the apartment building that Ben Hassan called home. I handed Mahmoud two thousand dirhams—despite his protests that his employer had told him I wasn't to pay him—and asked him to wait for me outside for an hour.

"If I don't come downstairs by one a.m., you can head back to Marrakesh. But if I do need you before then . . ."

"I'll be waiting."

The truth was, I knew that, without the false foreign travel document that Ben Hassan could provide, I had hit the end of the line. Still, just in case Ben Hassan was out for the night, or if the situation turned tricky, at least Mahmoud might be persuaded to drive me to Tangier. I would then have to find a black marketer for a way out of the country. My hope was that, by flashing ten thousand dirhams in front of him, Ben Hassan would come up with the necessary goods and even get me north onto the ferry for Spain by morning.

I got out of the Mercedes and loitered to the side of the front door until a young couple came out of the building. Before the door could slam behind them I raced inside and up those four flights of twisted stairs to Ben Hassan's apartment. I rang the bell. No answer. I rang it again. No answer. So I held it down for the better part of a minute.

Then, out of nowhere, the door opened. Ben Hassan was there, looking as if I had just gotten him out of bed, his capacious caftan stained with sweat.

He looked just a bit confused to find a woman in a niqab standing in front of him. I pulled the veil away. The shock on his face was considerable. But he quickly wiped it away, replacing it with his usual menacing irony.

"So . . . the most wanted woman in Morocco drops by to say hello."

I pushed by him into the apartment, saying, "I need a shower and a passport."

TWENTY-SEVEN

HOT WATER FROM a shower spray. Proper soap and shampoo. A toothbrush and toothpaste. A large towel. A bed with clean sheets. And before that, a late-night supper and several very welcome glasses of wine.

Basic comforts can seem like huge luxuries when you have been denied them for a considerable amount of time.

As cautious as I was about being in Ben Hassan's presence, I also knew from before that he had a nurturing side. Seeing me exhausted and rank, he immediately aroused Omar from bed and got him working. I was shown the shower and handed one of Omar's freshly laundered light cotton djellabas. Given his slightness—and all the weight I'd lost—it actually fit me. He also saw to it that the clothes I was carrying with me were thrown into the washing machine. While drying off in the bathroom, I inspected the scarring on my face and legs. The bruising from the beating had virtually vanished, but the cheekbone felt fragile to the touch, and the deep rings under my eyes, especially under the possibly fractured left cheekbone, made me look like a haunted insomniac. The facial sunburn was still apparent but subsiding, but there were still severe scars on my legs. I knew that I had to see a doctor as soon as possible about STDs and any lasting vaginal injuries. I also probably needed an MRI on my face and head, and to deal with the slight ringing still in my ear. Had he burst an eardrum when he slammed his fist against my left ear, then kicked me in the head?

When I emerged from the shower (I had spent almost twenty minutes under its blessed downpour), dried, and changed into the clean djellaba, I found that a small supper had been laid out for me in the living room. The wine was balming. And the pastilla—a pie made with cinnamon, harissa, almonds, and pigeon meat—was quite delicious.

I had decided on the way north from Marrakesh that my strategy with Ben Hassan would be to say nothing about Paul and the entire fraudulent loan for Samira's apartment. My desire here was to get a new passport and up to Tangier.

How much did Ben Hassan know of my ordeal? No doubt, if he called me "the most wanted woman in Morocco," he was aware that I was still being sought in connection to the disappearance of my husband. No doubt he'd also seen the television footage of the charred body in the desert. I knew, as he made his slow, belabored walk into the living room, that I would soon find out.

"I must say, from what I've learned of your exploits, you've been quite resourceful," he said. "Sorry about the abuse you received. Though I am hardly a doctor, my untrained eye tells me you might have a bone or two broken around your left eye socket. Still, your attacker did get his comeuppance, did he not? But, as I am not the police, who am I to pry into exactly how you burned that man to death? Or what you were doing with him in the desert."

I stared straight at his corpulent face.

"That young man and his accomplice seized me off a street in Tata, drugged me, drove me out into the middle of the Sahara, raped me, and left me to die."

"And you struck back."

"I didn't say that."

"Of course you didn't. Nor did his accomplice."

"So his accomplice has been found?"

"That's for you to find out. But as your hope is, I presume, to be out of the country tomorrow . . ."

"Can you facilitate that?"

"For a price."

"And what is your price?"

"Let's discuss that in the morning."

"I'd rather discuss it now. I need a false passport. You are the one person I know in Morocco who can provide me with such a document. Here I am."

"Availing yourself of my hospitality."

"I can leave, *monsieur*."

"And go where? Back into your native garb? How clever of you to go behind the veil to get through all those pesky checkpoints. How did you manage the identity paper problem?"

"I found a solution."

"I'm certain you did."

"So how much for a false passport?"

"We are all business tonight."

"I need to know your price."

"I presume you were robbed of everything."

"That's right. And I am not going to take out a loan with you."

"Smart woman. But if you have no cash on hand . . ."

"I have a little cash."

"And how did you manage to obtain that?"

"I sold what jewelry I had in Marrakesh."

He made a point of carefully studying my left hand.

"Ah, indeed," he said. "All vestiges of your marriage vanished."

"Except the emotional scars."

"You must have done well, given that your most collectible Rolex is also no longer present on your wrist."

"I had some debts to settle."

"Ah, yes, I also figured someone must have aided and abetted your evading the police. And he must have cost plenty."

"Actually, he might have been the most honorable man I've ever met."

"I'm so pleased for you—honorable men being so infrequent in your life."

"Present company included," I said.

"So . . . I am right in presuming that you have little money."

"You told me your standard price for a false passport was ten thousand dirhams."

"I also told you that if the individual was rather problematic—as in, wanted by the police—the price would treble. So I am afraid thirty-five thousand is the amount needed."

"Twenty-five thousand is what I can pay—and that must include transport up to Tangier. I'm certain you can get Omar to drive me."

"That will be an additional five thousand dirhams."

"It's only a four-hour drive."

"But think of the risks involved in getting you there."

"I can go back behind the niqab and use the ID papers I have. Then, when we're at the port, I'll change back into my normal clothes and use the passport you've given me to leave."

"My, my, you have this all figured out already. Most impressive. But there is still risk involved for myself and Omar. Still, as a way of showing goodwill, thirty thousand dirhams all in."

I put out my hand. "Deal."

He seemed supremely uncomfortable proffering his hand for me to take. As before it felt like a hot, bedewed cushion.

"What time can I get the passport tomorrow?" I asked.

"As it is now almost one thirty in the morning I will want to sleep in until ten a.m. It will take about an hour or so to put the passport together. I have the camera for the photograph. I will need to get you the appropriate entry stamp placed in the document, and also have it placed on the immigration computer system. That involves me contacting an associate who does this sort of thing for me. I have decided, given your facility with the language, that you will be French. But even at the Port of Tangier the immigration officers now have computers. My associate has a way of ensuring that your date of entry will pop up when they scan your passport."

"And does this cost extra?"

"Of course not. It's all part of the overall fee. Tomorrow we can choose a name for you. Nothing too absurd. We'll sleep on it."

"Fine. I could use sleep."

"The bed awaits you."

"One last question . . . in my absence have there been any sightings of my husband?"

"None whatsoever since you tried to chase him down in Ouarzazate."

"How did you know about that?"

"I have my sources."

"Like his other wife?"

"Perhaps. And I know full well that you are now desperate to ask me why I didn't give Samira the money that Paul borrowed for her apartment. And did I contact Paul, telling him that, by helping buy his daughter and grandson an apartment, he could atone for his absence from Samira's life?"

"Did I even indicate I was concerned about this?"

"My source in Ouarzazate informed me that you certainly seemed vexed by it. The truth is—"

"The truth, *monsieur*, is that dealing with you is like walking through a hall of mirrors in which nothing is ever concrete or real. So be it. I don't need to know why Samira didn't get the money. Or if you set all this up as a trap to ensnare my now vanished husband. Let that be on your conscience . . . if you have one. You will be getting close to four thousand dollars from me tomorrow for one hour's work and a drive to Tangier, which you yourself won't have to make. Our business is therefore done for the night. I thank you for the hospitality."

A very long silence followed, during which Ben Hassan got up and poured us both an *eau-de-vie*. Then he finally spoke.

"I don't entirely agree with your character assessment of me, *madame*. Yes, I do have my tricky side—and a very long memory for wrongs rendered. But I am also an excellent friend. As I was to your husband all those years ago. And the result . . ."

He held up his battered, deformed hands.

"We all have our ways of dealing with the injustices and sorrows piled upon us, *madame*. We all have our ways of getting through the day. And we all have our moments of malevolence . . . even if, in your recent case, the malevolence you meted out on your attacker was wholly merited. Pushed to the wall, some of us surrender to the brutal inevitable. Whereas there are others—like you, like me—who turn feral. And who fight back with the same brutality visited upon us. Because we know that, in life, the central preoccupation is still the one that existed when we all once lived in caves: survival. You're a survivor, *madame*. I salute you for it. But don't try to capture the high moral ground here. You are exactly like me. You killed to stay alive."

"You killed as an act of revenge."

"Unlike you, I didn't have the opportunity to strike back immediately. Two crushed hands leave you at a profound disadvantage. But I did strike back eventually . . . to prove I would never be cowed by such animals ever again. And to let my little community here know that too . . . not that I ever admitted to anything. I didn't need to. Everyone knew. Everyone also knew they could never pin the crimes on me, because I was too circumspect in my plotting to get caught. But the real lesson that everyone around here gleaned was that I would kill to stay alive."

Five minutes later, I was alone in the guest bedroom. As much as my analytic side wanted to deconstruct the skewed logic of Ben Hassan's attempts to draw a parallel between us, exhaustion won out.

I had started the day at four in the morning, hearing my friend Aatif being beaten and robbed. I crawled into the first bed, between the first sheets, I had slept in for weeks. Sleep came quickly.

Then I was awake and wondering where I was, and thinking that I had been unconscious for a very long time. Getting up and wandering out into the hallway, I passed Ben Hassan in his office.

"My, my, you certainly needed your beauty sleep, didn't you?" he said.

"What time is it?"

"A few minutes before noon."

"Oh my God . . ."

"Not to worry. Have your shower. I will have Omar arrange breakfast for you. Meantime I have a few phone calls to make . . . and then we can get down to business."

"Will there be enough time?"

"To take care of everything and get you packed off? Absolutely. Now off you go. The sooner you are showered and dressed . . ."

I hurried into the bathroom, noting with pleasure that, as before, a hair dryer had been left there for my use, as well as all my freshly laundered clothes. Ben Hassan was a dangerous customer, but he also knew how to play the thoughtful host. Twenty minutes later, showered, dressed in clean clothes, I was sipping coffee and eating two croissants in Ben Hassan's kitchen. At which point I heard his front doorbell ring. As Omar went to answer it Ben Hassan came into the kitchen.

"Enjoying your breakfast?"

I heard voices down the corridor.

"Do you have visitors?" I asked.

"*We* have visitors. Last night, after you went to bed, I thought about our little exchange. I also considered the complexities of risk, and the fact that there are some clients who are just too hot to handle. Which, on reflection, is most certainly the case with you. Another little matter entered my thinking: I need to keep my friends and associates happy. Helping you flee the country might anger several of the men now at the end of the corridor, all of whom want to talk with you, as they are members of the Sûreté. Or, as you Americans might put it, the feds."

"You bastard," I hissed.

"I won't contest that. At least be thankful that I allowed you a shower, a good meal, and an excellent night's sleep before calling them."

Then he shouted something in Arabic down the corridor. Moments later I was surrounded by three men in suits and a police officer in uniform. One of the detectives spoke to me in French, asking me to confirm my name. I told him what he wanted to hear.

"Now, we would prefer not to use handcuffs," he said.

"I'll go quietly," I said.

"Very wise, *madame*."

With the two officers in front and two behind me, I was marched out. Ben Hassan insisted on accompanying us to the front door.

"Do say hello the next time you are in Casablanca," was his parting benediction. "And do remember there is a subtext to all this: survival is everything."

I was marched down the stairs, marched into a waiting unmarked car, accompanied by two police cars blaring their sirens as we shot across the city. Neither of the detectives with me said anything as we traversed Casablanca. I shut my eyes. *Why am I surprised it is ending like this?*

The windows on this vehicle were virtually blacked out, allowing me no idea of where we were heading. After a quarter of an hour I saw through the windscreen that we were entering a modern block of buildings, and then driving down a tunnel into an underground garage. Once there, all the officers exited the vehicle before I was allowed to get up. The same deal as before: two officers in front and two behind me as I was marched to a doorway that only opened after one of the cops punched in a number code, and the door swung open. The walls inside were painted an institutional green. I was brought up a set of stairs, and then down another concrete corner until I was steered into a room furnished only with a metal table, four chairs, and a mirror that, no doubt, was two-way.

The cops deposited me in this room, then turned and left without saying anything. The door slammed behind them with a formidable thud. I could hear a bolt sliding into place outside. *Do you really think I'd try to make a break for it?* I felt like shouting. Instead I sat down in one of the chairs, put my face in my hands, and thought, Whatever you do, insist on a lawyer, and refuse to answer any of their questions.

I heard the bolt being slid back and the door opening. In walked a Western woman, late thirties, dressed in a crisp linen suit, a pressed white blouse, a bulging leather briefcase in her left hand. She came over to me, her hand extended.

"It is so good to finally meet you, Robin."

I accepted the outstretched hand, trying to work out who this woman was and why she was here in a Moroccan police station.

"Alison Conway, assistant consul at the US Consulate here in Casablanca. Now, we don't have long, as Inspector al-Badisi and the translator will be here in a moment. But what I wanted to explain before he got here—"

She didn't have time to finish that sentence, as the door swung open and in walked a man, with thick black hair and a groomed moustache, wearing a light brown suit. He extended his hand and informed me that he was Inspector al-Badisi. He had a dossier of documents with him, which he put down on the table. I asked for water. He shouted out to someone in the hallway. Meanwhile a woman joined us—dark suit, black hair tied up in a tight bun, severe features.

"This is Madame Zar," the Inspector said, "who will be translating for me today."

"But we are speaking in French now."

The assistant consul, now seated next to me at the table, put her hand on my arm.

"I felt it was better, for clarity's sake, if all discussed here was translated, so there would be no ambiguities."

"What's going on here?" I whispered to her in English.

"Just let the inspector speak," she whispered back. "All will be explained."

The water arrived. The door was closed. The inspector sat down and opened his dossier, bringing out several copies of what seemed to be the same document. Then he looked up and regarded me with formal severity. As he spoke, the translator waited for a pause every few sentences before rendering his words into English for me.

"*Madame*, on behalf of His Majesty and his government, I wish to offer you our sincere condolences for the ordeal you have been put through. We have been, as Assistant Consul Conway can attest, working very closely with the US Consulate here in Casablanca in the search for you. We are immensely relieved and pleased to have you here, alive and, I hope, reasonably well."

I said nothing, just nodded acknowledgment.

"Now, I regret that we must discuss the events that occurred in a sector of the Sahara some forty-three kilometers from the town of Tata. We do know what happened out there—"

Suddenly I flew off the handle. "How can you know what happened there? I was there. What happened there was inflicted on me."

The assistant consul gripped my arm tightly. I shut my eyes for a moment, gathering myself, then opened them and said, "I apologize for interrupting you, Inspector. It has been a very long few weeks."

"There is no need to apologize, *madame*. On the contrary, we should be apologizing to you, considering what you've been put through. But as I was saying . . . we are aware of what happened in the desert."

With that he pulled over what clearly was a prepared statement. And began to read it to me. In it he recounted the "facts" of the case. How I had been searching for my missing husband in the Sahara and had been drugged with chloroform while leaving my hotel in Tata to catch the early bus to Ouarzazate. The two "criminals" were named Abdullah Talib and Imad Shuayb, both twenty-one, both from Marrakesh, both working on a road work project in Tata. They beat and robbed me, knocking me unconscious. But after that, the two thieves argued over how to split the money and goods stolen from me. A fight between them broke out, with Imad stabbing Abdullah to death, and then, in a panic, setting fire to the body and returning to Tata. When he tried to sell my computer and passport some days later in Marrakesh, a merchant notified the police. Imad Shuayb confessed everything after his arrest and was so ashamed of his crimes that he hanged himself in the prison cell in which he was being held, awaiting trial.

When the inspector reached this part of the narrative, my shoulders stiffened. I was about to say something—but again Assistant Consul Conway put her hand on my arm, letting me know that silence was the best option. Of course I knew immediately what the inspector was reading me: the official version of what went down, eliminating the nasty public embarrassment (especially in such a tourist-based economy) of the revelation that a Western woman had been abducted and raped and left to die under the Saharan sun. I could only begin to wonder if, after having had his confession beaten out of him, that dreadful young man had truly taken his own life or was conveniently "suicided" to close the case entirely. While part of me was outraged that the rape had been left out of the official statement, the other forensic part of my psyche also understood what the authorities were doing. They were giving me a way out, and one in which no possible legal charges could ever be directed at me, or an investigation demanded by the assailants' families. The loose narrative ends were being tied up in a manner in which the case would be closed permanently.

The inspector continued on, explaining how, having been left unconscious in the desert, a Berber family rescued me, nursed me back to life, and eventually helped get me back to Casablanca. Again the thought ran through my brain: Did they actually know the name of my saviors or was this just more official-story-speak? I interrupted him at this point.

"That is what happened, *monsieur*. I owe my life to those people who saved me and the man who drove me up here."

The inspector's face twitched, as if he had been caught unawares by this revelation. That's when I knew: they had been totally unaware of Maika and her family, of Aatif and the way I was smuggled up here behind the niqab. They had just invented the Berber part of the story as another way of explaining why I had gone missing for several weeks. So my Berber friends would not be receiving unwanted visits by the Sûreté posing all sorts of questions. They would be left alone.

Assistant Consul Conway shot me a look, telling me that I should let the inspector finish.

"I am pleased that you were helped by our citizens," he said. "And I would just like to say—those men who attacked you, those criminals . . . they are not us."

"Believe me, *monsieur*, I know that," I said. "I know that so well."

"So we have prepared an official statement in English, French, and Arabic, which Assistant Consul Conway has examined in all three languages to confirm they are one and the same, and which we would like you to sign . . . after, of course, you've had the chance to peruse them. We would appreciate it if you would pose for a photograph with me; a photo that will be released to the media to show that you are alive and well, as there has been considerable concern here and elsewhere in your disappearance. We were in contact with the hotel at which you and your husband were staying in Essaouira. All your clothes were packed up and sent north to Casablanca, where they will await you tonight at the Hôtel Mansour. It is an excellent hotel and you will be our guest tonight. When Imad Shuayb was arrested, we also recovered your passport" (which he now pushed across the table to me). "We also discovered that you had a reservation back to New York on Royal Air Maroc some weeks ago that you never used. We have contacted the airline. They have changed the flight, at no charge to you whatsoever, to tomorrow at midday. We will also arrange for complimentary transport to the airport—and anything that you want tonight at the hotel you just sign for."

So Ben Hassan had probably called his police contact early this morning while I was still asleep, telling them he had me at his place, but to wait until I was up and ready before showing up to take me in. In the meantime the assistant consul had been contacted and everything put in motion to wrap this story up as quickly as possible and get me out of the country tomorrow.

"That's all very thoughtful of you," I said. "One important thing remains outstanding: Have there been any sightings of my husband, any sense whatsoever of his whereabouts?"

The inspector pursed his lips and reached for another file.

"On August second your husband checked out of the Oasis Hotel early that morning and was seen walking out of town. A local tour guide named Idriss was heading to work in his jeep and saw Monsieur Leuen heading directly into the desert. He stopped and asked Monsieur Leuen if he could offer assistance, as he was heading into a barren area without oases, and as he was wearing no hat and carrying no backpack or canteen. Your husband told the guide, 'I'm fine,' and kept walking into the Sahara. That was the last sighting of him."

"And that was at what time?" I asked.

"The tour guide said it was around seven twenty."

"But that's impossible," I said. "I arrived in Ouarzazate at seven and caught sight of my husband at least three times that morning."

"Did you speak to him?" the inspector asked.

"No—he always eluded me. And the woman at the hotel told me he returned there at four o'clock and was heading to the bus depot to catch the four ten to Tata. I followed him. I saw him in front of me. I missed the bus and took the next one."

The inspector pulled out more documents, scrutinizing them with care.

"I have here the statement from the tour guide and the woman at the hotel. Again I repeat, she said your husband checked out at seven, and the tour guide confirmed he had his conversation with him at seven twenty. It's all here."

"But I saw him."

"But if you saw him," the inspector said, "then why didn't he answer you?"

"He was avoiding me. But that woman at the hotel . . . I remember the conversation I had with her when I came back from seeing . . ."

I stopped myself from saying anything more. Because to do so would, I sensed, begin to raise questions about my sanity, questions that I myself didn't want to answer. I closed my eyes. There was Paul, eluding me on the streets of Ouarzazate. There was the scene at the hotel reception desk, after visiting his other wife. "You've just missed him," the woman at the desk told me. And the sight of his bobbing gray hair and his tall frame in the distance as I raced to catch him before he boarded the bus. Everything else that had happened to me after that was so real. I still had plenty of physical scars from the attack. They'd found the burned body. Opening that passport in front of me, I saw that it was my own. All tangible, all real. I had lived this story. It was all verified. But those hours in Ouarzazate when Paul was everywhere and nowhere . . . surely that couldn't have been a hallucination?

"Are you all right, Robin?" Alison Conway asked me, her hand on my shoulder.

"No," I said.

Leaning toward me, she whispered in my ear, "I cannot give you official counsel, as that is not in my diplomatic remit. But, speaking personally, if I were you, I would sign the statement. I had one of our legal people and one of our translators look at all three versions. They all match up, and they all let you leave Morocco with the matter entirely resolved."

So she too suspected (or, indeed, knew) that the burned body in the desert wasn't the handiwork of the accomplice who was then "suicided" while in custody.

"Give them what they want," she continued. "Put your signature on the statement, pose for the press photograph, spend the night in the five-star hotel they've arranged for you, take the flight home tomorrow. They are being very smart about all this. Very conscientious. I strongly advise you to do the same."

I shut my eyes again. Paul was there, sketching away on the balcony of our room in Essaouira, flashing me a seductive smile as I brought him a glass of wine, telling me he loved me. I blinked. Paul was gone. I blinked again. There he was dashing down that back alley in Ouarzazate, eluding me as always—but still so tangibly there. I blinked again. Nothing. A void as empty as the Sahara.

I opened my eyes. I saw the inspector staring at me with concern.

"Would you like some time to think about all this, *madame*?" he asked.

"No," I said. "I want to go home. Where do I sign?"

TWENTY-EİGHT

AT FOUR THAT morning I sat up in bed. I could not remember a single detail of the nightmare that snapped me into consciousness. All I felt was a dangerous, oppressive presence. Undefined. Entombing me.

But then I opened my eyes and found myself in this heavily over-upholstered hotel room. Hours earlier, upon being checked in here, I was brought upstairs to find the two suitcases that had been dispatched from Essaouira. It was a shock to see all my clothing intermingled with the garments of my vanished husband. Whoever had packed up our room had not separated his from hers. It took me just ten minutes to repack all of my clothes and lay out the items I would need until the flight tomorrow. While handling Paul's items I didn't feel rage or trauma. Just a profound numbness. Assistant Consul Conway—she insisted I call her Alison—had accompanied me to the hotel in the unmarked police car that the inspector had ordered after I signed the official statement and also posed for a photograph with him, showing the world "Case closed." I had extracted one request from the police—that the photo would not be released to the press until I was en-route to the States the next day. I didn't want stares at the airport. I wanted to be home by the time it was revealed that I'd emerged safely.

"You handled that all very well back there," Alison told me after we reached the hotel and the management offered us tea while the room was readied. "They wanted to wrap this up quickly, without fuss. They're pleased you played ball."

"What else was I going to do?"

"After an experience like yours . . . well, most people would be already showing signs of post-traumatic stress disorder. I am very impressed that you didn't break down in front of the inspector and were so contained."

"I've had several weeks to sort through the worst of it. And I need you to do me a favor."

I explained about the desert family who took me in. I told her the vague location of the oasis that they were calling home right now. I gave her the remaining forty thousand dirhams—and asked her to perform a minor miracle and get the money to them.

"I can't promise anything, but I will try," she said.

"I don't want the law involved. They're a bit wary, I sense, about anything to do with the government."

"Berbers?"

I nodded.

"It will be an interesting challenge finding them," she said.

"May I ask you a direct question?"

"Of course."

"Have the police conducted a search of the desert near to where my husband was last seen?"

"Absolutely. And they've found nothing so far."

By "nothing" I knew she meant: no body, no desiccated corpse, burned by the sun, fed upon by vultures.

"And that tour guide who saw him . . . he clearly identified Paul?"

"I read the report from the Ouarzazate Sûreté. He described a Caucasian male, around two meters tall—that's six-foot-three—thin, with long gray hair and several days' growth of beard. Does that sound like your husband?"

I shut my eyes and again saw his hair slapping the shoulders of his white shirt as he raced in front of me for the bus in Ouarzazate, my entreaties to him to stop only accelerating his pace.

"Yes, that sounds like him."

"Of course there could have been another Caucasian male of the same age and build and hairstyle who went out hiking in the desert that day. And I did check with my colleagues at all the other Western consulates and embassies here. There was no one of that description missing."

She chose her next words with care. "You still do maintain that you saw him on the streets of Ouarzazate, later that same day, several hours after he allegedly disappeared?"

"I saw what I saw. But what any one of us sees . . . is that ever the truth? Or is it just what we want to see?"

She considered this for a moment.

"Trust me—and I know this, because I lost my sister five years ago in a car accident in which I was the passenger—it's when you are beyond the initial trauma that it jumps up out of nowhere and grabs you by the throat. Don't be surprised if, now that you are out of danger, it begins to get tricky for a while."

At four that morning the trickiness had begun. That sense of a dark force in the room with me, about to encircle me and wreak havoc. But I couldn't pinpoint who or what it was. What I found myself doing, after getting up and pacing the room, was throwing on some clothes and heading downstairs with the suitcase containing all my husband's clothes. I went out to the street, passing a homeless man lying near the gutter, his clothes threadbare. I put the suitcase in front of him and handed him five hundred of the thousand dirhams I'd held onto for tips and incidentals. His eyes went wide when he saw the sum of cash I pressed into his palm.

"Why me?" he asked in French.

"Why not you?"

Back in the room I ran a very hot bath and sat in it for the better part of an hour. A long soak, during which I started to cry and couldn't stop until I was so wrung out that, after drying myself off, I forced myself back into bed with the hope that sleep might overtake me again. But I was wired and very wide awake. So I turned on my laptop and saw that Morton had answered the dispatch I'd sent to him after checking into the hotel, informing him that I was alive and would definitely be landing tomorrow (now today) in Buffalo at 8:10 p.m. I also mentioned that Paul was missing, presumed dead. Morton's reply was all business:

Will be at the airport. Very glad you are out of harm. Re: Paul. You should know that, under NY state law, a missing person cannot be declared dead for seven years. But there are some legal things we can do to protect you. More when we meet. Best—Morton. PS—I can finally sleep now, knowing you are okay.

Trust Morton to practice ultrapragmatism at a difficult time.

The rest of the day passed in a strange blur. An unmarked police car picked me up at the hotel, as arranged, at 9:30. At the airport I was checked in and brought through a special security line by the two officers charged with getting me on the plane. A representative of the airline met us at this checkpoint and escorted us to a private lounge. The cops stayed with me until the flight was called, bringing me to the gate and ensuring that I got on the plane. They wanted to make sure that I was leaving the country.

Eight hours later I was in front of an immigration officer at Kennedy Airport in New York. I had expected to be bombarded with questions—but it seemed that my "gone missing" status hadn't been filed against my name on the Homeland Security website (or maybe the US Consulate in Casablanca had already arranged for it to be pulled). The officer scanned my passport and asked me how long I had been out of the country. I said six, seven weeks.

"Were you only in Morocco?" he asked.

"That's right, just Morocco."

"Were you working?" he asked.

"Just traveling," I said.

"That must have been quite an adventure."

"Indeed it was."

Three hours later I landed in Buffalo. Morton was there to greet me. He gave me a paternal hug and told me I looked a lot better than he expected to find me.

Morton being Morton, he didn't push for details. On the way to my house he told me that the *Buffalo Sun Times* had reprinted international press service reports about my being found alive and well in Morocco. He showed me the clipping, which featured that official photograph of me shaking the hand of Inspector al-Badisi in Casablanca and looking shell-shocked. Morton said that there had been several calls at my office for interviews from former colleagues on the *Sun Times*.

"I took the liberty of telling them you wanted to be left alone," he said.

"That was the right call," I said.

That first night I was back I found I couldn't cope with the sight of all the detritus of my life with Paul spread around our dusty, shadowy house. Sleep evaded me. The next morning I called the manager of a downtown hotel whose accounts I helped straighten out. I asked him if he could give me a rate on one of his apartment suites for a few weeks. He came back thirty minutes later with a very reasonable price. I moved in that afternoon. I then contacted my doctor. She told me to get in to see her immediately. Dr. Hart had been my physician for a decade. A smart, no-nonsense woman in her late fifties, direct, canny, but also sympathetic. I could see her take in my face when I walked into her office. I asked if she had followed my disappearance in the press.

"Of course," she said, "not that there was much in the way of detail, except that you and your husband had gone missing. And then I saw the report yesterday in the paper that you'd been found."

I told Dr. Hart about the insomnia and the sense of oppressive darkness that had taken hold of me the last few nights. I came clean with her about Paul's betrayal. I also told her about the abduction and rape. But I stopped short of revealing what I had done in response to this attack. That was a secret that I knew I couldn't share with anybody. Not just because the Moroccan authorities had conveniently excised that denouement from the narrative, but also because a secret shared (even with the most trustworthy of friends or professionals) is no longer a secret. Even Alison Conway—who clearly knew the truth of the matter—gave me some advice, after checking me into the hotel.

"Speaking off the record . . . if I were you, I would be very selective about what you reveal about things that happened in the desert. The Moroccans have made it easy for you. They have provided an official version of events on which you have signed off. Silence on everything else might be a wise strategy."

I agreed with her reasoning. But by the time I saw Dr. Hart—only seventy-two hours after this conversation—I still had ongoing flashbacks of the rape and of reaching for the jerry can. In relentless slow motion, I relived the moment I grabbed the lighter from his accomplice's hand and tossed it on his gasoline-drenched body. And how—I'll admit this now—a huge sense of furious vindication came over me as I watched him ignite and writhe and scream in agony.

Ben Hassan might be a bloated moral black hole of a man—but he did touch a very exposed nerve when he pointed out that, like him, I had killed to stay alive.

The thought was hardly comforting. It was stalking me day and night. Especially the night. In fact, all night.

Over the next week I endured an entire battery of tests. I got lucky on several fronts. No parasites parading through my system. No sexually transmitted diseases. The gynecological exam showed nearly full recovery from internal trauma. I did not have a burst eardrum but had suffered a sort of concussion to the ear canal, which would subside in a few more weeks. A CAT scan did not point up damage to my left cheekbone. Nor did I have a dreaded "zygomatic fracture" of the eye socket (as the specialist called it), even though I still had a dark ring beneath my left eye. The dermatologist whom I saw next said that, though the facial scarring would largely heal, there might be some subtle but potentially discernible reminders of the damage done to my legs.

When my friend Ruth flew up to Buffalo the weekend after I returned, I put her up on the sofa bed in the living room of my hotel suite. I told her just about everything that had happened in Morocco, leaving out that one crucial violent detail. She listened wide-eyed and horrified, amazed by my fortuitous rescue and survival. When I mentioned that sleep was now an issue, she said, "You're back in the land of pharmapsychology. And you need to sleep. So ask your doctor to prescribe some pills. If I may say so, you should also consider talking to somebody professionally who can help you—"

"What? Find a degree of *acceptance* about what happened? *Closure*? I know that talking to a shrink can more than help. It's just—"

I broke off, not wanting to complete the sentence. Because what I would have said was, I am not going to sit in a therapist's office and somehow fail to mention that I burned my rapist alive and, in the moments before his accomplice kicked me in the head, I felt a frightening sense of avenging triumph. Still, I did accept Dr. Hart's offer of an antidepressant that also served as a sleep aid. She told me it might take a week for its efficacy to be felt. Actually it took ten days, during which that ongoing sense of foreboding stalked me. There were the flashbulblike memories that popped into my consciousness without warning, and left me seriously skewed.

But then sleep finally took hold.

I threw myself into work. Twelve- and thirteen-hour days. A rigor and a determination to function and cope and keep moving forward that saw me land a big corporate account—a chain of upstate New York hardware stores—the month after my return. After six weeks at the hotel, I moved back home. But it took another ten days before I finally walked into Paul's studio. On the drafting table where he worked was the package that I had sent back to my office from Casablanca. Morton had brought it with him to the airport on the night I arrived back, and I had tossed it into the studio when I got home.

Now, all these weeks later, I finally opened it, staring down at the notebook he'd left at Chez Fouad, forcing myself to open it and turn the pages, looking at his accomplished, intricate take on Essaouira and *la vie marocaine*. Seeing them all again slammed home the loss, the betrayal, the guilt, the horror of his disappearance, the horror of what was visited on me there, the fact that I was alone in our house, ruing so much, trying to keep the ongoing trepidation and rage and sadness at bay, and now, I broke down and cried for a good half an hour, the accumulated grief rushing forth.

When the tears finally stopped, I went into the bathroom and threw some cold water on my face and looked at myself in the mirror. I knew that, though the physical and emotional wounds might always be there, my work was to somehow achieve, in time, a degree of acceptance.

An hour later, nursing a glass of wine, I went online and found a cottage for rent deep in the Adirondack Mountains, on the shores of Upper Saranac Lake. It was available as of the next day—and the owner lived in nearby Lake Placid and said he could have the place cleaned and ready for my arrival by nightfall. He told me that the place lacked Wi-Fi and that cell phone coverage was, at best, spotty.

"Fine by me"—and we then agreed on a price for one month's rental. Negotiations completed, I packed one duffel bag with clothes, another one with a dozen books from around the house that I'd promised myself to read over the years. My last piece of business before I fell into bed was to send an email to Morton.

Sorry to drop another bombshell on you, but I have decided this evening to disappear to somewhere rural and hidden for four weeks. I will drive to a café with Wi-Fi every few days to see if there's anything urgent to deal with at the office. Otherwise I am going to be out of touch. Are you okay with this?

His reply arrived moments later.

Stay out of touch—and don't look at your email or cell phone for the next month. You need this time away for all sorts of obvious reasons. Go hide and think.

Hide I did. The cottage was simple, clean, idyllic. And isolated. It was located at the end of a half-paved road with no neighbors in sight. The nearest village—to which I drove twice a week for supplies—was ten miles away. I slept. I read. I cooked. I listened to classical music and jazz on the radio. I didn't open a computer or touch my cell phone for an entire month. There was a narrow walking trail just steps away from the cottage that followed the lakefront. Every day I did a three-hour hike along its shoreline. I also spent a lot of time thinking. About a certain rigidity that, prior to Morocco, had made me frequently look at life as a giant balance sheet, on which I was endlessly obsessing about reversing the loss column. And how I was always wanting to put things right. And how my wonderful, maddening father cast a shadow over so much. And how rational, hyperorganized me chose men whom I thought I could rescue from the impulse to self-destruct . . . which I was unable to stop my dad from doing.

The search for love—especially when it's been withheld by one parent—can lead you into all sorts of tricky rationalizations. Did I always go through life expecting to be, on some level, betrayed? And why, when it came to marriage, did I pick individuals whom I always secretly doubted would be able to give me the stability denied me as a child?

Life can change on a dime was one of my father's favorite epigrams. Because he was always hoping that the dime would finally come his way. Life changed utterly for me in the Sahara. It sent me to the darkest places imaginable, the absolute limits of endurance. But I did just that: I endured. I will never admit to anyone that I killed in order to live. That secret will stay with me forever. Along with a newfound knowledge that so much is surmountable if you choose to survive. The only way forward after great pain is fortitude.

So, in those weeks alone by the lake, there was a slow ebbing of that dark presence that had hovered over me from the moment I was free of danger in Casablanca. He wasn't knocking repeatedly on my psychic door as he had done so vehemently in the first months after my return. Which, in turn, gave me the space to examine that most telling and thorny of questions: *What do you want?*

And I began to formulate an answer.

When I finally returned to Buffalo, among the vast number of emails awaiting me, there was one that completely delighted me. It was from Aatif. Written in simple French, it arrived with a photo attached.

Hi Robin! Just wanted you to see a picture of my wedding and of the house we now live in. I will always be so eternally grateful to you. I even have a cell phone and an email address. Allah ybarek feek wal 'ayyam al-kadima.

The photos showed Aatif and a petite young woman who—if the snapshot was anything to go by—was clearly outgoing and spirited. They were both in formal Muslim wedding attire in front of a simple squat one-story house: concrete, painted that wondrous Moroccan aquamarine blue. I noted that laundry was already hanging on the line outside.

I wrote back an immediate reply: *Happiness is a wonderful thing, Aatif—and it is splendid to see you and your wife so happy.*

As I glanced once more at the photo of the proverbial happy couple, I couldn't help but feel a stab of loneliness and the sense that I was flying solo, but with a phantom still in the adjoining room.

There was also an email from Assistant Consul Conway in Casablanca. As promised, Alison was keeping me abreast about the ongoing search for my husband, and told me that the Royal Moroccan Army had recently been doing military exercises within the vicinity of the desert where Paul was last seen hiking into nowhere. They'd been conducting a comprehensive sweep of the area as part of their maneuvers and had found no body.

She also said, with regret, that the search for Jabalah and his family had turned up nothing. But now I had a means by which to make contact with them—and immediately sent her back an email with Aatif's coordinates, explaining that he knew the family and might be able to assist with their whereabouts. I then shot Aatif a second email, letting him know that he might hear from a woman at the US Consulate in Casablanca about trying to locate my saviors as she had a sum of money from me for them, and if he could help her locate them I would be hugely grateful.

Weeks went by, then out of nowhere, a further email arrived from Alison. She had finally heard back from Aatif. He told her he was heading to the oasis in a week's time—so, yes, he could deliver the cash to Jabalah and his family. The money had been dispatched by registered post to his home and she had received confirmation from the postal service that it had been received and signed for.

A month or so later I got a one-line email from Aatif:

Money delivered!

There was a photo attached of Maika and Aicha and Naima—the girl and her mother laughing and waving at the camera, Maika as stone-faced as ever. I printed the photo immediately and put it alongside the photo I'd pasted near my computer of Aatif and his wife. The only family I now had.

When I reached the six-month anniversary of my return home I had a second HIV test. Negative. Dr. Hart also did repeat swabs for all other potential STDs: all negative.

"You're in the clear," she told me.

On one level this was true. The discoloration around my left eye was now a thing of the past. And the facial scars had reduced to a point where you would have to study me closely to truly discern them. Still, the door to Paul's study at home remained closed. And the house had gradually lost some of its hushed eeriness—but there were still moments when I could feel Paul's presence.

Still, my determination to push through the worst of the post-traumatic stress paid off to the extent that I weaned myself off the pharmaceuticals, finding the one and only Chinese herbalist at work in Buffalo and switching to a strongly effective tea to help me sleep. At first, after I went off the prescription pills, there were moments of deeply unsettled regression and five days of insane insomnia. But eventually the herbal formulas kicked in. I could function profession-ally. I could sleep. A few weeks later, on a morning noteworthy for its cold clarity, I presented myself at a fertility clinic attached to the State University for a psychological evaluation. The interview and series of tests lasted over an hour. I was just a little nervous in the run-up to this crucial hurdle. Think of it as an audit, I told myself. Much to my surprise, I passed the evaluation. A few days later I returned for a series of examinations to determine whether, now approaching my forty-second year, I would be able to carry a pregnancy to full term. Again I was approved—though the doctor at the clinic with whom I subse-quently spoke did inform me that, at my age, the chance of a miscar-riage or other problems did exist. He warned me that, once I chose a donor, it could take at least three to five tries before I became pregnant.

The donor. I spent a good two weeks going through the one thou-sand or so possibilities on file, reading up on their family and educa-tional backgrounds, their professions, their hobbies and interests. It was so surreal, delving into the personal profiles of these men who had all masturbated into a sterilized cup and were now potential fathers for my much-wanted child.

Eventually I narrowed the selection down to four candidates—and scanned all their details to Ruth. Her pick was the same as mine: a thirty-three-year-old man listed as Michael P. An academic with an undergraduate and doctoral degree from the University of Chicago. A published writer. Athletic. His interests included classical music, cinema, and chess.

"I worry about the 'chess' part," Ruth told me. "Chess freaks tend to be obsessive-compulsive."

"It's rather absurd, isn't it, choosing a potential father the way you choose food at a Chinese restaurant: this attribute from Column A, another from Column B."

"And if you get pregnant you get a fortune cookie."

"If I get pregnant it will be a miracle."

"You've had one miracle already this year," Ruth said. "You got out of the Sahara alive."

"So why should the gods smile on me again?"

But they did—on the third try.

Trust me, it's a deeply lonely experience, having your legs up in the stirrups of a doctor's examination table, watching a nurse approach you with a tube filled with the sperm of the donor you've chosen. Lonely and so modern. No need to establish a rapport; to dance around each other at the outset, deciding whether to cross the frontier into sex; working out whether there is the hope for something more promising; the decision to set up house together (or not); the decision to reproduce (or not). Indeed, there will never be the memory of the intimate coupling that led to this conception. But I had no doubt whatsoever about the fact that I was making the right decision. Too much emotional debris in my past. Too much trepidation about trying to get involved with anyone right now. Maybe, in time, that would change. Maybe there would be a point in the future when I wouldn't be so closed off to that possibility. But for now . . .

The first artificial insemination didn't take. Four weeks later I was back for round two. When my period arrived two weeks later, my disappointment and despair were acute. But, dogged as ever, I returned fourteen days later for round three.

This time . . . bingo.

When my period was one day late, I bought a pregnancy test. At home that night I peed onto its chemically treated strip . . . and watched as it gradually turned blue.

So there it was: positive proof I was pregnant. But, being ever conscious of checks and balances, I ran a second test five days later. When it turned blue again, I called Dr. Hart. A week later she gave me the official confirmation—and hugged me at the end of our consultation.

"I know this has been your dream for so long."

And most dreams can only be fulfilled by yourself. It's a bit like happiness: you can never depend on someone else for that elusive state of being. In the end we are all directly responsible for our own happiness . . . or lack thereof.

I told nobody but Ruth for the first three months of my pregnancy, reading up extensively on everything and anything to do with baby and child care. When twelve weeks passed, I decided that the time had come to inform Morton and Kathy that I was expecting a child. And that after the birth I was planning to take a year off. Because, perhaps for the first time in my life, I wouldn't be flying solo anymore.

But I forestalled that announcement for a few days, as I suddenly had urgent business in New York. Business to do with my missing-presumed-dead husband. A week previously his gallerist, Jasper Pirnie, got in touch with me, telling me he had read about Paul's disappearance and regretted not contacting me before.

"I won't give you any sort of mealy-mouthed excuse about being too busy," he said. "It was bad form on my part, and you have my apologies for only contacting you all these many months later. But the reason I'm calling you now is because I have some interesting news for you."

The news was that one of Jasper's clients—a wealthy Korean industrialist—had, while in Manhattan, paid a visit to the gallery and spied one of Paul's early drawings (a Maine seascape, shaded by omnipresent clouds) that he immediately loved.

"So he asked me what I would want for it, and when I said twenty thousand he agreed on the spot. So, congratulations—you'll be receiving fifty percent of that."

As if reading my thoughts, he added, "Or, at least, Paul's estate will be receiving that. But here's the thing—this gentleman is quite the collector. Since returning to Seoul he's shown off the drawing to several of his high-spending colleagues. There is now a market for Paul Leuen's drawings. So my question to you is . . ."

Now it was my turn to jump in, and I told him about the sketchbook of Paul's final work that he left behind just before his disappearance, and how the thirty or so drawings were, in my opinion, absolutely extraordinary.

By the time I finished my spiel, I could almost hear Jasper palpitating, the way a smart agent reacts when the prospect of something significant and lucrative is about to land on his desk.

"Might you be able to FedEx the sketchbook to me overnight?" he asked.

It went out that afternoon. By the time he got back to me thirty-six hours later, Morton and I had already put into action a plan we had devised some months earlier for dealing with any possible sales of Paul's future work: a trust in his name that would legally revert to me in five years and a handful of months—i.e., after the seven-year time frame, at which point he could be declared legally dead. At the time, when Morton brought this up, we thought that maybe a few thousand dollars might trickle in over the years for his remaining work. But now . . .

When Jasper rang the next night he was no longer masking his excitement.

"You have given us a treasure trove. The brilliance and uniqueness of the composition, the absolute assurance of his line, the exceptional density of detail, the fascinating contrast between the representational and the abstract . . . and, dare I say, the tragic nature of his story, which will be a fantastic selling point when it comes to generating great press and critical interest in the exhibition we plan to mount of these final works . . . I think we are looking at a major public triumph, and one which will, of course, translate into a significant escalation of our asking price per drawing."

"Any sense of what that asking price might be?"

"At this juncture, I would probably be conservative about it and say, once we have drummed up the journalistic and collector interest I know we will generate . . . perhaps forty thousand per drawing."

I sucked in my breath. Fifty drawings at forty thousand apiece . . . two million dollars. Fifty percent to the trust set up in the name of Paul Leuen.

"That's impressive," I said.

"Might there be more of Paul's work left behind?"

"There must be a good sixty to seventy drawings in his studio upstairs."

"Could you get those packed up and dispatched to us immediately, please? And were I to offer you a flight and a hotel room and an excellent dinner, might you be willing to come down and meet with me early next week?"

I had my iPhone out and was already scrolling through my calendar for next week.

By the time I flew down on Thursday afternoon to meet Jasper, I already had in place a Manhattan lawyer whose specialty was art contracts. Morton, meanwhile, having been fully apprised of this windfall in the making, had found a supersmart trust and estates attorney who was finding a wholly legal modus operandi by which the funds from the sales of Paul's work could be made accessible to me. If, as suspected, I could be coming into close to at least a million dollars net of Jasper's commission, besides setting up a trust for the child growing within me and perhaps moving house, I wanted to honor Paul's desire to buy an apartment for his daughter in Casablanca. Only, this time I would be sidestepping Ben Hassan when it came to everything to do with this sale.

But talk is cheap. And talk about serious money coming your way is even cheaper. Until all the work started to sell, I was not doing or promising anything. As the Town Car sent to collect me from La-Guardia Airport emerged from the Midtown Tunnel and cruised into

Manhattan, I thought about Paul and his posthumous emergence as the major American artist I always knew him to be. He had such exceptional talent. But when it came to that other crucial ingredient—having the talent to have talent—he was living proof of a great truth: the greatest impediment we all have in life is our very own self.

I was checked into a hyperstylish boutique hotel located across from Jasper's gallery. The room was a monument to minimalistic chic. There was a bottle of champagne awaiting me, which I would bring out as a gift to Ruth tomorrow.

I surveyed the room and the cityscape panorama beyond its immense windows. I thought, He should be here, reveling in the fact that after decades of silently accepting his status as a creative also-ran—someone who had never achieved the critical and commercial status he knew he deserved—the door had finally swung his way. He was now being summoned inside with all the attendant fanfare accompanying his entrance into the realm he had so craved.

But instead of being in this room with me, he was out there, in the endless void that is the Sahara. The beckoning infinity into which he had run. A vanishing act from which there is no return.

I blinked and felt tears. I went into the bathroom and washed my face, reapplied my makeup, grabbed my leather jacket, and headed out into the Meatpacking District. Once I reached the pavement, I could see Jasper's gallery just yards away on the far corner of the next street. I walked to the corner, awaiting the changing of the traffic light. And that's when I saw him. On the other side of the street. Dressed in a white shirt, loose canvas pants, his gray hair cascading to his shoulders. I gasped. I told myself, This is not real, this is not him. I blinked again. Several times. And then focused my sight even more acutely on the man standing on the pavement directly opposite me. A man in his late fifties, six foot four inches tall, lanky, with a distinctive French pencil in one hand, a sketch pad in another. Without thinking, I shouted his name.

"Paul!"

He turned and stared directly at me. And smiled. So happy to see me.

Out of nowhere a cab shot between us, blocking my view for a second or two. When it raced away, Paul was gone.

I stood there, scanning all four corners of the immediate horizon. No sign of him. I dashed across the street, thinking he might have ducked into a shop or an apartment building. But there were no immediate entrances into which he could have vanished. Again I visually raked through every niche and recess of the area, running back to the hotel in case he had crossed when I wasn't looking, then racing across diagonally to see if, indeed, he could have headed down the street, or into Jasper's gallery.

I ran right into the gallery. There was a woman at the reception desk: hip glasses, a too-cool-for-school demeanor.

"Did someone just run in here?" I asked her.

She surveyed me wryly. "Not unless it was a ghost," she said.

"I'm here to see Jasper."

"Oh, really?" she said. But when I told her my name her attitude shifted.

"I'll be back in a moment."

I rushed outside, certain that as soon as I was back out on the street, he'd be there in front of me. Smiling. So happy to embrace all the good that was about to happen to him, to us.

But the street, though brimming with an early evening crowd, was not harboring Paul. I looked east, west, north, south. Only a minute ago he was in front of me. And now? Back into infinity.

It wasn't a delirium. An apparition. A mirage. He was there. I'd seen him. With my eyes wide open.

But when do we ever fully open our eyes?

ACKNOWLEDGMENTS

THE *BLUE HOUR* is my twelfth novel. And if there is one thing that links the disparate fictional terrains of those narratives, it is the realization that a novel is, in the end, the work of many people. Yes, writing is a singularly solipsistic métier. But only until you finish the last line of the first draft. At which point you truly need the canny critical eye of a brilliant editor. Which I certainly have in Sarah Branham at Atria Books. *The Blue Hour* marks our fourth collaboration—and Sarah could not be a better advocate for my work, not to mention so perceptive and astute when it comes to getting the best out of this writer. I owe her my great thanks. Just as I also owe a great debt to the head of Atria, Judith Curr, for publishing me so well.

At Atria, I would also like to tip my hat in the direction of Adene Corns, Suzanne Donahue, Jin Yu, Kathryn Santora, Arielle Kane, and Hillary Tisman. Just as, in Antony Harwood and Grainne Fox, I have two of the best literary agents imaginable.

All writers live with a personal demon (it's the nature of the profession). I am also fortunate to live with Dr. Christine Ury, my ever extraordinary and brilliant wife. Just as I would also like to acknowledge that my two children, Max and Amelia—now in training for creative careers of their own—are the best raison d'être imaginable.

Finally, a gentleman named Mohammed drove Christine and me in his 4x4 through the wild expanses of the Moroccan Sahara. He also got us out alive, becoming a friend during the journey. As such he served as a reminder that travel is not just about the otherness of the foreign. It is also about discovering a key truth: despite evident socio-economic-political-theologic disparities, we all share so many of the same dilemmas that comprise the human condition.

D.K.
Wiscasset, Maine
February 2016